MW01657007

Sons of Osiris

Book II

Regicide

MICHAEL WESTMORELAND

Sons of Osiris: Regicide by Michael Westmoreland

First Edition: December 2024

Copyright © 2024 by Michael Westmoreland

www.michaelwestmoreland.com

All rights reserved. No portion of this book may be reproduced in any form without permission from the publisher, except as permitted by U.S. copyright law. For permissions contact Michael Westmoreland at
westofthemores@gmail.com

This novel is entirely a work of fiction. The names, characters and incidents portrayed in it are the work of the author's imagination. Any resemblance to actual persons, living or dead, events or localities is entirely coincidental.

Michael Westmoreland asserts the moral right to be identified as the author of this work.

Michael Westmoreland has no responsibility for the persistence or accuracy of URLs for external or third-party Internet Websites referred to in this publication and does not guarantee that any content on such Websites is, or will remain, accurate or appropriate.

Cover Art design © Graphic Soul Art
Internal Map design © Graphic Soul Art
https://www.instagram.com/graphicsoulart/
https://www.graphicsoulart.com/

Edited by Dan Larsen

For Dad

EHTHILIA
MONSCARREN
KORZEG
DAECE
Nuuthracia River
Myladaece River
Hylonen River
VOLUUTIA
Nekroa River
SKULPOS
HOSTELLUS
THE
ORLESTIAN
SEA
Aeno Langdem River
N
W
E
S
MERRININE
OSIRIAN KINGDOMS

Regicide

Book II

- Prologue -

Before his ascension into godhood, Osiris, Child of Neshka, embarked on his fabled conquest to unite the Aznogsi clans that had rebelled against one another and sent the world back into damnation as it had been before their arrival. Osiris walked the earth armed with the divine power of the gods and the golden blade he used to channel it. A slave boy no longer, he used fury to drive fear into the hearts of his enemies. Neshka commanded him to right the world, and right it he did.

Many years passed since the days of war, and the Aznogs lost sight of themselves and allowed their once great civilization fall to chaos and ruin. Despite their dominance, the men from the mountains were outnumbered by the Eldish populations, the people of the Old World. They became hard to control, and, in turn, rebelled against their masters. Osiris saw the corruption and evil spreading like a disease, sneered in disgust, and took matters into his own hands.

The first village to fall was a mining town at the base of the Lunendar Mountains where Osiris claimed the Sword of Kings. He wasted no time, descending from the cliffs with rays of bright light beaming from his eyes. Any Aznogsi tribesman who saw him drew their sword at first sight. No one man ruled over them; they forbade it. Their ignorance proved fatal, though, as Osiris wielded metal and magic to slaughter them like cattle. In an hour, Osiris leveled an entire town. A thousand lied dead, annihilated along with their home. He left none alive. There was no reason to.

Word of the 'sword carrier' reached all corners of the Aznogsi-controlled states. Small armies rallied to challenge him in the first few weeks until Osiris reached the capital of the western territories, Horroscova, the cradle of evil and corruption. There, ten thousand gathered to put an end to his campaign. He only sneered at their pathetic defiance. Like a bolt of lightning, he flashed through the city, using every power Neshka had given him, to douse it in holy fire. The sinners of Horroscova screamed as their flesh melted from their bones. Osiris hovered over the burning city, basking in a golden glow, and stared into the flames.

His victory only angered the Aznogsi warlords further, but it also gained attention from others. Eldish slaves, monks, and those who wished to seek freedom from Aznogsi rule flocked to him in waves. They bowed before Osiris, offering him gold, livestock, and precious silks. Smaller kingdoms pledged their allegiance to him, and his most devoted subjects erected temples in his honor. Soon, Osiris began to rewrite the law of the land, claiming his conquered territories for his followers. A month passed, and he had pulled a dozen once divided nations into his fold. In the areas he liberated, the Aznogs dared not tread. And so, true peace bloomed like lush flora in Osiris's garden. He circled back to the destroyed city of Horroscova, ordered his massing armies to rebuild the fortress, and renamed it Maelensis. From this fortress, he launched his future campaigns into the eastern lands where the Aznogs stood with their back to the sea, much like the Eldish did when the men from the mountains first invaded. With every kingdom he absorbed, his power and influence grew. His followers became fanatically loyal, praising him as a god, and gave him the title of 'The Holy Uniter,' the one who brought peace to the world.

None of the Aznogsi warlords hoped to defeat his divine wrath. They tried to bargain with him to ask for a truce. Osiris found their weakness repulsive and hung the messengers sent to plea from stone pillars by their ankles to suffocate under their own weight over several hours. Desperate, the warlords needed a plan of action. They called a summit to discuss their retaliation against Osiris, seeing they only had one choice for survival. However, as history tells, their meeting ended with a grisly conclusion.

Osiris marched his armies through every settlement he could find from Maelensis to the Orlestian Sea, conquering Aznogsi strongholds like Nostas, Jovozeg, and Teleklesta. The days of the men from the mountains waned; Osiris expelled them from his sight and replaced their ideologies with his own. He elected to honor the Aznogs, though, favoring their language and military tactics over the Eldish people. Even with the absence of the warlords, the Aznogsi culture flourished.

The world had been righted as Neshka commanded. Over three hundred years passed since he first grasped the Sword of Kings, and the land he called Osiria remained in perfect harmony. However, as time progressed, the divine power the fueled his extended life started to outlive his mortal body. He decayed while still alive, muscles weakening, bones becoming brittle, and skin peeling off like bark on a tree. His acolytes wrapped him in silk from head to toe, covering every square inch of him to preserve what they could. The Holy Uniter knew his time on the earth as a human dwindled.

Osiris then prayed to the high goddess, Neshka, who called him to the island of Aeladaecia. There, he underwent a ritual known as an ascension ceremony to fully complete his transition into a god. The ceremony erased the last of his humanity. He traded his ability to walk through his kingdom like his children to become omnipresent. His physical body was destroyed, his soul plucked from the flesh by Neshka's hand, and he elevated to her level of divinity.

In Year 327, holy Osiris emerged from Aeladaecia in forms of golden light. His spirit watches over the world, still protecting it from unseen realms.

The legend of Osiris's conquest has been cemented in the minds of his Son's until this day. Many claim that their ancestor's march was nothing less than an act of heroism; they see his actions as divine intervention, the will of the gods. Others condemn that ideology. Thousands died at the hands of the Holy Uniter regardless of the peace he brought after vanquishing the Aznogs. That amount of death is difficult to justify in the eyes of the less devoted.

And then ... there are those who wish to repeat his chapter in history.

Osiris demanded that his eight heirs rule over their respective lands with the promise to progress the world into a brighter future of peace and prosperity. Peace cannot last forever, though; there are those who desire more. The ambitions of men often outweigh the kinder virtues they once stood for, and one king is determined to claim the prize he's been dreaming of for over ten years.

Chapter 1

The Invasion

Day 3 in the Month of War, Year 973 in the Age of Steel

After days of assaulting the Ehthilian border north of the Nekroa River, King Matticus sat tall on his horse in front of his gathered armies. Battle commands and the sounds of siege weaponry rattled in his ears. Overhead, massive chunks of stone hurled toward the fortress bearing the Ehthilian flag. Mind tinkering with thoughts of leveling his cousin's kingdom to the ground, Matticus kept his soldiers at bay as the city in his view crumbled.

"Mangonels, advance!" a soldier shouted as dozens of foot archers fired over the walls.

"Oil on the rocks!" Matticus said, bellowing in a deep voice.

On command, siege engineers poured pitch into several buckets. Another crew brought torches and tossed them in. The roaring flames danced in Matticus's eyes as his hunger for domination grew.

Commander Nysis trotted up from the left, and the king looked over for a report.

"No sign of surrender from Serkonan, Your Majesty," Nysis said.

A boulder from the trebuchet planted in the ground behind the army crashed into the side of a wall tower. Chunks of crumbling stone fell to the earth, forcing clouds of dust and debris into the air. Matticus squinted while keeping his focus on the castle.

"They are foolish to resist."

He studied the rubble and heard a few muffled shouts that reached his ears from a quarter mile away.

"The first wave is ready to march, my king," Nysis said. "Shall I give the order?"

"Wait another moment," Matticus said. "The sun will shine over them soon. Let the light blind them."

The mangonels fired their burning rocks behind the outer wall from their forward position. Matticus shifted his gaze to the mounted paladins in front of him aching to charge the weakened enemy. Every so often, a small team of Ehthilian archers managed to find cover and sling arrows toward his knights, but the protected siege engines quickly turned to obliterate them.

Hostellian flags fluttered in the air as their bearers signaled for infantry to advance. A bright beam of light highlighted the interior of the fortress, giving Matticus a clear line of sight to the cracks in the walls. His soldiers quaked the earth in their strides, the broken wooden gate of the fortress flew open, and Serkonan's defenders rushed to meet the invaders.

King Matticus watched with a curious eye as the Ehthilians fell to the dirt like weeds under the boots of Hostellus's professional army. Peasants and farmers were no match for his elite soldiers, and Matticus quickly realized that King Ambrose had called his knights home to defend against Grimm's forces. The Bandit Lord had held up his end of the deal; Ehthilia's border remained vulnerable to an attack.

Half an hour passed, and his soldiers marched over vanquished foes into the castle, killing all who clung to the grasses begging for mercy. This was an easy task, one that hardly satisfied his warmongering mind.

A soldier in white raised the standard of Hostellus high in the sky atop the ruined gatehouse, and Matticus let a faint grin break out on his face once he saw it. Victory was at hand.

Though proud of his men and their ability to sweep through the fortress, he knew that more skilled enemies lay in wait on the road ahead. A handful of other fortresses stood along the path. The pieces of Matticus's plan inched closer together as he envisioned the razed villages on the way. Still, though, he looked further into the future, to his cousin's castle. To Maelensis.

Matticus knew overthrowing Ehthilia's capital was the only way to secure control over the entire kingdom. He craved something far greater, though, something his heart longed for more than anything: culling the weakness infesting his bloodline. Murdering King Ambrose.

Nysis rode beside him once more and held out a piece of parchment marked with the surrounding landmarks.

"It'll take days to search this place," the commander said. "Finding Caedus may prove to be more difficult than we thought."

"Caedus isn't here," Matticus said, keeping his watchful gaze on the Ehthilian civilians taken captive from the front lines.

"You're sure of that?" Nysis asked. "How so?"

Matticus glanced at the doomed expressions on the Ehthilian's face. They told the story well enough.

"There's nothing here left fighting for."

A few cries from the soldiers ahead jerked his attention to them. They brought out Serkonan's measly riches and dispersed the wealth among themselves. Matticus cared not for their petty greed, but the plundered goods kept their spirits high. Gold proved to be the best motivator in the eyes of a soldier, second only to the king's command.

"Nothing worth their lives, at least," Matticus said, spurring his horse forward.

"What of the prisoners?" Nysis asked.

Matticus slowly turned his head to the Ehthilians kneeling against the cold earth.

"Hostellus takes no prisoners."

Sounds of cold steel slashing flesh and bone echoed as King Matticus rode ahead and surveyed the road that led to Maelensis. Each defeated castle laid another brick in the road to the Hostellian Empire. His dream for domination became clear, blackening his heart, and the screams of dying men soothed him.

Sudden movement drew his focus; his eyes fixated on a hazy sight. A rider escaped from the right side of the crumbling fortress of Serkonan, furiously galloping away toward the forest to the east.

"He's going to warn Ambrose of our advance. Should we ride after him?" Commander Nysis asked him.

"No," Matticus answered after a pause.

He corrected his posture and held his chin up high. Dismounting his horse, he hit the earth with a thud. The Hostellian king walked forward and observed the razed fortress one last time. His skull buzzed at the sight of ruination, and Matticus removed his helmet to gain a better view, the white, feathered plume flowing in the wind. The indent left by a stray arrow from one of Zededia's archers weeks ago fueled his daunting appearance.

"Let them know," Matticus said as he caressed the indent with his index finger and cast his gaze toward the Ehthilian capital. "The conquerors are here."

Chapter 2

Lost

Day 10 in the Month of War

A group of drunks blabbered in raucous laughter inside the tavern of a shoddy town high in the mountains between Hostellus and southwestern Merrinine. They watched with smiling faces and greedy eyes as two hulking men squared off against each other, fists in the air and sweat dripping from their arms. The man on the right held a cock-eyed gaze while the one on the left smirked with a loose stance.

Provoking the other fighter, the man on the left grinned at his opponent, the bleeding lips and purple eye sticking out from across the makeshift arena. The sharp tune of a poor-quality lute filled his ears. Behind, several members of the crowd slapped and patted his bare, cheering him on in the brawl. He waited for the other man to approach, side-stepped a right cross, and backed away into the other side of the ring where more peasants yelled and placed their bets on who would win the fight. The man took a flagon of beer from the counter over the shoulders of the bystanders and poured it into his mouth; trickles of it ran down from the corners of his lips.

As he turned back to face his opponent, a swift punch nearly cracked his jaw. A hint of red glowed under his chin, but he kept it hidden from everyone else. The mocking attitude he carried to gloat evaporated; the grin faded to a blank expression. The second man advanced with another hasty punch, but, this time, he blocked it with ease, returned with a haymaker from the right, and rocketed his knee into the other man's abdomen before pushing him to the floor.

Victorious in the bar fight, he raised both arms, and a roar from the crowd followed. The lute player stood from his chair and presented a more upbeat tune. Walking to the tavern keeper, the fighter collected his winnings, and the gamblers around him shuffled pouches of coins back and forth.

The rotten floorboards creaked under his muscly figure, and he drunkenly took a seat, signaled for a tall drink and cracked the bones in his neck.

"I haven't seen anyone beat Adomire in a brawl in almost four years," an older man said from the adjacent seat. "No one here has even gotten close."

The man nodded and smiled as he took a hold of his alcohol. He tipped his head back and let it drain into his throat.

"Well, I'm not from around here."

"Where did you learn to fight like that?" the older man asked.

He set his stein on the bar top and wiped the foam from his lip. Memories of intense training that included hour after hour of brutal physical combat circled through his mind. The man's grin melted away as he thought of prior days filled with bloody lips and broken ribs.

"In my former life," he said, "I was forced to master hand-to-hand combat. Having two older brothers will do that to you."

"And what were you? In your former life?"

He smiled again and twisted his head over, looking around to make sure no one else was eavesdropping.

"I was a prince."

A slightly surprised face peered back at him, but Lucien downed the rest of the ale, stood from the chair, and left a gold kor next to his cup. He stumbled toward the door with several townsfolk patting his shoulders and praising him for filling their pockets with coin. Their salutes meant little to him, though; he cared not to linger around them any longer.

Out in the cover of darkness of the night, Lucien struggled to eye the shack he called his home. The wind blew by, almost knocking him off his balance. Like a distant parade, the commotion from the tavern still rang in his ears. Blinking away his intoxication, he couldn't pry the images of Matticus and Zededia in their youth when they once cooperated with each other from his thoughts. Now one lay dead, and the other scoured the entirety of Osiria in search of a weapon of war with hate guiding his strides; more than enough to shatter the strongest of hearts. Lucien's despair stemmed from his desire to see his family whole again. But, like the sting of a scorpion, the painful reminder that he would never see those days again stabbed at him.

He neared his run-down hut and stepped onto the worn path. An eerie hoot from an owl in the wooded area surrounding the town bounced between the buildings of the crooked alleyway as the crescent moon's light cast a dim aura through the planks.

Lucien pushed the door to his shack open, the rusted iron hinges piercing the air with their squeak. For a moment, he thought he saw a dark figure in the corner, but he dissolved the worry and blamed the hallucination on his drunkenness. The blurriness prevented him from seeing the wooden chair in the shadows, thus allowing his foot to crash into it with a thud.

"Damn bloody chair," he said under his breath. "Stupid ... piece of shit ..."

"What would your mother say if she heard you talk like that?"

A bolt of fear froze Lucien in place; he nearly jumped out of his skin.

"Who the hell–" he asked before tripping over the clutter on the floor.

He tumbled onto the hardwood and banged his head on the wall. Dazed, Lucien leaned against the side of the shack and cast his weary gaze out at his mysterious visitor.

The outline of the figure he had seen before shifted ever so slightly. A small orange flare of burning embers broke the darkness followed by a hazy cloud of smoke that dispersed across the ceiling. Lucien rubbed his eyes as a sense of familiarity spiraled through him.

"I wondered where you had ended up after you abandoned your home, but I never imagined I would find you here of all places."

Lucien fumbled to grab a lantern, but he managed to find one, light it, and hold it up with squinted eyes.

An aging gray beard emerged from the shadows behind a water pipe.

"Thancred?" Lucien asked. "Where in the–why are you here?"

"I could ask you the same question, Prince Lucien."

"Don't call me that."

Lucien set the lantern on a table and took a seat across from his old friend.

"That life is beyond me," he said, his voice softening.

"And so, you spend your days peddling for money and drowning yourself in ale?"

He frowned at the old man and turned his head.

"You cannot run away from your responsibilities to Hostellus," Thancred said.

"There's nothing for me in Hostellus, Thancred. Nothing but pain and disappointment. I'm not a prince, I'm not meant to lead, I'm not a–"

"You are a Son of Osiris!" Thancred said with a stern voice as he stood from the corner of the shack. "A beacon to all others around you, someone who is supposed to lead them out of the darkness of hate that plagues humanity."

Lucien sighed.

"I haven't been looking for you for over a month just to see you waste away like a town drunk," his elderly friend said in a more friendly tone, like that of a concerned mentor.

"Why have you been looking for me, Thancred?" Lucien asked again, rubbing his temples.

A sharp cough followed as the old man puffed another cloud of smoke.

"Your people need you, Lucien. Hostellus has grown darker in your absence."

Confused, the prince leaned forward. Surely, the state of his kingdom couldn't decline so rapidly.

"What are you talking about? What's going on?"

He looked at Thancred's grim expression that sent a spark of fear racing through his mind. The doctor put down his pipe, tossed the ashes, and cleared his throat while Lucien sat in bewilderment.

"Hostellus has declared war on Ehthilia."

"What?" Lucien asked, an astonished look on his face. "That's–Matticus would never do such a thing."

Lucien waited for an explanation, but silence followed.

"What drove him to this madness?"

"My prince, you must have seen this coming. Matticus has been using Grimm and his army of thieves to weaken Ehthilia for this very reason."

The daunting reality of his influence on his older brother increased his guilt. He remembered the dark dealings Matticus had involved himself with in secret meetings even he wasn't allowed to attend. At the time, Lucien thought nothing of them; the less he knew, the better.

"Hostellian troops have marched over the Nekroa, and by now, they've secured the entire southern border. Ambrose moved his armies to fend off Grimm's advances to the west, leaving Maelensis ripe for the taking," Thancred said. "Your brother is attempting to unite the Osirian kingdoms under one flag as Osiris did long ago. What he thinks is holy intervention is mistaken for insanity. Matticus has become increasingly obsessed with your ancestor's ideologies. He believes he's saving the world when in reality he's using Osiris's doctrines to justify war. He's delivering tyranny and calling it mercy."

Lucien's defeated gaze dropped to the floor. The painful reminder of Zededia's absence suffocated him. The consequences of his brothers' feud came to fruition; without the Black Prince to oppose Hostellian rule, nothing stood between Matticus and the rest of the world. Suddenly, an old conversation the prince shared with Zededia flashed by.

"Be wary, Lucien," his brother had said nearly ten years ago on the prince's fifteen birthday. *"Matticus's ambitions have grown beyond our father's throne. His eyes lay elsewhere, places they do not belong."*

Lucien hardly understood what Zededia had meant back then. That was before he had learned of the true nature of their rivalry. It all made sense now. His brother's wisdom continued to teach him, even after his death. As the dots connected, they only compounded his sorrow.

"What can I do, Thancred?" he said, a darkness growing in his voice. "This is all my fault...."

He stood from the floor and walked over to a high shelf. After he reached to search for the jar he had kept around for emergencies, a bottle clinked. Lucien yanked it down with a staggered pull, ripped the cork off, sniffed the toxic fumes, and turned the bottle up to the ceiling. He heard Thancred stand from the corner but stepped away as the liquor dripped down his chin.

"For the gods' sake, Lucien, put that down!"

Defending his obsession, Lucien tried to run out the door, but he tripped over the rubble littering the shack.

"No!" he shouted as he crashed into the floor, scattering debris in all directions.

Thancred's weathered hands reached for the large bottle in his grasp, but the prince wrestled it away.

"Leave me be!"

His strength forced Thancred to retreat, and he took another swig, giving no care to the intense burn in his throat.

"Just ... just let me ..."

Lucien's grip on his consciousness faded. He groaned and struggled to keep the liquor bottle from slipping out of his fingers. The sharp sound of glass rolling on the floor intensified his headache. Spiraling, the prince drowned in his own thoughts of despair.

"Lucien," Thancred said, "you cannot remain here like this. Drowning your anguish in the bottom will only lead you further down the path of ruin. Your people need you."

"I have no people," the prince said.

"Am I not your people?" Thancred said, a hint of anger in his tone. "Forget me, is Livia not your people? Or those in Hostellus who resist the warmongering machine that is the Vaedorian army? What about the thousands of people in Ehthilia and Monscarren, Neshka forbid Matticus ever make to the Daece?"

"There's no point...."

A new kind of torment that Lucien hadn't ever experienced choked his thoughts. His left eye produced a single tear that streaked across his temple. Despite his best attempts to push the guilt to the back of his mind, it clawed at him.

"My prince," Thancred said.

Lucien felt a hand on his forearm. The notion nearly broke his last defenses against the rivers of water pooling in the corners of his eyes. Everyone who looked up to him, he had failed them all. The light of his youth hid behind the veil of his bleeding heart. Gleaming smiles transformed into hopeless faces in each memory that passed by, distorting his perception of happier days. The old man squeezed his arm and leaned closer.

"I have watched you grow from the joyful child you once were into the man you are today, and through all these years, I have seen every one of your troubles. I know the pain that you carry, the same pain Zededia carried. Your brother's death was a tragedy, and I know the guilt that riddles you because of it. It is unbearable, and I do not blame you for trying to escape it."

The words from the old man were soothing, but Lucien remained unmoved.

"However," Thancred said, continuing, "you must move forward. You must face your agony. You cannot allow the despair that Zededia passed to you spread to others."

"How? I can't save anyone, much less help them. How am I to keep such darkness at bay?"

He heard Thancred released a thick sigh through his beard.

"There was something that your father told me long, long ago, when I asked him the same question. He held this dear to his heart after your mother died."

Lucien closed his eyes, trying to defend himself from the thought of his mother's death, as the salt on his eyelashes stung him.

"Place one foot in front of the other," Thancred said. "In times of darkness, smile in the face of anger. Soothe the cries of loss. And keep moving. You will never ease your suffering while you remain lost to the world."

Recognizing the quote, Lucien sat up.

"Zededia used to say that to me," he said.

"That doesn't surprise me. Matias and Zededia didn't always see eye-to-eye, especially on how to rule a kingdom ... but the hole left by your mother drew them closer together."

For the first time in weeks, a sincere grin appeared on Lucien's face. The pieces of his broken heart started to come together again. All the lessons Zededia had tried to imprint on him that he had forgotten during his rambling in south Merrinine rushed back to him. The hope, the perseverance, the will to overcome so legendary in his family, it returned. However, Lucien understood that words were just words.

"Their advice, that's easier said than done, Thancred," he said, shaking his head and running his fingers through his hair. "My father and Zededia-"

"Have been exactly where you are now and have gotten themselves out," Thancred said, cutting him off.

Lucien scoffed.

"I suppose but look where they are now."

A swift hand smacked the back of his head. Alarmed, Lucien looked at the old man's stern face.

"You are a fool to mock the wisdom of your family," Thancred said. "Especially wisdom from those who have acted as your guides and have given you nothing but their love from the day you were born."

Lucien blinked and retreated. He sent a large breath through his nostrils, regretting his cynical attitude.

"Well. What do you expect me to do, exactly?" he asked. "I doubt anyone other than you is paying attention to me."

He watched Thancred struggle to rise out of the chair to his feet.

"Your father is watching you, Lucien Osiris. Zededia is watching you."

Lucien's eyelids trembled for a moment, his mind replaying his brother's death over and over again. For a moment, he felt the grittiness of his brother's blood coating his hands. The prince instinctively looked to his right as if to glare at Zededia's pale face and lightless eyes as he had done in the cave of Talion's Tomb. His subconscious urged him to pull Zededia's corpse into his shoulder, thinking it was still in the cave. The depressive trance started to tug him back under, but a movement caught his eye.

The prince looked up and saw a hand reaching out to him.

"He is counting on you to finish what he started."

Lucien finally started to fight his guilt. His lungs beat irregularly as he tried to regain control of his thoughts. After a moment, he channeled his pride and took hold of Thancred's hand.

Seeing a way out of the abyss thanks to his mentor, Lucien stood on fresh ground and forced a fake smile onto his face. Thancred shook his hand with a light smile under the dense gray hair on his lips, giving the prince enough courage to start the journey to redemption.

"All right, Thancred. I will follow you," he said.

"I'm afraid we won't be returning to Vaedor Sellos, my prince."

"Oh? Where are we going, then?"

Thancred stepped away to grab the lantern from the table.

"We have a long road ahead of us, but our first journey takes us where the few friends we have left have gathered."

Lucien frowned as he tried to list any and all those he could trust outside of Vaedor Sellos. His brother's armies, maybe, but he doubted they would be open to trusting someone so close to Matticus. The liaisons in the city had been executed, his ties to the Black Legion cut.

"I didn't think we had any friends?" he said, coming up empty.

"With luck, Matticus hasn't extinguished them all just yet."

"That doesn't answer either of my questions."

Thancred walked past him and opened the door, the shadows stemming from the lantern casting faint shapes over Lucien's face.

"We mustn't keep them waiting any further. I've delayed too long already," Thancred said. "Our hosts are growing impatient at Anzagaar Nostir."

The name of Zededia's former home forced Lucien to stop for a moment. Though he had never been within the walls of the Home of the Dead Witch, the thought haunted him for a moment. Stories from his mother and father about the previous tenant had stuck with him since his childhood. Before Zededia moved in, death and decay were the only things spawning from Anzagaar Nostir. The old witch's castle had been converted into a teeming fortress, though, and perhaps the fearsome soldiers of the Legonae counted him more as an ally than he gave himself credit for.

Regardless, more pressing matters were at hand. Lucien gathered his cloak and walked over to the back portion of the shack. He removed a loose plank and eyed the item underneath. As the shining silver hilt of his longsword peered back at him, the prince grabbed the sheath, held it for a moment, and eyed the jewel in the gauntlet. He remembered the day his father had gifted him with his sacred blade. Though it had never tasted the bitter blood spilled in war, the years he had spent training in Vaedor Sellos perfected his skills. Lucien grinned and followed Thancred out of the hut, ready to venture back home.

Chapter 3

The Order of the Black Legion

Day 14 in the Month of War

Lucien rode behind Thancred out of the thick forest of Hostellus as a clearing neared in the distance. Eying the smoke columns, he knew the end of his journey from Merrinine neared. Anzagaar Nostir seemed like a myth to Lucien. He'd never seen the walls of Zededia's home for himself; only rumors of its existence passed through his ears. He thought of the letters his deceased brother had sent him over the years from the fortress in the mountain. As he reminisced over the letters, Livia popped into his mind. He smiled as he imagined the way Zededia would talk about the queen. Lucien grew tired of his brother's endless rants about Livia's beauty when the Black Prince first started to pursue her, finding the high level of detail in Zededia's description of her body disturbing. He welcomed those conversations now, though. He welcomed any conversation with his brother for that matter.

He dismissed the sentiment after a moment just like every other notion of the past. The tall, dark walls of the castle that housed the Legonae became clear through the leafless trees. Lucien's lips parted in amazement as he deduced that the fortress could rival Vaedor Sellos in terms of defensibility. No wonder Matticus failed to breach its exterior in four years of assaulting it.

As he and Thancred neared the Home of the Dead Witch, Lucien heard a faint horn sound off from the gatehouse. A sharp creak blistered his ears as the massive iron gate ascended from the ground. Shouts from the guards caught the prince's attention.

"With Zededia gone," Lucien said as he steered his horse onto the cobblestone road from the forest path, "I'm assuming Caedus now leads the Legonae?"

Thancred gave him a strange look.

"I'm unsure," the old man said. "They've alienated themselves for the rest of the world, called all their agents back home. The only reason I know they are gathering in the first place is that I happened to run into one of their spies."

Lucien sighed, trying yet again to shed the husk of shame that had consumed the past month. Inside the main courtyard of his brother's fortress, dozens of armed soldiers rallied to form a crowd. He deemed their attitudes neutral, though, as he noticed that their blades remained sheathed. One came over to take the reins from him, and he glanced at Thancred as the old man dismounted. Lucien followed suit, grabbing his pack of belongings from the saddle and keeping a hand on his sword for safekeeping.

"Come along, Prince Lucien," Thancred said in a louder tone to announce the prince's identity.

As his name left the doctor's mouth, the soldiers murmured among themselves and presented a more friendly welcome. He looked himself over, thinking that they didn't recognize him. Without a proper bath or shave in over a month, filth and grime coated him in a shell of disgust.

He followed Thancred to the keep of the city, and the guards standing outside pulled open the wooden doors, revealing the vast hall and banquet table in the center of the room. Lucien squinted through the shadows blanketing the hall, eyeing a few familiar faces among the people seated in their respective chairs. Systian Ursa with his youthful, light beard turned to him first, followed by Orleus Ammonladus with his monstrous stature and distinct appearance. The officers of the Legonae stood from the table, looked at him for a moment, and walked toward him. Captains Redding, Seether, Sykas, and Corso tailed the pack.

Lucien's throat closed, a hint of anxiety freezing his bones as he remembered the last time he had seen all these men together: Zededia's funeral. The somber atmosphere of the procession depressed him, and for a moment, he felt the haunting chill of the rain bearing down on his head from that day. He wriggled his fingers to clear them of sweat and battled to find the strength to put on a happy face.

"Ah, Captain Ursa," Thancred said, stretching out a hand. "I am pleased to say that I have finally arrived with our guest of honor."

"It's good to see you again, Highmaster Thancred, but I'm afraid I'm a captain no more; I've taken Zededia's place as head of the Legonae."

Lucien frowned, finding it hard to believe that Ursa would surpass Caedus as the next commander of his brother's army. Several questions bubbled in his thoughts, mainly "why." The prince opened his mouth to speak, but Zededia's successor beat him to the punch.

"Welcome, Lucien Osiris," Ursa said with a grin.

A firm hand grasped his in a handshake.

"I was wondering when we would meet again."

"You are acting commander?" Lucien asked.

Realizing the unintentional disrespect in his tone, he retracted his hand.

"Forgive me, I mean not to cast you any disdain, I merely expected someone else to take that title."

Ursa sent a half smile at him followed by a sigh.

"As did we."

Captains Ammon and Redding approached from each side and extended their salutes to Lucien, and he took them gratefully.

"So ... if you've taken Zededia's place, where is Caedus?" the prince asked.

An awkward pause fell over the room as he watched the three men in front of him share a grim look with one another. Lucien's stomach churned with nervousness, and Ursa looked back at him with a raised eyebrow.

"We were hoping *you* could tell *us*."

"What?" Lucien said. "Why me?"

"Well," Commander Ursa said, "you were the last person to speak to Caedus."

Lucien crossed his arms with a puzzled expression.

"What do you mean?"

"Lucien," Captain Redding said after a moment, speaking up for Ursa. "Caedus is gone. He vanished after we cremated Zededia."

A dark feeling of worry wrapped around Lucien's mind. He looked at Thancred, who shared the gloomy expression.

"Well, uh ...," Lucien said, replaying the last interaction he'd had with Caedus. "I don't ... I don't know. Nothing he told me led me to believe he would disappear."

Three disappointed faces cast their gaze to the floor.

"All right," Ursa said in a saddened tone while turning to the banquet hall. "Our arms are open to you, regardless. I'm sure the road has been long and tiresome. You are welcome to walk the grounds, or you may bathe in the springs if you desire."

A bath sounded like heaven to the prince in his current state. He missed the amenities of Vaedor Sellos that came with his life as a royal. Commander Ursa walked back toward the center of the chamber, and Lucien followed to venture deeper into the tower.

"Dinner will be served at sundown," Ursa said. "We expect our final guest to arrive then. All the other members of the Order have already arrived."

Lucien thought back to the conversations he had overheard between Thancred and the agents working in Vaedor Sellos. He wondered how far the arms of the Legonae's spy network truly reached. The mysticism behind the Order of the Black Legion still intrigued him. Knowing he had much to learn, Lucien told himself to keep a sharper eye out for the clues they left behind.

"Are the other highmasters here, then?" the prince asked.

"Yes," Ursa said. "All eight are here now, one from each kingdom. The rest are biding their time in the city somewhere."

The prince's worry started to fade once he guessed some sort of plan was in action if such high-ranking officials were present.

"Wait a moment," Lucien said. "Zededia headed the Order of the Black Legion, correct?"

"That's right," Thancred said. "But we can proceed without him once our final party member is here as Commander Ursa stated."

Lucien planted his foot on the stairs ascending to the second level of the tower.

"And who is that?"

Thancred's confident grin beamed at him.

"The new grandmaster."

Curious, Lucien widened his eyes.

"Go, my prince," Thancred said, his playful smirk lingering. "Warm yourself in the springs. I'll fetch you once it is time."

~ ~ ~

After washing away the filth from his body in the hot spring of Anzagaar Nostir, Prince Lucien wandered around the bathhouse nude, examining the ceiling of the room that twinkled. His mind retreated to when he had escorted the queen to the illumination chamber within the mountain behind Vaedor Sellos. Livia hadn't entered his thoughts in quite some time. He wondered about her well-being if she had decided to depart from the Hostellian capital while Matticus marched through Ehthilia.

Amid his journey around the damp, limestone floor, he heard a set of light footsteps approach around the bend. Lucien turned his head, and a young maiden appeared from the other side of a column and blushed.

"Oh, forgive me, Your Majesty," she said, sending her eyes straight to the right wall.

Lucien grinned, having not been addressed in such a fashion in weeks. He walked over to the young maiden as she held out a bundle of clothing, his shoulders and broad chest dripping with water. Feeling the fabric, the prince took a firm hold of the tunic.

"I've been ordered to present these to you," the maiden said, trying her best to meet his gaze and keep her eyes from wandering over Lucien's lean, powerful body.

"Thank you," he said.

Lucien hastily slid the tunic over his torso and inserted his legs into the pants. Once clothed, he noticed that the maiden loosened her sight restrictions and faced him more clearly. After a moment of silence, Lucien lowered his chin and pointed his green irises toward her.

"Is that all?" he asked as the girl stood there trying to find a place for her hands obviously distracted by the prince's stunning appearance.

"Oh—um, my lord, Commander Ursa requests your presence within the tower when you are able to speak with him."

She curtsied before turning to the entrance of the spring, and Lucien wiggled his shoulders in the tight tunic that promptly displayed his pectoral and deltoid muscles. The late winter sun cast a ray of light into the bathhouse, causing the wet pathway to glisten. After Lucien made his way to the grand archway, he surveyed the grounds of his brother's fortress. A teeming city, Anzagaar Nostir and her streets bustled with life as merchants and tradesmen carried out their various tasks.

Prince Lucien stepped down the stone staircase and faced the tower to the right. He crossed the courtyard and wriggled his toes in the new pair of leather boots provided for him. The crowds here were different from those back home; he didn't feel much of a need to hide his identity. He felt fewer sets of eyes on him, and he assumed that most people here had grown accustomed to having a prince roam the common grounds.

He heaved open the doors to the keep and ventured inside. Captains Ammon and Seether sat at the table in the main hall, and Lucien looked at them once he gained their attention.

"Ursa's upstairs," Ammon said, pointing to the staircase. "You should go and find him."

Lucien nodded and turned for the second floor of the tower. Servants hurried around, attending to the matters of keeping a court afloat, a scene he had almost missed.

The black marble floors of Zededia's castle sparked an interesting thought in his mind. Heavily opposite to the white decorum of Vaedor Sellos, Anzagaar Nostir displayed the differences between his brothers' tastes. Atop the stairs, he took a good look at the main hall of the keep, eyeing the sturdy column supports, stained glass windows, and darkened brick walls.

"Very fitting for you, Zededia," he said to himself, a smile faintly stretching across his face.

"It is indeed," a voice said from behind.

Lucien turned out of slight shock. After studying the shadows of a nearby hallway, he saw an outline of a man approaching. Commander Ursa appeared from the shadows, hidden under his cloak from shoulder to ankle.

"Zededia called this place our home," the commander continued. "Turned a dying, empty husk into a fruitful sanctuary."

Ursa stepped next to him.

"Your brother found this place amid our wandering in the winter of nine sixty-nine. Abandoned, open, in reach with other settlements nearby. It was the perfect place."

"Was?" Lucien asked.

Ursa's sadness from Zededia's absence leaked through his tough exterior. For the first time, Lucien noticed that his brother's death had affected more than just him. It only added to the weight of his grief to know that the hearts of others had broken as well.

"Forgive me, my prince. I misspoke. It is the perfect place."

Though Ursa covered his tracks, Lucien remained skeptical. The commander turned his back to him.

"Come on," Ursa said. "I want to show you something."

Lucien followed him deeper into the castle. He climbed several flights of stairs scaling the inside of the rounded central tower. A month of drinking himself to death and picking fights with peasants in the Merrinine village had crippled his physicality. His heart pounded, and his lungs ached, but he didn't dare allow Ursa to know.

Finally, his guide veered off onto a floor that held one singular door. Though Lucien's body screamed at him, primarily in his calves, he forced the pain away and surveyed the stone archway in front of him. A wall lantern hung over the prominent keystone caught his attention with its low flame. Down below, Lucien observed the lock securing both sides of the door in place. He soon realized where Ursa had taken him.

"No one has been inside since Zededia's death," Ursa said. "We've been reserving that honor for you."

"Me? Without ever knowing if I would come to Anzagaar Nostir?"

He received a light grin from the commander.

"We knew. Thancred assured us that he'd find you and bring you here if it meant doing so with his last dying breath."

Confused, the prince stepped closer to the door as if some great mystery lay beyond it. Ursa jingled a set of keys, jostled the lock free, and removed it from the handle. Lucien paused as the memory of his brother's abandoned room in Vaedor Sellos came to him. The chamber in front of him seemed as desolate as the one back home, and he noticed a strange resemblance to now and the days after Zededia's exile that had brought a damning sense of loneliness, the kind of loneliness that tore his family apart.

Lucien pressed his fingers on the door, bracing himself for the trauma that had assaulted him on the night of his father's death and Zededia's banishment, and pushed it open. Inside, a musky scent of dust infiltrated his nostrils, and the silk curtains over the bay window fluttered from side to side.

"I'll ... leave this to you," Ursa said. "When you are ready, dinner will be served once the grandmaster has arrived."

The prince nodded but kept his focus on Zededia's room. He slowly walked through the middle of the chamber, twisting from side to side to glance at the tapestries hanging from the walls. After the next step, his foot crashed into the leg of a table on the left. The large map sprawled across the hardwood drew his attention. Lucien placed his flat palm on the table and ran it over the coarse parchment until he touched Vaedor Sellos's secluded position on the eastern side. Several handwritten notes and markings surrounded the white city's emblem. Lucien, bewildered, glanced over his brother's writings but struggled to agree to their existence. After weeks of purging his brother's memory from his head, he hardly believed anything of Zededia's was real.

Lucien lifted his head and looked at another, smaller table. Strewn over it, a handful of cream-colored letters contrasted with the dark oak, and a quill and vial of ink rested next to them. Eyes glued to the papers, he pulled the chair out from under the table and sat down. The coarse texture of the parchment grated his fingers as he picked the top one off the pile and studied what his brother had written.

Livia, he read to himself in his head.

Intrigued, Lucien read over the letter Zededia had dedicated to the queen. Paragraph upon paragraph of his brother's love for her poured from the words. As Lucien neared the conclusion, he frowned, realizing the shift in Zededia's tone. The letter ended with a heartfelt farewell in the sincerest form.

Why would he be saying goodbye? Lucien thought.

Lucien grabbed the next letter.

Caedus, the top line read.

A wildly different tone, this letter included Zededia's appreciation of Caedus's fierce determination and undying loyalty. Seeing how his brother labeled Caedus the greatest ally he could ask for cheered him up, but, again, the letter's final paragraph spoke of a good-bye. Noticing the theme, Lucien grabbed the next few letters.

Systian ... Orleus ... Nox....

Soon the prince reached the end of the letters and found only blank pages. He held them all in one hand, glancing over them once more to study their meaning. Nothing added up.

"You wrote these," Lucien whispered to himself, "as if you knew ... you'd be gone?"

A gut-wrenching thought shot into his mind like a bolt of lightning. For a moment, he seriously entertained the idea that Zededia had planned his death. Why on earth he would carry out such a plan evaded Lucien, and he cast that notion aside with a soft shake of his head after closing his eyes. Anger took the place of his confusion. The prince slammed his fist full of letters on the table, sending most of the inkless ones gliding to the ground. Lucien let his gaze roll over the room as he sat in deep thought, battling the theory that invaded him. As he mindlessly glanced around, something caught his eye.

The last letter, hidden below the others at the bottom of the pile, held a dark spot on it in the upper left corner. He leaned forward, scanned the page, and read over the lone word Zededia had written.

Lucien.

Eager for his turn at closure, the prince scoured the page for anything else. He darted his eyes back and forth, hoping something would magically appear. However, the letter remained blank after the comma that followed his name.

Lucien scowled, trying to stave off the tears that started to pool in his eyes. Zededia had left nothing for him, not another word. Everyone else received the love and care they deserved, the final caress Lucien so desperately craved. Hands trembling and breaths shaky, the prince contained the rage in his heart fueled by grief and disappointment.

Am I not owed a valediction?

Before the prince gave any more thought to the matter, a loud horn alerted the fortress and rang deep into the valley. Lucien glanced over at the bay window, walked over to it, and pulled the silk curtains back to survey the land below. He looked outside and saw a column of mysterious riders approaching. Assuming this was the "final member" of the Order, the prince tabled his sorrow for another day. On his way out of Zededia's chamber, he grabbed the letters to distribute them to their recipients and slid them into the inside pocket of his gambeson.

Lucien made haste toward the stairs and descended as fast as his feet allowed him. Captain Seether stood on the balcony overlooking the main hall as the prince stepped out from the spiraling tower.

"Who is here?" the prince asked.

"An ally."

Several of the keep's guards rushed toward the main doors. Lucien jogged down to the first level and slowed his pace as he walked to the banquet table. He noticed Thancred seated on one side in the center of the room, smoking a pipe while nodding at him. Nearing the table, he stopped to observe.

Anzagaar Nostir's guards opened the towering main doors, and an envoy of soldiers all bearing the same sigil entered like a silent parade. Lucien eyed the light green tree encompassed by a perfect circle and recognized the symbol from the history books his father had read to him as a child. These were men from Daece.

As the black of night started to push the sun out of the sky, Lucien couldn't distinguish their faces under their hoods. At least twenty men separated into two groups to the right and left, leaving a team of armored knights in their wake.

Lucien cast his eyes over some of the largest warriors he had ever seen, their pauldrons reaching incredible widths. Heavy metal boots clanked in the keep, capes flowing behind as well. Once the armored men grew closer, they split as the first group did.

After, a lone figure emerged, dressed in a prestigious cloak with a shining metal helmet decorated with a large green gem on the crown that signified his status as royalty.

"Be respectful, Lucien," Thancred said in a low voice. "This man outranks both you and me by a large margin."

With a firm stance, the prince tilted his chin slightly in the air and held his hands behind his back. The cloaked man stopped a few feet away from him, waited for a squire to take his garments, and removed his helmet.

A cleanly shaven face hosting a charismatic smile peered

"The people of Anzagaar Nostir welcome you, Your Majesty," Commander Ursa said as he walked forth from Lucien's left. "We are most grateful and humbled by your presence."

"Thank you, Commander. Though I don't plan to linger for long, I hope my company will not be a burden for your court."

Ursa stepped back, giving Lucien a full view of the guest once more. "Your Majesty" rang through his head, and a couple of possible candidates for the title stuck out in his thoughts.

"Prince Lucien," Lord Ursa said, holding an open hand out toward the royal, "it is my esteemed pleasure to present to you: King Atlas Osiris, ruler of Daece."

"Atlas?" Lucien asked. "Why, it's been ... it's been years since I've seen you. You were still a prince then, I believe."

The man chuckled and stretched out his hand, not the usual greeting for a king. Lucien took a firm hold of Atlas's hand regardless and shook it with a half-smile, trying to think of his most recent memory of his cousin. He remembered how much Zededia bonded with Atlas being the same age as the Daecian king, whether they roamed each other's lands during visits or combed through endless texts in grand libraries until the sun rose over the valley.

"It's great to see you here, Lucien," Atlas said. "Your brother's told me quite a bit about you since I last traveled to Vaedor Sellos."

Lucien stepped back and smiled, a warm feeling blossoming in his heart after hearing Zededia had talked about him to others.

"I assume you are here in response to the Ehthilian invasion?"

"I'm afraid so," Atlas said. "But we can discuss that later. For now, we rest and rejoice."

Surprised at the large number of men Atlas brought with him, Lucien started wonder how many others supported the Black Legion outside of Hostellus.

"We were growing anxious of your arrival, Your Majesty," Commander Ursa said as Atlas walked by.

"Ah, yes, forgive me, Commander," the Daecian king said. "We made a detour to a small town north of here. There was someone we needed to collect on our way."

"Oh?" Lucien asked. "There are others?"

Atlas grinned and took a firm hold of the prince's shoulder. As the crowd of guards followed the king farther into the keep, Lucien noticed shadowed movement in the dimness of the entrance to the tower.

The prince squinted, eyeing hints of white and blue silk. Several young women ventured inside, and Lucien's mind wandered back to the members of the Vaedorian court. A curious thought sparked.

Making their way toward him, the maidens smiled, and then, from the group, a veiled woman appeared with a child in her arms. Pulling back the fabric covering her face, she revealed her wide, amber eyes. Lucien stood from the table, and a grin sprouted.

"My Lady," Lucien said as he took a step closer.

Livia approached with a jovial expression; Ender's infant face buried in her chest as Mattox waddled behind.

"How it soothes me to see you again, Lucien," Livia said. "I started to think I had lost all three of you in such a short time."

The joy in Lucien's face slightly faded. Though he sensed happiness in the front she displayed, something about the vacancy behind Livia's eyes told a sadder story. He thought back to when she had asked him to dine with her and noticed the same emptiness now as he did then.

"Three of us?" he asked. "What do you mean?"

Livia's grin vanished.

"I'd rather not speak of that here," she said. "I've chosen to leave Hostellus behind; there's nothing left for me here.

Lucien's stomach knotted, feeling guilty of abandoning Livia to Matticus after realizing she might have longed for his calming presence. The queen's delicate hand softly grasped his arm.

"Come, I've grown tired of traveling."

Following Livia to the center of the keep, he watched the servants hastily bringing out all the tables and chairs they could find to accommodate Atlas and his small army. Smells of roasted chicken and deer filled the air, sending Lucien back to the feasts he enjoyed in Vaedor Sellos. Most of his recent meals consisted of stale bread and cold stew if there was any stew to be had at all.

After a few short minutes, tables lined the entire hall in the keep with decorative cutlery. Lucien looked around for a place to sit, but he shied away from the main table where Atlas and Livia had taken their places. As the prince tried to wiggle his way to the back of the forming crowd, a massive thud slammed into his back, nearly knocking the breath from him.

"You're going the wrong way, Prince Lucien," Captain Ammonladus said with a wide smile.

Lucien formed a confused grin himself.

"Come," Ammon said. "You are no less welcome at this table than any of us."

Thoroughly coerced, the prince walked near, and he eyed a vacant spot next to the queen. Music from lutes and lyres sang through the air, servants brought out platters of food and drink, and Lucien knew the festivities had begun. He hesitantly took a seat next to Livia with King Atlas on the other side of her.

A merry feeling lightened the mood as well as the prince's heart. He sat back in his chair and allowed the kitchen staff to finish their duties. As Lucien glanced up, he studied the men on each side of the table. Mixed in with the captains of the Black Legion, Highmasters of the Order and their personal squires filled the remaining seats.

A graceful hand touched Lucien's wrist.

"Seems we're unable to escape the festivities of a court," Livia leaned over and said in a hushed tone. "However, this doesn't resemble a Vaedorian banquet very well if you ask me."

Lucien chuckled and eyed the widespread happiness among all the guests.

"Not exactly," he said. "Seems we're missing the malicious politicians. And the clerics with a pike up their ass."

Livia's laughter warmed him. Comfortable in the scene, Prince Lucien dug his fork into his hearty meal, wrapped his other hand around his wine goblet, and relaxed.

The musicians of Anzagaar Nostir continued to play their joyous tunes, opening the atmosphere to a full party. Lucien spent the next half hour basking in the merriment. His wine goblet ran dry from time to time, but a servant made sure to refill it.

Though the prince never initiated a conversation, he eavesdropped on story after story from the men at the table, some of which retold the recent battles between the Legonae and the Hostellian armies in the Month of Snow. Notions of Zededia dampened his mood whenever someone mentioned his brother, but Lucien's attention wandered to the next tale shortly after.

He glanced over to Livia to gauge her mood. Despite the smile on her face, the prince knew the emptiness lingered. As Livia took a bite of food, he reached over and placed his hand on hers. She wrapped her thumb around his, and her real state of mind started to appear in her broken gaze. Livia shook her despair, however, and released his thumb. Knowing she shared the deep grief that afflicted him, the prince wanted to comfort her, but the queen dismissed him after showing her fake grin.

As the prince turned away, concerned for her, King Atlas stood from his chair and raised his goblet.

"On the behalf of the Black Legion, I must express our gratitude to Commander Systian Ursa and all peoples of Anzagaar Nostir for preparing this feast," Atlas said.

The crowd simmered, and the music faded. All eyes flew to Atlas, including Lucien's as he swallowed his worry for the queen.

"I wish I could say that we are gathered here under better circumstances, but let it be known that those who are courageous enough to stand against evil stood in these halls as free people."

Atlas raised his goblet higher into the air.

"Join me in a salute," the Daecian king said.

Lucien grabbed his cup and held it at eye level.

"Hail to the Order and those who protect it. Hail to our freedom and those who have died for it. Hail to ..."

Atlas's gaze fell over Lucien mid-sentence. The prince locked eyes with him and shared a moment of remembrance of his brother. In the silence, he nodded at Atlas as if to give him permission to finish his toast.

"... to Zededia."

A warm feeling rushed through Lucien at Atlas's words. Everyone around him finished the salute and drank their fill of whatever their goblets held. The prince hesitated for a second before sipping his red wine. He had almost forgotten that Atlas had known Zededia for years. However, despite that, his brother's relationship with him remained a mystery to him. Wondering why Zededia hadn't mentioned Atlas much in their youth, he told himself to keep an open eye on the Daecian king.

Lucien centered his attention on the other men at the table as Atlas sat back down. The feast declined in excitement as everyone reached their limit of good food and potent drink. Those not associated with the Highmasters at the table departed first, leaving the kitchen staff to clean their places. Next, Ursa and his captains dismissed the common soldiers.

Prince Lucien looked at Livia and expected her to exit the keep as well, but she maintained her position next to him. Soon, only King Atlas, the Highmasters, and the elites of Anzagaar Nostir remained.

Nightfall's darkness seeped into the keep, battling the dimly lit torches for space on the walls. As the outside guards secured the main door, a thud echoed throughout the hall. Everyone fell silent afterward, and Lucien patiently waited as King Atlas cleared his throat. Without the distraction of a party, the underlying tone revealed itself. Lucien scanned across the faces of Zededia's soldiers, and they all held the same grim expression.

"Now, my friends," King Atlas said. "The time has come where we must decide how to handle the Hostellian aggression rampaging through Ehthilia. As your Grandmaster, I will hold each of you to your oath to defend not only your kingdoms but Osiria in its entirety."

A wave of head nods surged across the table, and Lucien followed suit.

"Unfortunately, the circumstances around my position as head of this Order are far grimmer than I had ever thought."

Prince Lucien dropped his eyes to the middle of the table, dreading the statement to come.

"Grandmaster Zededia has been slain," Atlas said. "His soul has been put to rest and sent forth to Elysia. However, there are darker things at hand."

Each man present kept perfectly still as Lucien glanced around. An eerie quiet loomed over the chamber like a creeping shadow. The prince looked at Atlas's face as the candlelight from the table flickered across it.

"King Matticus has declared war on Ehthilia, his armies march on Maelensis's doorstep as we speak. Thousands have been slaughtered already with more than half a dozen fortresses sieged in the past week. He has no intention of stopping and no regard for the treaty our forefathers signed into law. Peace among the Osirian kingdoms has been broken."

The murmurs that had spread before elevated to soft conversations. Lucien perked his ears to tune in, but he couldn't decipher the whispers.

"As an order dedicated to the betterment of Osiria, we have the responsibility to act for those who cannot," Atlas said. "Ehthilia will fall in the coming days, and there is little we can do now to intervene."

Lucien wriggled his fingers as his anxiety returned. The others around him held sullen expressions.

"Matticus will then turn his eyes elsewhere," Atlas said.

"He'll come for Monscarren next," a gentleman from down the table said.

The prince shifted focus to the Highmaster he assumed hailed from the Red Hills to the north of Ehthilia.

"Monscarren doesn't merit such a campaign through her towering mountains," Commander Ursa said. "He'll target who threatens him the most."

"Who would that be?" Captain Seether said from under his balaclava.

Though there was a small list to consider, no answer followed. Lucien filed through the candidates and tried to place himself in Matticus's position. No one knew his brother like he did, after all. The prince tried his best to ignore the militaristic side of Hostellian politics, but he became wise to all Matticus's plots one way or another. He thought back to the time he wandered into Vaedor Sellos's war chamber high in the keep. He remembered the map laid upon the table and the growing list of information of each kingdom's armies that the spies brought back from their adventures of secrecy.

All the evidence danced around Lucien's thoughts, and as he saw a familiar pattern, one name rose above all others.

"He'll go to Voluutia," Lucien said quietly.

The attention gravitated toward Lucien; he started to regret his words.

"I agree," Atlas said. "He may also choose to attack Korzeg for their siege engines. Matticus could march south of Monscarren while also avoiding Voluutia's main armies. After conquering Korzeg, the Hostellae will not only be the most powerful ground army in the world, but they will also have machines of war no fortress can defend against."

A couple of the Highmasters spoke up after Atlas's point, diving the table into a mild dispute. As Lucien watched Atlas attempt to ease the concerns brought up, the memory of his presence at Matticus's war meeting months ago clawed at him. Though he aimed to diffuse the situation entirely, he left with far more information than he needed to know. The debate heightened, pressuring Lucien's thoughts. Fear of a trap arose.

"Matticus has no need to conquer Korzeg," he said over the others.

Atlas sent a concerned frown his way. The others looked at him again as well.

"What makes you think that, Lucien?" Commander Ursa asked.

The prince stood from the table and straightened his tunic, swallowing his nervousness. Twenty pairs of eyes locked onto him; he had never felt this influential in his life given the statuses of the men seated around him. After looking at each of them, he cleared his throat.

"Hostellus and Korzeg maintain a hidden alliance," Lucien said. "Just this year, thousands of our soldiers returned home from the north to fend off a series of attacks launched by the nomadic clans above us."

"This isn't new information, my prince," Atlas said. "Any Osirian kingdom that is under a direct threat from a foreign entity is always met with aid from the others. It is the eighth law that Osiris distributed to the Sons. Daece and Voluutia sent soldiers as well."

"Yes, but the law states that unafflicted Osirian kingdoms are to provide support without the requirement of compensation or debt, isn't that right?" Lucien said.

Though Atlas provided an argument, the prince stood his ground.

"That's right," Atlas said.

Lucien paused, weighing the decision to reveal the critical information he held onto, the information that drove the majority of his guilt in knowing he could have prevented this from happening. Sweat formed on his forehead, and his fingers tapped the hardwood. Livia's hand brushed over his on the table, calming him enough to speak.

"Three and a half years ago, when the Hostellae were sent to Korzeg, Matticus and Holthiem signed a pact between themselves, one kept secret from the other kings. I remember Matticus discussing the details with me because he entrusted me with Hostellus's copy of the parchment."

Lucien's explanation gained momentum, and he noticed Atlas's raised eyebrow.

"The pact dictates either kingdom to come to the aid of the other if an internal war is declared. They are to join the war effort regardless of the circumstances prior to," Lucien said.

More murmurs rose from the men, and, this time, the prince picked up on the nature of the whispers. He heard them question his loyalty.

"I am not here to sway you from standing against Hostellus or to trick you into falling for some sort of scheme."

The murmurs ceased.

"Matticus and Holthiem could have created this pact with their kingdoms as a safety net, yes; other Osirian kings have done so to ensure support after a recession," Lucien said. "But the pact states that it becomes null and void after five years since it was signed."

Atlas's intrigued expression shifted to shock.

"We are approaching the fifth year after this document's creation," Lucien said. "This was planned before Hostellus flew to Korzeg's aid. Matticus has already bought Holthiem's armies for his war and will use that secrecy to his advantage in conquering Voluutia."

Prince Lucien sat back down in his chair, but he maintained the attention of everyone at the table.

"That's impossible," an elderly man said. "We would have known of such a thing."

"If there's one thing you need to know about my eldest brother, it's that he is as shifty as any man I've ever met. He may hold the appearance of a brute, but Matticus has grown more cunning over the years. He hungers for his war."

"There is no proof of this document you speak of," another man said. "Why should we trust what you are saying as someone so close to King Matticus? You could be here to feed us this lie so we count Korzeg as an enemy."

Lucien's anger rose at even the notion of betrayal. After a moment, the majority of the table broke out into a heated debate, mostly in support of Lucien as a traitor. The prince felt helpless and watched the groundwork for a plan he provided wash away. Their bickering suffocated his defensive instincts. Trying to regain control of his racing mind, he focused on what Zededia would do in this situation. He couldn't simply retreat like a boy. He needed to rise like a man.

"Enough!" King Atlas shouted.

To the prince's delight, silence followed.

"Prince Lucien has demonstrated his devotion to the Order plenty of times before. He is responsible for Grandmaster Zededia's escape from Vaedor Sellos and prevented Caedus Redstone's discovery on his journey to fetch the Sword of Kings."

Lucien froze when Atlas hinted at the murder he committed. That decision still haunted him regardless of its necessity. Wondering how Atlas knew so much about his dealings in Vaedor Sellos, he met eyes with the man.

"He has earned my trust, and that is all he needs."

"Yes, sire," several of the men at the table said after a long pause.

Coughs and sniffs echoed in the quiet. Lucien knew many of those around him didn't agree with Atlas's statement, but he didn't care. The Grandmaster had spoken.

"My liege, if we are to take this information into account, what are your orders?" one of the Highmasters said.

The prince sat back down in his chair, satisfied with his participation in the meeting, and glanced over. As Atlas rubbed his chin, Lucien sensed a brewing plan.

"A meeting has been called," King Atlas said. "All the living Sons are to gather in the hall of Amuun Drall in Voluutia on Day 20. Raed has summoned the other kingdoms to discuss a counterattack on the Hostellian invasion, no doubt. As a Son of Osiris, I will represent Daece in the matters at hand."

Lucien studied Ursa's conflicted expression. Captain Redding leaned over and whispered something to the Commander, but Lucien couldn't quite hear it. After a moment, the prince deduced that the two men had formed a plan of their own.

"Grandmaster," Ursa said. "The Legonae are at your disposal. We are ready to march to Ehthilia upon your request."

The Legonae had bested their Hostellian counterparts on multiple occasions in the early winter, Lucien remembered, but he feared a slaughter. They wouldn't be fighting near the mountains where they could retreat and regroup, they'd be cut off from Anzagaar Nostir entirely.

"As much as I trust your ability to fight against the Vaedorians, I don't believe the wisest decision would be to throw you to the wolves without any support."

Suddenly, several members of the Order placed their palms flat on the table, a curious sight for Prince Lucien as he watched them do so one by one. Soon, every man, including Commander Ursa, held their hand face down.

"My men will follow your command, Grandmaster," one of them said.

"As will mine."

"And mine."

Lucien felt a little safer knowing that so many would come together to oppose Matticus. It gave him hope that others would rally as well.

"I salute your servitude, my lords," King Atlas said. "But we must protect those under our flags before we challenge another. The people of Anzagaar Nostir are no longer safe in Hostellus, nor are those of us who reside in Voluutia."

"What do you propose then?" Livia said, making her debut in the conversation.

The prince wondered the same.

"An exodus, my lady," Atlas said. "To Daece. My people can protect you there, the forests are dense and strong. If we are to face the worst of circumstances, you will have port access to the Orlestian Sea which you can evacuate from."

Atlas stepped away from the table, walked around behind the various elites, and paced with hands behind his back.

"In fact, all women and children of those associated with the Order of the Black Legion should ride to Daece, including the Legonae. We will all depart from here in the morning and make way for Amuun Drall. There, we will go our separate ways. Highmasters, collect all who follow you. Safe havens in Osiria are shrinking in number. We need to stay ahead of the warpath. Rest tonight. Tomorrow, we make our leave."

Just like that, the lords of the table stood and gave their salute to King Atlas. Lucien sat by, slightly confused by how easily a solution came about after growing accustomed to the years of sitting around conniving politicians trying to plead with Matticus. Usually, it took a week or more for any matter in the Vaedorian court to find a resolution. As Atlas started to walk away where his ensemble waited for him, the prince rose from his seat with one question lingering in his mind.

"Your Majesty," Lucien said.

He met Atlas's eyes as the king turned around.

"Where am I to go during all this?"

King Atlas gave him a confident grin.

"You're coming with me."

Chapter 4

The Siege of Maelensis

Day 18 in the Month of War

The Hostellae rampaged through southern Ehthilia over the previous week, ransacking castles and burning villages as they went. Like a plague, they swept over the valley with the kingdom's capital in sight. Now came the time to finish Ehthilia for good. Only Maelensis remained, and King Matticus narrowed his gaze upon its crumbling exterior as his ferocious armies stormed the grounds outside the castle. Mangonels pelted the outer wall, weakening the defenses so his men could pour through. Next to him, a massive siege ram slowly rolled up the stone road to the main gate. Ladder men raced to the lower sections in pairs to give the infantry an entry point.

"To the walls!" Commander Nysis shouted to order the men to proceed with the attack.

Up the ladders and through the ruined castle towers, hordes of white and silver surged through every opening they could find. Matticus watched his army disperse like a colony of ants devouring a corpse. As the ram moved closer to the wood and metal gate, a chunk of stone larger than a horse smashed into the tower directly to the right of the gatehouse, causing it to collapse in on itself. Clouds of dust erupted into the air, and Matticus squinted as it wisped over him. The Ehthilian arrows raining upon the Hostellae dwindled to near none, allowing for a proper advance.

Dozens of engineers sprinted to the ram to bash open the gate. One by one, the Ehthilian flags waving atop the castle walls fell as the Hostellae progressively captured more territory. The outer shell of Maelensis cracked under the onslaught Matticus orchestrated.

"Heave!" a soldier yelled from inside the ram.

The engineers pulled with all their might, raising the arm of the siege engine higher and farther away from the gate. Metal gears cranked until the ram clicked into a fully charged position. Matticus grinned in anticipation.

"Release!"

After a notch snapped, the steel-capped head of the ram slammed into the gate, wooden splinters and chunks of the metal frame rocketing out like a volcanic eruption. A deep chill rushed down Matticus's spine as the crushing sound of the impact rattled his armor. He exhaled in ecstasy, and a devilish grin appeared.

Though the gate still stood after the first collision, the soldiers and engineers pulled on the ropes once more. The chants from everyone around the king elevated to screams of war, and the blood on the white and silver steel of his men fueled his desire to press on. Behind the inner wall, his target lied in hiding.

King Ambrose's forces fled like wounded dogs away from the gatehouse. Matticus expected his cousin's army to at least put up a fight, but perhaps Grimm had been a deeper thorn in the Ehthilians' side than he realized. No matter, easy pickings accelerated his plan for unification.

The ram crashed into the gate again, and this time, Maelensis's battered defenses stood no chance. Matticus eyed the inner city through the cracks between his siege weapon and the archway of the gatehouse. Horns sounded from the other side, a call for the remaining Ehthilian soldiers to band together.

"Move forth, Hostellae!" King Matticus shouted in a booming voice, the red shine in his veins climbing up his neck. "Slay them all!"

As his soldiers charged through the gatehouse, Matticus grew tired of sitting idly on his horse. The sounds of war enticed him.

Moments later, a behemoth of a man stood at the chokepoint in the gatehouse, hurling a great two-handed sword around in circles to deter the Vaedorians from advancing. A proper enemy arose from the meek.

With a scoff, Matticus dismounted, shook the stiffness from his shoulders, and grabbed his helmet from the saddle of his horse. He glared at his enemy through the slots after sliding it over his head, the wind brushing through the fluttering white feathers in the plume.

The Ehthilian in his sight heaved the massive blade in a cumbersome manner, but it kept the attackers at bay. Matticus channeled his focus, blotting out all other sounds than his thundering footsteps, and marched toward the city like a giant in slow motion.

Anger building, the king tightened his fists. On either side of him, his soldiers roared. As Matticus primed the divine rage boiling in his veins, a faint red glow seeped through the thinner parts of his armor.

He carried immense strength in his hulking body, strength that easily rivaled a bear twice his size. However, he knew he could enhance it further. Matticus hadn't recited the sorceries his ancestors used in years, thinking back to the last time he summoned Osirian magic long ago as a student in the Vaedorian Military Academy. He had always refrained from resorting to magic to win his fights, favoring strength over all. Now, though, as he stood upon the doorstep of destiny, he welcomed the destructive powers of the gods.

"Pyrang kar, maauntelzes, belang kar zanto zrekos. (Heed me, ancient ones, grant me your wrath,)" Matticus said in a hushed tone through clenched teeth. *"Nnusa kar gaz lett diaenzaporrsir. (Bath me in the blood of the divine.)"*

An aura of red whirled around Matticus's arms. He approached the challenger under the gatehouse, sneering under his helmet. The Ehthilian waved his sword around as the assaulting Hostellae made way for their king. Matticus picked up speed and elevated his slow march to steady strides. Lungs pounding and heart beating, he charged and ripped his longsword from its sheath.

As King Matticus barreled into striking distance, his opponent swung his greatsword from right to left in an awkward stroke. He sliced with his blade over his head to meet the Ehthilian's at chest level. The enemy soldier staggered back and barely held onto his weapon. With ferocity, Matticus used his strength to bully the giant soldier to the back of the archway, nearly breaking the blockade to the inner city.

The defender, back against the open streets of Maelensis, made his final stand and bull-rushed him with his shoulder. Matticus sidestepped the charge and hacked clean through the man's leg mid-calf. A cry of agony rang through the city's lower level, the Hostellae outside erupting with bloodlust.

Matticus walked a circle around his prey, scraping the tip of his longsword against the stone road. The Ehthilian crawled away and left a trail of gushing blood from his cleaved leg. Tilting his head like a predator toying with his food, the king followed the bleeding soldier to his right. In a desperate last attempt, the Ehthilian savagely flung his sword behind. Matticus caught the blade with ease thanks to the thick gauntlet covering his hand. He reinforced his grip on the sharp steel and yanked it from his opponent's hand.

Wielding two swords, Matticus flicked each of them to reverse grip and pressed his heel against his enemy's back. He held his arms stretched out in a glorious pose for his men watching with eager eyes.

"Matticus! Matticus! Matticus!" they chanted.

Hell guided his hands as he swiftly lifted both blades over his head and drove them through the Ehthilian's back, skewering each lung clean through his ribcage. Blood spewed out from the man's mouth in a dying gasp. The city had been breached.

Matticus slowly turned his gaze to the terrorized Ehthilians massing to defend the city. Their quivering legs only angered him more. He inhaled, filling his lungs to full capacity, and pointed at them.

"Feed!" he bellowed.

The Hostellae poured into the city as the king stood over the maimed Ehthilian. He pried his longsword from the corpse, leaving the other sticking straight up as a symbol of his cruelty.

Matticus stepped into the courtyard just inside Maelensis's walls. Eyeing the buildings in the upper city, flinging arrows from the archers perched on the roofs nearby alerted him. The last ranks of the Vaedorian infantry flooded the streets like waves of steel, and Commander Nysis rode up beside him.

"The Ehthilians are retreating to the keep," Nysis said, "and we have no ranged support to outmatch theirs."

Scanning his surroundings, Matticus looked for a weakness to exploit.

"Redirect the mangonels to target the inner streets," he said. "No buildings left standing."

"That will hinder our foothold of Maelensis, are you sure? We find use in the resources here."

Matticus stared at his commander with red glowing eyes.

"Destroy the city."

"Yes, sire," Nysis said hesitantly.

The Hostellae moved swiftly through Maelensis, cutting down all who stood in their way with ease. Matticus searched for the fastest route to the heart of the city, his thirst for blood growing into an obsession.

"Are you going to remount, my liege?" Nysis asked.

Matticus looked beyond the slaughter in the courtyard and eyed the central stronghold in the distance. Just the sight of it nearly drove him mad.

"No," he said, the depths of his rage rising to the surface. "I'm going to find Ambrose."

As the two armies viciously brawled for control of the inner city, King Matticus marched over the bodies with his sword in hand. Arrows skewered the ground near his feet, but he never walked into lethal range. His soldiers pried the enemy archers' attention away from him—that was their purpose. Each Vaedorian that fell in battle inched him closer to victory. With his gaze fixated upon his prize, he gave no care to the dead men around him.

The rubble under his metal boots crunched, and, eventually, the Hostellae broke through the line of defenders dying in a losing battle. Through the alleys, the king pressed on. He marched at a steady pace, confident and determined. The dominance of his armies fueled his pride as they cleared a path for him to Maelensis's keep.

A scream rang out from above, and an Ehthilian archer plummeted to the ground next to him, splattering blood across his leg armor. Matticus glanced to the left and glared. Body broken and skin mangled, the man stared at him with a plea for mercy. Matticus frowned, the sight of weakness angering him further. Stepping on the archer's throat, he pressed his heel to the earth. The wincing, sorrowful eyes of the Ehthilian bulged. Matticus pressed harder, cracking the man's spine and rupturing his esophagus. A wicked smile replaced his scowl as the archer gurgled a dying breath.

Something in the king's heart snapped as he dispatched the Ehthilian into the void. His sneer dropped to a blank stare, but his helmet hid it from those around him. He sensed the evil spread through him, though; he felt it. He felt the eerie ecstasy of murder usurp control of his rational thoughts behind hollow eyes.

The Vaedorians advanced toward the inner city, securing building by building. Matticus walked up the inclined road that led to keep. Maelensis's architecture reminded him of that of his own city. He recognized the craftsmanship of Monscarren's stone masons and assumed that the Ehthilian kings long ago called for expert builders to construct the capital city.

Suddenly, Matticus heard a loud boom followed by a rumbling in the ground. He stopped to steady his balance and scanned ahead. Rocks crashed into the street from the left, and Matticus realized that an entire building had collapsed. Dust and rubble cluttered the air, blocking his view.

He hadn't ordered for the engineers to bring out the black powder, and the trebuchets couldn't reach this far from their stationary position outside the walls. Only one thing could have caused such a disaster.

"Ambrose," Matticus said while gritting his teeth.

"Sire, your orders?" one of the knights next to him said.

King Matticus paused to analyze the situation, realizing his cousin called upon Osiris's magics to defend the keep. Every Osirian held the power of their great ancestor, but only the adept could wield it so efficiently. Harnessing such sorceries required spoken chants, sturdy tools, and knowledge of the ancient spells. With Ambrose's ring in possession, Matticus could control darker, more formidable magics. He knew he needed it to conquer Voluutia if *Osirisigniros* didn't present itself in the ashes of Ehthilia.

"Stand aside," Matticus said darkly. "A king is needed here."

The ruins of the building Ambrose tore down blocked his path, but Matticus's warpath would not be stopped so easily. Sheathing his longsword, Matticus walked toward the mountain of rubble and took a deep breath.

"Sunzer ish tul ene zot sen comosetag. (Stone and earth are mine to command,)" Matticus said under his breath. *"Kogzang nal, folst, ish mnaka! (Break away, fall, and crumble!)"*

As the king finished chanting, he slammed his open palms on the ground near his feet, and a titanic shockwave exploded from his position, blasted the rubble free, and scattered it down the street. The path to Ambrose became open once more; Matticus glared down the road after raising his head.

Matticus unrelentingly continued his march toward the keep. The Hostellae sprinted all around him. All momentum pointed to the lone structure ahead.

After backing the Ehthilians into a cage by surrounding the stronghold with thousands of steel-clad soldiers, Matticus centered his gaze upon the crenellated wall where Ambrose rallied the last of his men. Dozens of Vaedorian swordsmen ran out to protect their king as he proceeded into the open where the lines of Ehthilian archers could easily pick him off. They held their fire, though, as a moment of peace arose with the two armies staring each other down from across the street between the keep and the rest of the city.

The gate to the stronghold opened to reveal a band of Ehthilia's strongest warriors ready to face him. Matticus, behind rows of his infantry, ordered them to make way. He accepted their challenge, stepping out from the Hostellae and drawing his blade. The Ehthilian elites bolted from their position and charged toward him. Matticus took his *Igni* stance and marched on.

The first Ehthilian cocked his arms for a devasting blow as he sprinted. Matticus cleaved the man in half in one stroke with the help of his empowered strength. Mauled, the carcass tumbled across the ground to the side, horrifying the rest of the defenders who halted in their advance. They ran straight for him after a moment, though, and Matticus released his true aggression run rampant. Enemies flocked to him in groups of two and three, but he cast them aside like helpless sacks of meat. He hacked, sliced, and slashed his way across the street, using the domination of the *Igni* fighting stance to carve a path forward.

Eventually, Matticus became so enraged in battle, he released a maniacal scream through his helmet as he seized an attacking Ehthilian's arm, placed his heel on the man's chest, and heaved with all his might. Like a savage bear, he tore the limb from the man with ease as it jerked at every severance of muscle and ligament.

The king's scream shifted into a sinister laugh. Body after body littered the clearing in front of the keep. Matticus's armor gained a new coat of red, the silver shine on his chest hardly able to reflect midday's sun overhead. None of Ehthilia's strongest remained, and he searched around for a new target when he heard a faint shout from atop the stronghold's wall.

Hundreds of arrows screeched from the sky in his direction. Without a moment to think, Matticus lifted his hands to the sky.

"Basteletang kar, lucidenhororizgir. (Shield me, guardians of light,)" Matticus whispered to himself.

After calling forth another enchantment, an energy field warped around Matticus, and he shoved it toward the volley of arrows. Each one bounced off and twirled to the ground. Those unafflicted landed well outside of reach.

King Matticus returned to his upright stance, flipped his sword to reverse grip, and forcefully planted it in the ground. The entire castle shook violently, knocking the Ehthilian archers on their backs. None of Maelensis's defenders stood a chance against him, and he knew they were running out of options.

"Ambrose!" Matticus shouted.

Both armies lowered their guards, allowing a swift silence to sweep through the street.

"Enough of your cowardice!"

In the eye of the storm, Matticus waited for a response, but he only heard the rustling of metal armor and the faint breeze of wind. He sheathed his sword and removed his helmet, the red glow fading from his eyes.

"You cannot hide behind your walls forever!" he shouted again.

Another calm silence followed. He waited, nonetheless.

Finally, after another moment, Matticus noticed movement in group the Ehthilians on the wall. A glimmer appeared over the stone, and he recognized it as King Ambrose's jeweled crown.

"Matticus!" Ambrose yelled. "The gods will strike you down for this! How dare you invade my lands with the peace treaty intact!"

Matticus chuckled to himself.

"What brought you to this madness?" Ambrose asked in a desperate shout. "Slaughtering my people like sheep? Ransacking helpless villages? Have you no honor?"

The Hostellian king remained unmoved. He shifted his weight to the other foot, growing a darker expression on his face.

"This isn't about honor. This is mercy."

"You murdered the entire countryside at first sight!" Ambrose yelled. "Not once did you show my people any mercy, even as prisoners of war!"

The previous week of culling Ehthilia's weaker towns crossed his mind. Matticus sneered.

"Your people are weak, Ambrose," he said. "Too long has your kingdom crumbled from within. Too long have you sat at the throne corrupting *my* legacy as an Osirian."

King Ambrose didn't respond.

"Ehthilia has ensnared its people in an endless cycle of poverty and crime. I am simply here to liberate it."

"By killing all who oppose you?" Ambrose shouted. "By laying claim to my kingdom with some demented sense of union and burning it to the ground?"

Matticus smiled.

"Exactly," he said under his breath.

The wind picked up, whistling through the corridor outside of the keep.

"You are no longer fit to rule over these lands. Your territory now belongs to the Hostellian Empire!"

"Empire?" Ambrose said. "You are delusional Matticus. None of the kings would ever bow to one nation. Certainly not me."

"Don't worry," Matticus said as he put his helmet back on and pulled his sword from the sheath. "You won't have to."

Banners flying behind him, Matticus raised his sword in the air. Horns and shouts of war followed as the Hostellae continued the assault. Matticus watched for a moment and allowed his soldiers to take the lead. The mangonels in position just behind the inner wall hurled their rocks toward the keep. After the second projectile crashed into the gate, it slammed into the ground, destroying the last obstacle between Matticus and his target.

The Hostellian king stepped forward, his soldiers surging forth and overwhelming the Ehthilians. After a moment, the arrows from above ceased as the enemy retreated deeper into the keep. Matticus pressed on and walked underneath the gatehouse of Maelensis's final line of defense. He studied the crowded courtyard as his men swarmed the castle.

Just as the Hostellae reached the door to the main hall of the keep, Matticus heard a familiar language in the distance. Though unable to decipher the exact phrase Ambrose spoke, he knew what followed the chant spoken in Aznogsi.

The ground shook under him, and multiple shockwaves rippled through the keep, sending stones flying through the air. Ambrose sacrificed the structural integrity of his castle to obliterate the Hostellae. Many of Matticus's soldiers fell to their feet while the unlucky few in high places fell to their demise. Seconds later, chunks of the wall rained upon the courtyard like a storm from hell.

Matticus planted his feet, stared at the sky as if to will the boulders away from him, and survived unscathed. Through the clouds of dust, he looked around at his soldiers splattered across the pavement. He diverted his attention, though, once he saw King Ambrose racing across the wall to escape inside the keep behind a crowd of Ehthilians.

Scoffing, King Matticus made his way toward the large wooden doors ahead.

As he climbed the stairs to the inner castle with the second wave of his soldiers behind, he knew Ambrose had nowhere left to run. Matticus stabbed his sword through the marble patio under his feet, cracking it several inches in multiple directions, and placed his hands on the door. The power in his blood flowed through his arms and legs as he heaved. Matticus pressed, the sheer anger in his heart allowing his godlike strength to push the door open. Eventually, splinters scattered, the hinges bent, and the light of the main hall shone through the gap he created. The Hostellian king peered through the tiny opening to dozens of frightened enemy soldiers. He stood upright once more and clenched his fist. Matticus then cocked his arm back, tightened his fist, and crashed his knuckles into the weak spot of the door, shattering it as the glow in his veins shone the brightest.

Matticus entered Maelensis's great hall after yanking his blade from the ground and allowed his soldiers to rush behind. A pause occurred as he witnessed the definition of weakness in the eyes of the men across from him.

"Enough, Matticus," Ambrose said, emerging from the crowd. "These men do not need to die. You have bested me."

"Sacrificing yourself will not alter my decision to absorb your kingdom," Matticus said, pointing his sword behind him to the thousands of dead Ehthilians in the streets. "Your army has been slain; your city razed."

"Perhaps," Ambrose said. "My foolishness has led my people to ruin as you have so boldly demonstrated."

Matticus waited, squinting in skepticism.

"But this can end, now. Please. If any mercy still lives within you, may you show it to these men behind me."

"I did not come here for them," Matticus said with a dark tone. "I came here for you."

King Matticus took one step closer, and Ambrose did the same.

"Then fight me," the Ehthilian king said, "and let my life act as payment for their freedom."

Matticus remained silent but lifted his blade to his *Igni* stance. Accepting the duel, he marched forth. Ambrose plucked his sword from his side and neared at a quicker pace. A swift stroke from above fell upon Matticus, but he side-stepped the attack and sliced across his body. Ambrose somersaulted forward to avoid his cold steel. Matticus's blade crashed into the keep's floor before he pulled it back to regain control.

Looking into his opponent's frenzied eyes, Matticus gathered himself to a neutral position. He waited for Ambrose to launch a brutish strike and parried it with ease, forcing his opponent to stagger. Immediately after, he grabbed Ambrose by the top of his shoulder with his free hand, stomped forward with his left foot, and crashed his right knee into his cousin's chest. Matticus's thick leg armor carved a dent in the insignia on the cuirass.

Matticus dropped his sword as Ambrose hacked and wheezed, longing to toy with him. Once his opponent shakingly stood upright, he grabbed the sword pointed at him and yanked it away before swinging it with the blade at Ambrose's shins.

He knocked the Ehthilian king to the floor, sweeping Ambrose's legs out from under him with the hilt. The defending soldiers gasped in fear.

"This is exactly why I am here," Matticus said.

He grabbed his opponent by the hair sticking out behind the crown. Ambrose winced in pain. Caring not for sympathy, Matticus pried his cousin off the ground.

"You are weak."

The evil corrupting Matticus's heart urged him to prolong Ambrose's death, and he took a liking to the idea. He shoved his free hand onto the Ehthilian king's exposed throat with his metal gauntlet and held him higher in the sky. The fury of hell pulsed in his hand, the shine from his red eyes seeping through his helmet.

Ambrose wriggled and clawed at his arm. Matticus squeezed tighter.

"Ehthilia will not be spared from my wrath," King Matticus said.

He stared into his cousin's panicking eyes and watched the blood vessels burst from lack of oxygen. Feeling Ambrose's spine crack as he squeezed tighter, he pulled him closer.

"Neither will you."

Matticus clenched his fist, crushing the last morsel of life from King Ambrose. The Ehthilian's face shifted from red to pale white, and his limbs fell limp. Tossing his cousin's carcass to the floor, he eyed the rest of the defenders quivering in their armor.

A Vaedorian captain approached him from behind.

"Your Majesty, the city is captured. What are your orders?"

He looked at the surrendered soldiers one more time. Their scared expressions enraged him further.

"Slay them all," he said as he turned back.

Matticus picked his blade off the floor and made his way toward the exit of the keep. Cries for help rang in his ears as he left followed by the sounds of clanging steel and tearing flesh.

Blood filled the streets. Maelensis had fallen.

King Matticus looked upon the destroyed city and inhaled the ashen air. At last, he could call himself an emperor with two territories under his control. But more land awaited. More enemies lied in his path to unity.

Matticus favored the growing rage that he unleashed upon Ehthilia, and he longed to unleash it again unto the other kings.

Chapter 5

Voluutia

Day 19 in the Month of War

After the Order of the Black Legion made their plans to disperse from Anzagaar Nostir, Prince Lucien traveled with King Atlas and a majority of those present in the meeting on a journey for Voluutia's capital city. The Legonae, led by Commander Ursa, followed shortly behind as they waited for further instruction, and the remaining citizens in Zededia's fortress vacated as well. Those heading for Daece rode adjacent to the party stopping in Voluutia and would linger near until the Hylonen River branched off from Lake Mulduur, the largest body of fresh water in Osiria where the Voluutians founded their greatest city, Amuun Drall.

During his travels, he spotted Queen Livia with her sons and group of maidens following around to cater her every wish. Despite every suggestion to travel straight for the high forests to the northeast, Livia insisted on riding to Voluutia for the Meeting of Sons. Lucien knew that she would be safer in Daece, but he was grateful for her presence. Having a friend nearby that didn't hide behind a suit of armor or a sword gave him a pleasant feeling.

Once King Atlas had led the envoy of thousands out of the Lunendar Mountains between Hostellus and Merrinine, Prince Lucien laid eyes upon the vast landscape of Voluutia for the first time in his entire life. The reigning peaks and endless forests shifted to small, grassy hills and cliffs.

In the distance, Lucien saw smoke columns from a village and traced the river down near the edge of the mountain where a massive lake separated the forests from the rest of the kingdom. The fog concealed the far side of the lake, but the prince narrowed his vision on several fishing boats and a faint dock through the haze. He counted three small towns on the outskirts of the lake in his view, all likely aligned to the capital of Voluutia that he had heard stories about as a boy.

"I suppose that's how Amuun Drall feeds its people," Lucien said to himself, watching the fishing vessels sail to and from the dock behind the fog. "I can smell the fish from here."

"Don't be so gloomy, Prince Lucien," Thancred said to him on his left.

Lucien looked over to his friend as they rode down the path leading out of the mountains.

"There are plenty of other worries for your mind to focus on aside from the fish," the old man said.

Lucien scoffed.

"Ah, yes," he said. "That's comforting."

Ahead of the convoy, Prince Lucien caught a glimpse of the white silk wrapping Livia's shoulders. He sat deep in thought for a moment, a frown appearing on his face.

"I don't suspect that it's just the fish that troubling you, eh, my prince?" Thancred said.

Lucien kept his eyes upon Livia when she bobbed into view.

"Why do you believe the queen decided to travel with us to Amuun Drall instead of Daece where she will be safe?" he asked.

"If there is one quality that Her Majesty possesses, it's determination."

The prince raised an eyebrow and looked at Thancred.

"I don't follow."

Thancred's pause confused him further.

"If I were to guess, I'd say the queen feels partially responsible for Matticus's actions and wishes to see the resolution to the end. She may not have a chance to speak among the Sons, but she isn't the type of woman to sit idly by in a far away castle ignorant to the plan at hand. She'll want to know how they are going to deal with Matticus."

Lucien sent a sharp exhale through his nose.

"How do you think they'll agree to handle the situation?" he asked.

Immediately after, Thancred chuckled.

"What?" Lucien asked.

"The Sons of Osiris hardly agree on anything. It'll be a miracle if they leave the meeting without sparking a war themselves."

"But there's been peace across the Osirian kingdoms for hundreds of years now." Lucien said. "They would allow that to happen so quickly?"

He waited for Thancred to reply, sensing Thancred tried to find the proper explanation.

"There's something you need to learn about politics in Osiria."

"And what is that?" the prince said.

A breeze wisped by, and Lucien's ears fixated upon the thuds of his horse's hooves.

"War never ends, Lucien," Thancred said, "and it never changes. The battlefields may fall silent, and borders may remain the same, but far worse actions take place behind closed doors."

Lucien's mind wandered to the suspicious activities shadowing the elites in Vaedor Sellos's council. He started to regret sitting by and allowing such schemes to come to fruition under his own nose.

"Espionage, treason, sabotage," Thancred said. "These are the seeds from which wars grow, and they are planted at every chance. The Osirian kings may publicly live by a code of peace and honor, but they spend every moment inside plotting against one another."

Lucien's view of his familial lineage soured. Everything made sense, however. Matticus's years of devising plans and the treaty he signed with King Holthiem proved Thancred's point. He soon assumed that it only took one king to catalyze the process. Civil war was inevitable; it simply mattered who started it. Lucien clenched his lips, feeling the curtain of innocence slip away from him. The sheltered life in Vaedor Sellos that Matticus and his father provided kept all notions of evil and sinistry away. He wondered if Matticus had made his life easy on purpose so he wouldn't feel a need to act upon what happened behind closed doors.

The thought sickened him. There was nothing to do about it now, though. Lucien steered his mind toward current and future events and glanced over to the endless lake at the bottom of the mountain path. The trees grew thin in number, and the grasses stretched to the sky like slender arms reaching for the clouds. As Lucien rode onto flatter ground, the mass of people traveling in a column split into two streams. One diverged to the left of the lake toward the distant land of Daece, and the other pooled outside of the closest town. Most of the voyagers continued on their path to the northeast, and Lucien guessed that King Atlas and his selected soldiers pulled off to the side to regroup.

Lucien followed Thancred and a few of the Legonae captains, and he watched Queen Livia venture ahead of him as if he needed to see her decision to linger in Voluutia for himself.

"This way, my prince," his old friend said.

A watery aroma filled his nose, but not that of a coursing river. A stagnant, mildewy scent overcame him instead. He flared his nostrils and tried to calm his stomach. The Hostellian landscape never gave him the chance to explore the oceans or lakes of the Osirian kingdoms, a trait of his home that he started to appreciate.

King Atlas's shining crown stuck out in the distance as Lucien joined the gathered crowd halted just before the lakeside village. Some of the commonfolk emerged from the palisade wall to greet him, but Lucien kept his gaze on Queen Livia. He rode up to her and quickly dismounted.

"Here, My Lady," the prince said, offering his hand.

Livia's smile warmed him. However, as he carefully helped the queen to the ground, he knew the emptiness within her lingered.

"Thank you, Lucien," Livia said.

"How are you fairing?" he asked.

Lucien took her arm and started to walk toward the town as Thancred approached behind.

"Oh, I suppose I'm fine. Spending nearly every moment of every day on a horse has made me appreciate the finer things of being a queen, though."

The prince chuckled.

"A month ago, I had talked to a graceful woman about how she despised life in a court. I wonder where she's run off to?"

"She's wondering how hard it would be to find a good meal. The road hasn't provided much these last few days."

Notions of Livia's behavior in the past and the coldness behind her eyes now reinforced Lucien's theory that she was more troubled than she wished to seem. He thought of himself for a moment, sensing the same feeling within himself.

Lucien knew life after Zededia's death had been different. He felt the pain lurking around him on the endless search for a hole in his defenses. Despite attempting to drown the reminders, seeing Livia's subtle dread heightened his.

"I'm sure Her Majesty will find great comfort in Amuun Drall," he said. "Though, I don't suggest that you stay in Voluutia for long."

"You wished that I had chosen to ride to Daece instead?" she asked.

The prince hesitated.

"Yes," he said. "I'd sleep better at night knowing that you are as far as possible from the war my brothers have caused."

"Matticus would never allow harm to befall me, Lucien, regardless to my protests against his actions."

"It's not Matticus I'm worried about, Your Majesty," Lucien said.

He sensed Livia's confused expression looking at him.

"After years of humiliating defeats from the hands of the Legonae, the Vaedorians have grown ... eager ... to reinstate their militaristic dominance across all Osiria. If Matticus has led them to Ehthilia, they will have slaughtered them without a second thought."

"What are you trying to say, Lucien?"

The prince shifted his eyes around to make sure that no one would eavesdrop.

"I'm saying that Matticus may not be able to protect you if the Vaedorians reach you first. They've been defeated too many times and have developed a bloodlust. I could see it in their eyes shortly before..."

Lucien trailed off, unaware that he had started to venture into a dark place in his mind.

"Before Zededia was slain?" Livia asked.

The prince nodded. He hadn't realized how difficult his brother's death would be to discuss. Just mentioning it again knotted his stomach.

"Yes."

A silence swept over Lucien as he tried to keep his demons at bay. He felt Livia's grip on his forearm tighten.

Soon after, the prince caught up with King Atlas and the rest of those traveling to Amuun Drall. Lucien mingled with the crowd until he reached the front. Commander Ursa greeted him with a hand on his shoulder, and the prince met eyes with three other Black Legion elites behind.

Lucien maintained a tight hold on Livia's arm. While he fully trusted the men around him and knew they would protect the queen at all costs, he still felt the need to keep her close. Atlas made conversation with an official from the town in front of him, and Lucien squinted as the king walked back.

"We've been granted safe passage to Amuun Drall," Atlas said. "We will board the fishing vessels docked in the harbor and proceed from there. You may gather your belongings, but the horses must remain here."

The news lifted a light burden from him. Livia's complaints about riding horseback amused him, but he longed to travel on his own two feet as well. King Atlas motioned for everyone to head for the town, and twenty men grabbed what they could to initiate the voyage.

Ramshackle buildings and uneven roads stuck out in the prince's view like a sore thumb. Voluutia had never been a poor region. Lucien remembered the stories from his father and reports from his brothers describing the kingdom's intricate infrastructure, so seeing a crucial checkpoint to the capital city in such a state surprised him.

"I thought Voluutia was relatively well off," the prince said. "Not a loosely bound series of townships falling apart at the seams."

"As I said before, Prince Lucien," Thancred said quietly from his left. "The war has continued in other areas."

Lucien raised an eyebrow as he escorted the queen through a square.

"What are you hinting at?" he asked.

"Voluutia's economy has all but been reduced to rubble after years of supplying money and troops to Korzeg."

"Rather ironic that Korzeg is about to turn around and point their swords at Voluutia," Lucien said with a smirk on his face. "What a bloody mess this world is."

"That it is, my prince," Thancred said. "Count yourself lucky that Matticus has shielded you from it. Most other Osirians are thrown into chaos before they can walk. Mythian murdered his own brother before he was ten to secure his right to the throne of Merrinine."

Though Lucien struggled to keep dark thoughts of his eldest brother from eating away at him, he found delight in the positives that Matticus provided him with. It gave him hope that somewhere in the Hostellian King's heart lay remorse if not redemption.

"I suppose I am lucky then..." he trailed off while his mind wandered.

The cracks in Lucien's internal integrity started to deepen. Up until this point, he had presented an unbroken stance aside from his conversation with Thancred and his time alone in Zededia's chamber, one that gave no trace of despair. The weight of his bottled grief started to creep in, clawing at him. His strength waned. Eventually, he would reach his breaking point. He kept that fact foremost in his thoughts, trying to prolong that day for as long as he could.

As the parade approached the harbor, Lucien shook off his worry and focused on the journey. Several fishing boats lined the docks, fishermen dragging their haul off by the basket. Atlas stepped aside as his guards pointed the way.

"This is the best we have to work with on such a short notice," the Daecian King said.

Lucien surveyed the mediocre ships and felt uneasy.

"This is better than walking to the city?" he asked.

"Much," Atlas said. "Saves us a half a day's ride at least."

Atlas gave him a sly grin.

"Besides," the king said, "there's only one way into Amuun Drall, and you can take a guess as to what that is."

"Great," Lucien said with a frown.

"Against sailing, Prince Lucien?" he asked. "You're starting to sound like your brother more and more."

Lucien leaned over the edge of the stone path and peered into the murky lake and then to the rotting hulls of the fishing boats.

"I'm less against sailing and more against drowning. These ships look one step above rotten."

Half an hour later, Lucien found himself standing on the deck of a rickety boat surrounded by Atlas's men. Thancred stood in his usual position to the prince's right, giving him the comfort that even if he drowned, the old man wouldn't outlive him by much. The ship embarked for the capital city, and Lucien's mind raced with the possible experiences he would find there.

Night fell quicker than the prince thought. He stood by the edge of the ship resting against the railing of the hull. Thancred lingered by to give him company. The calm water below disturbed only by the oars of the sailors cast a mirrored glaze. Lucien stared at his blurry reflection. He hardly could look himself in the eye, a heavy dose of shame plaguing him still. As he glanced off to the east, he knew Matticus marched somewhere on the other side of the mountains. Lightning flashed in the dense clouds looming over Ehthilia in the distance, deepening his worry.

The outline of Amuun Drall crept into view as more of the city revealed itself through the fog by the lit torches planted on the outer walls. Just as he imagined himself lying on a soft bed, someone approached the railing in his peripheral vision several yards away.

Lucien glanced over while Livia removed the silk hood from her head. The moonlight illuminated her face in a way he had never seen. Despite living with her for years, Lucien hadn't felt this close to the queen. Something about her emptiness, the way it reminded him of his own, spoke to him.

"Do not worry about the queen, my prince," Thancred said softly in his ear. "She will manage."

Lucien sighed to himself and looked back to the massive city growing on the horizon.

"I'm not sure it's the queen he worries for," King Atlas said as he quietly walked from behind.

The prince turned and cast a sharp gaze at everyone.

"My worries are my own at the moment, no one else's."

"Of course," Atlas said. "I did not mean to intervene."

Atlas pivoted on his foot and turned away.

"Wait," Lucien said.

Recognizing his defensive behavior that he learned from Zededia to shield his emotions, the prince released his held breath. His regret forced him to open up, a trait he loathed.

"I, uh ...," Lucien said, "I've been meaning to talk to you about something."

Atlas leaned against the railing, and Lucien took another look at Livia as Thancred walked away to give them privacy.

"How may I be of service, Prince Lucien Osiris?" Atlas asked.

The question caught him off guard.

"Well ... actually that's one thing that's been puzzling me," Lucien said.

"Oh, do explain."

Lucien supported his weight on his elbows on the railing and exhaled.

"Why does a man of your position and power still maintain such a serval attitude?"

A pause swept between them.

"I'm afraid I don't understand?"

Lucien bit his upper lip and tried to muster a different approach.

"All of my life," he said after a moment. "In all the years of royalty and living among those of the court, I've come to understand that our humility fades as we obtain more power, yet, with you, it seems to remain. My father tried to teach me humility, tried to mold me into a respectable man as if respect was never to be something I would receive."

"Respect isn't something that someone receives, Lucien," Atlas said. "Or at least it shouldn't be. That's the problem with politics of today's world."

The churning waters underneath the ship snagged Lucien's attention for a moment as he processed the king's answer. He had heard that once before, but he couldn't remember who from.

"Respect is earned," Atlas said. "Regardless of-"

"Status, position, or skill," Lucien said in unison with the Daecian king.

Atlas smiled at him.

"That's right. I suppose I shouldn't be surprised that's a phrase you're familiar with."

"Yes, but ... I'm having trouble recollecting where I became familiar with it. Where did you learn it?"

Atlas smile widened as he leaned back over the rail.

"The first time I ever met him, your brother said that to me."

Lucien looked at Atlas, and his blank face shifted to a frown as the pain he had been trying to contain leaked through.

"He, Matticus, and your father had traveled to Daece on a diplomatic mission to meet with my father when he was king. Matias brought Matticus into the meeting, and Zededia and myself were left to the city on our own."

Hearing the memory of his family before the great divide that followed his father's death wore down his ability to hide his emotions. A warm rush washed over his face, building underneath his eyes.

"Zededia and I spent the entire night sneaking around the castle and trading stories. We must have driven the guards crazy after they tried to chase us down, unaware of who we were while we acted like criminals skulking about."

A pool of water gathered on Lucien's eyelid. He noticed the chuckle in Atlas's voice, sensing the happiness that Zededia left behind in the memories of his loved ones. The prince's own memories of sneaking around on adventures with his brother lit his thoughts ablaze. Caught in an endless circle of repeating scenes from his childhood, he sniffed and kept his chin up high. Oh, how Lucien longed for those days to return. Back when the world wasn't so complicated. Back when his family lived in harmony and prospered in the love they shared. Back when Zededia was alive.

"Finally, we had been caught," Atlas said. "My father's personal guard, Thestalus, a bitter old man, cornered us in the keep's pantry. I was about to stand and apologize and take responsibility for our actions, but ... Zededia spoke first. I didn't understand why since I easily could have gotten the two of us out of trouble in an instant by ordering Thestalus to stand down."

"I'm guessing that's not what happened," Lucien said.

"No, it's not," the Daecian king said.

A half-grin formed on the prince's face as he started to detect where Atlas was leading him with the story.

"Zededia spent the next three hours inside of a prison cell underneath the keep; he didn't inform Thestalus of his status as an Osirian. I walked out with nothing more than a stern look."

Atlas broke out into a bigger laughter.

"Holy Neshka," he said as Lucien listened. "Your father nearly tore the castle apart looking for him. It took me half the night to work up the courage to explain that his beloved son was sitting in chains forty feet below him."

"Wait ...," Lucien said. "I remember this story. When Father returned with my brothers, he tried to convince my mother that the Daecians had taken him prisoner and were plotting to overthrow Hostellus."

Lucien leaned back, holding himself upright with a steady grip on the railing, and let the stars shine over his face.

"Not a bad plan if Daece wasn't so damn far from us," Lucien said.

"Nevertheless, I'm quite glad King Matias never returned with his armies," Atlas said. "I'm not sure if Daece could withstand so much Vaedorian steel."

"Back then ...," Lucien said, "we believed in the peace among the kingdoms. Father fought to keep things that way up until his last breath."

"I spoke to your brother once he was released, and I asked him why in hell he did what he did."

Atlas's sincerity forced Lucien to refocus. Hearing of Zededia's selflessness made him proud of his brother.

"I told him that Thestalus would have respected me since I was a prince, and he looked back at me with that stupid smirk of his and said: 'Respect shouldn't be something that is merely given. It's earned, regardless status, position, or skill.' I was speechless. A seventeen-year-old boy from a distant country managed to humble me in seconds. I didn't understand, still don't in a sense. All I could think was 'damn you, Zededia.'"

Lucien chuckled.

"That was a common phrase spoken about him."

"Oh, I believe you," Atlas said with a scoff. "But, um ... from that moment on, I looked up to Zededia. I knew that he was a man I could follow. A man I would fight for given the chance. Years of friendship later, when he asked me to join a secret organization he planned to create, I volunteered without hesitation."

Lucien struggled to find a response. He only clasped his hands together, squeezed, and tried to keep his composure.

"Your brother was quite special, Lucien," Atlas said.

"Yeah ...," the prince said, his voice watering.

He swallowed the spit in his mouth and shifted his lips.

"Yeah, he was."

As Lucien started to succumb to his pain, a loud, deep bell echoed across the lake. He looked up and watched the ship glide toward a dock in the great city's harbor, and the crew hurried about to prepare for landing. Atlas left his side, as did Thancred, and Lucien forced his emotions back into the pit of his heart.

No time for mourning now, not when more pressing matters approached. The void cracking his heart would have to wait. Hopefully, he thought, he could use the grief he felt for Zededia to ignite his courage for the coming days.

Lucien gathered his belongings and mingled with the soldiers around him as the ship sailed in. The journey to Voluutia had nearly ended, but Lucien knew the hardest steps had yet to come.

Chapter 6

The Plan

Day 20 in the Month of War

The night on the docks of Amuun Drall cleared without a sound, bringing a red dawn rising over the mountains that spread its rays across the lake. Lucien followed King Atlas and the rest of the group toward the inner city where King Raed and the rest of his court prepared for the Meeting of Sons. Feeling out of place, the prince tried to blend in with the soldiers and elites around him. He had always been a royal in his own court; being a guest dampened his view of his status.

Eventually, Lucien made his way through the city until the keep rose above all other buildings where a wide, man-made river circled it and the adjacent structures. The prince compared the mercantile and militaristic zones of Amuun Drall to the Vaedorian counter parts and found several similarities. Just by walking through the main street, however, he deduced that the Voluutians placed most of their effort into bolstering their mounted warriors rather than infantrymen by how many stables and heavy armor shops he passed.

King Atlas stopped the party at the edge of the outer bank of the moat, and Lucien saw a guard give the signal to the gatehouse. Shortly after, a drawbridge lowered, granting them passage. The prince looked down into the water to gauge its depth, but he couldn't see the bottom despite the relatively clear water. The guards kept their shifty eyes on him. Chills ran down his spine.

"Fear not, my prince," Commander Ursa said from his right. "We are welcome here."

Lucien watched the Voluutian soldiers with caution regardless. Inside the walls and past the heavy security, he scanned the clustered buildings and their unique architecture. The fluid, smooth design of the houses differed from the rough, strong edges of Vaedor Sellos.

A thousand men could live within these walls without ever leaving, a thought that sickened Lucien and his sense of adventure. Out from main doors of the keep, an emissary bearing the mark of the Voluutian court approached.

"Welcome, King Atlas Osiris and the followers of Daece," the messenger said. "We have anticipated your arrival and are happy to offer our hospitality."

Atlas stepped forward and conversed with the man. Lucien took a firm hold of his pack and started to take a step himself, but Thancred stopped him for a moment.

"The Meeting of Sons won't take place until tonight, my prince," the old man said. "We had best ready ourselves and leave Atlas to his affairs."

"Yes," Lucien said. "Though, I'm unsure if I'm going to attend the meeting at all."

Thancred gave him a surprised look.

"I'm not sure that's your decision, Prince Lucien."

Lucien frowned.

"What do you mean?"

"All able Osirians are required to make an appearance when a meeting is summoned. You, especially, as a representative of Hostellus."

"Thancred, this gathering is to discuss what to do *about* Hostellus, why would my input be of any value?"

"Because," the doctor said. "You may be the only one here who can bargain for the future of our home when this war is over. If Matticus is defeated, Raed will start a rampage on his own and burn Hostellus to the ground out of sheer spite. You are needed to remind them that Matticus started all of this, not the people of Vaedor Sellos."

Lucien clenched his lips.

"I suppose," he said. "But I doubt my reason will have much weight."

"Atlas will support you, my prince, and more will follow. You don't need everyone to agree, you just need to ensure that they don't decide to raze Hostellus unanimously. If one opposes, others will too."

"Look how that turned out for the Ehthilans. I'm sure they opposed to being conquered."

He heard Thancred sigh.

"That isn't the same," the old man said. "Greed leads men to commit terrible acts, but revenge ... revenge can destroy the world. Matticus's rage runs deep like rivers, but Raed's outmatches his. If the Hostellae are beaten, seven kingdoms will descend upon Vaedor Sellos like vultures cleaning a corpse. Believe it or not, Matticus isn't the quickest Osirian to go to war with his kin."

Lucien thought deeply about Thancred's statement. He wondered who else among his cousins plotted in the shadows and if his home ever rested in their sights. None of the others could hope to conquer Hostellus alone, but seven kingdoms, seven armies, could easily do so. With the grim outlook on the way things seemed to work in Osiria, the prince shook his head and mustered forth.

The mass of people in the courtyard dispersed, and Lucien watched Atlas in his direction. The prince shifted his hand around his pack to ensure that he hadn't left anything behind and took a step forward.

"That went better than I expected," Atlas said.

"It could have been worse?" Lucien asked, a confused look overtaking him. "They're expecting us, aren't they?"

"Correct," Atlas said. "But the Voluutians aren't always as ... inviting ... as they appear to be."

Lucien frowned.

"But, the Voluutians summoned this meeting? Why would they dismiss our presence?"

King Atlas smiled at him.

"Welcome to politics, Prince Lucien," Atlas said with a laugh. "Follow me, I will escort you to your chamber where you will stay until we depart from the city."

As he hesitated to walk in Atlas's path, Lucien surveyed the keep and made eye contact with one of the guards. A brutish gaze stared back at him, one that sent an eerie feeling down the back of his throat.

Over a gravel-paved walkway, Lucien approached a raised, railed platform surrounded by various plants and decorative garden work. He scaled the low steps and grazed his hand across the wood support. Atlas disappeared through a silk curtain that flowed under an archway. As Lucien sifted through it, he moved his eyes across every crevice of the hall, studying its details. The gray tones and smooth floor invited him inside, but he still felt out of place.

Soon after, down the hall, as Lucien peered through the windows to pick up a few details about the keep's exterior, Atlas stopped in front of him. Several maids and other servants passed by from the adjacent chambers. Lucien deduced that Atlas had requested to give him a room close to the other party members. He walked up to the doorway and bowed.

"Thank you, Your Majesty," Lucien said.

"Don't thank me," Atlas said in a joking tone. "Thank the Voluutians."

Lucien opened the door and stepped inside. The room was quite small and bleak, save for an open window pointing toward the town and the mediocre inscriptions on the walls that symbolized royalty and prestige.

"Not quite what I've been used to," Lucien said. "But better than a rundown shack."

A thick hand heartily patted his back.

"Don't worry, Lucien," Thancred said. "I will be next door. If you will allow me to rest these old bones, I will join you in a moment."

Lucien grinned and looked back to Atlas in the doorway.

"Take the rest of the day to yourselves," the Daecian king said. "It may be the last time you have that chance for a while. I'll summon you once the Meeting of Sons has begun."

Lucien nodded.

"Good day, Prince Lucien," Atlas said as he started to turn away from him.

"Good day, Your Majesty."

Atlas vanished once more, leaving the prince to explore the room on his own. He walked over to the bed in the corner and kneaded it to feel its complexion. Softer than he expected, the bed caved under the pressure of his hand and left an impression. Lucien sat down and sank into it. A deep exhale left his mouth, and as a moment of peace arose, so did the thoughts in the back of his mind that he'd been fighting off for weeks. Forced to face his agony without any sort of external stimulus to distract him, he started to dart his eyes back and forth. He couldn't pry away the image of Zededia's dead eyes, the sensation of his brother's blood on his hands reemerging. The last words Zededia spoke to him circled his head like children around a maypole.

"Find your light, Lucien. Protect it."

Deeming the task impossible, the prince fell deeper into his despair as he realized he couldn't uphold his brother's dying wish. It ruined him knowing that he allowed the evil silently consuming the world to infest him. The darkness that Zededia carried spread to him. The once jovial expression Lucien proudly wore collapsed into a sullen gaze. It took everything in him to hide it from everyone nearby.

With a sigh, Lucien reached over and set his pack at the foot of the bed, but it started to lean over and slipped open, allowing the bundle of letters he found on Zededia's desk to fall to the floor. One by one, the coarse papers unfolded and scattered across the room. Lucien glared at them for a moment; he had nearly forgotten them since he left Hostellus. A gust of wind fluttered through the open window, blowing them farther apart. Lucien stood from the bed, eyes dull and depressed, and walked over to collect them.

Like he did in Zededia's room, he skimmed over the various names for whom the letters had been written. He touched Livia's for a moment and then Atlas's, contemplating whether or not to distribute them. Caedus's lied under those, and the realization that his brother's best friend had been missing all this time electrified his thoughts.

Where the hell are you, Caedus?

Lucien thought hard on his last encounter with Caedus, remembering what Commander Ursa asked him as he arrived to Anzagaar Nostir. The last thing he saw was the back of Caedus's head as the captain walked away from Zededia's funeral. He let his eyes drift across the stone floor as tried to place himself in Caedus's position, trying to figure out where he had gone and why.

"Keep it safe."

The simple phrase haunted him. On one hand, Lucien felt grateful that Matticus hadn't obtained *Osirisigniros* so easily, but on the other, he feared his eldest brother's lethal determination to find it. The invasion of Ehthilia surely sparked once Matticus discovered Caedus's treachery. The prince then asked himself how far Matticus would go to find it after being so close to its power.

Before he could give any more thought to his question, Lucien heard a knocking from his door. Scrambling, he gathered the letters and tried to stuff them back in his pack. Thancred stepped into his side view, but he concealed the parchments just in time.

"My prince, what are you doing on the floor?"

Lucien hurriedly climbed to his feet, still trying to cover his tracks.

"Nothing, just picking something up from my pack."

He looked at Thancred and noticed the small bundle in the old man's hand.

"What have you got there?" Lucien asked.

Thancred stepped further into the room.

"I, uh, thought you might like to unwind a little after our weary travels."

The prince studied the contents of the bundle and glanced over two pipes. A strong herbal scent stung his nose.

"King's Leaf?" he asked. "How in the world did you sneak that in here?"

Lucien always hated the smell of his father's preferred narcotic as a child. However, when he first smoked it, he was introduced to a world of relaxation. The plant relaxed his body and calmed his nerves and tasted slightly sweet similar to honey and peaches. Pairing it with brandy often made for a wonderful evening. After it became outlawed in Hostellus, Lucien made sure to memorize its appearance so he could find it outside the castle. Seven fan-like leaves spread in a complete circle on every bud, resembling the crown of a king where the herb received its name.

"Are you forgetting who I am?" Thancred said with a light frown. "If I can smuggle King's Leaf past the immense security in Vaedor Sellos, I believe I can do so here."

Lucien sat back down on his bed.

"Ah, yes," he said, taking a pipe from his friend. "Forgive me."

Thancred handed him a portion of King's Leaf, and the prince packed it into the end of his pipe. He waited for the doctor to strike a spark from his flintstone. A minute passed by, and Lucien's lips became tired of holding the pipe. He took it out and watched Thancred try again and again. The old man grew more frustrated. Lucien then realized how much his friend's strength had declined over the years. The journey through the mountains didn't help.

Suddenly, a strange sensation took over Lucien's mind. He unwillingly clenched his hands, and his eyes started to glow a bright green. Thancred's hand twitched as the prince allowed his concentration to sink in. A moment later, Thancred grunted, and a spark flew off the flintstone next to Lucien's pipe, igniting the herbs inside. His head throbbed as the intense pressure faded away. Lucien brought his free hand to his forehead and winced.

"By the gods," Thancred whispered. "Your eyes, Prince Lucien."

"What?" he said in a daze.

When Lucien fully came to and understood what he had just done, a shocked expression spread across his face.

"I-I, uh, I didn't intend on-"

"How long have you been able to do that?" Thancred sporadically said, cutting him off.

Lucien froze, the memory of Spymaster Rachtus's grisly death in the keep of Vaedor Sellos rocketing forward.

"You ... were in my head, controlling my hand," Thancred said.

Shame spiraled through him. He associated the action with murdering the Spymaster, hastily deeming himself evil. The first instances of his practiced sorceries were used to slay a man and manipulate another. Quite the reputation already, he thought, a fact that haunted him.

"Have you finally been blessed with your Osirian magic?" the old man asked. "Your brothers received their gifts at an early age; here you are at twenty-five demonstrating your abilities yet again."

"What?" Lucien said.

Thancred started to chuckle.

"When you came to me that day in the upper city telling me how you watched Spymaster Rachtus drive a knife through his own neck, I had my suspicions," the doctor said in between a puff of his pipe. "But, uh ... now, I suppose I can make sense of what you saw."

Lucien sat stunned.

"Osiris's blood truly flows through you at last," Thancred said.

The old man sat up in the chair opposite Lucien's bed.

"And you're a Mystic. How wonderful indeed."

"What does that mean?" Lucien asked.

He received a raised eyebrow from his friend.

"In all the years you spent with Zededia, how did you not learn of the sorcery classifications?"

Lucien remained silent and leaned over as thancred reached over to light the prince's pipe.

"I suppose I should not be surprised given that your father attempted to bury Osirian magic after Zededia became a Shadewalker."

"He wasn't too fond of that," Lucien said, picturing his father's scowl the first time his brother managed to resurrect a soul.

"Well, I don't blame him, exactly."

"Why not?"

Thancred exhaled a plume of smoke.

"Some of the most infamous Osirians in your family's entire history have been Shadewalkers. That's why your forefathers started to cull them from the breeding pool around year 400."

The prince drew in several inhales of King's Leaf as he pondered over the reputation Shadewalkers carried. He looked out the window and gazed at the light shining brightly against the other buildings lining the circular wall of the keep's grounds.

"Zededia would have taught you," Thancred said during the silence. "He longed to teach you the secrets he knew."

Lucien couldn't reply. The sweet, intense taste of the King's Leaf kept his tongue dormant. Each moment he spent with Zededia as his brother talked about the depth of Osirian magic passed through his thoughts. At those times, he simply wished Zededia would shut his mouth as the constant lectures bored him to madness. Looking back on those moments now made him wish he had paid attention.

Half an hour filled with soft exhales and smoke clouds passed. Lucien's body loosened as the King's Leaf circulated through his system, but his mind continued to race. He looked over to his pack, the letters inside urging him to take another gander. Lucien darted his eyes to Thancred, who kept his focus on the sunny courtyard outside.

"Well, my prince," Thancred said after a moment. "I believe I will retire."

Lucien watched his friend stand from the rocking chair and headed toward the door. A firm hand gripped his shoulder as Thancred looked at him with a sincere grin hiding under his bushy beard.

"May you find peace in this day."

As Thancred turned the latch, the prince opened his satchel.

"Wait a moment, Thancred," Lucien said.

He took the bundle of letters from it and sifted through until he found the right one. His mentor turned back, and Lucien reached his hand out with the parchment between his fingers.

"What's this?"

Lucien hesitated for a moment, still unsure of his decision as he refused to acknowledge the reason for the letters' existence.

"It's from Zededia," the prince said, forcing his gaze away as if it hurt to look at. "I found it on his desk in Anzagaar Nostir. It's his final words to you."

"Oh, um ..." Thancred trailed off.

His friend struggled to take the letter. Lucien saw the pain in Thancred's face and knew right away what he was feeling. Seldom had he ever seen a sullen expression from the old man. Seeing it now troubled him.

"Thank you, my prince."

A subtle nod was all he could muster while trying to hide his own agony from Thancred. He locked his fingers in between themselves and dropped his head. Thancred left, and the door closed, sealing the prince in with his thoughts. The flowing wind from the window whirled in his room. Lucien closed his eyes and listened to the song brought by the invisible currents.

Prince Lucien spent the remainder of the day in his chambers. Traveling as a vagabond and on horseback for the previous month gave him a new appreciation for a consistent place to rest. He sat by the window in a chair, watching the shadows eat away at the sunlight. His mood declined as nightfall approached. The thoughts of the surrounding circumstances infesting his mind gnawed at him in his solitude. He longed for Thancred to come back or for Atlas to finally summon him for the Meeting of Sons. Company sounded nice, but Lucien didn't want to admit it.

Nocturnal birds cast their calls throughout the city with the moon slowly scraping across the black sky. Lucien looked around into the courtyard in search of a party of interest as his boredom reached a new peak. He tapped his fingers on the windowsill when, suddenly, a faint knock at his door alerted him.

Lucien snapped out of his trance. After a moment, it opened, and Thancred stepped inside with King Atlas behind.

"Has the meeting been called?" Lucien asked as he stood up.

Thancred and Atlas shared a concerned look between themselves, confusing the prince.

"The Meeting of Sons has been delayed," Atlas said. "Holthiem and Mythian have requested that we begin tomorrow morning."

"What?" Lucien said. "Why?"

"We don't know," Thancred said. "But it draws suspicion nonetheless."

Lucien took a step forward and frowned.

"Do you think they are gathering in secret before the meeting?" he asked.

"It's possible," Atlas said. "Which is why Raed has mandated that they remain in their chambers. However, that won't necessarily stop their emissaries from communicating. Mythian has ... unconventional ways of collecting information."

Treachery leaked from the news, but it distracted the prince from his former worries.

"It seems the lines of the war are already drawn," he said.

He received a nod from Atlas.

"This gives credit to your claim that Korzeg will unite with Hostellus. And if that happens, Merrinine won't be far behind."

"But then ... there won't really be a war, will there be? Those three forces combined can erase all others and rewrite the Osirian legacy," Lucien said.

"We mustn't burden ourselves with that now," Thancred said. "Nothing has been decided yet."

Lucien placed his hands on his waist.

"All right, well, if the meeting has been delayed, why are you here? Surely you have better things to attend to in preparation for tomorrow."

"There's someone here you need to talk to, Lucien," Atlas said. "We've come to fetch you."

Who in the world would I need to speak with? the prince thought.

He stepped forward regardless but turned back to his pack. The bundle of letters stuck out to him. Something told him to grab them, and he did. After taking a deep breath, Lucien followed Atlas and Thancred out the door.

Through the halls of the outer buildings, the prince walked behind the two men who had come to summon him, and he looked around at every new face to see if he could recognize anyone that fit the description of who he needed to talk to. Only the servant staff remained in the halls as everyone else retired to their rooms. Guards stood by, but Lucien hardly guessed that anyone residing in Amuun Drall permanently knew of his existence much less wished to speak with him.

Eventually, Atlas and Thancred stopped in front of a door that looked similar to that of his room, and Lucien followed them inside. Much like the door, the interior held the same theme. However, instead of a bed, a table lay in its place, and an archway stood on the right wall with a curtain covering the entrance. Lucien looked around in confusion.

"We'll leave you here until you are done," Atlas said as he turned to Lucien.

He received a sincere grin from the Daecian king, but saddened eyes told a different story. Thancred gave him the same look, further muddying his thoughts.

As quickly as the two men entered the room, they left, leaving the prince by himself. The door shut, and Lucien looked around again, shuffling his feet across the floor. From the open window, the moonlight danced and cast a white glaze over the stones. The sight reminded him of how he and his brothers would watch the stars from their bedrooms in the keep of Vaedor Sellos.

Lucien walked over to the windowsill and placed his hands on the wooden outline. He exhaled and waited for his company to arrive. Several figures passed through the streets across the moat, and the prince watched them as they went about their nightly tasks. A small grin cracked on the prince's face as he reimagined the citizens of his home city wandering around. He longed for a chance to disappear into the masses once again, to remove the pressure of life from his shoulders.

"Reminds you of better days, doesn't it?" a voice asked from behind him.

Startled, Lucien jolted and turned. The voice rang in his ears; he recognized it. Footsteps sounded off from behind the thin curtain in the archway. As a rugged hand moved the fabric, Lucien studied the familiar face in the shadows.

"Caedus?" Lucien asked with a bewildered expression. "Is that really you?"

Caedus came into full view and leaned against the wall.

"Where the hell have you been? Half the damn nation has been looking for you! Do you have the Sword of Kings? Is it safe?"

"Yes, the sword is safe," Caedus said, cutting Lucien off from any further questions. "And the Order has been made aware of my presence in Voluutia. That's all you need to know for now."

Lucien faltered, unsure of how to proceed. Caedus was the last person he'd expected to see here after he departed from Zededia's procession. He blinked, astonished, and scoffed.

"What are you doing here?" he said.

He watched Caedus cross his arms.

"Carrying out Zededia's orders."

Zededia's orders?

The prince paused for a moment, trying to rethink everything he could about the last interaction he had with Caedus that day in the forest. The same phrase he thought about before sprang out in front of all else.

Keep it safe.

A sudden realization dawned on him.

"You have the sword, don't you?"

Caedus's subtle nod relieved him

"I knew Matticus didn't find it in that tomb, not the real one. That's assuredly what led him to Ehthilia after he-"

Lucien couldn't bring himself to finish his sentence.

"Killed Zededia," Caedus said.

The prince sighed and let his gaze fall to the floor. Caedus moved closer, but he wanted to retreat. Lucien slid his left foot backward and crossed his arms.

"Yeah."

An awkward pause arose.

"I've heard that, um," Caedus said. "Zededia's death has ... afflicted you."

Lucien scoffed.

"I'm fine."

"No, you're not."

The prince's defensive nature overcame him, forcing a frown on his face. He stared at Caedus with agitated eyes.

"If you were fine," Caedus said, "Thancred wouldn't have found you rotting away in the shoddiest part of Merrinine."

Retreating still, Lucien fought the turmoil surfacing in his mind. Caedus was right. However, he hid his shame behind a wall of anger.

"What's your point, Caedus?"

"My point, Prince Lucien," Caedus said, his tone darkening, "is that I know you have not been able to find closure after Zededia's death. Because of that, I've decided to seek you out."

"Why?" Lucien asked, his eyes narrowing to a squint.

As Caedus fiddled with the cloth on the table in the center of the room, the prince scanned the hesitant look on his face.

"As a servant of your brother," Caedus said, "I have a responsibility to you as he did."

"You don't need to look after me, Caedus," Lucien said, turning his head away to further drive away his emotions. "I'll deal with my brother's death like I've dealt with every other death in my family: alone. The circumstances will make sense soon enough."

Lucien faced out the window and focused on the churning water of the moat below.

"What do you mean 'circumstances?'" Caedus asked.

Falling into his own trap Lucien clenched his lips and knew he couldn't dismiss the thoughts. The dozen questions that hunted him like a pack of wolves closed in. He couldn't hold them off any longer. Lucien sharply exhaled, the tip of his nose reddening as tears welled in his eyes.

"I don't know, Caedus," he said, sniffing the cold air. "I keep running over what happened in the tomb over and over again. Some of things Zededia said to me in his final days curdle my blood. Nothing makes sense. So much of what happened puzzles me."

"Like what?"

The agony in Lucien's mind crept closer.

"Just that Zededia's death seemed ... unexpected."

"He fell in war, Prince Lucien," Caedus said. "Death is always to be expected."

"I know, I mean...."

Lucien stumbled over his words as he couldn't catch up with his racing thoughts.

"I mean that when I spoke to Zededia as he literally sat in chains fifty feet below Vaedor Sellos ... he convinced me that everything was going to be okay. He convinced me that he had this master plan and that he was going to make it out alive and that-that there was hope of peace. Peace like we had in our childhood again. For one stupid fucking second, I actually believed things would go back to the way things were before Mother died. I *believed* in him."

The tears in his eyes spilled over, leaking down his face. Lucien's breaths staggered as he masked his grief for his brother with hatred. He hated that Zededia lied to him. He hated that Zededia let him down. He hated the world Zededia abandoned him to. So much anger brewed in his heart, enough to corrupt the purest of souls.

"Well," Lucien said in a watery voice as he nodded his head, "his plan didn't work. Nothing went back to how it was, there's no hope of peace, and he bloody died. And that above all is what I don't understand. My brothers have dueled constantly over their entire adult lives, and Matticus has rarely been able to best him in *all* that time. I understand how he was able to so easily this time."

"Your brother's plan worked, Lucien," Caedus said.

Lucien frowned and turned around.

"What do you mean his plan worked?" he asked, anger taking over his tone. "Of course it bloody didn't. Look around, Caedus! He's gone! Dead! Burned and scattered!"

He uncrossed his arms and started to flick his hands with his words.

"Matticus is razing half of Osiria as we speak, the other kings at each other's throats themselves! All Anzagaar Nostir was forced to flee for safety, Livia is in shambles and can barely hold herself together, and the fate of the entire nation rests in the hands of six greedy, spineless politicians who would sooner throw their people to the wolves than band together! How can you possibly say that his plan worked?"

Caedus's dismissive expression agitated him. How in the world Zededia's greatest friend could act so casually about the situation maddened him. Weeks of suppressing his pain leaked through, intensifying his anger. As the captain remained silent, Lucien clenched his teeth. The hell in his eyes demanded an answer.

"Lucien," Caedus said after a moment. "Zededia's death ... and everything he put in motion as a result was ... intentional."

The prince's eyes instantly transformed from a squint to wide open. A new flame sparked in him.

"What?" he said with a dark voice.

"Your brother's plan ... worked," Caedus said with a soft nod and a sullen face.

Just the thought that Caedus would insinuate such a theory sent him into a frenzy. The rage he forced himself to swallow for two entire months burst free from its cage. Lucien sneered, his fingers trembling.

"What do you mean it worked, Caedus! Are you trying to tell me that Zededia devised a scheme that would lead to his death and that he held this goal in mind the entire time!"

The weight of Caedus's explanation nearly caused Lucien to explode. His entire body shook, and he used all his strength to hold himself together.

"Zededia came to a conclusion ... he needed to retrieve the sword and send it as far away from Matticus as possible," Caedus said. "He was convinced that there was only one way for the Sword of Kings to slip through Hostellus unnoticed. He told me that keeping the sword safe would cost him his life, and I was to tell no one else of it. I didn't expect him to actually find it, but ... he did. And from that moment on, there was no changing his mind. Zededia fell into a dark place, Lucien, one I couldn't pull him from. He told me he wanted a way out. And he found it."

Lucien's back hit the wall with a thud. He turned to place his palms on the smooth wood and dropped his head.

"It was ... the plan."

"It was suicide, Caedus!" Lucien screamed from the tops of his lungs as he turned back.

A single tear trickled down his right cheek. He glared at Caedus.

"Zededia! Committed! Suicide!"

Everything came together. The letters, Zededia's demeanor in his final days, Caedus's swift disappearance. He couldn't keep his head from shaking, and the veins in his arms started to glow. The conversation he had with him in the dungeon of Vaedor Sellos mocked him, and he watched the memory of the life fading from Zededia's eyes on repeat.

"My brother willingly walked into darkness!" he shouted. "Knowing that death would claim him!"

In the outrage, Lucien paced back and forth.

"For years, I let him waste away in a godforsaken tower, constantly surrounded by the reminder of his damnation! Matticus cast him out to wander the wastes like a lost dog, exiled from life itself! The one person he loved was ripped away from him the same day our father died, half the people supporting him turned a blind eye overnight, and those he counted on couldn't save him from banishment! He spent the entire last four years hidden away in the shadows, doomed to a life of isolation! He was drowning, and I didn't see it! I didn't see his cries for help! The letters he wrote me, the despair in his eyes! I didn't see a bloody thing!"

The lone tear turned into a small river on his cheek.

"And you!" he shouted, directing his attention to the captain. "You knew about it! How long, Caedus! How long did you know this is what he wanted!"

Lucien stepped forth in anger, grabbed Caedus's shoulders with force, and shoved the captain to the wall.

"You knew about all of this!" Lucien screamed, the veins in his face glowing bright red. "Zededia told you what he was going to do! And you just-just ... let him!"

After he assaulted Caedus, Lucien expected retaliation. Only a sorrowful gaze looked back at him. Caedus didn't fight back like the prince wanted him to; he wanted an excuse to further take out his anger on him. His shaking arms held him to the wall, and the glow in his face seeped into his eyes. Lucien looked for a reason to send Caedus flying through the wall, but he couldn't bring himself to do it.

"Damn you!" he shouted, pressing the captain harder into the wall. "Damn you, Caedus!"

Caedus's remorseful glare weakened him. After a moment, Lucien released his grip on the captain, stumbled backward, and fell to the floor with his back against the wall yet again. He sat motionless, his anger fading into despair. As his strength drained, Lucien dropped his gaze to the floor.

The fury that drove him flew from his body like a ghost. He simply felt empty.

In Lucien's peripheral vision, he detected Caedus taking a seat next to him. Unable to pay him any attention, Lucien let loose a shaky breath.

"I'm sorry, Lucien," Caedus said as the prince let a lone tear fall to the floor. "Your brother set a course that I could not change."

Lucien heard Caedus's words, but they bounced off of him like an echo.

"I pleaded with him ... for years. Begged him, even. But he wouldn't listen to me."

Caedus's voice broke through eventually and pulled Lucien's interest. He slowly turned his head toward the captain.

"He made me swear on pain of death that I would keep his secret between the two of us."

"Then why are you telling me now?" Lucien asked, his voice at the deepest it could reach.

"Because you needed to know."

Lucien raised his head and leaned it against the wall. Caedus addressed some of his concerns, but others lingered.

"Why did he go through the trouble of luring Matticus into a private duel just to die?" Lucien asked. "Why didn't he just ... do it himself?"

Caedus sighed beside him.

"I don't know, Lucien," the captain said. "But I'd imagine your brother wanted to leave this world with his dignity intact. Falling in battle to his greatest adversary ... well ... I suppose that seemed like an option that would honor his legacy."

Lucien picked at the dead skin on his hands as he listened. The silence that followed stung him like a wasp.

"Your brother was plagued, Lucien," Caedus said. "Plagued by a darkness that not even he could defeat."

For a moment, Lucien thought he heard the captain sniff. As he looked over, however, the captain's stone face dissolved any chance of a display of emotion. Caedus wouldn't allow such a thing to arise.

Moving on to the next question he held onto, Lucien reached into his tunic pocket and felt around for the bundle of letters he grabbed. With the papers in hand, he unraveled them, filed through until he found his name, and plucked it from the stack. The empty page mocked him like a bad joke. He stared at it like he did when he first found it, Zededia's unique calligraphy sticking out. Lucien brushed his thumb over his name, cherishing it one of the last things Zededia touched.

"Why is it blank?" Lucien asked under his breath.

He rolled the paper in his fingers

"Hmm?" Caedus said.

"Why did my brother leave a final remark for everyone else ... but not me, Caedus?"

The fact that Zededia hadn't left him anything at all broke him more than his death.

"Why wasn't I enough to keep him here?" he said. "Did I not give him enough reason?"

Lucien's eyes dried and ached. He heard Caedus clear his throat.

"Your brother was never good at goodbyes, Lucien," Caedus said. "And of all those who he left behind, you were the one he couldn't say it to at all.

"Why?" Lucien said, his face straining.

He looked at Caedus, who met his gaze with the same sullen expression he always carried.

"Because he loved you the most."

Caedus stood from the floor, and Lucien titled his head up. Despite the captain's usual lack of emotion, he could tell that Caedus felt a deep pain for Zededia just as he did. Once his anger disappeared, he understood.

"Rest while you can," Caedus said as he walked away. "You will need your strength to face the Sons."

Lucien tried to collect himself, but he remained numb on the floor. Caedus lingered in the doorway after Lucien heard the iron hinges squeak. He glanced over and studied the captain's pause.

"Keep your spirits high, Prince Lucien. Better days are ahead."

Chapter 7

Prophecy

Day 21 in the Month of War

Later that evening, Lucien fell into a deep sleep the instant he laid his head down on his pillow. Filled with grief and despair, the prince tried to calm himself with steady breathing. The silence of the city lulled him and soothed his ears and allowed a dream to form in his mind. Images of what troubled him flashed by in a sort of haze, and the prince tossed in his sleep at their sight.

Lucien's vision turned from the whirling memories to a slow, meditative-like state. Suddenly, he stood on a grassy hill as a brisk current of wind blew by. He looked around, trying to gather his bearings or find a landmark, but an endless field stretched on as far as he could see. Slowly, he proceeded up the hill, squinting as a bright light shined from the other side. The breeze brought an eerie chant laced in its whistling. A chill crept down his spine. Lucien gained awareness rather quickly, understanding his place in the dream and able to make conscious movements. However, something else tugged at his soul. The green fields held an ethereal feeling to them. Almost like the spiritual planes of Elysia. Lucien hadn't purposefully wandered into the other realms ever before, much less now. This wasn't just a dream, though; he recognized the sensations of the afterlife from how Zededia talked of its effects after his many adventures there.

Lucien summited the hill, and a phantasmic sight entered his view. An island rose out of a tropical ocean and stretched on for miles in both directions. A dense fog covered portions of it, barring his view of the forest that blanketed the lower landscape. He didn't recognize it as any place he had seen before; something wasn't quite right. The trees were deformed, bending in ways they shouldn't, and beaches of black sand moved like currents in a river. As Lucien looked down at the water, he noticed the waves flowing in the opposite direction toward the open sea.

"What the ...," Lucien said quietly.

Occasionally, shadows danced across the face of the mountain that soared high into the sky. The fog clouds shifted as if they had a mind of their own, and monstrous, four-legged beasts clamored in the distance on the edge of the forest. Lucien's skin crawled as he realized they mimicked no beast of Osiria. Their alien appendages told of a different origin.

The prince panned his gaze across the beaches, watching for further signs of life, when a faceless figure stood motionless in the sand. As Lucien studied the humanoid being, familiar features morphed on its face, and it stared back at him. He knew those bright blue eyes from anywhere.

"Zededia?"

Lucien stepped forward toward the island, but as he approached, the being faded, and another became visible behind. He stopped and moved his gaze over it. A tall, majestic deity hovered in the air with her hands held out beside her wide hips. Neshka floated before him, the unmistakable crown on her head that concealed the top half of her face gleaming. Her eyes brightened like a star under the shining metal mask, nearly blinding him. A strange hum filled Lucien's ears, the ground started to shake, and the chant carried by the wind grew louder. Suddenly, two more figures faded into view like black shadows on either side of the goddess. The edges of their bodies flowed like low flames of a fire, and their top-heavy ovate heads eerily turned to stare into his soul. Lucien wanted to shout as the black figures raised their arms to the sky and tilted their heads back. A blaring, metallic cry pulsed from each of them, piercing his ears. Whirling auras of white light circled them as they sang. The prince's mind struggled to comprehend any of what he saw. He looked back at Neshka, and the goddess slyly smiled at him in the chaos. A bright light shined in the center of her chest and grew rapidly, the humming reaching deafening levels.

Lucien jerked awake a moment later. His heart pounded, sweat poured down his forehead, and his fingers gently vibrated.

What the hell? he thought, trying to piece the fading fragments of his dream together.

He had heard stories of the lucky few blessed with prophecies by the gods. The empowered realism, the ethereal images, the sightings of the gods; it all came to him in one neat bundle.

Could Neshka have reached out to me?

Lucien glanced down at his hands and noticed a faint glow in his veins.

Perhaps. But why?

From outside his room, footsteps stomped all around. The prince looked to the window, and, judging by the dim sunlight, had guessed the morning routine had begun.

Standing on weary legs, he tried to collect himself. After taking a moment to tidy up his appearance, Lucien cleared his throat and made his way for the door.

Though he readied himself to greet the day, the presence he felt in his dream still pulled at him almost as if it stood in the room behind him, watching his every move. It sent chills down his spine, Neshka's acute smile branding her mark in his thoughts. Lucien pressed his hand on the door, and a still image of his dream flashed across his eyes like lightning. He shuddered.

Several soldiers marched through the halls, but Lucien couldn't find any sign of a royal emissary or the of kings' guards. He assumed they had gathered in the main hall already.

Lucien pulled the cloak he had been gifted with during his time at Anzagaar Nostir tighter over his shoulders. His leather boots clicked against the stone as he walked. Occasionally, he caught a glimpse of one of Atlas's men in their Daecian armor. However, the king was nowhere to be seen, nor Thancred or Livia. As he approached the corridor that emptied into the main chamber of the keep, Prince Lucien heard muffled voices ahead.

The hallway decreased in foot traffic, likely an order from King Raed to keep the common soldiery away from the Meeting of Sons. Once Lucien stepped into the next room, he eyed the faces he had been searching for. Thancred sat down on a bench, smoking his pipe, and Caedus joined him while leaning against the wall. Other servants and important figures in Atlas's entourage gathered on the other side of the room.

Lucien walked over to his company members, the shouting from inside the adjacent hall ringing in his ears through the grand wooden doors.

"It seems they've already started," he said.

"Started but haven't moved," Thancred said as he exhaled a plume of smoke.

Lucien peered over his shoulder and looked at the decorated doors, booming voices pounding from beyond them still.

"I take it they haven't been able to construct a proper solution?" he asked.

"Oh, there are plenty of solutions," Caedus said. "They just can't agree on one."

"What are the leading candidates?"

"Well," Thancred said, "King Raed insists on marching his armies east to greet the Hostellae before they can descend from the mountains into the valley. However, as Atlas and Taalpin have brought into evidence, the Voluutians cannot match Matticus's strength alone."

Lucien released a deep exhale and looked around.

"The Daecians and the Merrins wouldn't arrive until Matticus has already reached Amuun Drall," Caedus said. "And by then, it's pointless trying to squeeze as many bodies into the city as the streets can hold."

"Holthiem said that he would merge his armies with Voluutia, but, still, that might not be enough," Thancred said. "If Voluutia and Korzeg lose, there won't be a standing army large enough to oppose Matticus in time. He would be able to roam across the plains of Merrinine like a wildfire without any hope of containment. He'll then take Skulpos, and with that, the entire Orlestian Sea.

"Holthiem isn't going to merge his men with Voluutia," Lucien said with a sigh, hinting at the notion of a treaty between the Korzegi and the Hostellians.

His mind raced with panic. As he filed through the premonitions of Matticus pillaging Osiria's landscape, the harrowing image of the twin shadows from his dream ate at him. Lucien blinked rapidly to wash them away and rubbed his eyes.

"Are you all right, my prince?" Thancred asked.

"Yes...," Lucien said. "I'm just thinking about ten things at once."

Lucien looked at Caedus. He hadn't forgotten the captain's mysterious nature pertaining to the events surrounding Zededia's death. Caedus kept quiet as always but gave him sincere eye contact.

The prince longed to further question the captain, but before he could, the doors of the meeting hall burst open, exposing him to the unbridled savagery within. The prince turned as he heard footsteps behind him. King Atlas descended the stone stairs, and as the doors shut once more, the bickering died down to muffled shouts.

Lucien stepped toward Atlas with arms crossed.

"Seems everything is going smoothly," he said sarcastically.

"Yes ...," Atlas said, visibly distraught. "I remember now why I've always hated these gatherings. Raed and Holthiem are insufferable."

"They insist on marching to war, then?" Thancred asked.

Atlas held out his open hand toward the door behind.

"Come," he said. "We need to offer a solution to combat theirs before there's no Voluutia to defend."

Atlas, Caedus, and Thancred climbed the stairs leading to the meeting hall, and Lucien tagged along shortly behind to a clearing right in front of the door. The Daecian king whistled, and when the prince twisted his head around, he watched the guards there to protect them scurry off out of view.

With no outside ears listening in, Lucien opened himself to whatever Atlas had to say. A deep sigh seeped from the Daecian king's nose, hinting at dismal news.

"Voluutia is going to march to war," Atlas said. "I've been unsuccessful in supplying King Raed with another option."

A dark mood fell over the men around him.

"Lucien," Atlas said.

"Hmm?"

"If what you told me in Anzagaar Nostir is even half true, then Raed is walking into a trap."

Lucien slowly nodded as if he didn't believe his own theory.

"The problem is ... I can't exactly relay that information in a private forum. For multiple reasons. Holthiem would deny any accusation and the Order of the Black Legion would be exposed to the leaders of every kingdom in this land. And, if there's one thing the other Osirians despise more than a rival king, it's a rival faction outside of their lineage."

"Raed can't order multiple kingdoms to war without an agreement from the other kings, not even a defensive war," Thancred said. "Who's given him their support?"

"Uh, well," Atlas said as he paced. "Holtheim, Taalpin, and Mythian. That's four. More than enough," Atlas said.

A deep pulse ached in Lucien's head. He winced from the minor pain.

"What do you need to sway them," Caedus asked behind him.

"Any bloody solution would work," Atlas said. "But no one else has been able to provide one, so Raed's is the only choice. My only offering has been to evacuate Voluutia and regroup to buy more time, but the land between Matticus and the sea grows thin. We haven't anywhere to go, not with this many people."

Lucien struggled to pay attention.

"Simply put, we don't *have* a solution," Atlas said. "Raed's plan will assuredly fail, so, I'm all ears for a suggestion."

As Thancred and Caedus started to give their advice, Lucien faltered as the images from his dream echoed through his thoughts. He met his palm to his forehead and bent over on his knees. The others continued to bicker, but their words bounced off his ears.

Lucien's mind faded in and out of the ethereal realm the gods revealed to him, crossing the veil of the spiritual world repeatedly. His vision blurred, the sight of the island and its strange features flashing like lights. Neshka's soft smile flickered by as well. A moment later, Lucien slipped into his dream completely.

Black beaches appeared as crystal clear water rolled along the banks. A vast forest towered over the shore, but Lucien couldn't quite picture the trees. He only saw vague shapes that seemed to move on their own. The prince's breath quickened, and he snapped back.

"The Black Legion could merge with Voluutia, but Raed would have to accept Ursa's rule over them," Caedus said.

Lucien lightly gasped for air, still bent over as the men around him argued.

"That's a little risky," Thancred said. "If the Legonae are lost to us so soon—"

The prince coughed harshly.

"Lucien, are you all right?" King Atlas said as he shifted attention over.

The prince blinked and grunted as he returned to his feet. He regained control over his racing mind.

"I'm ... I'm fine," he said. "My ... my sleep hosted strange visions last night. I think they are still haunting me."

He met the eyes of all three men and saw their concerned faces.

"I'm fine," he said. "Just a bad dream."

"I don't believe ordinary dreams can affect a man to this degree, my prince," Thancred said. "Much less an Osirian."

Thinking through Thancred's logic, Lucien faced the reality of his spiritual encounter.

"Are you pained anywhere else, Lucien?" Atlas asked.

"No, I-I just have these ... visions," the prince said. "They're stuck in my head, flashing by like lightning."

Lucien leaned against the nearest wall and with a frown on his face as he concentrated on clearing his mind. But just as he tried to analyze the hallucinations, they slipped away from him, lingering in the murkiest regions of his memory.

"What did you see?" Caedus asked.

He glared at the captain, assuming he had a reason for his question.

"Why do you ask? It's just a dream."

Caedus shifted his weight and crossed his arms.

"Well," Caedus said.

Lucien kept a keen eye on him and noticed that Thancred and Atlas were doing the same.

"Zededia used to ... see things ... during the day after he meditated for long periods of time," Caedus said. "What he saw during in his stasis seemed to follow him. Sometimes, they alluded to present and future events, often surrounded by holy sites and places where spiritual beings had dwelled. Other times ... nightmarish visions arose, sending him into a frenzy whenever they struck."

The prince raised his eyebrow but maintained his concerned expression.

"My point is," Caedus said. "Is that whatever you saw likely has meaning to it if it's lingering this long. And since I'll assume you haven't cast yourself into a deep meditation, I'm willing to wager that these visions have even more meaning."

"Prophecies," King Atlas said. "The gods send them to their favored heroes in times of need. Perhaps one has favored you enough to grant you clairvoyance."

Stunned, Lucien loosened his firm stance. Caedus took a step closer.

"So," Caedus said. "What did you see?"

Lucien closed his eyes for a moment and exhaled.

"I, uh ..." he said in a soft voice as he tried to pull from the depths of his memories. "I saw ... a meadow. A large, green meadow."

He looked at Caedus, but he sensed that his description didn't satisfy the captain's curiosity.

"I was walking up a hill, and over it I saw ... an island with black beaches and towering trees that ... moved."

"What else?" King Atlas said to Lucien's surprise with an urgent look on his face.

The prince met eyes with Atlas, who seemed to meet Caedus's level of interest.

"Um ... the water was ... clear, but the waves moved in the opposite direction. The mountains in the distance were sharp and craggy," Lucien said.

"Did you see anyone there?" Atlas said. "A man, a woman?"

Just as the king's question hit his ears, the image of the feminine figure from his dream shot back to him along with his headache.

"Yes, actually" Lucien said. "There was a woman there ... her eyes as bright as stars as she glared at me from above the beach. She held her hands out wide at her hips, like she was inviting me. And there was a light in—"

"-in her chest," Atlas said, finishing the thought.

Lucien nodded.

"You know of what I speak, then?" the prince asked.

Atlas remained quiet for a moment, but Lucien kept his attention on him.

"You have been blessed with a vision, Prince Lucien, but none other than Neshka, the Goddess of Creation. What you've seen is an interpretation of Aeladaecia, a home of the gods."

It took Lucien a few moments to fully grasp what Atlas had explained, but he recognized those names from stories and fables he was told as a child by his father and the clerics of Vaedor Sellos. He squinted, trying to build the connection between his dream and the current events Caedus insisted was there.

"So ... what does that mean, exactly?" he asked.

Atlas shrugged his shoulders and raised both eyebrows.

"I can't speak for the gods, Lucien," the Daecian king said. "I don't have the slightest inclination as to why Neshka has suddenly surfaced in your dreams."

"But it's for a reason, right?" Lucien asked, looking at Caedus as he spoke.

The captain nodded.

An entirely new perspective flooded the prince. Questions, theories, and predictions alike fired through him.

"Your Majesty," he said after a moment of concentration.

Atlas gave him his full attention.

"What significance would Aeladaecia have to an ordinary man?" Lucien asked.

"Uh, well, nothing that comes to mind. It's rumored to be the home of all of Neshka's creatures that she decided not to send out into the earth. Beauties and horrors beyond our comprehension ... nothing more than that, really."

The king's answer didn't supplement any of Lucien's ideas. He stood in silence for another several seconds and frowned.

"But ...," Atlas said.

Lucien's eyes beamed up to him.

"But what?"

Something in Atlas's expression gave Lucien a slight chill.

"Seven hundred years ago, Aeladaecia was essentially the birthplace of our lineage."

"What do you mean?" Lucien asked, stepping forward with an intense curiosity.

"So, as all of us here know, Osiris was the first Osirian," Atlas said. "Otherwise, we wouldn't be called Osirians."

"All right," Lucien said, his patience fading. "And?"

"And, to become the first Osirian, Neshka pulled him from our realm as her chosen son and performed what practitioners of ritualistic sorcery would call an 'ascension ceremony.' Aeladaecia is where this took place."

Lucien started to put the pieces together.

"How is the ceremony performed?"

Atlas looked a little lost for a moment, but Lucien kept his attention on him.

"According to legend," Atlas said. "The soul of a man is taken from his body, cleansed in the light of the divine, and then put back into a new body in the image of the gods. Theoretically, you don't even need a physical body in the first place, as evident with the gods themselves. When Osiris transcended into his ethereal form, Neshka slayed his physical body, sifted his soul from it, and built a new one. She *killed* Osiris so she could create him."

As Atlas finished his thought, Lucien's mind flew back to his knowledge of *Ozek Monns*, the plane of the damned in Elysia, and the souls of all the fallen kept there within.

"Wait," Lucien said. "Are you saying that any soul that is willed for Ascension can be given a new body to roam the earth with in the image of the gods? Free to walk just as you and I do?"

Atlas shifted his sight from one side of the room to the other.

"I suppose that's correct," Atlas said. "Not much is known about the ceremony, though."

It all made sense now. Lucien cracked a smile. A brilliant idea sprang to his mind.

A dead man ... can be remade?

"We can take a lost soul, from someone who has passed, and bring it back to life?"

"Again, theoretically, but Lucien—"

"Our issue with Matticus is that we don't have enough bodies to throw at him to stop him or even slow him down," Lucien said, his problem-solving skills kicking in as he further developed his idea to revive a dead soul. "What if what we need isn't a larger army? What if we can defeat Matticus with the men that we have?"

"Lucien," Thancred said. "What are you talking—"

"What if all we needed was someone smart enough to defeat Matticus because they had faced him before ... and *won*?"

"To my knowledge, in the rare instances where Matticus has been challenged in combat," Atlas said, "no one has *ever* beaten him."

Lucien smiled again.

"Someone did," he said, shifting his gaze to Caedus as his grin widened.

Caedus frowned, but Lucien knew he understood what he meant. He knew Caedus started to piece together the plan he founded from his desperate desire for a lost loved one.

"King Atlas, you can return to the Meeting of Sons," the prince said. "We have our solution."

Chapter 8

The Meeting of Sons

Day 21 in the Month of War

The grand doors to the meeting hall opened wide as the guards heaved on them once Prince Lucien and company approached. He followed Atlas inside, and the eyes of the other kings fell upon him. Lucien felt a trickle of anxiety crawl down his spine. He met the stern gazes of his distant cousins. Shortly after, though, they turned their attention back to one another and continued their bickering. The prince waited while Atlas walked over and took his seat at the other end of the room. Feeling alone, Lucien struggled to find his confidence. His eagerness to join the meeting melted away.

The prince took a step backward, bumping into Thancred before he could retreat out the door.

"Relax, my prince," the old man said. "You have nothing to fear."

Lucien scoffed.

"Nothing but cynicism from the most powerful men in the world."

Thancred's heavy hand embraced his shoulder, comforting him as he scanned over each of the six kings.

"I can't even tell who is who," the prince said softly.

As he surveyed the room and all the guards standing by, he noticed a familiar face hiding among her maids in the corner directly to his left. Lucien frowned, having guessed that Queen Livia wouldn't be allowed entry to the Meeting of Sons. She gave him a blank look, but he knew that she needed to maintain a cold front to keep the others from walking over her in a place such as this.

Thancred ushered him forward, forcing him to break his concentration on her.

"You've already met King Atlas of Daece, of course, so I suppose you should become wise to the others," the doctor said.

Moving his sight to the leftmost king to him, Lucien glanced over a hulking, short-bearded man that looked like he could crush a human skull with one hand. The man reminded him of Captain Ammon in stature. But, an Osirian of this size made for a much more dangerous character.

"That is King Taalpin of Monscarren," Thancred said in a low tone in his ear. "He rules over the Red Hills. Mostly keeps to himself."

Taalpin met eyes with him for a moment, which intimidated him more than he'd have liked. The scar on Taalpin's right eye that left it gray and milky disturbed him, and the slight sneer didn't help.

Lucien then glanced to the next king, a tall, wide-shouldered man with an incredibly defined muscle tone. The light stubble on his face parted on the lower left side of his lip from a thick scar as well. Lucien quickly realized how battle-hardened the men around him were.

"That's Neptabyss," Lucien whispered as he crossed his arms.

"Correct," Thancred said. "His Majesty holds sovereignty over the entire Orlestian Sea from the shores of Skulpos to the Eastern Isles as well as all external trade from outlying regions."

Atlas's serious expression came next.

"Of course, you know who Atlas is," Thancred said.

Like a bull ready to charge, an older, gray-bearded man stared at him with a grimace on his angered face. From his glare, Lucien guessed that Raed had already taken a hostile position against him, perhaps simply from his association with Matticus.

"That must be King Raed," Lucien said. "His menacing appearance holds true to the legends."

"I'm afraid you're right, my prince," Thancred said. "It would be wise to stay in his favor. Only Matticus can rival Raed's ferocity among the Osirian kings. He may be brutish and headstrong, but he rules with an iron grasp and an unbreakable dedication to discipline and resilience. His courage is unmatched, perhaps to a fault on some occasions."

"What makes you say that?" Lucien asked.

Thancred paused for a moment.

"Let's just say that if Matticus's army reached Amuun Drall, Raed would fight to the last man to defend his city, even if imminent doom closed in around him. He'd sneer at your brother the entire time, even with a sword in his chest."

Lucien slowly inhaled as he took in Raed's daunting presence. The Voluutian king released his fierce gaze soon enough and returned his attention to the meeting.

"Next to Raed is King Holthiem of Korzeg. You already know quite a bit about him from Hostellus's support in their war against the northern tribes."

Holthiem appeared even older than Raed, his face heavily wrinkled and just as sour.

Bitter old men, Lucien thought.

"And finally," Thancred said, directing the prince's attention to the closest man on his right, "King Mythian of Merrinine."

Like a sore thumb, Mythian stuck out from all the other kings in Lucien's eye with dozens of shining gems on his crown and garments not even he could find. Such a pompous sight made him feel ill. Even Matticus and his obsession with conquering all in sight didn't reek of such greed.

"You could see his crown from a mile away," Lucien said, frowning.

"I believe that is the point, my prince," Thancred said.

Neptabyss and Raed continued to argue, pulling Lucien's focus.

"Seems Skulpos doesn't exactly agree with the Voluutian plan of action," Lucien said. "Neptabyss appears skeptical."

"Then he will be your first target," Thancred said.

Lucien frowned again and turned to the doctor.

"Target?" he asked. "What do you mean?"

"In order for any sort of action to be taken as a result of the Meeting of Sons, the party of proposal must receive aid from at least half of the present kings. Otherwise, the motion fails, and you likely won't be heard from again."

After years of letting Matticus deal with nobles and members of the court alone, Lucien started to see what a complicated government Osiris had installed in his kingdoms. He became aware of an entirely new perspective of his eldest brother.

No wonder Matticus lost his mind.

"You'll need to convince three of these men that whatever plan you've conjured up is worthy of their time and effort," Thancred said. "Everyone here has gathered to stop Matticus—you need to persuade them on how to do that.

Lucien slowly shood his head, doubting his influence already. His brilliant scheme felt hollow and weightless in the presence of the six Osirian kings. He swallowed the dry spit in his mouth and took a step forward.

Despite making himself known by approaching the table, no one paid attention to him. Scanning over the kings' angered faces, he met Atlas's silent gaze. The Daecian king nodded at him and circled the air with his finger, signaling him to press on.

The prince cleared his throat as a bead of sweat trickled down the back of his neck. Lucien darted his eyes around, waiting for the proper moment. His impatience pushed him on, though, and he slapped the table with an open palm.

A dead silence followed.

All eyes turned to him, glaring at him like shining daggers. A rock sank in his stomach. Lucien waited for someone to speak, but he realized he would have to initiate after so boldly interrupting the arguments. Thankfully, Atlas's reassuring expression gave him enough courage to stand proud.

"Your Majesties," Lucien said, finding confidence in his voice. "If you will lend me your ears, I have come to you, to this court, with a proposal to answer the Hostellian aggression shown to Ehthilia."

Another awkward pause followed. Lucien waited for a response, only receiving the same stares as before. The seconds ticked by like they were stuck in pitch.

"Who is he who deems himself worthy to speak at the Meeting of Sons?" King Raed asked, a fixated stare cast at the prince once again.

"This is Matias's youngest," King Neptabyss said before he could answer. "Prince Lucien Osiris. Of Hostellus."

Stunned that the Skuplin king knew his identity without meeting him, Lucien struggled to find a response. As soon as his origin was made known, a few murmurs slithered across the table.

"You look exactly like your father," Neptabyss said. "Let us pray that you are more like him than your brother. If you have come to reason with this court on the notions of your aforementioned aggression, that moment has passed. We must prepare for the war that has been delivered to us. Now, share with us what you have to say."

Though his tone was harsh, Lucien thanked Neptabyss for granting him an opportunity to speak with a nod. He leaned over the table, pressing all ten of his fingers into it.

"As you are all aware, Matticus has invaded the land of Ehthilia to conquer it for himself. That's why we are here," he said. "But my brother will not stop there. He will march his armies across each kingdom until all flags follow his. His twisted vision of a united Osiria drives the very madness that sent this campaign into motion."

The prince scanned the kings' faces once more, and he knew he had gained their full attention. Lucien then looked at the empty chair to his right where King Ambrose would be seated. If he was still alive. While thinking over the circumstances around Ambrose's absence, all he could picture was the might of the Hostellae rampaging through the valley. He closed his eyes, trying to remove the image of Matticus's villainous gaze from his mind.

"With all the respect you are owed, Your Majesty," he said, directing his focus to King Raed facing him on the other side of the table. "If you lead your men to the mountains below Monscarren in an attempt to ambush Matticus, every soldier under your command, including yourself ... will die."

The sentence poisoned his tongue as it scraped out.

Be brave, not arrogant, he reminded himself.

Raed sat up in his throne and raised his chin.

"You are as stupid as you look if you wish diminish the Voluutian army," a man spat from behind his king.

Lucien watched as a thick-bearded, muscular man stepped forth.

One Voluutian rider could easily defeat five of the strongest Hostellians," the man said. "Your people reek with cowardice marching under a crooked king."

"Enough, Roan," the Voluutian king said.

Prince Roan, son of Raed, Lucien thought to himself.

He had chummed the waters quite efficiently, King Raed's sneer intensifying.

"With all the disdain that *you* are due, Lucien, son of Matias," the Voluutian king said in an angered tone, "your soldiers will fall like weeds under my boot. I will vanquish the precious Hostellae and make an example out of Matticus for all those who dare stand against me. Your brother will die, and Hostellus will burn. Your line will be erased from history."

"Hostellus is not to blame for this war!" Lucien said, his tone becoming more desperate. "This is one man's obsession for power, and with that obsession, he wields an army of ten-thousand strong to slaughter as he pleases. The people of Hostellus are not responsible; you will be killing thousands of innocent people who want nothing to do with this war."

"And what of the thousands of innocent people that Matticus has already slain, hmm? What of Ehthilia?" Raed said. "Where were you when they needed someone to save them from his savagery? Where were you when Maelensis crumbled to dust?"

Raed's question hit Lucien hard. The guilt he carried from allowing Matticus to reach this point sickened him. Lucien's thoughts collapsed on themselves, eating away at his internal strength. He knew he failed the Ehthilians; for a moment, he started to think he had failed the world. Atlas's look grew more concerned, and the prince silently begged him for help with the agony in his eyes.

"Matticus Osiris has committed regicide. Ambrose has been slain," Raed said, the anger building in his voice. "The peace between our kingdoms stands no more, and for that, Hostellus will fall."

"Raed, our fight is not with the Hostellian people," Atlas said.

"Silence!" Raed shouted. "After I kill that bloody traitor, I will—"

"If you wish to prolong this war into the Hostellian territory and target its citizens!" Atlas shouted back, standing from his chair, "then you are no better than Matticus! Daece *will* intervene."

Lucien widened his eyes. He knew that Voluutia could easily overrun Daece if the circumstances reached that point. Atlas's defiant stand silenced King Raed, regardless, allowing Lucien to continue.

"We are at war with Hostellus to *contain* Matticus, not follow in his footsteps," Atlas said.

After Atlas sat back down, the mood settled. Lucien took a deep breath and collected his thoughts.

"The Hostellae are more ferocious than they have ever been," Lucien said. "After warring with the Black Legion and suffering a humiliating defeat in their own fields, they no longer abide by the laws of conflict. They crave blood, and Matticus has promised them their fill."

Lucien directed his attention to Raed.

"Your warriors may be capable of defeating more than one Vaedorian, but a dozen more will replace the felled. Thousands of men eager for death bear the insignia of the White Eagle. When the horn sounds, they will pour out of the mountains from every valley, every road, every crevice that exists as the Aznogs did to the Old World. They will march through your lands, caring not for what lies in their path. You simply do not have enough men to stop them. The Hostellae welcome death as the reality of their conquest. Can you say the same?"

The secret pact that Matticus entered with Holthiem arose in his thoughts, but he knew he couldn't bring it up. Nervously, he glanced at the Korzegi king.

"You would be walking into a trap," Lucien said, maintaining eye contact.

Holthiem's emotionless scowl persisted.

"One that would cost the world its hope of freedom."

The Osirian kings weighed Lucien's plea, looking around at one another. Exhaling a steady breath, the prince calmed his anxiety, standing proud. He felt his father's eyes gleaming at him from Elysia. Leaning back off the table, he relaxed his posture.

"Very well, Prince Lucien," King Taalpin said with a dark voice and a heavy accent that enunciated the consonants. "What do you propose we do, then?"

Not thinking he would get this far, Lucien circled around the plan in his head. He knew he had to tread lightly in his next point.

"As I said, we don't have enough soldiers to defeat the Hostellae outright, and we don't have time to rally more before he reaches Amuun Drall," he said, scanning the room. "We don't need more men, though. What we need ... is someone to lead those we have. Someone who knows Matticus, how he thinks, and how to beat him."

Lucien waited in the silence that followed. He watched as all of the kings glanced at one another.

"Those who have stood against Matticus before are few and far between, and none of them are here," King Neptabyss said. "So, who are you suggesting fits that description?"

Despite his preparation for this moment, the prince found himself unable to speak. He clenched his jaw. Eventually, he overcame the stress by keeping his mouth shut, steeled his nerves and cleared his throat.

"Zededia Osiris."

Every face in the room frowned, gasps and whispers shooting across the table. Lucien peered over his left shoulder to look at Livia another time. The brokenness in her eyes brought him great unease. Bringing up his dead brother in front of her must have caused all the misery she buried to resurface, just as it did to him.

The kings appeared completely bewildered. Even Atlas looked puzzled.

"Unless I am mistaken, Prince Lucien, Zededia Osiris has been slain. *By* Matticus," King Raed said with his defiant tone. "That would mean that he, in fact, did not defeat him as you so claim, making your plan as null as mine."

Lucien's breath quickened in pace.

"Zededia's death was...."

Struggling to speak his next thought, Lucien feared how it would affect Livia and the others close to his deceased brother. He turned his gaze to Caedus leaning against the wall to his right.

"Planned."

Right after he spoke, he looked at Atlas, who let his lips part and jaw lower. It pained Lucien to say, and it pained him, even more, to feel Livia's sorrowful eyes boring a hole in the side of his head.

"What do you mean his death was planned?" King Taalpin asked. "Are you saying he did this intentionally?"

"Yes," Lucien said sharply.

The prince watched Atlas sink back into his chair and raise his hand to his chin.

"Why would Zededia do this?" King Neptabyss asked. "What did the world gain from his death? Or what did Matticus lose?"

Lucien glanced over at Caedus again. He waited for the captain to do something, as if he needed permission to answer the question. Rubbing his fingers together, the prince battled to make a decision. Then, as if Caedus had read his mind, he received a subtle nod. Another moment passed still; Lucien reviewed the consequences of revealing the truth. He didn't have a choice. He needed to convince the Osirian kings to give him their help.

"Zededia gave his life ...," he said, "to keep the Sword of Kings out of Matticus's grasp."

Another wave of shock surged across the room.

"So, it is true, then?" King Raed asked. "The Sword of Kings has been found?"

Lucien nodded, but in his sideview to his right, Mythian squirmed, a deep exhale pouring out from his nose. He wondered why that disturbed Mythian so greatly and pocketed that thought for the time being.

"That's right," Lucien said. "Zededia found it so he could keep it away from Matticus. And for that, he is the only reason Matticus hasn't conquered Voluutia already."

More whispers and murmurs arose, mostly between King Mythian and King Holthiem. Lucien studied their expressions, trying to find a hint of their hidden intentions. Their mischievousness elevated his curiosity and proved the point he brought up in Anzagaar Nostir about secret plans forming.

"Where is the Sword of Kings now?" King Raed asked.

Lucien rolled his tongue over his lower teeth.

"In a safe place," he said simply.

"A safe place, hmm?" Raed said. "And how are we to trust that what you say is the truth? For all we know, you could have the Sword of Kings. You could have delivered it to Matticus before arriving and are now here to trick us!"

Lucien's patience wore thin.

"If that were the case, and if I held those intentions," he said with clenched teeth while looking directly at Raed. "Then you would all be dead by now."

The severity in his tone dissolved Raed's skepticism. Perhaps the prince had earned a strange sense of respect for standing his ground. They feared him at that moment, even if that fear didn't last. The reputation of his father's intolerance for bullshit that Matticus waved like a flag aided him.

"Very well, Lucien," Neptabyss said. "But your point still fails. Even if the Black Prince had truly beaten Matticus and then decided to leave this earth as some sort of martyr or sacrifice, he is still dead, thus leaving no one who has defeated your eldest brother *and* lived to tell the tale. What do you propose we do, now?"

Eyes on him once again, Lucien thought quickly on how to translate his thoughts into a coherent statement. He took a deep breath and released it through his nostrils.

"We resurrect Zededia."

Lucien's reply managed to invoke a more volatile response. The kings started bickering at him over top one another.

"Resurrection?"

"It can't be done."

"It's blasphemous!"

"No one has been resurrected before."

"No one knows how to."

Out of the chaos, King Raed raised his hand and slammed it into the table. Silence followed, and Lucien looked to the Voluutian king, who stared at him with squinted eyes and an elevated chin.

"Resurrection ... is a forbidden magic," Raed said. "Even for Osirians. It was erased from our history before Osiris's children had children. So, how do you plan on conjure such power when no one in this realm is even close to capable of doing?"

Lucien's mind tinkered.

"By following Osiris himself," Lucien said. "An ascension ceremony."

Suddenly, Atlas gave him a curious look with a half-smile. He guessed that the Daecian king had connected the dots to their previous conversation in the other room.

"An ascension ceremony can only be performed in—"

"Aeladaecia," Lucien said, cutting King Holthiem off. "Yes, I know. We will have to travel to the realm of the gods, retrace the steps of Osiris's ascension ceremony, and bring Zededia back from the dead."

He scanned across the room and watched each king weigh his plan in their heads.

"This will be a taxing voyage," Lucien said in hopes of gaining ground, "but it may be our only option if we wish to defeat Matticus before he has killed us all."

The six kings looked at one another as Lucien leaned over the table.

"Make no mistake about it," the prince said. "Matticus *will* kill you if he has the chance. There will be no mercy, no quarter to those in his path. He seeks the complete annihilation of any who would threaten the dream of his empire."

Raed squinted his eyes at Lucien once more, giving the prince an eerie feeling that crawled along the back of his neck. Soon after, another quarrel arose, and the kings around him broke off into their own arguments with one another. Lucien waited by as the bickering continued for nearly a minute. Hopeless, he sighed. Finally, to his surprise, King Neptabyss stood from his throne and raised both hands in the air.

"Enough!" he said.

Everyone ceased their disputing, and Lucien looked at the Skulpin king with a raised eyebrow.

"If this is what you have brought to the Meeting of Sons for us to decide upon, then let us decide," Neptabyss said, looking Lucien dead in the eye. "I will summon this motion brought forth by Prince Lucien Osiris, son of Matias, for the current Osirian sovereigns to act upon. Speak your decision, and let it be as it was spoken for the remainder of the motion's necessity."

King Neptabyss sat back down.

"Allow me to speak first," Neptabyss said.

The prince's rising anxiety peaked, causing his hands to tremble. The seconds after lasted for hours to him. He waited, although, with no other option than to stand there and let the fate of his plan be decided by six of the most powerful men on earth. Neptabyss leaned back in his chair and interlocked his fingers as Lucien stood there in his sweating skin.

"While there is no evidence that Zededia is able to be resurrected ... and there is no guarantee that he can defeat Matticus if he is," King Neptabyss said, "I would rather place my faith in the hands of those who wish to heal the world than those who wish to destroy it."

Lucien raised his eyebrows; hope returned.

"Skulpos will aid you in this affair, Lucien Osiris. The harbors of Shirico are yours to use—and you will need a ship to reach Aeladaecia."

A massive weight eased off his shoulders. One down, two to go. He looked around to see if any of the others had reached the same decision and caught a glimpse of Atlas's sly smile.

"Daece will aid you in this affair," Atlas said, seeming almost proud of him in this moment. "I will see that this mission is carried out, and I will guide you through the spiritual enigma that awaits in your path."

Excited, Lucien shifted his gaze to the other kings.

"Monscarren," King Taalpin said with a doubtful face, "will remain neutral in this affair."

The kings could either support or decline support by remaining neutral. Perhaps easier to say than just 'no,' Lucien thought. Though he expected at least one if not all to reject his idea, Taalpin's response jaded him.

"Voluutia will remain neutral in this affair," Raed said, forcing Lucien to snap his attention over.

The expected no hit hard as well. Lucien's heart sank. He glanced at the last two remaining kings, and, unluckily for him, one of them had secretly aligned themselves with the enemy.

"Korzeg will remain neutral in this affair."

Just like that, Lucien's dream of seeing Zededia alive again shattered. Only Mythian remained, and if the prince knew one thing about the Merrin king, it's that he isn't exactly the charitable type.

The thin layer of sweat on his forehead shifted to a thick blanket. His stomach became knotted, nauseating him to the core.

Lucien stood there as Mythian tapped his fingers on the table. The feeling of helplessness ate at him.

"Gentlemen," Mythian said in the midst of the tensest moment of the meeting.

Glaring at Mythian's powdered face with the life of his plan in the balance, Prince Lucien shifted his sweaty fingers.

"What can one man do against such a force that Matticus controls? It is unlikely that Zededia will be able to make much of a difference, and if he can, we will be trading one brother for another. What are we to gain from this journey?"

The pessimistic perspective deflated Lucien's aspirations. He closed his eyes and prepared for the worst.

"But ... on the other hand," Mythian said.

Lucien opened his eyes, hanging on to the Merrin king's every word.

"What are we to lose?"

Mythian gave him a raised eyebrow after a nod of his head.

"Merrinine ... will aid you in this affair."

The relief of tension nearly caused Lucien's heart to burst. However, he maintained his composure and filtered his overbundence of joy through a tight smile.

"I will fund this voyage you wish to embark on. Whatever you need, Merrinine will provide."

It seemed almost too good to be true. Lucien managed to convince three of six Osirian kings to give their support for his plan. Although, knowing Mythian's history and lack thereof when it came to working with others, he kept a tab on him in the back of his mind. He cared little for that right now; he became ecstatic at the news that he had the chance to bring back Zededia.

Those in favor of Lucien's idea expressed their joy as well through smiles and handshakes. Now that he had the means, Lucien started to think of what to do next.

Before he could converse with those in his corner, however, King Raed stood from his throne.

"Your motion may have passed, Prince Lucien," Raed said. "But I cannot allow you to leave until you abide by a condition of mine."

Lucien paused. He knew Raed had an angle to exploit.

"Before you may depart on your journey to Aeladaecia," Raed said, "you are to surrender control of the Sword of Kings to *me*."

The other kings at the table shot their eyes at him, an eerie pause suffocating the room.

"How are you sure I even have it?" Lucien asked in protest.

"The crows speak to me," Raed cryptically said with a sly smirk. "And they have seen your sword-carrier in my city. I know he is here."

The prince's eyes widened.

How had he learned of Caedus's identity so easily? Did he overhear our conversation?

Caedus's stone face shifted to a cautious expression. Lucien struggled to reply as he looked at the captain. Giving Raed the Sword of Kings defeated all of Zededia's plans to keep it safe, but he didn't have any other choice.

"If we are to trust that this plan of yours is to succeed, Voluutia will need a way to defend herself while you are gone. Give the sword to me. I will use it to strike Matticus down and lay waste to his army."

"The entire point of Zededia's scheme to smuggle it out of Hostellus was to get it as far away from Matticus as possible!" Lucien said, pleading with the Voluutian king. "What if you can't best him, even with the sword? You'll be handing it right to him, and Zededia's death will be in vain!"

Raed gave him a sneer.

"You either hand *Osirisigniros* over to me," he said, "or I will bury you and your followers in the foundation of my city."

Lucien looked around for any sort of support from the other kings, but they remained silent. The prince released a deep exhale.

The air stilled, and Lucien still felt trapped in Raed's dead stare. Reluctantly, he looked over at Caedus and nodded. The captain closed his eyes for a moment, and Lucien realized his blindness to the predicament he had gotten himself into.

After a moment, Lucien watched Caedus walk out of the meeting hall as everyone kept their eyes on him. The prince dropped his head, playing out every consequence of handing Raed the Sword of Kings. Every outcome spelled disaster.

The doors to the meeting hall opened once again. Lucien's heart skipped a beat with each of Caedus's steps. He looked up, glanced at the bundle in the captain's hand, and watched him toss it on the table. Though wrapped, the weapon clanked on against the wood. Caedus walked away, but Lucien kept his eyes on the wrapped sword, curious of it like everyone around him.

Raed slowly grabbed the fabric and flicked it aside. A shimmer of gold washed across the room, reflecting in the kings' eyes as Lucien looked around. Many of them gasped; the prince nearly did so as well. *Osirisigniros* hadn't had a master in centuries, its aura calling for a hand to grasp it once again. Lucien admitted that the alluring charm of his ancestor's blade tempted him to take it. He understood now how much his bloodline craved it. The familial obsession came to light.

As soon as King Raed grazed the hilt, a wave of energy surged through him. Everyone gasped as the Voluutian king's veins glowed a bright red. He held the triple-corkscrewed blade up to his face and smiled, sending a damning sensation down to Lucien's stomach.

An eerie hum resonated from the golden sword as it reunited with an Osirian. The other kings watched in awe, but Lucien shook his temptation away. The fabled weapon couldn't corrupt a heart as pure as his. He merely stood there, desolate and disappointed.

Though the door to Zededia's resurrection cracked open, Lucien feared the days to come.

If Matticus pries the Sword of Kings from Raed's grasp, he thought. *Zededia won't even be able to stop him.*

Chapter 9

Separate Ways

Day 22 in the Month of War

King Matticus marched his armies onward beyond Ehthilia into the mountains that lined the southern border of Monscarren. Waves of thundering footsteps echoed off the hillsides, banners flowed in the wind, and battle drums beat behind each battalion.

With Ambrose's blood on his hands, Matticus grew hungry for more. In the distance, he eyed the northern territory of Voluutia just a couple of days ride from his position. He then looked to his left, to the higher mountains that kept Monscarren isolated from the other kingdoms.

Conquering Taalpin's territory was on his list, but Voluutia came first. With Raed eliminated, nothing separated him from linking his armies with the Korzegi engineers, masters of the finest siege weapons that were crucial to overthrowing heavily fortified towns like Merrinine's capital, Pyla Sellos. After that, Monscarren would easily fall.

As Matticus swept his gaze over the ocean of silver around him, he heard a horse trample behind him. He turned to look over his shoulder and saw Commander Nysis's prestigious insignia on the crest of his armor.

"My liege," Nysis said.

Matticus met eyes with his commander.

"Six thousand have already emptied into the valley," Nysis said. "The rest will descend by nightfall."

"Our reserve troops are mobilizing?" Matticus asked.

"Yes, Your Majesty. Eight thousand strong from our first wave are here, and four thousand more are on their way from Hostellus. A group of survivors from Ehthilia have also decided to join the war effort. Seems snapping the neck of their king provided a little motivation."

"How many?"

"Two thousand or so; more trickle in each day."

The sudden addition of troops gave him more confidence as he prepared for the assault on Voluutia. Winning a war against a crime-ridden, divided kingdom was one thing, winning a war against Hostellus's strongest militaristic rival in all Osirian history was another.

"We need move into flatter terrain," Matticus said. "Our numbers will mean nothing if we can't outflank the Voluutians."

"Yes, sire," Nysis said. "Is there anything else?"

Matticus released a deep exhale.

"Ride out to Korzeg ahead of the army," he said. "Call upon Holthiem to fulfill his oath. I will lead the army to Amuun Drall."

The dead trees of the valley swayed all around him; Matticus sensed the aura of battle grow in the air.

"We're one step closer, Nysis," he said, his eyes widening with a crazed look.

The twisted evil sprouting in Matticus's heart spread through his mind. He dreamed of the specifics of war rather than it as a whole. Murder, power, domination; they pushed him closer to the edge of his evolving insanity. The scent of blood filled his nostrils as he imagined himself walking through the corpse-ridden streets of Amuun Drall.

"Our time in Ehthilia will not compare to the damnation I will bring to this land. The Hostellian empire *will* endure."

"How do you plan on persuading the Voluutians to join our ranks, Your Grace?" Commander Nysis asked. "Their loyalty to King Raed will be difficult to break."

A devious grin cracked on Matticus's face.

"We don't need their loyalty," he said, staring at the smoke columns rising from the Voluutian capital.

"Sire?"

Matticus reached his hand inside his cuirass, sliding his fingers over a piece of parchment tucked away in a hidden pocket. He pried the folded paper out and studied it for a moment.

"What is that, my liege?"

Unfolding the paper, Matticus scanned over the inscription titling the page.

Morvvos Sinistas, he read. *The Hive Mind.*

Matticus studied the passage written below that described one of the most powerful sorceries of all Osirian magic. The seventy-third spell of Osiris's great tomes had been forbidden to conjure since his death, a sorcery deemed too unholy for any man to wield. As he held the left side of the page where the torn sections created a jagged edge, Matticus thought back to the day he ripped *Morvvos Sinistas* from Zededia's book of spells. He saved this sinister magic for over twelve years, locking it away until days like today. For twelve years the seventy-third spell burned a hole in his mind, constantly tempting him to unleash it upon the world.

He read over the text time and time again as he had done ever since he learned of the spell. The forbidden magic in his possession had been erased from history; few tomes in all Osiria still contained it.

The image on the page depicted a detailed drawing of a man holding his open hand out over five others. From his downward facing palm, a tentacle slithered out and punctured each of the lower men in the back of their skull. Matticus took in the full terror of the art, the gasping faces and milky white eyes of the five men displaying horrified expressions. He moved his attention to the man towering above them. As he stared at the wicked smile from the man standing over the rest, he compared himself to him, seeing himself in the man's place like he was looking in a mirror. Subconsciously, Matticus's right fist opened, and his fingers spread out wide like the claw of a bear.

"'Dominate the world, O mighty one,'" he whispered to himself as his eyes followed along with the last sentence in the description passage.

Matticus looked out over the landscape once more, focusing on the smaller villages on the edge of Voluutia's great lake far in the distance.

"'Cast your judgment ... upon the weak.'"

~ ~ ~

The morning after the Meeting of Sons, Prince Lucien stood in the courtyard of Amuun Drall's keep surrounded by soldiers, squires, and nobles alike. He lingered close to those he knew, the unfamiliar faces unsettling him. King Atlas and his men gathered off to his right and left him no opportunity to engage in discussion, and the captains of the Legonae all did the same. All but one.

"So, where do we go from here?" Lucien asked Caedus as the captain approached.

"We're headed to Merrinine," Caedus said. "Three days' ride to a port just outside Pyla Sellos. From there, a ship will take us to the harbors of Shirico in Skulpos on the other side of the Aeno Langdem. Then, once we resupply and sail out into the Orlestian, your guess is as good as mine."

Lucien shifted his focus to the Daecian king close by.

"Hopefully Atlas can provide his expertise," he said.

"Would have been nice if a map was included in your vision," Caedus said with a gripe.

The prince sighed.

"Can't have things too easy, can we?"

Caedus grunted next to him.

"Word is spreading that Mythian has hired a mercenary fleet to escort us across the sea," Caedus said, hints of skepticism in his tone.

"That bothers you? Why?" Lucien asked. "Not fond of mercenaries?"

"Mercenaries, I'm fine with. They're easy to understand—their loyalty lies with whoever pays them the most coin. It's Mythian I don't trust."

Though Lucien understood Caedus's weariness, he detected an underlying reason for further mistrust.

"He seems shady, sure," he said, making sure to keep his voice low. "But he's already made his decision to aid us. Is that not good enough?"

As Caedus took a step closer, Lucien lowered his ear.

"There is always an angle with Mythian Osiris," Caedus whispered. "He longs for the sword as much as Matticus."

"You say that like you've had experience with him," Lucien said, raising his eyebrow.

Caedus's conflicted hesitation made him wonder what the captain really knew.

"Let's say I have."

Lucien froze for a moment as he tried to process Caedus's cryptic allusion. Caedus started to walk away, and a peculiar sight caught his eye. A dark, shadowy substance leaked out from Caedus's sleeve at his wrist like a misty tentacle. Frowning, Lucien squinted to study it further.

"Caedus?"

Caedus turned around a few yards away.

"Hmm?"

Something kept Lucien's tongue in his mouth, like he knew he shouldn't ask. The black mist quickly seeped back inside Caedus's sleeve.

"May the gods be with you," the prince said with a near stutter, trying his best to avoid his original question.

Caedus nodded at him after a moment, gave him a curious look, and walked away.

What the hell was that? Lucien thought.

The memory of the black figure at Zededia's execution in Vaedor Sellos flashed through his mind like a strange sense of Déjà vu.

"Lucien," a womanly voice said, jolting him from his train of thought.

As the prince glanced over, he beheld the queen in her full beauty surrounded by her maidens. Prince Ender slumbered against her chest, and Prince Mattox looked upon him with curious eyes in the arms of one of the maidens.

"Your Grace," Lucien said, lowering his head in a light bow.

"You are off to Merrinine, then?" Livia said.

The prince nodded. He searched for the emptiness that dwelled in her saddened eyes since he saw her at Anzagaar Nostir, but as she held her head up with pride, he only found hope in its place. Perhaps the plan to revive Zededia from the grave enlivened her spirits; it enlivened his in an instant.

"It warms me to see the life in your face once again," he said.

Livia reached her soft hand up and grazed his light beard.

"How I have missed the peace that you bring me."

Lucien grinned.

"Tell me, if you will, are you confident this plan will work?"

Running over his thoughts from the Meeting of Sons, he gathered his confidence in the vision Neshka blessed him with.

"Yes."

"I must admit I am not familiar with the magics at play beyond this world," Livia said. "How are you going to resurrect him?"

Lucien sat in concentrated thought for a moment. He faced the fact that he didn't actually know the exact details.

"We're sailing to Aeladaecia," he said. "According to Atlas from what he told me last night, to get there, we have to enter something he calls the 'Cradle of the Colossus,' a gateway left behind by the old gods before Osiris's time. He didn't tell me much more. For the ceremony itself, the only written details of how to ascend a man lie in a handful of texts scattered across Osiria. Luckily for us, Voluutia had one—Altas already grabbed it and is studying it like a madman. We're going to recreate the ritual that transformed Osiris from a king to a god. The ritual only requires a soul to complete, so I'd imagine we'll have to find Zededia's in Elysia somehow."

The more he explained his plan, the less he believed in it. Numerous obstacles stood in his path to Zededia, obstacles he didn't even understand. Regardless, he had set his mind on the journey before him. Livia's future days remained a mystery, though.

"Now that you have seen this gathering to its end, where will you go?" he asked.

"I will make my leave for Daece," Livia said. "That's the most secure place I can take my sons. They will know nothing of this war as long as I take breath."

The road ahead split in two, and Livia couldn't follow him. Lucien longed to stay with the queen to protect her and provide the peace she claimed to miss, but he agreed with her decision to travel east. Matticus wouldn't turn his eye to Daece for quite some time even if Voluutia falls. She would be safe there until he returned. Or so he hoped.

"Then I will wish you safe travels, My Lady," Lucien said.

He took her hand in his and kissed her knuckles. The maidens behind her began to disperse toward the rest of those heading east, and the soldiers traveling to Merrinine gathering their wares to mobilize as well. Livia lingered and sent a sincere gaze at him like a beacon of light. Lucien lightly frowned, curious about what final message she had for him. The queen's tender touch on his forearm magnetized his attention.

"Lucien," she said, her voice trailing off.

"Yes?"

Livia stepped closer, her eyes slowly watering.

"Bring him home."

The task was up to him. Lucien knew in the back of his mind that the fate of the world depended on his success, but Livia's statement placed a heavy weight on his shoulders. Unable to find a response as he choked for words, Lucien nodded. Livia squeezed his forearm as a last caress and then turned away from him. The prince watched her mingle into the crowd of citizens departing the city. His lungs pushed a deep exhale through his nostrils as he wondered when he would see the queen again. He had a mission to return with her beloved, and he would carry it out if it was the last thing he ever did, if not for the world's sake, for hers. Livia grew farther apart from him with each second. Lucien kept his eyes on her still, holding himself to her word.

"Farewell, My Lady," he said.

Livia disappeared from his view, and he became eager to start his journey to Aeladaecia. Lucien picked up his pack that rested at his feet and shifted his focus to Caedus and the others.

To Merrinine.

Chapter 10

Captain Vederosa

Day 25 in the Month of War

For three days, Captain Caedus Redstone rode over the green plains of Merrinine to the port on the bank of the Aeno Langdem, the river that ran through the heart of Osiria. He boarded a transport ship to make haste toward Skulpos where Mythian's mercenary crew waited for the departure to Aeladaecia. As he looked over the railing of the boat at the churning water below, he took a moment to reflect on his thoughts.

The weeks of wandering through Osiria wore on Caedus. Since his commander's death, he had been on the move from one town to the next, never staying more than a night in any of them until he reached Amuun Drall. The conversation he had with Lucien before the Meeting of Sons ate away at his composure. He could have prevented Zededia's death; perhaps if he tried harder to alter the plan, his friend might still be alive. Caedus hardly let such thoughts afflict him, but he was human like everyone else. Guilt corroded his heart as it did any man. The years he spent pleading with Zededia to take a different course of action meant nothing to him now. They only reminded him of his failures. He knew Lucien felt a similar way, given the anguish he saw in the prince's eyes during his enraged outburst as he told him that his brother wanted to die.

Caedus cast his gaze across a hundred miles of tall, thin grass sprouting from the fertile soil of Merrinine.

Damn you, Caedus! he thought, picturing the prince's trembling eyes as he replayed that part of the conversation in his head.

Lucien's words broke him, even if he didn't show it. Caedus carried so much pain with him on his journey and always forced it away with the distraction of taking the Sword of Kings to Daece where King Atlas could keep it safe. Since that plan never had the chance to play out, he lacked a purpose to fulfill. No order to follow, no army to serve, no master to answer to. Just the hope that whatever lay on the other side of this voyage would bring him peace.

Caedus picked at the callouses on his palms just below his fingers when the black mist hiding in his sleeve started to trickle out.

"Lett signiros ed raenas sen zigni. Osiria ed proyznek. (The sword is lost to us. Osiria is doomed,)" the voice of Osinian said in his head.

Caedus took a deep breath.

"Nossek dem. (Not yet,)" he said.

After Zededia's death, Osinian's tether to the physical world vanished. Caedus was forced to act as the spirit's temporary host until he found a way to liberate them both. He paid little attention to that over the last few weeks as it wasn't high on his priority list. Keeping his word to his friend was all he cared for.

Several benefits came from his partnership with the shade, mainly the opportunity to learn Aznogsi. When he first met Osinian, he understood few words of the ancient language, but, after having a proper teacher living in his head, he graduated to semi-fluent. Osinian also gave him powers no other man could possibly hope to obtain. His veins didn't carry the empowered blood that Osirians possess, so Osinian could only grant him a handful of sorceries that required them both to enact.

"There's still hope," Caedus said.

Osinian's essence retreated back up his sleeve. Caedus lightly winced as the black shadow burrowed into the pores of his skin.

Hours passed, and Caedus remained in the same position. Without a change of scenery since he boarded the Merrin ship, he started to think he had lost his mind. The coursing river provided a bit of an audible distraction, but the endless fields of grass bored him.

Just as he started to doze off against the rail, a sailor in the crow's nest blew a high-pitched horn, startling him. In the distance, Caedus saw a faint structure and assumed it to be the outer fortification of Skulpos's capital city, Shirico. As the boat sailed closer, he fixed his eyes upon two massive stone statues standing on either side of the river. Each of them held up a flat hand toward inland, as if to act as a deterrent for any unwanted visitors. The smell of the sea stung the air; salt and fish filled his nose.

The sailors on board prepared to land in the port city of Shirico and called for the barriers to retract. Caedus watched as giant chains poured out of the sides of the stone statues and loosened. The metal net blocking the entrance to the city sank in the water.

"Make way! Raise the sails!" he heard the quartermaster shout followed by various other orders.

As the boat passed over the sunken chains, Caedus caught a glimpse of the waterside city ahead. Not quite as prestigious as Vaedor Sellos or even Anzagaar Nostir, the Skulpin capital held wonders of its own. The founders of Shirico built their city on the side of a cliff a thousand feet above the Orlestian sea; Caedus had heard stories of the incredible feats of engineering that allowed their ships to lower to the Orlestian via a complex system of pulleys and platforms.

The Aeno Langdem provided massive amounts of wealth for Skulpos in the form of trade. As the ship progressed through the city, Caedus saw why all external commerce flowed through here. Nothing but markets, workshops, and artificer guilds rose over the river on each side for over a mile.

In the heart of the city, after passing the bustling Merchant's District, a grand harbor came into view. Caedus lost count of the docks that lined the circular port and glanced from ship to ship. Fishing and trade vessels mainly occupied the harbor, but he occasionally caught a glimpse of the Skuplin warships that patrolled the Orlestian Sea. Defenders of Osiria from naval invasions, these great ships trivialized any he had seen in the western kingdoms. Three masts held up thick sails like capes draping drown from wide-stretched arms, the hulls held dozens of windows for the oarsmen to propel them into battle, and fearsome weapons made for oceanic combat jutted out over the tips of their bows. Caedus found it ironic that the galleons of Osiria preferred Liquid Fire, as the Skulpins called it, as their weapon of choice on a battlefield made of water. A combination of sulfur, oil, and black powder, it could spew out onto enemy ships at a great distance and engulf the deck in flames. Those not carrying the equipment for Liquid Fire mounted sturdy ballistae to puncture enemy hulls with harpoons.

The ship transporting him from the port in Merrinine came to a stop just before the circular harbor and docked, and Caedus gathered his belongings to disembark. With nothing but a pack over his shoulder, a pouch of gold kors at his side, and the clothes on his back, the captain hopped onto the stone street and walked toward the rest of his company Lucien's head rose over the crowd by a couple inches, so he set a course for him first.

"That wasn't so bad, hmm?" he said to the prince.

"I suppose. I'm not accustomed to traveling by water," Lucien said. "Too much motion for me."

Caedus cracked a half-smile.

"You'll get used to it," he said.

He saw Lucien raise an eyebrow.

"How do you know? There aren't waterways like this in Hostellus."

A particular memory sprang up in Caedus's mind as he remembered the time he set sail on the Orlestian Sea long ago when he served a different commander as a soldier of the Hostellae. He elected to keep that to himself, for now.

"When we have more time, I'll explain. I've seen more of this world than most men."

"I'll take your word for it," Lucien said.

After a moment, the group started to disperse, and Caedus eyed King Atlas making his way through the crowd toward him.

"All right, His Majesty, King Neptabyss, is currently making arrangements for our journey. You should take the time now to resupply for the days to come."

Caedus took a moment to take inventory of his belongings and realized he lacked the most important tool for a soldier.

"This way," he said.

"Where are we going?" Lucien asked.

"I need a sword."

With Lucien in tow, Caedus caught up to the other captains of the Legonae close by. Ursa and Redding greeted him with a grin while Seether gave him a squint through his wrapped face, the usual gesture from the Black Legion's most feared bowman.

Ammon placed his massive hand on Caedus's shoulder; he missed the behemoth that was his friend, even if he intimidated him slightly.

"We haven't had much of a chance to collect ourselves, Caedus," Commander Ursa said. "But I'm sure we'll have the time once we set sail for Aeladaecia."

Caedus nodded.

"We'll meet you here," he said.

Into a teeming crowd of Skulpin citizens, Caedus ventured off into the markets. As he passed by some of the vendors, he recognized some of the weaponry. Swords and shields from Merrinine took the majority of the batch as he expected. However, occasionally, he ran his eyes over a Vaedorian longsword or a Daecian bow.

None of the weapons on the tables matched what he needed. Everything was either too bulky or not a sword at all. He grunted out of disappointment. Ursa and the others stopped at a table of food and wine to restock next to him, and Caedus moved on.

Eventually, the captain stumbled upon a strange looking man sitting in a dark corner in a small alcove between two buildings. The man kept a tight cloak around his face, similar to Captain Seether, and Caedus squinted to meet his bright green eyes. Into the shadows, he stepped, and the man kept his gaze upon him.

"Aye," the man said. "Welcome, master traveler. How can this old pirate be of service?"

Caedus shifted his focus to the table nearby that held several unique pieces of weaponry different than the other booths. Spears, gaffs, and other equipment found on a fishing vessel rested next to one another. While they looked lethal enough, he needed a blade.

"What else do you have?" Caedus asked.

The man eyed Caedus for a moment before reaching down to grab a roll of leather from behind his booth. As the merchant unraveled it, Caedus observed armaments more akin to what he was used to. He saw daggers and shortswords worthy of a professional army, some of which he recognized as those that the Merrins or Skulpins used. A Vaedorian assassin's stiletto stuck out the most, but even a handful of Hostellian steel didn't quite charm him enough. Caedus tapped the table with his fingers, unable to decide.

"Nothing here fits your standards?" the merchant asked.

Caedus shook his head.

"I know a quality soldier when I see one. And a quality soldier deserves a quality sword."

The merchant intrigued him at least.

"Come with me," the man said.

Squinting, Caedus glanced around but found no visible alleyway or door nearby. The merchant leaned away from the wall, turned around, and pressed his hand into a loose stone at eye level. A lever cranked, and a section of the wall jostled free.

"This way," the man said, pushing the hidden door open to reveal a passageway behind.

Beckoned forward, Caedus walked around the table.

"Wait here," he said to Prince Lucien, standing by while paying half attention.

Caedus ducked his head and proceeded through the corridor into a dimly lit chamber. The arms merchant waited for him with crossed arms and invited him to take a look at his higher quality stock. Caedus took the invitation and saw numerous crates stacked on top of one another around large table in the center of the room that held a bundle of silk in the middle of it. The pirate stepped over to the table and pinched the edge of the fabric; Caedus followed, eager to see what was worthy of so much secrecy.

"Perhaps one of these might suit you better."

As the man flicked the silk wrap open, glimmers of silver and steel filled Caedus's eyes. He glanced over each blade, touching them with his fingers to see which one felt right. After a moment, Caedus found most of them displeasing for one reason or another. Then, at the last sword, something called out to him. A certain insignia engraved into the rounded pommel tested the captain's memory of the soldiers from ancient times.

He moved his hand across the symbol that he recognized as those worn by the temple guardians charged with protecting the holiest of Osiris's sanctuaries when he roamed the earth. Selectively bred like the mighty Aznogs, these men carried an unbreakable devotion to their profession, priding themselves on their unmatched combat skills. The Black Legion modeled their training regimen on theirs, something the captain had become quite familiar with. Their ferocity echoed through legends across Osiria's history. Caedus respected that. More importantly, he knew of the sacred bond between the warriors and their blades; the smithies that crafted them inserted their very souls into the metal.

"Now that's a particular one, there," the merchant said. "One of many crafted by Haagaestas, the fabled blacksmith of Osiris himself."

The gleam of the blade reflected in his eyes. Caedus focused on its complexion, unable to find a single imperfection in the metalwork. A sword better than his own, it forced a rare smile from him. On the edge of the blade near the hilt, he noticed a small inscription.

He who carries this sword judges not who is slain, he read. *For judgment has already been cast by the worthy, holy, and divine.*

A fitting phrase for a man of few words, the inscription created a bond with Caedus. Seldom did a smile ever appear on his face, but he couldn't help but grin at its magnificence.

Caedus grabbed the pouch of kors tucked away in his belt and tossed it on the table, offering the entirety of his gold as payment for the sword regardless of what the merchant asked for it.

"I'll take it," he said.

The sword felt weightless in his hand similar to the Sword of Kings. He reminded himself that both blades contained the same level of expert craftsmanship.

"Here," the merchant said.

Caedus looked over as the man handed him a sheath.

"Should fit just fine. Looks about the right size."

"Where did you obtain this weapon?" Caedus asked.

The man shrugged.

"Must have found its way here on a ship," he said. "Just like you."

As Caedus started to familiarize himself with his new sword, a horn sounded off from outside, one that he had heard hundreds of times before as the call sign for the soldiers of the Legonae.

"Is that for you?" the man asked.

"Aye," Caedus said.

He nodded at the mysterious merchant, thanking him for showing him his exclusive collection. Caedus held a tight grip on the ancient blade, turned to fetch Lucien in the streets, and made his way through the smuggler's tunnel.

"Good fortune on your travels, soldier," he heard from behind as he stepped into the light. "May your sword serve you well."

Back in the busy streets again, Caedus looked around through the gathered citizens. Prince Lucien waited idly by.

"Did you find your sword?" the prince asked.

"That I did. Now, stay the hell away from it."

"What? Why?"

"In the last seventeen years, I have wielded only two blades—one, I was forced to give to Matticus, and the other, you volunteered to Raed without even consulting me. Your family has a history of taking swords from me."

"I guess it's Zededia's turn to liberate that one from you," Lucien said with a light chuckle.

"Which is why if we manage to resurrect him," Caedus said, weaving his way through the crowd of people in the street, "I'm going to bloody hide it from him."

He eyed Captain Ammon's unmissable appearance ahead near the harbor and steered in that direction. The rushing currents of people reminded him of his days in Vaedor Sellos. Though he missed many parts of that life, the endless crowds weren't one of them.

As he neared the harbor and noticed that everyone had gathered, he looked for King Atlas to give him news of a ship.

"Are we leaving already?" Lucien asked.

"Seems that way," Caedus said, studying the various ships passing through the harbor. "I suppose our travel plans have been arranged."

Caedus panned his view and tried to guess which ship Neptabyss had secured for them. None of them stopped to dock, though. Shortly after, he saw the Skulpin king arrive to converse with Atlas, and he stepped forward with Lucien at his side.

"Prince Lucien," Neptabyss said, "I've summoned my greatest warship to transport you to Aeladaecia. You'll won't find a finer vessel suited for traversing the Orlestian in all Osiria."

Looking out to see what Neptabyss referred to, he scanned the harbor. Nothing new stuck out in his view. Overhead, the pulley system that hauled incoming ships up to the Aeno Langdem from the sea below activated. Another vessel arrived.

"This will be your ship," Neptabyss said as a hundred metal chains churned to heave up something far heavier than any other in the harbor.

Watching in anticipation, Caedus glanced at the tip of a central mast appearing over the rushing current of the waterfall. His mouth fell agape, eyes widening, as the largest galleon he had ever seen came into view. He frowned in confusion after noticing the dark red paint coating the ship's hull, another unique feature to add to the list of others along with *four* sets of masts instead of the usual three.

The chains rattled as they pulled the ship over the river. He couldn't help but stare at the marvelous sight, scanning over the white sails etched with red insignias of a giant, sinister looking sea monster. Rays of angelic light bathed it in glory; the ship struck him with awe.

As the pulley lowered it into the harbor, Neptabyss ushered the party toward it. The sailors aboard tossed a ramp onto the dock and started to unload their cargo. Those who Caedus managed to catch a glimpse of looked like some of the toughest men he could imagine. Scarred, hulking, and hardened by the sea, the sailors might even be a match for the Legonae if the occasion arose.

"Gentlemen," Neptabyss said, holding out a hand toward the ship.

Caedus traced the king's gesture to the central mast that nearly scraped the top of the structure that covered the bay and held the rope system.

"This is The Leviathan," Neptabyss said. "This is the best I can offer you for your journey."

Stepping near the ramp next to Lucien, Caedus glanced around for the ship's captain. He craved to know who would be leading them on such a voyage.

"Will you not be joining us, then?" Atlas asked.

Caedus turned, curious as well.

"I'm afraid so," King Neptabyss said. "I must remain here. If the Vaedorians break through Voluutia before you return, I will be required to defend Shirico. My duty is to my people."

Caedus understood, and he knew Atlas did as well. He glanced at Lucien and found that he didn't share the same respect given the look of disappointment on his face.

"I am sorry, Prince Lucien," Neptabyss said. "But you are in hands of my most veteran captain. She'll ensure you make it to Aeladaecia.

She? Caedus thought, darting his gaze in the direction of sharp footsteps clicking against the wooden ramp.

Dark red hair grappled his attention as it flowed below wide yet feminine shoulders. Caedus traced the outline of sunlight around her figure, his eyes lingering on her bare, lean abdomen. Her face remained shadowed by her feathered tricorn, increasing his curiosity.

As she proceeded down the ramp, her hips swayed with a fierce attitude, and her plentiful chest bounced just inside the thin white shirt she wore under a cropped leather vest. Caedus hadn't ever seen a woman as daunting as her; she stopped at the edge of the ramp, placed her hands on her hips, and lifted her chin, revealing a sneer on her perfect face.

"It is my honor to present you to you: Captain Vederosa," King Neptabyss said. "She's the most feared captain to ever sail the Orlestian Sea."

Caedus blinked to break the intense eye contact she engaged with him and looked at Lucien. The poor prince struggled to contain his confusion and awe as well. To save him from disrespect, Caedus elbowed him, knocking him out of the trance.

Vederosa shifted her weight to one side, forcing her hip to stick out even more. She bowed after a moment, and Caedus realized that someone even as intimidating as her answered to an Osirian.

"Your Majesty," she said.

Her strong yet smooth voice rang in Caedus's ears; it reflected her fierce personality.

"Vederosa knows these waters better than I do," Neptabyss said. "And, more importantly, she's loyal to me over Merrinine gold."

Caedus met eyes with her again, the dagger-like stare intimidating him still. He nodded as a sign of respect and submission to her command. Her stern expression loosened a little, revealing a graceful nature for a split second. However, he understood the front she chose to display and elected to remain neutral himself.

"There is where I leave you," King Neptabyss said.

Caedus looked over and saw him shake hands with some of the men in his party.

"King Atlas, Prince Lucien," he said. "Good luck to you. The fate of Osiria rests in your hands."

As Neptabyss departed from the docks, Caedus turned back to his new commanding officer. She barked orders to her crew in a harsh tone. The sailors scurried about, and Caedus was amazed at how easily she could force dozens of brutish sailors to perform at her will. He waited for her to strike the fear of the gods in him, mildly stuck in a trance.

"You may have earned Neptabyss's favor," she said to address everyone, panning her steely gaze across the crowd of men, "but this is as far as that will take you. From here, you are no more important to me than the rats who feast on rotten fish. Get aboard."

Vederosa marched up the ramp, and Caedus took a moment to allow the hairs on the back of his neck to lay down. He shared a bewildered look with Atlas before the Daecian king climbed onto the ship as well. The rest of the party followed with Lucien tailing the pack.

"Things are continuing to grow stranger," Lucien said.

"Yes, yes, they are," Caedus said, exhaling through his nose while mentally preparing himself for life at sea. "Let's see where this adventure takes us next."

Chapter 11

Salt and Mist

Day 27 in the Month of War

Lucien stood upon the deck of The Leviathan as he looked out across the endless waves of the Orlestian Sea. Land lay a hundred miles behind, and as the harbor city of Shirico grew farther away, his motion sickness increased. From time to time, the churning water under the ship splashed his face with misty spray as they crashed into the hull.

All around, the prince heard the sailors hustle about, performing their various tasks to keep The Leviathan in top shape. Occasionally, Lucien caught a glimpse of Captain Vederosa on her perch behind the wheel of the ship on the upper deck.

She fascinated him; he couldn't quite determine why. Her flowing scarlet hair pulled him in, as did her strong yet curved figure. He had experienced lust before, but his immediate thought of the captain didn't fall under something as simple as a sexual desire. A part of her intense masculinity that drove the sailors like a master's whip frightened him. One wrong look might be the end of him. Regardless, Lucien risked peeking over from the corner of his eyes.

To his right, he heard someone approach and turned.

"Still not used to sailing, yet?" Caedus Redstone said.

Lucien nodded and braced himself against the railing of the bow.

"I'm not used to nausea, more like," he said while turning his head in Captain Vederosa's direction as sneakily as he could. "But, I'm not sure it's the water that's making me ill."

He looked back at Caedus, who also took a glance at her at the helm. Caedus lightly raised his eyebrows as him.

"Be careful, Prince Lucien," Caedus said. "That type of nausea can lead to trouble. You'll end up in more pain than it's worth."

Lucien frowned. For a moment, he saw a hint of pain in Caedus's face, and then, he realized he talked from experience.

"Do you long for someone?" Lucien asked.

A pause arose for a brief moment. Caedus's gaze fell to the water as the prince waited.

"No," Caedus said with a sharp tongue.

Lucien easily saw through the response, but he declined to pry further and kept quiet. Clouds rolled in from the north, catching his attention as a current of wind breezed by.

"So," Caedus said after a moment. "Thancred let me in a little secret of yours."

The prince squinted, wondering what in the world Caedus meant.

"He told me you've finally been blessed by the gods. That there's a bit of magic in you after all."

"Oh, uh ...," Lucien said. "I suppose you could say that."

"That's a shame."

Lucien glared at Caedus.

"A shame?" he asked.

"Yeah," Caedus said. "I always wanted to be the one to slit Rachtus's throat."

Lucien chuckled after realizing what Caedus truly meant.

"I'm sorry to have taken that opportunity from you, then," he said. "But, in all honesty, I don't exactly know when and how to conjure it again."

He looked at Caedus, who subtly nodded.

"I, uh ... helped ... Thancred light his pipe in Amuun Drall, but ... other than that, I've been quite unsuccessful at doing much. I've always wondered how Zededia became such a powerful Osirian mage. As a child, I'd always ask him how he did things, and he just said-"

"Through force of will," Caedus said.

Lucien paused as Caedus finished his sentence.

"Yes ... through force of will," he said. "I still don't fully understand what that means."

"It's all right," Caedus said. "I don't really understand either. I just know that your brother dedicated himself to his ancestral powers with discipline, practice, and meditation."

Memories of finding Zededia sitting perfectly upright in the dark of night surrounded by lit candles arose. He had wondered where his brother ventured off to, the stories he heard about the spiritual planes only providing so much information.

"Did Zededia meditate frequently after his banishment?" Lucien asked. "I recall some of his journeys to Elysia, or at least what he told me about them."

Caedus hesitated, making him glance over in confusion.

"Yes," the captain said. "He traveled to the spiritual plane quite often. Too often, if ask me."

Lucien raised his eyebrow. He knew Zededia roamed to the other worlds frequently, but he couldn't remember any that carried a negative consequence.

"Why do you say that?" he asked.

Caedus sighed next to him.

"Not long after we stumbled upon Anzagaar Nostir," Caedus said, "Zededia found a hidden sector underneath the city."

As the waves and mist rolled by, Lucien squinted to protect his eyes.

"It was an old ritual chamber used by Nel'vaela Oordune, a necromancer from before Osiris's time."

The prince recognized the name. He pictured his father's collection of books on mystical beings, thinking back to when he first learned that others outside his familial line possessed otherworldly powers.

"I've never smelled more mildew or rotten moss in my entire life," Caedus said, breaking his train of thought. "Though, I suppose that's what it would smell like after being abandoned for a thousand years.

Lucien softly chuckled.

"Anyway," Caedus said. "Your brother took a liking to it for some reason. Something about the ... atmosphere ... he enjoyed. And, so, he restored the ritual chamber to working condition. But it wasn't really the chamber itself that he was drawn to. It was what he found."

"And what was that?"

"The Seal of Elohiir."

The archaic name puzzled the prince. That was one he *hadn't* heard of before from the archives in Vaedor Sellos.

A few sailors walked by, carrying out their various chores as Vederosa barked her orders, forcing Lucien to pause. After they wandered out of range, he lifted his head.

"What's so special about that?"

"The Seal of Elohiir is as powerful a tool as the Sword of Kings. It unlocks the darkest of magics in he who activates it. The only difference is that it's carved into the floor, and it required nearly all his mana to use, so he wasn't able to exploit it nearly as frequently. *Osirisigniros* is a direct connection to your ancestor's limitless power. The seal, on the other hand, draws from a finite source of energy stemming from the old gods who ruled this realm before Neshka; its effectiveness dwindles with each activation."

Lucien's eyes widened. Struggling to fully understand what Caedus explained, he tried to keep up.

"Zededia used the seal to ... enhance his meditations. He mixed his Osirian sorcery with black magics the world hadn't seen in a millennium to perform rituals that ignored the laws of our gods. Armed with the essence of the old gods, he traveled to places no one has ever been, to do what no one else had ever done. Or so he claims, at least. But, like all things in life, there are consequences of every action. There are things that reside in the spiritual planes that are never meant to be reached. Not by man."

"Did he find something that troubled him?" Lucien asked, detecting Caedus's darker tone.

"Some*one*," Caedus said. "Not some*thing*."

Lucien hadn't spent much time around spirits or gods before. While he was wise enough to understand that the spirits of men roamed Elysia after death, he couldn't imagine one so troublesome to disturb a seasoned Shadewalker like Zededia.

"Who?"

Caedus's eerie stare sent a chill down his spine.

"Apollyon."

Like a boulder, the name smashed into him and muddied his racing mind.

The World Ender, he thought, digging up the name in his deepest memories of Osirian lore.

Fear overtook him.

"It was my understanding that—"

"Apollyon was destroyed?"

Lucien nodded.

"Mine, too," Caedus said with a sigh.

Gulls overhead screeched, and the waves repeatedly beat against the bow of the ship.

"Well," Caedus said, continuing his thought, "Zededia found him. Somewhere in the void of Elysia where gods don't even dare to look."

"Intentionally?" Lucien asked.

Lucien turned his torso to Caedus, fully invested in the conversation.

"He never said. If he *did* seek him intentionally, everything I thought I knew about your brother's pain ... was wrong."

"What do you mean?" Lucien asked.

Another pause fell over the men.

"Apollyon haunted your brother, Lucien. Appeared in his dreams like a phantom. I've never seen him so frightened on some of those days. I'd find him sitting against the wall of this room, arms wrapped around his knees ... eyes hollow and lifeless. Slimy, cold sweat coated every inch of his face. He wouldn't move or speak for an hour after that."

Hearing of such a harrowing encounter sent Lucien into a mild panic. He had been unaware of his brother's internal struggles for years, but learning of such agony made him realize just how ignorant he was.

"I don't know what he saw," Caedus said, "but it held him in constant fear. Your brother went back to Elysia before I found the sword, but, before that, he hadn't been in years because of that."

A slow exhale left through the prince's nose. He meshed his fingers together and looked out to the horizon.

"I'm not trying to alarm you," Caedus said as Lucien watched the flowing sea. "I'm just saying ... if you choose to pursue the same avenue as your brother ... be careful."

If Lucien ever wanted to explore the realm of Elysia, that desire evaporated. He knew he would have to march through the spiritual realm before this journey ended, though.

"There are places no man should ever wander," Caedus said.

Lucien tightened his grip on the wood railing as the ship rocked back and forth. The waves died down; calmer waters approached. He took Caedus's words to heart, but that didn't dissuade the disturbing nature that came with them.

Before Lucien could think over the conversation any further, he heard Captain Vederosa's indistinguishable voice echo across the ship. Her orders set the sailors on a different path, one that allowed them to relax for a moment. The prince glanced to his left and tried to eye her without drawing attention to himself. She stepped away from the wheel and made her way toward the stairs that descended to the main deck.

Mustering his courage, Lucien stiffened his shoulders. As she neared, he darted his gaze forward out to sea. Vederosa turned in his peripheral vision, giving him a chance to ease his eyes over once more. He saw her push open the door to her quarters and seal herself off from the crew. The urge to seek her presence crept into his thoughts. Something about Vederosa kept him in a state of awe, something he didn't quite understand.

"I'm not sure that's a much better place to wander," Caedus said.

Lucien flicked his head back to Caedus.

"What?" he said.

A faint smile stretched across Caedus's face.

"I said I'm not sure that's a much better place to wander. I think I'd rather take my chances with a spirit rather than her. I've never seen a woman so ... fierce."

Lucien gave him a light frown before shifting his attention back to Vederosa's chambers.

"Neither have I ...," he said. "Yet my curiosity remains."

A couple of sailors blocked his view of the decorated door of the captain's quarters.

"Well," Caedus said. "If you stare at her any longer, she may simply throw you overboard. I'd like to not be next to you when that happens."

"Hmph," the prince said with a smirk.

He leaned away from the rail and looked around for a moment.

"It might be a good idea to see what she knows about where we are going," he said. "Atlas hasn't given me much to go on."

"Perhaps," Caedus said. "While you do that, I'm going to find some food. Try not to get yourself killed."

"Don't worry about me, my friend," Lucien said, shifting gears to focus on his charisma. "Don't worry about me."

As Caedus walked away, Lucien made his way for Vederosa's chambers. Passing several pirates on the swaying deck, he sent sharp exhales through his nose to clear his nostrils of the salt water sprayed up from the sea.

He approached the door and eyed the serpent insignia that matched the one on the sails. The faint red eyes, sharp fangs, and black scales beast fit perfectly with atmosphere of the ship.

Lucien raised his closed fist and knocked on the hardwood. The commotion from the crew on the main deck forced him to listen carefully for a response.

"What?" a muffled voice shouted back.

Hesitating, the prince suddenly forgot his plan of action. Keeping Vederosa waiting seemed like a rather poor decision, though, so he had to come up with something. Lucien pressed his palm on the door and pushed. As it cracked open, the sunlight peering through the stained glass in the rear wall gleamed across the floorboards.

Lucien's eyes adjusted and scanned over a pair of thick black boots facing away from him. Frozen, he stared at the most beautiful woman he had ever seen as she leaned over a table with a map stretched out over it.

Holy Neshka.

His heart beat faster, and he traced her strong curves from her calves to her powerful thighs. The dimples in her lower back rested over her perfectly rounded ass clearly visible through her skintight pants. Lucien allowed his lips to part as he took in her alluring appearance. Face flushed, he shook his head to free himself from the lust flooding his thoughts.

"Quartermaster Sovo, if you've nothing to say to me, then get the hell out," Vederosa said while keeping her eyes on the map and her hands flat on the table.

"Your quartermaster is busy," Lucien said, squaring his shoulders and slightly pushing out his broad chest.

Vederosa whirled around, sending a sharp glare back at him. She gave him a once over as he did her moments before, but if she held any lust for him, she hid it well. Only skepticism showed in her face.

"I am—"

"I don't give a shit who you are," she said, cutting him off. "You're not part of my crew and you're not my king."

"Are you always this cynical to new people you meet?"

"Do you always barge into places you don't belong, such as my mission to—"

"This is *my* mission," the prince said with a bold tone, matching the severity in her eyes. "Everything about it concerns me, including you."

Vederosa squinted at him, keeping her same scowl.

"You must be the prince. Lucy," she said after a moment. "You're the one who put this little team together."

"*Lucien,*" he said, correcting her. "And, yes, this journey was my idea. I've simply come to see our progress."

"Well, as you can see, Prince *Lucien,* the ocean still surrounds us on all sides. Does that satisfy you?"

Lucien took a step forward, the gleaming light from the windows cascading over his short beard and chiseled jaw.

"I suppose. I trust that you know where sailing to?"

"Aeladaecia," Vederosa said. "The Cradle of the Colossus. While I personally think you're all bloody morons for setting such a course, Neptabyss made his orders quite clear."

"Morons? Why do you say that?"

Captain Vederosa crossed her arms and leaned against the wooden table, tilting her chin up ever so slightly.

"Aeladaecia is a fool's errand," she said. "It doesn't exist."

"Wha—of course it does," Lucien said with a scoff. "How do you think Osiris came to be what he was?"

"You and your gods ... Osirians are all the same. Following legends that are no more than myths. The blood in your veins may grant you sorceries, but there is only one power in this world that everyone bows to."

Lucien raised his eyebrow.

"Gold," Vederosa said.

"Is that why you've agreed to sail to a destination you believe isn't real?"

"I am sailing to your island," the captain said as she stood upright and walked around to the other side of the table, "because I was ordered to."

"You seem to take Neptabyss's orders rather seriously given your dubious view of Osirians. Why is that?"

"Simple."

Lucien stepped up to the table and glanced down at it while Vederosa turned her back to him to fetch something off her shelf. When she faced him again, he noticed the bottle of dark liquid in her hands.

"I owe Neptabyss for the life I have. My ship, my crew, I wouldn't have them if he hadn't decided to spare me."

She popped the cork out with her teeth and took a gulp. Lucien smelled a familiar scent, one he smelled each time he drank a glass of liquor. As he watched her wipe the rum from her lips, his craving for alcohol surfaced. The prince admired how easily she threw back a strong drink, another thing to add to the list of what attracted him to her.

"I'm sure as a woman of your status could bargain her way out of this quest," he said.

"I don't exactly want to be on the mainland right now."

Oh yeah. The war, he thought.

"And if the world is really going to come to an end, I might as well greet it on the sea."

"The world isn't going to end," Lucien said. "I won't allow it."

"Ah, yes," Vederosa said. "You won't allow it. I'm sure bringing back a dead guy is going to solve all our problems."

Lucien shot his hand to her wrist, restraining her from lifting the bottle to her mouth.

"You may not respect me," he said in an increasingly hostile tone, "but you *will* respect those I love."

He glared at her as she did he. After a moment, he released her arm and saw a hint of understanding in her eyes. Lucien retreated and regained his composure.

"Very well, Osirian," Vederosa said in a calm voice, giving him more open glance. "Family is all we have, after all."

The prince sighed, feeling a sense of shame for allowing his emotions to break through so easily.

"I did not mean to disturb you," he said, bowing his head.

Lucien turned started to make his way to the deck outside. He felt her cautious gaze on him as he walked away.

Just as the prince reached the door, a sudden jolt rocked the ship and rippled up his leg. Lucien frowned, curious about what made such a thud. He twisted his head over his shoulder to look at Vederosa, and she shared the same expression of concern. Another bump followed seconds later with much greater intensity, nearly knocking him off balance. The curiosity he held jerked to panic. He stumbled toward the table, another thud crashing into the ship from the ocean below.

"What the hell was that?" he asked.

When he glanced at Captain Vederosa again, she darted her eyes across the chamber and released rapid breaths, seemingly aware of what was happening.

"Steady yourself, Osirian," she said in a hasty voice. "We've entered deeper waters."

Chapter 12

Horrors of the Deep

Day 27 in the Month of War

Lucien staggered into the captain's chambers, the tremors from below rocking the ship even more. Muffled shouts and hurried footsteps sounded off from the main deck.

"Move!" Captain Vederosa said as she shoved her way past him.

A massive impact rattled the loose items on the nearby shelves and knocked Vederosa off her feet. Lucien reached out and grabbed her wrist, saving her from the concussion the wooden doorway waited to deliver. She gave him a look of stern appreciation and stood upright. Without another word, she stormed out onto the deck and left him in her wake. The door swung open, allowing Lucien to catch a glimpse of the commotion outside. He stepped into the doorframe, leaning on it with both his hands.

Huge waves of misty saltwater splashed up from each side of the ship, creating tiny rivers in the cracks of the hardwood. Lucien watched as the crew frantically sprinted about, and a deep, guttural roar bellowed beneath the churning sea. The prince covered his ears to shield them from its incredibly low pitch. When he looked up, he tried to step forward on the shaky ground as the sailors dashed around like madmen.

"Man the harpoons!" he heard Captain Vederosa shout. "Sails at full mast!"

Lucien tried to find a way to help, darting his gaze to Vederosa hastily climbing the stairs to the helm. A towering wave crashed onto the main deck, and the ship teetered side to side, both obstructing his view of the scene. Through the haze as he regained balance, he eyed King Atlas stumbling near the primary mast. He tried to make his way to him, but a ghastly sight froze him in horror of the port side. A hulking creature breached the surface, arching and turning to reveal its thick, scarred fin. He studied its dark navy color through the mists of seawater. The prince's eyes widened in panic as he guessed that the animal had reached at least half of the ship's size in length.

"Lucien!" Atlas shouted. "Hold on!"

Finding himself in the middle of the deck with nothing to grasp, he searched for a lifeline. He slipped to his hands and knees and crawled over to the right staircase. Water soaking him to his core and face dripping, Lucien hugged the newel post. His vision blurred in the chaos, and his ears rang.

Another deep roar boomed from the sea beasts beating against the ship and shook him from his trance. Lucien wobbled as he struggled to keep control of his balance. He pulled himself up and reached for the port side railing.

As he leaned over, the sea splashed his face, forcing him to retreat. Lucien persisted, though, and studied the water to find out what monstrosities had risen from the depths of the Orlestian. Shadowed figures coursed underneath the surface, varying in size from a fully grown man to as wide as a building. He counted over a dozen frenzying creatures and eventually gave up trying to keep track. One breached the surface like before, and Lucien stared in horror at the large, solid black eye on the side of its head.

It crashed back into the sea, and Lucien noticed the scale-like plates on its back. Several inches thick, the armored hide of the beast rose to a fine edge to act as its dorsal fin that resembled the edge of a great axe.

After studying them, the prince realized they swam in frantic patterns, bumping into one another as well as cracking hull of The Leviathan. Another sea beast exploded from the sea right under Lucien's nose and sent him flying on his back. He dropped back onto the deck, coughing for air as his breath had been beaten out of him. One of the sailors tumbled over the side of the ship and screamed as he plummeted into the merciless ocean.

An arm slid under each of his and hoisted him up. On his feet, Lucien looked beside him to see Caedus with the same expression of frightened concern.

"What the hell are these things!" he shouted.

Caedus's hesitation panicked him more.

"I don't know!"

Lucien's feet slipped across the soaked wooden deck; his leather boots unable to find a footing.

Suddenly, a loud, mechanical clank sounded from the center of the ship. An opening appeared in the main deck after several wooden slats retreated underneath in a spiral pattern. Half a dozen sailors heaved on thick, woven ropes to raise a platform from below. A menacing-looking weapon emerged from the heart of the ship; The Leviathan finally bared its teeth. Lucien kept his eyes on the serrated harpoon nestled in the largest ballista he had ever laid eyes on.

Another clank followed a jolt as the sailors released the ropes and lodged the weapon in position. A soldier that matched Ammonladus's stature climbed into the seat and fastened himself in.

"What to feed her, Captain?" another sailor shouted.

"Arm the explosive bolts!" Captain Vederosa yelled back. "The ocean will bask in black fire!"

Lucien turned to plant his shocked gaze on her.

"What the hell is she going to do with those?" he said. "Blow a damn hole in the sea?"

The sailors reached up to switch out the ballista's ammunition, and Lucien eyed the strange head at the end of the new bolt. Instead of a razor-sharp blade, a flat, wooden box took its place. The crank turned as the mounted sailor sneered and shifted the weapon toward the port side. A quiet calm appeared like the eye of a storm. The rampaging beasts continued to breach and fall back into the water, but the men aboard grew quiet.

Lucien saw the sailor in the ballista chuckle as he braced himself. After another second, a lever on the great weapon flicked backward, releasing hell itself toward the sea. Lucien followed the bolt as it soared through the air with a low-pitched screech that curdled his ears.

The calm pause erupted into a fiery explosion on impact, sending a shockwave through Lucien's body that rocked him more than the creatures' strikes. With blistered ears, he placed his hands on each side of his head to steady his jarred brain. The sailors around him raised their arms and shouted with a cheer. More deep roars pulsed from the dark waters of the Orlestian, and Lucien stumbled over to the side and noticed how the beasts scattered away from the ship in all directions.

"Another!" he heard Vederosa shout.

Like before, the sailors loaded a second explosive bolt. The ballista aimed lower. Lucien braced himself for the shot. Scraping along the insides of his ears yet again, the second missile met a more solid target. A horrid yelp sang through the air like a symphony for the dead, and Lucien scanned the water as one of the massive creatures writhed near the surface, a gaping hole blown into its side with low flames burning around the edge of the wound. The scent of seared sea flesh hit Lucien's nose like a lightning bolt and seized his sense of smell. His stomach tossed, and he wanted to hurl over the railing.

He looked on in agony and caught a glimpse of the poor fish as it faded into the blackness of the sea. Mouth agape, it gave him a murky view of hundreds of razor-sharp teeth. Somehow, seeing the rows of white blips sink into the depths haunted him more than anything.

After the second explosion, the beasts learned their lesson and rampaged away from the ship. The ballista cranked again as the sailors heaved on the wooden posts on the base of the platform to turn it.

"Starboard side!" Captain Vederosa said.

While everyone else seemed to find a way to help, Lucien felt completely lost. He froze trying to decide whether to aid the sailors or simply try to stay alive.

"Make yourself useful, Osirian!" Vederosa yelled down to him.

Her mocking tone irked him, but he knew she had a point.

"Grab another bolt!" the sailor mounted in the balista shouted while pointing to a crate nestled under one of the staircases to the upper deck.

Gaining a grip on himself, the prince stepped forward and searched through the ammunition crate until he found one just like the previous two. Lucien wrapped his hands around the bolt and hauled it into the open. The weight surprised him. Strong as he was, he struggled to maintain control of the awkward distribution of weight. Eventually, Lucien managed to carry it over to front of the great weapon, careful not to bump the highly explosive head on anything or anyone.

Two sailors took it from him and nestled it in the indention in the ballista. The sea beasts shifted course to the other side of the ship, and Lucien stepped back to let the other men work.

As the ballista turned and aimed down to the water, he planted his feet to brace himself. However, before it fired, one of the creatures breached the sea, its plated spine carving its way up the starboard side of the hull. Everyone screamed and lost their footing. The massive shark nicked the edge of the ballista's bow arm and knocked the explosive bolt free, sending it summersaulting upward.

Time slowed to a crawl. Debris from the ship flung through the air, and the muffled warning cries from the sailors drew his attention to the imminent doom plummeting toward the deck. Lucien's eyes widened in shock as the reflection of the explosive bolt spiraling down headfirst shined in his pupils. That singular second lasted for an eternity to him. Panic overcame him, his legs buckled, and he had no time to find cover.

The bolt landed from freefall and instantly detonated, blowing Lucien off his feet and shards of wood into his forearms as he raised them to protect his face. He flew back and crashed into the wooden railing on the port side. The explosions before already rang in his ears despite their distance; this one deafened him. Lucien came to his senses after losing consciousness for a moment, wincing at the bruise he felt on his lower back. Blood trickled down toward his hands from the wood shrapnel in his arms, fire roared at the impact point, and the survivors in close proximity shouted in agony. Though he felt the vibrations of their cries, he couldn't hear a word.

Lucien looked ahead to where the bolt landed. His hands trembled in horror, and his mouth fell agape, the sight of severed limbs and splattered intestines traumatizing him to his core. He couldn't pry his eyes off the bloodied piles of meat. Beside him, a hand attached to half of a forearm twitched with its final movements, the fingers jaggedly flicking toward the palm.

Frozen in place, he then saw Caedus slip and slide his way to him.

Lucien! he read on Caedus's lips. *Get up!*

Caedus's voice started to fade in along with the hellish sounds booming across the ship.

"Lucien!"

He darted his shaky gaze to Caedus as the captain heaved him off the deck.

"Come on!" Caedus said. "Get up!"

Adrenaline kicked him back into gear. The crew of The Leviathan scurried to make repairs for damage control, their voices becoming clear as well. That, though, is when he noticed that someone's was missing: Captain Vederosa's.

He looked at wheel of the ship; it spun back and forth without a master. Lucien bolted from his stance and took a firm hold of the supports on each side of the staircase. The beasts in the water continued their assault on the hull, shaking his ability to climb in a timely manner.

Once he leapt onto the upper deck, he searched for Vederosa. He stepped forward and took a firm hold of the wheel to keep it steady while he frantically glanced around. He eyed a woman's leg sticking out from under a loose plank, and the tricorn hat she wore lay several feet away. Lucien clenched his lips, the urge to protect her rising. He waited until one of the sailors could take control of the wheel and then ran over to her.

Stumbling down to his knees, Lucien lifted the wooden plank off. Vederosa didn't appear to have any immediate injuries. The prince assumed she had hit her head after the explosion and prayed that she was all right. He took her hand in his, feeling how weak she had become. She slowly opened her eyes, and Lucien held the back of her head in his palm. For the first time since they met, Lucien noticed that Vederosa's outer shell had faded. The strong, sneering expression she displayed for the world shifted to one of pain and agony. Lucien's heart warmed as they shared a tender moment.

However, her stern frown quickly returned, painting her in a coat of dominance and power. Lucien understood and helped her to her feet.

"We won't last much longer!" Lucien yelled. "What do we do now!"

Vederosa's sharp eyes looked out across the ship. Lucien waited for orders while trying to keep his balance.

"We need to let them pass," she said after a moment. "With the ballista gone, our only hope is to ride out this frenzy and focus on repairs."

Breaking apart with each passing minute, the ship sank lower in the water.

"Hoist all sails!" Captain Vederosa shouted, stepping closer to the wheel.

Lucien walked over to the side and noticed that the sea rose higher and higher in relation to his position.

"And get this soddin' water off my ship!"

Suddenly, a jagged crack sounded off behind the prince. He twisted his head around and cast his worried eyes upon the splintered mast of the rear sail; it swayed as the sailors hauled on the ropes. A sense of danger alerted him, and, as he studied the breaking wood, he traced the anticipated trajectory of the boom resting at head level right to where Vederosa stood.

The mast snapped before he could warn anyone. Without hesitation, he lunged at Vederosa, shoving her out of the way just in time. He tried to turn, but the boom bashed into his chest as soon as he did, nearly cracking his ribs and lifting him off his feet with ease.

He grunted as a coppery taste spread on his tongue, and his vision blurred as he whirled through the air. Half a second later, the backs of his legs slammed against the side of the hull, knocking him overboard into the raging sea.

Like a stone, Lucien plunged into the water and fought with all his might to stay conscious. The salt of the ocean stung his eyes and nostrils, the blood in his mouth seeping out and leaving a trail from the surface to his lips the deeper he sank. The sunlight above waned, allowing the darkness of the ocean to suffocate him in murky shadows.

Lucien waved his arms around, trying to rise to the surface. His lungs begged for air, burning beneath his ribcage that throbbed with an intense pain. The blue water above him turned purple. As the depths choked the last strands of light around him, Lucien reached his hand toward the surface.

Fatigue overcame him, allowing the currents of the ocean to flip him face down. Through squinted eyes, Lucien gazed into the black abyss below. The endless chasm sparked a primal fear in his mind, a fear greater than any he had ever experienced. It paralyzed him, freezing his desire to swim toward the surface.

Lucien started to drift into an unconscious state as the oxygen supply to his brain ran dry. The pain in his chest and the sting in his eyes became the least of his concerns.

However, just before the prince fell into death's hand, something grasped the back of his cloak and heaved him up. The jolt brought him to life for a moment. As his reserve levels of energy coursed through him, he frantically looked around and thrashed his arms. A horrifying sight beneath him froze him in terror, snaring his attention from the gaping void clawing at his sanity.

Something about the abyss below changed. Lucien frowned, not paying any attention to the water filling his mouth and nose. After carefully peering beyond the shadowed veil, he realized that the darkness *was moving.*

By the gods ... what the hell is that? he thought.

His eyes widened, the sea stinging them more, and saw massive plate-like structures slowly peeking through the shadows of the depths resembling something akin to the carapace of a centipede.

Lucien ascended toward the surface, a muscular arm hauling him up by him the shoulder. The sun's bright light returned, and soon enough, his head broke the plane of the sea. He spewed saltwater from his mouth and blinked rapidly to clear his vision of the blurriness.

Hacking like a dying man, Lucien clung to his savior for dear life.

Over the roving waves, a lifeboat appeared in his view. He had never felt such love for a vessel in his entire life. Shakingly, he reached one hand over the side. The sailors in the dinghy dragged him aboard, and he hit the hardwood with a thud. Horizontal, the prince coughed one more time, blood rushing to his face and sea water spilling over the corners of his lips. He took short, rapid breaths of the fresh air, finding an appreciation for it that he had never expected. The caws of seagulls overhead filled his ears once the water drained, and he felt the firm hand of one of the sailors on his shoulder.

"We've got ye, Your Majesty," the man said. "The sea won't claim ye yet."

Lucien lowered his head to rest on the bottom of the boat. He heard someone else climb in and assumed it to be his rescuer. After mustering his strength, he leaned his head back up. With rivers of ocean water pouring off him, Caedus Redstone panted in exhaustion. Lucien was too tired to think, but he realized what an incredible feat his ally had just completed.

Wanting to express his gratitude, Lucien tried to force the words from his burning throat. However, he couldn't manage to speak and simply nodded. Caedus nodded back to him, and the prince lowered his head once again. Now able to rest, his mind circled back to the creature he saw crawling along the bottom of the sea. He struggled to decipher if he really saw some sort of titanic monster or if he simply imagined it.

If that was just a part of its spine ... how large could it truly be?

The rowboat neared the damaged hull of The Leviathan across calmer waters, and the pod of mysterious sea beasts had vacated the area. Lucien found comfort in the shade as the ship blocked the sun from his eyes. He found his strength again and pulled himself upright. From above, ropes cascaded down, and the sailors next to him tied them to the notches on the ends of the dinghy to hoist it up.

Once parallel with the main deck, Lucien waited for the others to step off before standing. He scanned from the front of the ship to the back and took note of the damage. Plenty of cracked or broken planks in the floorboard came into view along with chunks of wood splinters scattered about, but nothing compared to the jagged hole next to the decommissioned ballista that nearly fell through the upper deck to the level below. Lucien walked by the blast site and watched a group of men try to clean up the remains of their friends. They scraped the tattered pieces of flesh off every surface and tossed them overboard.

Lucien felt surprised at their nonchalant nature. He couldn't imagine having to pick through the corpses of his friends or family and come out on the other side fully sane. Caedus's sturdy hand gripped his shoulder, and Lucien nodded at him once more. The prince then focused his attention on the wheel of the ship where he had last seen Captain Vederosa. Another sailor had taken her place, so he assumed she had retired to her chambers.

Meandering over toward the captain's quarters, Lucien tried his best to flush out all the pain in his body. He gave no effort into greeting her with a professional courtesy and pushed on the decorated door without hesitation. Inside, he caught Vederosa's stone-cold face looking up at him from beyond the map table. He then noticed King Atlas standing with his back to him as he surveyed the map with her.

"Leave us for a moment," Vederosa said.

Atlas turned after pausing and made his way outside, giving Lucien a nod of respect as he stepped by. After the door behind him closed, Captain Vederosa stood completely upright and raised her chin. While he had expected a softer greeting, her sternness started to grow on him. He kept the smile off his face, nevertheless.

"That was an incredibly senseless thing you did," she said.

Lucien frowned.

"I saved your life," he said with a chuckle. "I don't know if I would call that senseless."

Vederosa shifted around the table and approached him. He stood his ground.

"Listen to me, and listen good," she said in a quieter yet firmer tone. "You are not built for the sea. You are ignorant of its dangers and how to evade them. Count yourself lucky that your friends care for you so deeply. If not for Caedus Redstone, your bones would be rotting along the ocean miles away from the dimmest speck of sunlight."

"Had I not acted, that would be *you* in my place," Lucien said inching his head closer to her, growing agitated.

"If the sea wills me dead, then by the gods, let it be. You have no right to rob me of my fate. If the world should end, I will meet that end aboard the best damn ship that has ever sailed. Your attempt to spare me made me appear weak. Like I couldn't handle a simple shiver of Naguzii sharks."

Lucien flared his nostrils, the anger rising in his face.

"If that is how you show gratitude for someone willing to die for you, then you deserve whatever fate you so desperately crave," he said through clenched teeth.

"I don't need you to protect me!" she shouted in his face. "My orders are to protect *you*!"

And there it was. The silver lining behind her confrontational personality.

"You were ordered to protect me?" he said, lowering his voice.

Vederosa crossed her arms.

"If you die, Osirian, then this mission is lost. I know of the war in the mainland. Neptabyss told me everything. Matticus, the ascension ceremony, ... Ehthilia...."

Lucien loosened his shoulders and looked at her with kinder eyes. Something about her last word opened a door to darker thoughts. He knew then that Ehthilia meant something to her for some reason.

"He also told me that you may be the only person who can put an end to the war."

Lucien scoffed.

"No, the only person who can put a stop to it is who we are going to get."

"And you're who's been charged with that task. So, for all our sakes, you can at least *try* to stay alive."

The prince took a deep breath to calm himself. Perhaps Vederosa had a point, he concurred.

"Very well," he said.

His patience invited the opportunity to calm down. She relaxed her torso and flicked her head to clear her hair from her eyes.

"Where are we off to next?" he asked. "Is that what you and Atlas were discussing?"

She nodded.

"We're going to dock at the port city of Talluna," she said. "There, we'll make repairs and have a chance to recollect ourselves."

Though he had never heard of the destination, he trusted Vederosa's knowledge of the area.

"That's a friendly port?" Lucien asked.

"As friendly as they'll get from here. It's controlled by the pirate lords of the Orlestian, one of the last of its kind. You won't find many friends, but you won't find any enemies, either."

Oh, brilliant, he thought sarcastically.

"You should find Atlas," she said while walked past him toward the door. "He'll be able to heal you far better than anyone in Talluna.

As her leather boots clicked against the wood floor, the harrowing vision from the black abyss of the ocean crawled to the front of his mind. He hesitated to follow her, the monster he saw holding him in place with just a memory.

"One more thing, Captain," Lucien said over his shoulder.

He turned as Vederosa did the same.

"These sharks ... do they cause this much trouble often?"

She squinted at him.

"Not usually," she said. "Naguzii sharks hunt deep along the ocean floor where the sun has never shone. I've only ever seen so many near the surface once before."

"Why do you think they rose from the depths? Seems like they had a reason."

"I don't know, but I don't really care either. You don't have to anayzle the behavior of every creature. Sometimes an animal is just an animal."

"I think I know why," he said.

The captain stepped closer and narrowed her eyes.

"What do you mean?"

Lucien hesitated, thinking that she knew something he didn't.

"Well, as I nearly drowned, I saw something so ... massive ... that the shadows of the deep followed it like mist. I think those whales, whatever you called them, were fleeing from it."

"What did it look like?"

He paused, regretting putting himself in a position where he was forced to recall what he saw.

"Just these gigantic ... scale-like plates. Moving and shifting like segments of armor. No fins, no arms, no legs. I didn't even see its head. It almost looked like the tail of the largest lobster I could possibly imagine."

Vederosa's eyes slightly widened. Lucien frowned. She knew what he was talking about.

"Nyaka ... Viaentas...." she said under her breath.

"The what?"

Vederosa shot him a sharp glance.

"Nothing," she said, turning her back to him. "Go back to your duties."

"Now, wait a moment, if something's out there then—"

Twisting around in the blink of an eye, Vederosa shoved her hand to his chest and pushed him into the hardwood of the doorway.

"Silence yourself," she said in a quiet yet menacing tone. "There are many rumors that spawn from the depths of the Orlestian, and when they reach the ears of a crew, they spread chaos and mutiny. If I so much as hear a word about some sea monster lurking around in the shadows, I will cut your tongue out with my cook's rusted filet knife. Am I clear?"

Lucien nodded, not having much of a choice.

Vederosa's tone sent a firm message, but the prince detected a bit of fear in it as well. He kept silent and stood by, watching her storm out of her quarters onto the main deck. The conversation produced more questions than answers, the air grew thick with a rank smell, and Lucien's body ached to the point of exhaustion.

He followed Vederosa's path onto the deck and kept a worried eye on each of the crewmates. The sea's raging waves died down, the Naguzii sharks already out of his view. With no indication on how long it would take to sail to Talluna, Lucien sighed. Not having an immediate course of action tested his patience much like his days wasted in the halls of his father's keep.

A breeze blew by, chilling his exposed hands. Lucien wrapped his damp cloak around his shoulders and tried to keep warm. King Atlas walked up next to him with a similar expression of concern and weariness.

"Well, all our people are still here," Atlas said. "I can't say the same for the crew, though."

"Do you think Vederosa will mourn her men?" Lucien asked.

"In time, perhaps. But she strikes me as the kind to mourn in solitude. Besides, in this line of work, death is to be expected. I'm sure she's prepared for the loss of her men and has lost plenty before."

Lucien remained quiet for a moment as he stood with the king. He shivered from time to time as the cold sea water lingered in his clothing. Her anger after mentioning what he saw in the ocean intrigued him intensely.

"Atlas?" he asked.

"Hmm?"

"You're fluent in Aznogsi, right?"

"Yes. Why do you ask?"

Lucien licked his lower lip and sniffed.

"Vederosa mentioned something ... a phrase," he said. "It sounded like an Aznogsi phrase."

"What did she say?"

"The, um ... the *Nyaka ... Nyaka Viaentas*?" Lucien said, looking to the floor. "Something like that."

"She said *that?"* Atlas said. "You heard her say that?"

The Daecian king's worried tone disturbed him.

"Yes, right before she threatened to throw me back to the sharks for speaking it around the crew."

"Is that so? She must think it's real, too."

"Think what's real? What does it mean?"

Atlas looked at him with a smirk.

"Big damn bug."

Chapter 13

I am Death

Day 28 in the Month of War

Word had spread far of Matticus's advances through Western Voluutia. Every town, village, and settlement abandoned their homes to seek shelter in the capital, allowing the Hostellae to proceed while met with little resistance. The great walls of Amuun Drall invited a challenge, rising above the low fog that hovered over the lake adjacent to the city. Just the sight of his rival's castle boiled his blood. To the north, his ally, Korzeg, marched into the Voluutian valley and camped on the other side of the city. Matticus knew that Raed had called for their aid long ago, but with Nysis's presence to remind them of their allegiance, the Korzegi warriors would soon turn their blades against him. A calm quiet washed over the grassy hills, the steel helmets of the Hostellae all pointed toward the fortress of Amuun Drall.

Battalions of footsoldiers stood in formation, ready to march at their king's command. Matticus crossed his arms, rubbing the thick metal plates of his armor together. The horses in the mounted divisions neighed restlessly. Still in the early phase of spring, the weather cast a light frost across the land and a chill over his skin. After a moment, the sharp sounds of wood and steel shifting together alerted him, and Matticus turned his head and watched the packed trebuchets roll forward through the alleys between the gathered soldiers.

Horns and orders from his generals sang through the air, and the standards bearing Hostellus's insignia of the gilded eagle fluttered in the light wind. In the distance, Matticus observed the activity along the top of the outer wall protecting Amuun Drall. Torches lined the crenellations, archers stood in their positions, and a lone mangonel atop a squared tower swiveled toward his direction.

"The Voluutians are preparing their defenses, my liege," General Komm, leader of his cavalry units, said. "Shall we begin the siege?"

Matticus squinted his eyes as he gazed upon the Voluutian capital. He envisioned Hostellus's flags stretching to the sky atop the gatehouses. Drawing in a deep breath through his nostrils, he savored the morning air. The might of his ancestor flowed through him; Matticus felt the power of the Holy Uniter crawling in his veins within his crimson blood. He longed for the destruction of Voluutia, to wipe it clean and start anew. Seeing the battlefield after years of planning fueled his rising aggression. His armies were ready, the day was young, and the thought of leveling Amuun Drall to the ground sent him into a restrained frenzy.

"'Come, now, you wicked. Deny not your salvation,'" Matticus said, speaking a direct quote from Osiris he memorized from the poems of the Chosen Scribe, Ozamendelas.

The king's eyes reddened with rage. Hell emerged in his heart.

"'Hasten thy end, scream for the heavens. Water in the ground, your blood will nourish my kin and make them whole. For I am flame. I am fury. I am death.'"

"Release trebuchets!" General Komm shouted, taking Matticus's response as an order to launch the attack.

All around him, beasts of wood and metal screeched as immensely heavy counterweights dropped from their locked positions. Seconds later, stones larger than the horse he rode on hurled through the air. Matticus tilted his gaze up and observed their descent; the deep pitched screams hummed in his ears. The outer wall of Amuun Drall exploded into a rain of debris as the boulders crashed into the fortifications. Tremors shook the ground beneath his feet. The siege had begun.

Subsequent boulders crashed into the wall soon after, creating an opportunity for the Hostellae to penetrate the first line of defense.

"Swarm the city," Matticus said, a trail of frost blowing through the slits in his helmet.

The horns of the Hostellae blared, commanding the infantry to surge toward the crippled wall. To meet his charging horde, the Voluutians sent forth their initial wave of soldiers wearing light armor and crude swords. Matticus remained unimpressed, expecting more a formidable foe to appear. The elite waited deeper in the city, he thought, to protect their king at all costs.

A thousand Hostellian swordsmen clashed against the Voluutians on the front line. They cleared a path for the cavalry to charge, and Matticus drew his longsword for battle. He spurred his horse forward with hundreds of armored knights behind. Arrows flew from the wall, ash ascended in columns of smoke, and the shouts of dying men shrieked across the battlefield. All sounds of war, he savored each and every moment.

As Matticus led his rampaging cavalry, he reached the frontline in less than a minute. Trampling the Voluutians in his path, he surged his horse forward and slashed his blade at any who stood within reach. Blood coated his shining silver armor, and a red glow glistened through the eye slits of his helmet under a plume of white fluttering feathers.

Bodies bounced off the metal pauldrons covering his horse's shoulders. One Voluutian hadn't noticed him barreling over the dead grasses and turned his head just in time for Matticus to cleave his skull in half from chin to forehead.

Matticus rode deep into the Voluutian front line and carved his way through them like an anchor dredging the ocean floor. His enemy became wise to his tactics, though, and deployed a row of halberdiers to counter the heavy cavalry. The Hostellae galloped too fast to react properly, falling right for the trap that the Voluutians had set. Matticus tried to steer his horse between two pikes, but one of them skewered his mount clean through the chest. The horse buckled under him and collapsed.

Plummeting to the ground, Matticus twisted midair to roll across the hard sod. His cape wrapped around him as he tumbled, and he landed in the belly of the beast.

The Voluutians surrounded him but kept their distance to respect his lethality. A mistake, they allowed him to regain his senses. Matticus pushed himself off the earth and climbed to his feet. His hulking body rose, a heavy gust of wind blowing his cape to one side. As the Voluutians cut off every path of escape, Matticus tightened his grip on his bloodied longsword. He eerily lifted his chin from his chest, breathed deep, and glared at the fear growing in their eyes.

"Fools."

Matticus heaved his longsword into the air and slashed at the nearest Voluutian in front of him, tearing his abdomen open like a knife through a ripe peach. Sensing attacks from multiple sides, he quickly took his *Igni* stance, ducked to evade, pivoted on his heel, and swiped all around to put distance between him and the enemy soldiers circling him. He threw them in disarray, breaking their formations and charging at them head on. Matticus sidestepped a thrusted spear, pried it free from his attacker's grasp, and plunged it through its master until intestines spilt out through the hole wound in the man's back. He then parried the next Voluutian and shoulder charged him, knocking him to the ground. Another advanced to his left. Without time to hack with his blade, Matticus balled his fist and shattered the man's skull with a devastating punch.

Realizing they couldn't hope to outmatch the Hostellian king's rage, the Voluutians started to flee. The group of thirty that surrounded him before dwindled to twenty, the rest either retreating or slaughtered. Twenty became ten, and ten became two.

Standing in the middle of a pile of corpses, Matticus trembled with anger. Blood coated his blade and hid the glimmer that usually shined in the perfect steel. The two Voluutians quivered before dropping their weapons to surrender. One sprinted away with a horrified gasp, and the other tried to follow. Matticus quickly raised his free hand and curled his fingers toward his palm.

"Helsoc. (Ensnare.)"

The sod shifted beneath the Voluutian's feet and swallowed them. Matticus walked forth, stepping over the bodies, and narrowed his sight on his target sword in hand.

"No, no, please!"

The king ignored the pitiful cry and cocked his arms to one side. With one fluid strike, he unleashed his full might through his sword and hacked the Voluutian clean in two at the waist. The man's torso spun to the ground several feet away, spraying the grasses underneath with blood and viscera, and his legs twitched before caving in on themselves.

Matticus absorbed the carnage with his red gaze before looking on ahead. The Voluutians sounded for a full retreat, pulling all survivors back behind the outer wall. Arrows ceased flying, and his siege engines paused their barrage. Standing alone in a field of dead men, the king turned around to see his armies advancing. Many of his knights lay slain from the halberdiers, but that didn't matter to him. Ten more would replace each of the fallen.

The outer wall protecting Amuun Drall a mile outside the city's edge crumbled, allowing for the Hostellae to pour through before their main assault. Matticus walked up the low hill to gaze upon the ruins. His boots clanked against the stone pathway lining the outside of the wall. The rest of his army shouted behind him and rallied to charge the fleeing Voluutians. Kicking the loose rubble, Matticus trudged through a wide gap in the wall and looked out across the cobblestone courtyard that separated the outer defenses from the city. The Voluutians gathered in the distance, preparing for a fierce counterattack. Thundering footsteps beat against the ground as the Hostellae climbed the hill to join their king. Matticus waved his hand at eye level, though, signaling for them to halt.

Malice burned inside him, his sharpened gaze fixated upon his enemy. A hundred Voluutian soldiers sprinted at him to retaliate with another thousand ready to charge right after. Filling his lungs with the cold air, he closed his eyes to pray.

"Pyrang kar, Aenaolae. Nnusa kar gaz Zanto zrekos. Ini lett onnokas ir bosch saarna yuoznae Zant ... ish Zanto diaenzamog. (Hear me, Great One. Bathe me in Your wrath. Let the enemies of this land witness You ... and Your divinity.)"

Matticus's skull buzzed with fury. He felt the raw energy of his ancestor channeling through his veins, and wisps of red mist appeared and whirled around him. After sheathing his longsword, he held out open palms at his side. He slowly marched toward the battalion of Voluutian soldiers, basking in a red aura of divinity like a god. His soul cried out to Osiris as Matticus walked the very steps he did so long ago. He who conquered nations roamed the earth once more; the Holy Uniter returned!

"'Come, now, you wicked!'" Matticus said, bellowing his deep, demonic voice across the stone plains.

He siphoned his power into two red orbs of light hovering above his hands.

"'Deny not your salvation!'"

The Voluutians rushed toward him, swords held overhead.

"'Hasten thy end! Scream for the heavens!'"

Matticus summoned the most powerful sorcery he possessed, amplified by Osiris, who watched over him, an angel of war on his shoulder.

"'Water in the ground! Your blood will nourish my kin! And make them whole!"

His roar pulled from the depths of his rage, darkening his tone further. The red aura revolving around shook with violent trembles.

"'For I flame!'"

His enemy neared—just a hundred yards away.

"'I am fury!'"

A crimson glow shined brightly through his veins.

"'I am ... DEATH!'"

Matticus slammed his palms together to initiate his arcane magic, and as soon as he did, every single Voluutian in sight burst into white flames from head to toe. Shrill, agonizing screams sang through the air like the choir of hell. The burning Voluutians flailed in the reflection of his eyes like a chaotic ballroom dance. Matticus couldn't pry his gaze from them, watching their pink flesh char to black as they dropped to the ground. His pupils grew larger, taking in as much of the purifying light as they could. Soon, the screams ceased. All that remained were the sounds of flickering flames dispersing into tiny columns of smoke above the bodies.

Something deep in Matticus snapped. He had slain and slaughtered plenty in his life as an Osirian, but nothing compared to the devastation he just unleashed. An obsession sprouted from the cracks in his heart, an obsession for *more*.

He stared at the corpses scattered before him for a long while, falling into a mild trance. A horse's trot broke his concentration after a moment.

"My king!" General Komm said as he rode nearby.

Silence followed as Matticus allowed his officer to observe the view.

"Sire, are-are you all right?" Komm said, audibly disturbed while the dying white flames melted away the last bits of flesh.

Matticus released a deep breath through his nose.

"'The heathens are vanquished. The land is cured,'" he said, further quoting the ancient text he resorted to earlier in the day. "'May the colors of spring ... rise from the ashes.'"

Komm's horse poked into his sideview.

"The-the Voluutians have fled to the inner city. We now occupy the outskirts of Amuun Drall."

The news bored him. He kept quiet, losing himself in the corpses in front of him.

"Commander Nysis has returned as well. He brings word from the Korzegi forces and seeks an audience with you."

"Good," Matticus said in a slow, menacing tone. "Now the real work can begin."

Voluutia suffered a slaughter at the hands of King Matticus. Though they brought out their weaker soldiers to soften the blow of the Hostellian assault, they fell to their superior counterparts like blades of grass. The Voluutian flag still waved atop the keep of Amuun Drall, a fact he would have to correct in the coming days. The extent of Matticus's power had revealed itself to the world, and he knew no one could hope to withstand it.

Chapter 14

Talluna

Day 1 in the Month of Rain

In desperate need of repair and supplies, The Leviathan sailed into the port of Talluna. A shoddy site, the city contained mostly tied together buildings wedged together from whatever washed up on shore. Hulls from shipwrecks, masts, even anchors decorated the pirate town at every corner.

Caedus stood firm on the deck of the ship as he scanned his squinted eyes across the hundreds of torchlights in almost every window. Darkness consumed the island town, covering its crooked outline in the black sky. Able to hear the commotion of the lawless land as the ship docked, Caedus frowned in disapproval. Life in the Black Legion demanded discipline, order, and respect; everything the people of Talluna lacked.

The ports of Skulpos and Amuun Drall appeared like palaces compared to this place. Rotten fish and stale beer stained the currents of air that wisped by. Caedus hopped off The Leviathan onto shaky planks of the docks that protected him from the dark water below. Just the thought of falling in sent chills across his shoulders. The encounter with the great sharks in the Orlestian Sea had scarred him more than he wanted to admit.

"What do we do now?" Prince Lucien asked from his right as he stepped off the ship. "It'll be days before we can set sail again. We're to just idle here until the repairs are complete?"

"Trust me, I don't like it any more than you do," Caedus said. "But we don't have much of a choice."

Caedus looked down beneath the slats of the dock and watched the water roll up and down with the tide. A wandering crowd of townsfolk walked by on land, catching his attention shortly after.

"Be wary here, Lucien," Caedus said. "This place will snap at you without warning."

"Have you been here before?"

Caedus glanced over the towering structures filled with gamblers, drunks, and pirates alike.

"Once," he said, taking a deep breath. "Long time ago."

Heading toward solid ground, he placed firm hands over his sword and pouch of coins attached to his belt.

"Come on. Let's find a drink."

As Caedus walked closer, the commotion from the town rang louder in his ears. Several men and women passed him by as he crossed the muddy road. He felt Lucien's presence behind him but looked over to make sure he hadn't been taken by the more unsavory denizens.

The tavern nearby seemed like a suitable place to lose himself. Caedus eyed a couple of men holding a pint and conversing between themselves outside under the low awning. They reeked of filth. One of them grinned at him and raised his pint, revealing a near-empty mouth of rotting teeth. Once inside, he lowered his chin and narrowed his eyes, keeping a tab on everyone in sight. The raucous nature of the tavern reminded him of the town he stopped in during his adventure through the Lunendar Mountains in search of the Sword of Kings. His thoughts instantly turned to Raeza, the thief girl he traveled with. As he meandered through the bar, the memory of her soft embrace spread down to his hands subtly squeezing as if she were there. He then remembered his encounter with the Vaedorian spy.

After a quick glance around, Caedus decided that the odds of an assassin lurking after him in the shadows were low, even in a town as dangerous as Talluna. He walked over to a table tucked away in the corner and loosened his grip on his sword. To restabilize his balance, he pressed his hands against the table and sat down. Multiple days aboard The Leviathan through rocky waters had skewed his perception of a firm place to sit.

Caedus leaned against the stone wall and cracked the bones in his neck. The setting felt even more familiar to him than when he had first walked here. Lucien sat down across the table from him, his broad shoulders blocking his view of the center of the tavern.

Lowering his guard, he scanned the townsfolk one by one as he moved his eyes from right to left. He then noticed Prince Lucien hunched over, unable to make himself comfortable.

"Something ailing you?" he asked.

"My back," Lucien said. "I can hardly sit or even stand right after crashing into that wooden rail. I'm not used to such ... abrasive ... adventures."

Caedus chuckled.

"Life's a little different outside Vaedor Sellos, isn't it?"

"I knew that would be the case," the prince said, a sly grin growing on his face. "But I had no idea how different it could be. Faces have changed, home has changed, even the food has changed. Ever since I rode out to Talion's Tomb after Zededia escaped, nothing's been the same. Seems like we can't ever find stability."

Caedus nodded in agreement.

"I said the same thing to your brother after our first year spent in exile."

"No one ever told me of what happened to the Black Legion," Lucien said. "Until I heard Zededia was making a nuisance of himself from some abandoned fortress.

"A nuisance?" Caedus said, cracking a smile. "We were fighting for our lives."

Lucien's mild panic amused him.

"That's not-I didn't mean to ... disrespect ... your survival."

"None taken."

An awkward pause arose for a moment, and Caedus watched Lucien's eyes fall to the table.

"Caedus?" the prince said.

Caedus raised his eyebrow.

"Zededia was an enemy of Vaedor Sellos. Doesn't that mean that he was my enemy as well?"

"Do you consider him one?"

"Of course not."

"Then he wasn't."

Lucien nodded his head in agreement, but Caedus detected a lingering bit of confusion. He tried to guess what the prince was thinking, placing himself in his shoes.

Perhaps Lucien considered the fact that Zededia openly opposed and warred against his own people and, in a way, him.

"I know your brother showed a great amount of aggression to Vaedor Sellos. But you must understand that all his anger, all his rage—it was directed toward Matticus. Every decision he made, he did with *Matticus* as the target, not you."

He saw the prince sigh with a gloomful face.

"Zededia never even came close to targeting you in any plot he carried out against the Vaedorians. In fact, there were several that he abandoned in fear that you would suffer the results."

"Like what?"

Caedus's memory whirled to find an example. The hours of private conversations and war meetings held in the banquet hall of Anzagaar Nostir replayed in his mind.

"Like, for instance," he said, "there came a time where Zededia grew bold enough to assault the city directly. In our first year of exile, with his hatred for Matticus at its highest, he wanted to storm Vaedor Sellos and take back what Matticus ripped away. He could have, too, with his powers. And we almost did. Upon reflection, though, Zededia changed his mind."

"Why?"

Caedus scoffed.

"I could come up with a dozen reasons. Eight-hundred soldiers? Storming the most fortified city in all Osiria outnumbered a hundred to one? No chance at all. I tried to reason with him to no avail until he suddenly dissolved that idea one afternoon. I thought he had finally just come to his senses."

He looked down and fiddled with the callous on his thumb as he remembered the exact conversation he referred to.

"But, um ... it wasn't until months later when I realized the real reason he decided not to."

"What was the reason?"

Caedus locked eyes with Lucien.

"You."

Watching the prince frown in confusion, Caedus waited for the weight of his response to sink in.

"We poured weeks into that plan. Down to the last man. Even when Zededia admitted that there were simply too many Vaedorians to overcome, his wickedly ingenious brain started to file over possible solutions. He became obsessive. Heartless. He finally came to me with a scheme that could even the odds. Something that would scare your nightmares."

Caedus hesitated, questioning his decision to bring up the evil that his commander had revealed to him years ago. Talking about it passively still soured his tongue.

"We, uh ... we were going to unleash ... the Green Lotus."

"What the hell is that?" Lucien asked.

"Neshka's deadliest creation. The Aznogs called it *Primarra Vivessta*, or 'prime evil.' It's a plant-like parasite that liquefies any non-botanical life it spreads to. We didn't even have any on hand. Too dangerous to keep around. But, if administered correctly, it could have wiped out the entire Hostellae, maybe even Matticus himself."

Lucien's eyes remained glued to him, and Caedus stiffened his shoulders.

"I asked him if that's what he wanted, to destroy everything he had ever known. He glared at me with hell in his eyes and said yes. He persisted still despite me mentioning that Livia would be at risk. I could tell from his hesitation that he gave her thought, but that didn't sway him. Then, I brought up you. That it could have killed you."

Caedus glared at Lucien with as much care as his stone face would allow. He watched Lucien's mouth fall slightly agape.

"Zededia abandoned that idea without any further discussion."

Another awkward pause arose. Lucien sank back in his chair almost in disbelief, and Caedus watched him process such heavy emotion.

"Zededia hated Matticus enough to destroy the world," Caedus said, "but he loved you more than he hated him."

"It's funny," Lucien said, a tear visible in his eye, "I've heard more stories about Zededia after his death than I did before."

"Good men live through those they affect. Especially after they're gone."

Lucien gave him another nod.

All the talk of sentiment heightened Caedus's desire for a stout drink. He glanced around to find the barkeeper through the bandits drowning themselves in ale. Clinking coins rattled in his ears, and he looked back to see Lucien pouring a few out on the table.

"I'm not sure your kors are good here," he said.

"What makes you say that? Kors are accepted worldwide, right? Wasn't that the entire point of making them?"

Caedus then saw the barkeeper appear from the back room. The man reminded him of his father in many ways with his strong chin and uninviting demeanor. Something peculiar happened a moment later. The barkeeper filled up a stein of ale and handed it to one of the grimmer looking pirates without any exchange of money whatsoever. Puzzled, Caedus tried to crack the code.

"These men aren't after gold. They don't value it like we do," he said.

"What do they value, then?"

Observing a group of men with drinks compared to a group without, Caedus took note of their contrasting physical appearance in the form of battle scars and missing body parts.

"Respect."

Caedus stood from the table.

"Don't worry, I think I can find us something to drink."

Caedus sifted his way past the miscreants in the tavern, keeping his eyes on each one to ensure that no one tried to pickpocket him. A few of the sailors he walked by gave him glares. One even pulled a knife from his belt. Caedus didn't flinch, however. He pressed on toward the bar with a stern expression.

The bartender continued cleaning the glasses and serving familiar faces, ignoring him entirely. Caedus cleared his throat and leaned over the counter.

"What do you want?" the barman said in a gruff voice. "We serve sailors around here. You don't look the part."

"I'm no sailor. But Talluna favors those who have served in other ways.

The bartender squinted at him.

"Your face is unfamiliar as it is ugly. You've no reputation here."

"Hmph," Caedus said, scoffing. "Perhaps you would recognize me better from behind."

Caedus turned around and held his cloak down to reveal the tattoo on the nape of his neck that marked him as a member of the Legonae. He heard a faint gasp followed by a hearty chuckle.

"Well, why didn't you say so?" the bartender said with a wide grin. "Black Legion soldiers are always welcome in my inn. Drinks for you and your men!"

Caedus grinned and held up two fingers. After a moment, the innkeeper returned with a pair of strong ales, and Caedus left a single gold kor as a friendly gesture. He then turned to make his way back to Lucien. Walking with both hands occupied made him nervous. The sailors around him kept to themselves, though, after hearing his prestigious title echo through the tavern.

He set both steins down on the table and noticed Lucien's bewildered expression.

"How the hell did you manage these?" the prince asked.

"I told you. Respect."

Taking a long drink of his beverage, he watched Lucien do the same. Caedus exhaled in delight and then set his stein on the table.

"So how is it that the Black Legion is known to people all the way out here?" Lucien asked.

Caedus sat in thought for a moment. He leaned over the table and shifted his lips to the right, the memories of the adventures of his youth rising in his thoughts. Tapping the bottom of his stein on the table several times, he tuned out all the noise around him.

"Do you remember when Zededia ventured off to explore the neigherboring lands a few years before his exile?"

"I do," Lucien said. "He was supposed to be gone for just short of half a year, but it took him fourteen months to return."

"Right, well, as you know, he didn't come back alone. He brought Seether and Ammon back with him. When he returned, he told stories of these outlying lands and how they differed from Hostellus."

Caedus took another drink of ale, wiping the froth from his lip.

"It was then that he had the idea to utilize Hostellus's bounty of soldiers and spread them to all corners of Osiria to aid others who lied in ruin, whether that be because of foriegn invaders, domestic enemies, natural disasters, anything. That's essentially what led to Hostellus's involvement in Korzeg's war with the northern territories. Anyway, Captain Ammon built upon that idea and suggested that we ... expand our horizons and extend our reach to those across the Orlestian, in the kingdoms founded by the Luzen tribes."

"Is that how you came to find Talluna?" Lucien asked, cutting him off.

Hesitating, Caedus wriggled his fingers.

"Not exactly," he said. "Just after its creation, a chapter of the Black Legion was sent out to explore the seas led by a man named Morren Mire. You might remember him as one of your father's personal guards before Zededia called him to serve in his army as *his* personal guard."

"Right, I remember Captain Mire."

Caedus nodded.

"Anyway, I was a part of Mire's crew to sail to the lands across the Orlestian and establish an embassy there. Talluna wasn't even on our map at the time. Just another port city in the middle of the ocean where retired sailors went to rest."

He tilted his chin up and finished his drink.

"But, um ... about halfway to Luzkuli, the capital city of the kingdom of Hiiel, a storm rampaged across the Orlestian and forced us to sail around it. We stumbled across this tiny island by pure chance. Tired, hungry, and eager to find land, we elected to dock here for a night. Everyone aboard thought the only people here were marooned sailors and old men waiting around to die."

"That wasn't the case?" Lucien asked.

Caedus slowly shook his head.

"Through the haze of the mist rose a gray flag bearing a wolf's head in the center of the docks. I hadn't ever seen it before, and neither had anyone in my company nor any of the crew we had leased from the mainland to assist us. As soon as we landed, we learned that the island had been overrun with mercenaries from a guild called the

Whitefangs, practitioners of ancient magics that originated well before Osiris's time. These men had enslaved the people of Talluna and turned the port city into a source of crime and terror in the Orlestian. We were lucky to not have seen their ships patrolling the seas prior to that point."

The flickering light from the lanterns nearby caught Caedus's attention for a moment, and he paused to collect his thoughts.

"Captain Mire took one step on the docks before he was greeted by the Whitefangs. He was ordered to surrender all arms and goods our ship carried and to march to the slavemaster to be put in their circulation. Four men surrounded him, and, if you know him as I did, you can imagine how little he appreciated such a greeting."

"I'm sure he made quick work of them," Lucien said.

"In a matter of seconds," Caedus said with a light chuckle. "And from that moment on, we slayed every Whitefang we came across. It became clear that they were a menace that needed to be eradicated."

"You slayed them all?" Lucien asked.

"Every. Single. One. Captain Mire made it his personal mission to see to the destruction of their clan."

Caedus took a deep breath.

"It took half a day to liberate Talluna, and her people praised us like kings. We accepted their reward in the form of food and drink and were gone by nightfall."

"Did you ever make it to Hiiel?"

A subtle laughter echoed off Caedus's throat.

"No," he said. "It turns out that the Hiielites were in league with the Whitefangs. They hired them to rob the seas and cripple any sort of trade network that existed outside of their influence."

"Ah."

"Not exactly the corruption we were sent to put an end to, but ... we did our job, nonetheless. We spent the rest of the Month of Sailing exterminating these pirates that had been infesting the waters around Osiria. Then, we sailed home."

"What happened to Captain Mire? I don't recall much of him after that endeavor?"

Caedus's thoughts circled around the uncomfortable memory of Captain Mire's disappearance. He hadn't ever told that story to anyone, the story of how he became a promising officer in Zededia's army.

"He didn't make it home," he said, electing to hold onto his secrets.

Caedus slid his stein away from him as he looked around the tavern once more. A few of the sailors from The Leviathan walked in through the swinging door. He watched as they greeted the others already in the inn and guessed they had made regular appearances in Talluna.

"What in the world are we going to do when we get to Aeladaecia, Caedus?" Lucien asked.

Caedus flicked his attention over.

"What do you mean?"

"I mean ... no one really knows how to perform an ascension ceremony, do they?"

"Perhaps you should ask the gods. They're who blessed you with their sight, after all. Who's to say they won't do it again."

An amateur at consoling those in mental distress, Caedus struggled to think of what to say next. Lucien sat across from him in silence as he watched the prince's face crumble to disappointment.

"Though, if that doesn't work, Atlas will likely be able to provide you with a solution. The book be found in Voluutia lays out the entire ritual, but he needs to translate it first. He'll know what to do."

"Maybe," Lucien said. "I suppose I should talk with him further."

Caedus nodded.

"It seems you are favored by the gods. Should you stray from the path they've given you, you'll end up back on it eventually."

"Something you've picked up on during your adventures?"

He shrugged.

"Maybe ... maybe. Osirians are Neshka's chosen children. I imagine that she gave you the idea to resurrect Zededia for a reason."

"For all our sakes, I hope you're right."

The doors to the tavern opened again, catching Caedus's curiosity. From the shadowed doorway, a familiar scowl appeared.

"When are we planning on departing from Talluna?" Lucien asked.

Caedus pointed behind the prince.

"I think she might have your answer."

~ ~ ~

Lucien twisted his head over his shoulder and traced Caedus's finger to a figure entering the bar. His eyes sifted through the crowd and focused on a hint of red. All worries he held onto flew to the back of his mind as he subtly stared at Captain Vederosa walking up to the counter.

The sailors in her path quickly moved aside and kept to themselves. Something about her daunting presence allured the prince. He let a tiny smile form in the corner of his mouth.

"Are you going to talk to her or are you going to ogle over her like a wolf glaring at a deer?" Caedus said behind him.

Lucien looked back at Caedus and frowned.

"Though, I'm not sure if you're the wolf in that scenario."

Lucien looked at Caedus and frowned.

"Very funny," the prince said, turning his head back to Vederosa.

Mustering his courage, Lucien stood from the table with his drink in hand. He kept a close watch on those around him as Caedus had inferred him to do, but his focus remained on Vederosa. As he looked, the bartender gave her a drink without a word spoken between them.

"Watch where yer steppin, boy," one of the pirates near him said in a raspy voice.

The bloodshot eyes of an old seadog glared up at him. Lucien swallowed his mild panic and pressed on.

As he approached, he tried to remain hidden from Vederosa's view. However, a keen eye glanced over at him from behind curvy strands of red hair. Lucien leaned against the bar top two seats down from her. Turned halfway in her direction, he took a drink of his ale. When he lowered his hand, he noticed Vederosa's attention slowly drifting over through a sly glare. He nearly choked on the words in his throat and licked the insides of his lips.

"It seems you're quite reputable in Talluna," he said as smoothly as he could manage.

Vederosa gave him her full attention and shifted her weight to the other hip. He grinned at her stern face.

"All sailors know me, Osirian," she said in a sharp tone. "I, along with my crew, am reputable everywhere the sea touches."

Lucien's grin briefly faded. He took a drink to dissolve the awkward pause.

"What do you want?" she asked.

Lucien stiffened his shoulders and set his stein down on the bar.

"I assume you've spoken with the harbormaster. How long until The Leviathan is ready to sail again?"

"By the morning."

Softly nodding, Lucien's eyes drifted toward the crowd of sailors to his right.

"That's a short amount of time to make the repairs we need," Lucien said.

"Well, if you had the chance to work on the most famous ship in the Orlestian Sea, wouldn't you take it?"

Vederosa's grim expression cracked into a grin as she spoke. Lucien's smile returned.

"I suppose I would."

He took another sip of his drink.

"Even still ...," he said. "That was quite the adventure we endured. Are you sure that-"

"She'll be ready. We'll resume our journey at first light, and we'll get you to Aeladaecia so you can bring your brother back. Then, maybe, the wrongs of this world can be made right."

Lucien squinted at Vederosa as he sensed an ulterior motive behind her words.

"I thought you weren't one for caring about life outside the sea."

He sneakily inched toward her.

"I-I don't," she said. "It's just ... just not right what the Hostellians are doing."

"Hmm."

Lucien brought his ale to his lips, pondering over her words. Before taking a drink, a sudden realization struck him.

"You have family on the mainland, don't you?"

A morsel of worry appeared in her eyes as Lucien studied her. It disappeared nearly as quickly as it arrived, though. At that moment, Lucien understood. Vederosa's position and prestige allowed no place for worry. She couldn't afford to think of anyone else not under her command. He knew the feeling well enough.

"Parents?" he asked.

Vederosa shook her head.

"A brother."

Lucien took another step closer, longing to comfort her and take her hidden pain away, but he knew she might despise any sort of consolation. He found common ground yet again; the door opened wider.

"Where?"

He waited for her response, her hesitation revealing more anguish than he realized.

"Ehthilia. Or at least that's where he was when I last heard from him. He was a soldier ... stationed in Maelensis."

Lucien froze in shock. Guilt riddled him. After hearing how Matticus rampaged through Ehthilia like a wild bear, he knew the odds of her brother's survival were slim. A deep sigh left his lips.

"I, um ... I'm-"

"Don't be. He chose his path, I chose mine."

Underneath the impenetrable exterior, Lucien sensed a caring heart. While the discovery of her brother's fate brought him agony in the form of her saddened eyes, he felt a bond forming.

"My reason shouldn't mean anything to you, anyway," she said.

"We all have a reason to be here ... we all have a say in what tomorrow looks like. Whether it means anything to anyone is irrelevant."

Vederosa looked at him through the corner of her eye, and Lucien saw her vulnerability peeking through her abrasive attitude. The tiny taste of her softer side sank its hooks into him. He knew better than to chase after it now. A proper time would arise.

"Don't get yourself killed while we're here, Osirian," Captain Vederosa said, voice slightly deflated, as she turned away from the bar. "There'll be plenty of chances for that once we get to Aeladaecia."

Lucien sat in thought for a moment, appreciating Vederosa's willingness to share a piece of her with him. He downed the rest of his ale, set the cup on the counter, and cleared his throat. Over his shoulder, he saw Caedus fast asleep in the corner leaning against the stone wall with crossed arms. Lucien smirked, admiring his friend's bravery to doze off in a place like this.

Eager to find a safe place to rest, the prince made his way out of the tavern and into night's darkness that consumed the island town. The quiet voices and dying lights of Talluna's lanterns comforted him. With a tinkering mind, Lucien analyzed his rapidly changing surroundings and the relationships he started to form with his companions. Despite trying to keep his eye on the task at hand, Captain Vederosa, with her endlessly beautiful features, rose to the center of his thoughts.

Just as he stepped out into the streets of Talluna, a strange feeling came over him, like someone was watching his every move. Lucien looked around, paranoia filling him to the brim. He saw too many miscreants to count, but none appeared to pay him any attention. In his peripheral vision, as he elected to lay the matter to rest, a peculiar sight hooked his attention.

Seated at a table outside the tavern, a hooded man engaged in conversation with another across from him. Lucien studied him further and focused on the faint purple glow in the man's eyes and skin around them. He had seen that glow before. It was the same that appeared on Thancred's face when he usurped control over the old man's mind. Lucien's thoughts raced, and the man gave him a side glance followed by a sly smile. He had only one thing left to determine: who was watching him? Who was on the other side of those eyes?

Chapter 15

Master of Puppets

Day 2 in the Month of Rain

Over the next three days, the Hostellae secured a perimeter around the northwestern border of Amuun Drall to allow for the preparations necessary to initiate the siege of the inner city. King Matticus stood on top of a section of the outer wall that hadn't been destroyed, using the fortified location as a makeshift command post. Half a mile of flat streets distanced his armies from the Voluutians stationed in the buildings on the edge of town. Both sides traded volleys of rock and arrow, but neither moved out into the open to engage. The main portion of his army occupied the hills adjacent to the lake while he sent his more elite battalions to take control of the port. Cutting off the city from trade, even for a few days, choked the Voluutians for resources. Matticus's thirst for war grew evermore. The Sword of Kings was here; he sensed its presence. Knowing his ancestor's mighty blade would be used to defend Voluutia only angered him further.

While Matticus kept his steel gaze locked on Amuun Drall, Commander Nysis studied a map of the city behind him to plan their next move.

"The city won't come easy," Nysis said. "It's built to dissuade any sort of frontal assault. The streets narrow and lead to the moat surrounding the heavily fortified keep surrounded by a moat. On top of that, the buildings are packed too densely to make a swift advance. We'll have to capture ground one block at a time."

"So be it," Matticus said. "Raed cowers in his castle, holding the very power I seek. If he wants his forefathers to watch me pry *Osirisigniros* from his hands in their sacred halls, then that is what I will do."

"You intend to march into Amuun Drall by yourself, my liege?"

Matticus's sneer intensified. Thoughts of rampaging through the streets of his most hated rival caused the shine in his veins to subtly glow.

"If I must."

Just as he envisioned Raed's head on a pike centering a pile of burning bodies, his common sense kicked in. He easily dispatched a group of Voluutians a few days prior, but thousands lingered in Amuun Drall if not more. He needed his grunts to lead the charge.

"If Your Majesty will heed me before storming through the city on a suicidal mission, I've discovered a weakness in the Voluutians' defenses that we need to exploit."

"Fine."

Matticus turned to observe the map Nysis had laid out. He noticed several lines leading to the keep from the outer fields and then a circle that connected them all at various points between buildings.

"Our engineers discovered these scattered in the hills outside the city."

"What are they?"

"Sewer tunnels."

The king's eyes slightly widened.

"Leading straight into the city."

"So, we penetrate underground, then?"

"In a way," Nysis said, crossing his arms. "There's a small issue, though. The Voluutians built these tunnels while considering the possibility of an attacking army utilizing their clear shot to the keep. They're guarded by a series of traps designed to stop any sort of advance from a large group. A system of plates lines the bottom, and if too much weight is placed on them, that section of the tunnel seals itself off. We sent a dozen men to explore the sewers two days ago. When the scout went to track them down, he told me he arrived just in time to watch a metal wall recede back into the ground and reveal the corpses of those twelve men. Apparently, the sewage from the previous two days flooded the chamber. They drowned."

Impressed at the wicked design, Matticus started to respect the Voluutians a little more.

"We can't send the entire army through the tunnels; they'll set off the trap," Nysis said. "But we can send a few at a time over the next day to the heart of the city dressed in Voluutian armor. They can infiltrate and sabotage whatever defenses they encounter.

That way, we can launch an attack on two fronts and confuse the Voluutians just enough to ruffle their feathers. With some luck, we'll be able to cut off the frontline defenders from reinforcements. The Hostellae can outmatch any army that opposes us. It's just a matter of shortening the playing field."

"Very well. Give the order. When we march upon the city, we'll—"

Shuffling footfalls interrupted his train of thought, the wooden scaffolding attached to the side of the wall creaking with each step.

"My king!" a voice said.

The guards stationed on top of the command post swiftly turned and held their pikes out to protect him. Matticus glanced over with a curious yet impatient expression. Running out onto the wall, a scout nearly tripped over himself.

"My-my king," the man said, bending over his knees to catch his breath. "An-an emissary approaches. Two, actually. They-they come bearing the sigil of a rearing horse—one we don't recognize."

"They must be Voluutians," Nysis said. "Perhaps they've come to make things easy for us and surrender."

"No," Matticus said with a soft sigh. "They're not Voluutians."

Matticus hadn't seen the unique symbol of the rearing horse in over a decade, but what it stood for became branded in his memory since that day.

Bloody Ponies.

The thought disgusted him, and what followed would sicken him more.

"They're Merrins."

"Merrins?" Nysis said.

"Yes. King Mythian's personal pets."

Why his most mischievous cousin would send an errand boy to him in the middle of his war with Voluutia puzzled him. Matticus knew of Mythian's parlor tricks well enough to detect a ploy. Despite his sense of caution, he remained curious of what message Mythian wished to give him.

"Let them through," he said.

The guards loosened their postures, and the scout descended the staircase. Matticus released a deep exhale, expunging the frustration that had already started to build in anticipation of his guests.

After a moment, a softer, calmer set of footsteps climbed the scaffolding. The king turned to greet the messengers and saw two of the most pompous men he had ever seen. Hair long and silky and cleanly shaven, they walked with pride, a condescending look of authority plastered on their faces.

"Greetings, mighty King Matticus," the lead emissary said. "The kingdom of Merrinine bids you a divine welcome. We are ever so gracious that you have accepted our arrival."

The emissary spoke in a calm, smooth voice, one that hasn't been scarred by war or poverty. Matticus scanned over the delicate fabrics and expensive jewelry covering the messenger that gave evidence of his lifestyle in the palaces of luxury under the protection of Pyla Sellos.

"My patience for Merrin politics is thin," Matticus said. "Speak your message. Pray I am merciful."

"Of course, Your Imminence," the messenger said, bowing his head low.

Matticus waited for him to rise, but, instead, the lavish man pulsed for a second, torso shaking, then went calm. The king studied the messenger intently and detected a shift in his demeanor. Something about him made him move more relaxed and charismatic than before. As the man rose upright and revealed his face, Matticus stared at the light purple glow that shined in his eyes and the surrounding areas like a ballroom mask. A cunning grin completed the smirk that followed.

"Mythian ...," Matticus said in slight disgust.

"Why such a sour face," King Mythian said through his puppet. "Doesn't it warm you to see your own family?"

Matticus grimaced. He despised his cousin's slimy use of Osirian magic. He hated all Mystics, really, but Mythian sat at the top of the list. Thinking back to the months prior during his latest search for the Sword of Kings, he wondered if Mythian had anything to do with its disappearance or Caedus Redstone's escape. Though that hardly mattered, Matticus reminded himself how slippery his cousin could be and proceeded with caution.

"Only the blood of the weak warms me. You repulse me."

"Ugh, always so *grisly*, Matticus, so melodramatic. Your attitude has a sharper edge than your sword."

The Merrin messenger walked over to the crenellation of the wall and leaned against it with a cocky posture.

"What ever happened to grace and elegance? Osirians used to be such proper people. I suppose I shouldn't be disappointed given how rash your father was."

Matticus twitched with anger.

"Not that my father was any better," Mythian said, forcing the messenger to glance at his decorative fingernails. "But, anyway, I'm sure you've better things to do than listen to me insult our precious predecessors. I've actually come to share a bit of news with you, news I have a feeling will pique your interest."

"You will not fool me into granting mercy to your people. I trust you less than I like you."

"Well, the good news for you, you fucking brute, is that you don't *have* to trust me," Mythian said through the messenger, temper rising with impatience to Matticus's blind aggression. "You just have to listen."

Though Mythian's words usually carried a sneaky reputation, Matticus felt inclined to believe him. Perhaps the all-seeing eyes of the Merrin king had something to offer.

"Listen to what?" Matticus said, squinting in skepticism.

The messenger's grin widened.

"Me, of course, and what I have to say. Your plan to conquer the nations of Osiria is quite perfect. You waited for the right time, you have the strongest army the world has ever seen, and, most importantly, you rid yourself of the only man who could stop you."

Zededia, Matticus thought.

"But," Mythian said, continuing, "there's one little thing that could ruin your fun. And I know what that little thing is. You see, I attended the Meeting of Sons that Raed summoned."

Hearing his rival's name enlivened his rage.

"The other kings formed a plan on how to defeat you. A desperate plan, sure, but a plan, nonetheless. And if they manage to pull it off, your ... empire ... won't be sitting on such sturdy ground."

Mythian's notorious pattern of betraying everyone around him worked in his favor; Matticus guessed he would eventually do the same if he trusted him now, but he could deal with that down the road. If he knew one thing about his cousin, it's that he wouldn't bring an empty bet to the table.

"And you've come to warn me of this plan?" he asked.

"Let's call it a measure of good faith. Believe it or not, I don't exactly benefit from your demise, so I'd like to support your little game while I can. I have my ... reasons."

Mythian always had reasons, a concept not foreign to Matticus.

"Fine."

Matticus calmed himself to listen to reason.

"What news have you brought me?"

"Ditch the muscle. Then we'll talk."

Weighing the risk of dismissing his soldiers, Matticus hesitated.

"Oh, come on, Matticus," Mythian said, "if I wanted to strike you down in the middle of this pissing contest between you and Raed, I would have brought someone a little more lethal than the boys I use to suck my cock. This information is simply for Osirian ears."

"Hmph."

Matticus waved his guards off. Shortly after, they vacated the command post. Nysis, however, remained.

"You, too, pretty boy," Mythian said.

Looking at Nysis's disdainful expression, Matticus nodded to dismiss his commander.

"Be wary, my king," Nysis said as he leaned in to whisper. "Where there are rats, there is plague."

The Vaedorian commander descended to the grounds below, leaving the two messengers from Merrinine alone with him.

"That's better," the emissary said.

"Be on with it."

"Before we get to the good part, I must have your word on something."

The heaviest sigh poured through Matticus's nostrils.

Of bloody course.

"Merrinine is willing to submit to Hostellian rule, but that comes with limits."

"Merrinine hasn't even crossed my mind. You're surrendering?"

"I'm no fool, Matticus. I know where your armies will turn once you've put Raed in the ground. Even if you elect to march to Daece or Monscarren first, you'll eventually roam to my territory. Why war with you when I can reason with you?"

Though Matticus preferred a more physical approach to forcing nations into submission, he saw the upside of gaining Merrinine as an ally. Mythian's wealth could fund his conquest for far longer if he needed more time to take control of the other kingdoms. Merrinine's army could also bolster his greatly or be used to defend one front while he attacked the other.

"What do you want?"

"In exchange for your word that my people are not to be harmed, I will offer you my kingdom's resources however you need them."

"Since when have you cared about your subjects?"

"Believe it or not," Mythian said with a stern tone, "I value the lesser people of my lands. I value their worth, more specifically. Without a healthy peasant class to tend my fields and dig my mines, my wealth evaporates."

Matticus crossed his arms.

"Very well."

"And I am to stay alive. That should go without saying."

"An empire is ruled by *one* man. You will be king no longer."

"Fine, fine. I will recognize your authority should you keep your dogs out of my cities. I can act as your advisor, though. Be your eyes and ears. That's essentially what I'm doing already."

Eyebrow raised, Matticus scoffed.

"Is that what you call ... this?" he said, referring to Mythian's use of mind control.

"I have eyes everywhere, Matticus. In places you would like them to be."

The Merrin king had a point. With Spymaster Rachtus eliminated, Nysis could only do so much espionage. Korzeg provided sturdy soldiers, but they lacked intelligence. A cleverer ally would do him much good.

"So," Mythian said, "do we have a deal? My information and resources for your word to stay out of Merrinine?"

Matticus took a deep breath.

"Deal."

He stepped forward toward the messenger, eyes still glowing purple.

"Now, tell me what you know."

Mythian's signature smirk appeared once more.

"As you are aware, nine days ago, on day twenty-one in the Month of War, Raed summoned the Meeting of Sons," the feminine man said. "There, the kings decided how to ... react ... to your advance into Ehthilia. Personally, I didn't mind it much. I've never liked Ambrose. Self-absorbed little bastard if you ask me, running his kingdom with the focus of being morally right rather than politically affluent. You and I both know that good-hearted men are not fit to rule."

A statement he had always lived by. Only the strong were meant to lead. Near the end of his life, his father showed signs of his waning strength. Matticus sunk back to those days for a moment, to the days where his hunger for power first blossomed. His father's illness opened the door and taught him how to usurp a throne. Now, here at the cusp of the war he had spent years creating, that mentality elevated to intoxicating levels.

"At first, Raed suggested that he send all Voluutia's able bodied men to ride out and meet you somewhere in the mountains, but that motion failed. Then, a peculiar idea was introduced."

Matticus hated Mythian's style of storytelling. Droning on like a play, the Merrin king made sure to draw out every ounce of drama he could.

"A voyage led by King Atlas," Mythian said. "To Aeladaecia."

Eyes widening, Matticus scoured his memories for where he had heard that name. It sounded familiar, like a term he had studied from ancient texts.

One of Neshka's islands? he thought. *Why would they go there?*

He scanned over the possibilities as to why Atlas would take a team to a spiritual dwelling. Then, it struck him.

Osiris's origin. Where men become gods.

"There's a ship commissioned by Neptabyss to sail through the Cradle of the Colossus to Aeladaecia. There, Atlas intends on performing an—"

"An ascension ceremony," Matticus said, cutting Mythian off as a mild sense of shock overcame him.

"Correct. They're going to retrace the path that Osiris walked prior to his ascension to bring back someone they deem is capable of defeating you. Someone you've lost to before."

Suddenly, the darkest parts of Matticus's anger started to surface. His eyes slowly reddened with a glow, his fists and jaw clenched, and his shoulders trembled.

"How one person can hope to save them from the hordes of the Hostellae is beyond me. It was sheer insanity to suggest such a thing."

Mythian playfully taunted him. Matticus barely heard him, though, mind buzzing with bloodcurdling rage. He pictured the face of whom Mythian referred to. The memory pushed him closer to the edge.

"They think they can resurrect the Black Prince ... *Zededia.*"

Then, as soon as Mythian said Zededia's name, Matticus snapped. He surged forward, eyes bright red while he roared, and dug his hands into the Merrin emissary, cocked his arms to the side, and hurled the man off the wall. Not so much as a scream echoed from below until a thud splattered from the ground. Matticus's chest heaved in anger. Glaring down, he eyed the spreading pool of blood that leaked from the broken Merrin.

"Easy, big guy," the second messenger said in Mythian's voice.

Matticus darted his gaze over and saw that his upper face had turned light purple just as the first.

"I only brought two of these, so if you want to hear how I can solve your little problem for you, you need to cage that bear inside you."

Taking a good pause to control his breathing, Matticus closed his eyes and allowed his anger to fade.

"Indulge me," he said.

Mythian forced his last Pony forward like the other.

"Luckily for you, I'm known for playing on both sides of the field. When Atlas and the others decided to set a course for Aeladaecia, I promised to supply a fleet to escort them through the more unsavory parts of the voyage. And before you jump to any conclusions, I did so to maintain control over the situation."

Matticus kept quiet. Speaking might let his dormant aggression spill out again.

"And if you so desire," Mythian said, "instead of their escort, this fleet can become their executioner. Their plan fails, your campaign continues uninterrupted, and our bargain remains intact."

Though he formed doubts on whether Atlas could even perform such a ritual and bring Zededia back to this earth, that wasn't something he could gamble on. The Black Prince stood in the way of his empire for most of his life. Empowered like a god, Zededia would be able to return with a swift vengeance. The Sword of Kings mattered even more in light of Mythian's information.

"The world is yours for the taking, Matticus. So. Take it."

The king leaned on the side of the wall to consider Mythian's proposal. As he thought, he looked for every chance something could go wrong. However, he also realized he might not have another opportunity to foil Atlas's plan if he and his team had already set sail from Skulpos as Mythian suggested.

"Call your fleet," he said in a quiet, eerie tone. "Hunt down Atlas's ship."

"A wise choice," Mythian said while lightly bowing. "I'll send word immediately."

His task to conquer Voluutia instantly became more complex. This wasn't just a fight for one kingdom anymore; it was a fight for Osiria. His enemies showed their true colors and proved their blasphemy. If they were willing to call upon the gods for aid, no hope of submission remained. Total war had been declared.

"With that taken care of, I'll leave you to your siege," Mythian said. "It seems you have your hands full here."

Matticus focused on the outskirts of Amuun Drall, the siege to come reemerging as his prime directive.

"Oh, there's one last thing."

He twisted his head over, curious of what else Mythian could possibly entice him with.

"The journey to Aeladaecia, the plan to resurrect Zededia ... it wasn't Atlas's idea."

Matticus frowned, sensing that Mythian deemed that relevant to say.

"Who's was it?"

The messenger's smirk grew to a devious smile. Matticus glared at the man in his sly, purple eyes, growing more tense by the second.

"It was your youngest brother," Mythian said, his grin cocky and irritating as ever. "Lucien."

Matticus's lips parted in disbelief. He hadn't heard from Lucien in over a month. A bit of shame started to creep in, replacing his anger.

"Made it all the way to Voluutia days before you did. Spoke to the kings as if he were one himself. I'd say you'd be proud of him if he hadn't openly betrayed you."

Stunned, Matticus battled with himself to accept the reality that his youngest brother, the one person he once relied on in his darkest hours, had gone against him to such degree. If Lucien traveled with Atlas on their journey to Aeladaecia, he would be the target of Mythian's fleet and the order he gave moments ago. The last morsel of good clinging to the fractured shards of his heart burst through. Memories of his fondest moments with Lucien flooded him. He thought back to the days in his youth before his mother died, when his family was last intact. The emptiness that tormented him, the love he lacked and so desperately craved deep down even though he'd never admit it, started to fight back against the rage that filled the void. His eyes softened and shoulders loosened.

"Well, it seems I've struck a chord," Mythian said, "so I best be on my way. Be a doll and make sure my Pony gets back to me safely. He's one of my favorites."

Matticus couldn't even look at the messenger. The conflict of emotions storming inside consumed all his focus.

"Ta-ta," he heard as muffled footsteps quieted down the wooden stairs.

His head throbbed with intense pain. For the first time since he set foot from Vaedor Sellos, he questioned himself and his motives. Mythian had gotten to him.

Matticus squeezed the rigid stones of the Voluutian wall to expel his growing afflictions. He knew he had come too far to turn back now. He had to proceed. To resolve the whirlwind of emotions torturing him from within, Matticus rose his head to the sky, eyes closed, and forced all thoughts of Lucien and sentiment out of his mind. Sieging Amuun Drall and conquering Voluutia slid back into control. Rage reentered; aggression emerged.

The turmoil tugging at his soul encouraged a darker sense of cruelty to appear. Matticus sent heavy breaths through flaring nostrils, eager as ever to slaughter Voluutia.

Chapter 16

The Way Is Shut

Day 2 in the Month of Rain

On the next morning after arriving at the port of Talluna, Prince Lucien stood on the town's docks once again. Hooded and arms crossed, he watched the sailors load supplies onto The Leviathan, mist blow in by the waves stinging his nose. Occasionally, he glanced at the top deck where Captain Vederosa stood tall and proud. A small grin crept across the side of his face, but he forced it away when Caedus approached beside him. Caedus's stone expression reminded him of what to focus on.

"Well, did you figure out who's the wolf and who's the deer?"

Lucien chuckled and looked beyond Caedus to the sea on his left.

"Not entirely," Lucien said, allowing his gaze to sway across Vederosa once more. Her cold yet inviting glare beamed down at him from a stern face.

"But, I'm not sure I want to that question to have an answer."

Caedus placed a hand on his shoulder. Lucien looked at his friend's subtle grin before Caedus stepped toward the ramp to board the ship.

"Move it, men!" Lucien heard Captain Vederosa shout from her post. "Or may your corpses wash in with the tides!"

The fierceness in her voice gave Lucien a chill. Though it frightened him for a moment, it entranced him.

Lucien uncrossed his arms and made his way for the ramp shortly after.

On board, he looked around for a moment in search of a place to linger. Spending his days among the roughest sailors he could imagine still made him rather uncomfortable. As he scanned across the deck, a familiar face greeted him with a smile underneath a bushy, gray beard. Lucien walked toward his friend leaning across the side of the ship.

"It feels like it's been weeks since I've talked to you, old friend," the prince said. "You've accompanied me all this way, yet I've been so ... distracted."

"You don't have to worry, my prince," Thancred said with his water pipe in his mouth. "I will be here whether you need me or not; that is the role of a mentor."

Lucien's mind raced back to the plethora of afternoons he spent in Thancred's apothecary in the company of a strong drink and lit pipe. The temporary escape from his current situation soothed him. For a second, Lucien felt himself sitting in the peaceful halls of Thancred's home in Vaedor Sellos.

"You've spent your whole life in my watch. I must say I do miss our quiet afternoons. Tea in hand, herbs in our lungs. Not a care in the world."

The prince smiled as nostalgia took over.

"It's been quite some time since we've been able to have a day like that," Lucien said, a trickle of sadness in his voice.

"Yes ... yes, it has."

A deep sigh left the old man's lips through a cloud of smoke. Lucien's worries deepened as he thought of the state of world and his place in it.

"Do you think our lives will ever be normal again?"

"I don't know, my prince. It's hard to tell. These are strange times and have been so for many years. I know you may think your time in Vaedor Sellos was nothing out of the ordinary, but to tell you the truth, no one's life has been the same since...."

Lucien raised an eyebrow at Thancred's pause.

"Since when?"

Thancred gave him a melancholy smile.

"Since your mother passed."

Thoughts shifting to his mother's death, Lucien's gaze sank. Matticus and Zededia's struggles with loss followed shortly after. However, when Lucien tried to revisit the mindset of his younger self, he couldn't remember the same darkness his brothers carried from Queen Niike's passing. The realization puzzled him.

"Why don't I remember grieving my mother's death?" Lucien said with a slight frown. "Why wasn't I affected like my father and brothers?"

He looked at Thancred for an answer, but the old man kept his troubled gaze pointed toward the water.

"I can't say for sure. But, if I were to guess, I'd say because your father and your brothers spent a great deal of their time shielding you from the pain that tortured them."

They shielded me? he thought.

Slightly offended at the notion that he needed protecting, frustration built beneath his skin.

"Why? Why didn't I have the chance to grieve? Didn't I deserve to feel as they did?"

Thancred gave him a side glance.

"No one *deserves* to feel that way, Lucien. They grieved to that degree ... so you wouldn't have to."

Tension rose in his throat. Conflicted on Thancred's opinion, he looked away.

"I understand how robbed you may feel," Thancred said. "Robbed of your chance to experience emotion.

Lucien turned his saddened eyes back to his mentor.

"But, my prince, your family–Zededia, Matticus, Matias–they endured the hell that burrowed a void in their hearts head on, and they placed you behind them."

After taking a moment to accept what Thancred had said, Lucien sniffed his nose.

"It's hard to imagine Matticus and Zededia standing against anything together, much less alongside my father."

"Believe it or not, your brothers used to get along quite well. Eerily well if you ask me. There was time where I thought Matticus and Zededia were inseparable."

"That's still impossible to believe," Lucien said. "For as long as I can remember, they've always been at each other's throats."

Thancred exhaled another cloud of smoke.

"If there is one thing in this world that can bring them back together," the old man said, looking directly at Lucien, "it's you."

Though Lucien knew he had acted as the mediator between his brothers for his entire adult life, that realization had never struck him so fiercely.

"If we are successful in Zededia's resurrection, this will be the farthest they have ever been divided. Two men will battle for the fate of Osiria with entire nations at stake."

The prince interlocked his fingers and weighed the severity of the situation, a solemn expression on his face as he stared out into the vastness of the sea.

"Lucien."

He looked over and saw the sincerity in Thancred's eyes.

"This war will change the course of history forever. Your brothers will need you in the end."

Lucien let a slow exhale leave his nostrils. Silence overcame him as The Leviathan pulled farther away from Talluna's docks. The rickety buildings grew more distant by the second.

As the prince absentmindedely scanned the port city fading away, a hint of purple caught his attention. Lucien squinted and saw a man standing on the cliff right above the shoreline. The purple glow shined faintly from under the man's hood on the upper half of his face. Troubled, Lucien quickly realized that the same man from the inn last night watched him yet again, this time with a more direct purpose. Something told him that whoever wished to keep a tab on him did so with not-so-good intentions.

Before he had a chance to give it more thought, thunderous footsteps creaked the floorboards of the main deck behind him.

"Prince Lucien," a deep voice said.

He turned and cast his gaze upon Captain Ammon's hulking stature.

"Yes?"

"King Atlas is looking for you. In the captain's chambers."

Lucien raised his eyebrow.

"What for?" he asked.

"I'm not sure," Ammon said. "But it seemed rather important."

Turning back to Thancred, the prince opened his mouth to speak.

"Don't worry, my prince," Thancred said, cutting him off. "I'll be here when you need me. Atlas likely has good news for us."

Lucien grinned at his old friend. Captain Ammon escorted him to Vederosa's chamber at the heart of the ship immediately after. As he stepped through the door, the darkness of the room swept over him. Even the light seeping through the crack underneath the door battled against the dense shadows crawling along the floor.

King Atlas turned around from the table in the center of the room. Lucien noticed the various ceremonial items scattered on it.

"Come in, Prince Lucien," Atlas said from under his hood. "There's something we must discuss."

Two of Atlas's men, dressed similarly to the Daecian king in thick, hooded robs, stood on the other side of the table. Lucien stepped forward, his bright green eyes lightly glowing in the darkness. As he approached the table, he observed a small copper bowl with a green flame flickering within. Seemingly lit from thin air, the fire danced roughly an inch above the bottom of the bowl.

As Lucien neared, he winced at the sharp pain in his spine. The black bruise that spread across his lower back after the encounter with the Naguzii sharks lingered despite the prince's days of rest to recover. His body ached all over, in fact. He hadn't quite acclimated to the life of an adventurer. Groaning in mild agony, he placed the back of his hand on his bruise.

"What's wrong?" Atlas asked. "You seem hurt."

"It's nothing. When I had my ... dive ... off the ship, I think I might have broken something."

The prince tried to man up and shake it off, but his wound persisted the more he walked around.

"Come here," Atlas said.

Lucien raised an eyebrow, curious of how he could help. The Daecian king spun him around quicker than he would have liked and lifted his cloak.

"Hey, what are you—"

"Shh."

A cold hand pressed against Lucien's wound. He flinched as the pain intensified.

"Easy, easy," Atlas said to soothe him.

Remaining still as best he could manage, Lucien steadied himself.

"Maena zur tazalin, hallas zur gual. (Heal thy flesh, mend thy bones,)" he heard Atlas say.

Like snow melting away, his soreness faded. Lucien hardly believed the ease he felt. Stiff no longer, he wriggled his back to test its range of motion. He quickly realized that every part of his body felt more relaxed, not just his back.

"You ... fixed me?"

"Well, of course I did," Atlas said with a subtle laugh. "I'm a Mender; that's what I do."

Lucien hadn't learned much about the other classes of Osirian mages. He knew even less about his own. Regardless, he greatly appreciated Atlas's aid. Aches and bruises had riddled him for weeks. Noticing the extravagant decorations Atlas had set out, He directed his attention back to the dancing flames in the copper bowl.

"It appears you're preparing for a ritual of some kind. Why have you called me?"

"I believe I've finally cracked the code in the text I found before we departed from Voluutia," Atlas said, walking back to the table.

"You've figured out how to perform the ritual?"

"Not quite."

Lucien's smile vanished.

"But I've discovered our way into Aeladaecia."

Atlas held an open palm out to him.

"Zaaonzelae, agnos inni sen lett luciden. (Realm of shadows, come out to the light.)"

A surge of energy pulsed from Atlas's palm, and a shimmering veil followed it and left an infinite void in its wake. Lucien struggled to perceive the cosmic scenery that had engulfed him, darting his vision back and forth between the specks of white and purple that seemed unreachable. When he shifted his foot, water splashed around him. The prince staggered, thinking that the ship had started to sink.

"Relax," Atlas said, soothing him. "It's merely an illusion."

Lucien stared at the red aura circling Atlas's open hand. His racing heart slowed.

"What is this place?" Lucien asked, shifting his eyes to the starry sky above.

"This, Prince Lucien, is Elysia," Atlas said. "Or a replication of it. We aren't actually standing in the spiritual plane; I'm simply casting a version of it around us. Have you never been here before?"

Taking a step away from the Daecian king, Lucien reached his arm out to the endless space. The empty feeling in his hand sent a chill down his spine.

"No," Lucien said in a soft voice. "Zededia was always the ... spiritual one."

He looked at Atlas, thinking back to the times that his brother meditated in Hostellus's Illumination Chambers for hours, sometimes days at a time. Zededia had mentioned something about the great astral planes of Elysia years ago. At the time, Lucien hardly understood what he was trying to describe. All he remembered was the awe that struck his brother whenever he spoke of this place. The same awe struck him now.

"Why are you showing this to me?"

Atlas beckoned him to follow with a raised finger. Lucien walked through the water that barely covered the soles of his boots, still mesmerized by his surroundings. After several steps, he watched Atlas raise his other hand.

"Bogrikrash, cost kar lett Athosbaraslos. (Bogrikrash, bring me the Gate of Creation.)"

Ignorant of the Aznogsi language, Lucien stood in confusion.

"Who are you talking to?" he asked.

Atlas turned his head and gave him a grin.

"A friend."

A portal appeared shortly after, and a massive stone gate took its place with a pulse of energy. Astonished, Lucien allowed his mouth to fall agape. Atlas pivoted to face him.

"This is the entrance to Aeladaecia," the Daecian king said. "The text revealed to me that this is the portal Osiris traveled through to find Neshka's holy island."

"Wait, we've been sailing for days now. You're just now discovering where we need to go?"

"The Cradle of the Colossus is gateway site. We would need to sail there regardless of *which* gate we have to go through. Through my wandering in Elysia, I managed to find the right one that the text describes."

Lucien tilted his head back to fully observe the titanic gate and analyze its features.

"It looks just like any other gate, like it was made by man. But, it's a ... a circle?"

Wondering how in the world Atlas planned to sail a ship through a perfectly circular doorway puzzled the prince. He scanned over the ancient runes carved in the outline and the triangular panels that met in the center.

"Correct," Atlas said. "The gate was made in our understanding—Osirians were the first to use them. Since the gods are able to pass between worlds much easier than we are, they've no need for this. Anyway, we'll summon the gate at the vortex of the Cradle and sail through it ... vertically."

"We're going to sail *up* above the water?"

Atlas's shaking head sparked fear in the prince.

"Down?" he said in a slightly panicked tone.

"Yes. If what the tome says is accurate, the gate will appear at the center of a powerful maelstrom. Currently, though, it's closed. So, unless we open it, we'll be sailing right to the bottom of the sea."

"I'll assume you're telling me this because you don't have a way to change that."

Atlas nodded.

"Unfortunately, Neshka forgot to bless us with the ability to open a gate when she allowed us to walk through them. Only the gods can open the gates of Elysia. And they rarely close to begin with."

"Meaning?"

"Meaning whoever decided to seal Aeladaecia off from the rest of the spiritual world did so for a good reason."

Lucien crossed his arms and thought for a moment. He glanced around into the endless black sky above him, still entranced by its beauty.

"What about who brought the gate to us in the first place? Your 'friend?'"

He watched Atlas clench his lips.

"I've already asked, and he's declined. It seems someone pretty high in the pecking order commanded for this gate to be shut."

A swift exhale shot through Lucien's nose.

"You see, Elysia is home to *all* spirits, not just a human's. All beings pass through on their way to one world or another, even the damned who roam *Ozek Monns*, the realm many people call Hell. The only reason a god would close a gate is that the realm it leads to has become too unstable. They would do so to protect the rest of Elysia."

Overwhelmed by the barrage of information from King Atlas, Lucien struggled to comprehend everything.

"So, if we can't open it, and no one will open it for us ... what do we do?"

After a few silent moments, Lucien looked at Atlas with a more intent glare.

"Well," Atlas said, gathering his thoughts. "We can try to *break* it open."

Lucien's confusion reached heights he didn't think possible.

"I'm going to skip passed why and go straight to how."

Atlas stepped closer to him, boots churning the inch-high water of Elysia.

"With you. And your magic."

"Me? How do expect me to do something like that if you can't pull it off? You're a far greater sorcerer than I—hell, I just learned I could even practice Osiris's magic a month ago. How am I supposed to achieve a feat only the gods can?"

"Because you're different."

Lucien gave Atlas a skeptical glare.

"I'm ... different. That doesn't exactly answer my question."

Atlas took a deep breath.

"Thancred told me about your stunt in Amuun Drall. He also told me what happened to the Hostellian Spymaster."

Feeling a sudden inclination to retreat from the conversation, Lucien started to perspire. Images of Rachtus's corpse in the keep of Vaedor Sellos flooded his memory like they did when he controlled Thancred's mind in Voluutia. Associated by default, guilt spiked his nerves.

"I-those were accidents."

"That only further proves my point."

"Which is?"

An astonished expression broke out on Atlas's face as if he still hadn't connected the dots.

"You have no idea how powerful you are, do you?"

The prince squinted in disbelief.

"What are you talking about?"

"Lucien," Atlas said, raising his hands to the prince's shoulders, "you are able to conjure your sorceries without so much as a spoken word, the foundation of all Osirian magic! Every mage who wishes to cast a spell must draw his power from within, but the invocations are what channels that power. Some of us use rings to help as well."

Zededia's ring, Lucien thought.

"Our magic has the risk of running rampantly out of control or failing completely when we don't use the tools that guide it. Yet, here you are, clear as day, with the ability to call forth some of the most advanced sorcery Osirians have ever used. *Without either.* Only one man in all our family's history has ever been to do that, and that was Osiris himself."

Atlas's explanation blew his mind as well as inflated his ego. He smiled; all the years of disappointment in himself for not being able to partake in the one thing that separated his family from all others vanished.

"Okay, so, I'm just supposed to throw the full extent of my power at the gate to crack it open?"

"You're a Mystic, Lucien, not a Conqueror. Brute force isn't in your nature. No, we're going to use your abilities for something far more incredible. We're going to control a god."

What? he thought, trying to convince himself that he heard Atlas correctly.

"That's blasphemous. I can't control a god!"

"With your talent and my knowledge, we can do whatever the hell we please. In this case, that means breaking into Aeladaecia to bring your brother back so he can stand up to Matticus and bring and end to this war he created."

Lucien turned away, the vast void of Elysia consuming his view.

"Something about that just doesn't seem ... right."

Sloshing footsteps circled around him. He met eyes with Atlas a moment after.

"Neither does slaughtering entire nations with the claim to unite them under one flag," Atlas said.

"Osiris did the same—"

"Osiris brought peace to a warring world. Matticus is bringing war to a peaceful one."

Pondering over the Daecian king's point, the prince shifted his lips.

"Neshka granted you her vision to save the world. How can we say we deserve to be kings if we don't act upon her wisdom?"

"*You* are a king," Lucien said, raising both eyebrows. "*I* am not."

"Not yet."

Lucien glanced at Atlas's hopeful grin, skeptic of his statement.

"But you will be."

"How can you be so sure?"

"Who do you think will take Matticus's place when he is gone, Lucien? Zededia? He's denied the throne already, and he won't take it if offered to him again. You are next in line. You are destined to save Hostellus's reputation in the eyes of the world."

An entirely new line of questions filled Lucien's thoughts.

Already? When?

However, he had little time to delve into that matter now.

"You *will* be king one day," Atlas said. "And moments like these will define your legacy."

"If you say so."

Atlas laid out a rather bold plan for their way into Aeladaecia. Lucien then realized the entire plan had been bold from the start and decided that changing his strategy before he needed to might dampen his chances of success. The cosmic aura of Elysia helped soothe his tinkering mind, and he paced around to consider the facts. Anything that stood in the way of his task to resurrect the Black Prince only further sent the world down the path of damnation. If he needed to control a god into defying the laws of the spiritual plane to bring Zededia back, then so be it.

"All right, Atlas. You've supported me on this mission from the start; I've no reason to dismiss your logic."

"Excellent. I'll have the rest of the text translated by the time we get to Aeladaecia. We'll know then how to perform the ceremony. For now, we just need to find the right god who's powerful enough to crack open the gate yet vulnerable enough for your magic to affect them."

Lucien still tried to come to terms with that idea.

"Do you have one in mind?" he asked.

A grin widened on Atlas's face as the prince turned back. The fanatical look appearing in the Daecian king's eyes gave Lucien the impression that he wasn't going to like the next part of the plan.

"Yes," Atlas said with a subtle laugh. "Yes, I do."

Chapter 17

Whispers in the Mist

Day 4 in the Month of Rain

As The Leviathan sailed across the outskirts of the Orlestian Sea, Caedus Redstone gazed out over the horizon from the upper deck. With one hand on a nearby rope, he held the other firmly planted on the hilt of the ancient sword he had purchased in Skulpos. The shouts of sailors and creaking wood acted as white noise in his ears; he had started to fit back into the mold of a life at sea as he once did in his youth.

A dense fog clouded his distant vision, and several pillar-like rocks jutted out toward the sky. Caedus looked at Captain Vederosa as she manned the helm and elected to trust her tested instincts. His hand tingled for a moment, and when he glanced down, a black mist seeped out of his sleeve.

"What?" Caedus whispered.

"Lett Volomi ed os bombanest melle. (The Cradle is a treacherous place,)" a mystic voice said inside his head. *"Oded frargess sen yorzetang lanz gaz os salcna ter tepi ola wislos. (It is dangerous to sail there in a vessel that depends on the wind.)"*

Though he hadn't quite mastered the Asnogzi language, the last few weeks harboring an ancient spirit had familiarized him with a few words. He knew what Osinian meant to say, but there was little he could do about that now.

Caedus leaned away from the rope and watched for an opportunity to approach the captain to consult her. No such chance arrived, though, as Vederosa battled the increasingly powerful currents. A nauseous feeling swelling in his stomach, Caedus felt his anxiety build in his sweaty hands. The ship sailed closer with each second, the dense fog creeping over the murkiness of the ocean.

A loud horn blared from the crow's nest high above Caedus's head. He winced at its deep pitch. Vederosa shifted from her watchful nature to paranoid and frantic. Caedus squinted, trying to decipher her concerns. Some of the sailors shouted up to the main deck, and he traced one of their pointed fingers to behind the ship.

Staggering, Caedus stepped to the back railing of the ship and clung to it. It took him several seconds to steady his vision against the bobbing, but, once he did, several white rectangles appeared in the edge of his view. Caedus studied the mysterious shapes and soon realized they were attached to larger objects beneath them.

"Ships," Caedus said.

Thick boots pounded the deck next to him. Caedus glanced over and saw Captain Vederosa intently scanning the distant horizon with her spyglass.

"Merrins," she said. "Our escort has finally caught up to us."

Caedus took the spyglass from her. He peered out at the gem insignia stitched into the masts.

"They're a little late to the party," Lucien said while jogging onto the upper deck. "There's not much to protect us from anymore."

"Roconomahylae. (Boarding galleys,)" Osinian said in his head. *"Tozi ad nonnen kell. (These are no friends.)"*

Taking a closer look, Caedus saw what the shade alluded to. A fleet of boarding ships escorted the command ship that dwarfed them in size.

"They're not here to protect us," he said in a troubled tone, moving his eyes over three mounted ballistae on the lead galleon armed with shining harpoons. "They're here to hunt. Mythian has changed sides, it seems."

"What?" Vederosa said, ripping the spyglass back.

Caedus took note of her astonished face. Red flags flickered in the low wind above white masts. Caedus understood what they symbolized. He had seen that naval formation before aboard a Legonae longship when he hunted the Whitefangs under the command of Morren Mire.

"Soddin' bastards," Captain Vederosa said in a shocked whisper as she lowered the scope from her eye.

Stepping aside as she marched back to the wheel, Caedus watched the Merrin ships largen on the horizon.

"All hands, to arms!" Vederosa shouted. "Mast to port! Get the wind on our side!"

The handful of sailors in Caedus's vicinity exploded into action. Ropes, pulleys, gears, and wood groaned as they heaved on the various mechanisms across the ship. Unsure of what to do, Caedus left kept his keen eyes on the approaching ships with a hand on his shortsword. Fog seeped around the ship and started to thicken. Though the haze barely stood against the unseeable waters that Osinian had warned him, not having a clear sight of his enemy made Caedus's skin crawl. The churning water under the ship's hull quieted, and he looked down to see that the wake's powerful waves weakened to practically nothing.

"We're losing speed," he whispered.

Darting his eyes to the masts above him, Caedus realized the wind had died in the fog. He glared back at the approaching ships and directed his attention to the dozens of oars pounding the water and resurfacing seconds later. The Merrins had the advantage of manual labor to thrust them into battle.

"Quartermaster!" Captain Vederosa shouted, stepping away from the helm. "Take the wheel! Steer us deeper into the fog."

Caedus glared at Vederosa as she walked to the aft-most part of the upper deck.

"Deeper?" Prince Lucien asked in shock. "You want to go *deeper* into the fog? Where our sails will mean even less than they do now?"

Vederosa boasted a devious half-grin.

"In case you haven't noticed, Osirian, The Leviathan is not a sailing vessel."

Caedus respected her grit and admired her decision to invite a fight rather than tuck and run. The splintering sound of grinding steel soared through the air as he watched her rip her rapier out from its sheath. He then caught her fierce gaze staring at him, knowing he shared her eagerness for a fight.

"She's a warship."

Caedus smirked and readied himself for combat. The hilt of his sword called for his hand.

The galleon churned through the water with relentless speed with its escorts maneuvering around it. Its massive size pierced the thickening fog. As it neared, Caedus caught glimpses of bright light reflecting off the enemy sailors' weapons. He waited for Vederosa's orders, but she remained silent.

"What's your plan?" Caedus asked.

Vederosa softly laughed.

"Patience, Caedus. Let me have my fun."

The fog grew denser, blotting out the lone longship less than half a league away.

"Douse lanterns," Captain Vederosa said in a quieter voice.

The sailors followed orders, and darkness swept over the deck. Caedus had no choice but to remain in his position, scanning the mist for when the Merrin ship would suddenly appear. Jagged rocks speared through the fog from time to time, but he stayed still as the others did. The next minute lasted for an eternity. Resorting to his training as a soldier of a Legonae, Caedus calmed his nerves to quiet his mind. Prince Lucien glanced around nervously a few feet away.

After adjusting to his surroundings, Caedus walked over to the edge of the ship. He listened for a sign of the enemy, but he only heard the waves crashing on the ship's hull and the rickety groans of the masts.

"First mate," Captain Vederosa said.

Caedus looked in her direction and saw the faint outline of her strong chin.

"Play us a tune."

A minute later, a crude melody from a lute broke the tension. Caedus's ears flicked and listened for the rhythm. Four notes in ascending order echoed across the ship followed by three more with a pattern of high, low, high. An eerie pause arose as the quartermaster ceased. Then, after the same duration of the tune's length, the lute chords returned with the same rhythm except for the final three notes that had a descending pattern. The mist muffled the notes as they bounced between the towering rocks, creating an eerie symphony that pulled his attention from all directions.

The first chord repeated.

"Hm-hm-hm-hmmm hmmm-hm-hmmm," the crew hummed, mimicking the tune.

The second chord played on cue.

"Hm-hm-hm-hmmm hmmm-hm-hmmm."

Caedus glanced around, trying to maintain his bearings. A longer pause arose, allowing the haunting atmosphere to sink further in.

"Shadows are crawling, anchor is falling," the quartermaster at the helm sang in a deep voice of honey.

"Heave'em away, heave away," the entirety of the crew sang in return, their words matching the rhythm played from the lute.

Caedus grinned, recognizing the old sea shanty he hadn't heard in years. A figure inched toward him, and Prince Lucien's face appeared through the haze.

"What are they doing?" the prince asked.

"The tides, they're a rising, skeletons writhing," the quartermaster continued.

"Heave'em away, heave away."

"Singing," Caedus said.

The scattered echoes from their song resonated from multiple places in the fog, confusing Caedus on his whereabouts despite remaining in place.

"Well, yes, but why?" Lucien said.

Caedus glanced around, picking up on the strategy Vederosa deployed.

"Send down the caskets, bodies, and baskets."

"Heave'em away, heave away."

Caedus looked around and noticed the sailors in his view remained locked in their stances, ready to act at a moment's notice.

"Because."

"The ferryman calls them, casts forth and trawls them!"

The quartermaster deepened his voice further and allowed the mist to carry his voice far beyond the ship's edges and louden the echoes.

"Heave'em away, boys, heave away!"

"Listen. Their song echoes through the mist like strange whispers. They're baiting them."

Captain Vederosa came into view after his eyes had acclimated to the fog.

"Coin in their pockets, bones in their sockets!"

Caedus quickly noticed her sealed lips and stern face as the sailors chanted.

"Heave'em away, heave away!"

"But ...," Prince Lucien said, "won't that alert the Merrins of our presence?"

As he kept his eyes on Vederosa, Caedus saw a faint grin appear on her face right after Lucien spoke.

"The lantern, she shines, grab hold of the line!"

"Heave'em away, heave away!"

"That's the point."

"Load the ballista," Vederosa said in a calm yet firm tone.

A large, clanking sound came from the middle of the lower deck, breaking the dull tension across the entire ship. Caedus peered over, squinted through the fog, and watched the sailors load a massive bolt into the mounted weapon.

"Farewell to the dead, boys, the voyage is red, boys!"

"Heave'em away, heave away!"

"Quartermaster, ninety degrees to port," Captain Vederosa said.

Caedus looked back at the ballista with a confused yet astonished smile.

"Lantern, aft side, captain," one of the sailors on the upper deck said. "Low to the water."

"Leave it," Vederosa said as Caedus glanced over his shoulder. "That's not our target."

The galleon, Caedus thought.

"For gold and for plunder, we pillage and plunder!"

"Heave'em away, heave away!"

Waiting like a stalking hunter, The Leviathan slowly glided across the water. Caedus stood in a sturdy stance, ready to burst into action.

"Call for the ferryman! Call for the ferryman!" the entire ship sang aloud.

A mast pierced the fog on the port side of the ship.

"Wait," Vederosa said.

Hints of orange from lanterns followed shortly behind. The confused shouts of the Merrins gave their position away rather easily. Caedus wriggled his fingers across the hilt of his sword, watching the hull of the Merrin longship sail directly at him.

"Heave! Away! Heave! Away!"

At the conclusion of the shanty, an unsettling quiet fell upon them. The Merrin ship's bowsprit closed in on Caedus's position. He stared at the enemy soldiers on board and remained motionless. The enemy inched closer to The Leviathan; the deafening silence ached in Caedus's ears.

"Fire!"

With a deep snap, the ballista hurled a bolt toward the Merrin ship and blew a vast hole in the front of its hull with a fiery explosion. Chaos erupted, and the bowsprit of the sinking ship stopped just over Caedus's head. Captain Vederosa leaped up onto it with her sword drawn. Equally amazed and perplexed with her strategies of warfare, he met her scowl with his stone-cold expression as she turned back to face him.

"And now, Caedus, perhaps you can be of use," she said.

Without further hesitation, Vederosa walked across the bowsprit in perfect balance. Caedus heaved himself up onto it as well and steeled his mind for battle. Sounds of clanging metal and splintering wood rang through the air, urging him to cross.

Halfway, Caedus nearly lost his footing, but he managed to stabilize himself. He looked down at the murky water and froze. Caedus studied the depths, shook away his fear, and took a deep breath as enemies flocked to the stern side of the galleon in waves. Captain Vederosa danced around the Merrin sailors, slaughtering them with a grace that reminded him of Zededia's nimble *Virtuo* fighting style.

Caedus finally jumped down onto the ship and clenched his teeth. With his shortsword in hand, he stepped to the first challenger. The sailor staggered to him, missing his poorly timed strike. Caedus leaned away to dodge the blade, swung upwards, and severed the man's arm in one fluid movement. He then planted his heel in the man's chest and kicked him overboard.

Another Merrin approached, but Caedus deflected the attack and drove his blade through the man's neck and out the back of his head. Blood splattered on Caedus's face, and he ripped his sword free. Battle elevated his senses; a frenzy overcame him.

Several more Merrins tried to best the finest swordsman in all Hostellus. Each met a grisly fate and fell to the deck mangled or in pieces. In a calm moment, Caedus looked around for his next opponent. A handful of sailors from The Leviathan and his allied captains of the Legonae had climbed aboard as well and charged into the fight and occupied all approaching enemies. Eventually, through the chaos, one narrowed in on him and sprinted. Caedus sank in his stance and readied his blade. Before the

Merrin soldier could reach him, however, an arrow flew into his left eye and out the back of his skull. Slightly annoyed, Caedus turned around as droplets of blood streamed down his face. A man concealed in a cloak and balaclava stared at him with yellow eyes and bow in hand.

"That one was mine," Caedus said, griping at Captain Seether.

"Come now, Caedus," Captain Redding said with a wide smile as he ran by with a hand on his shoulder. "You should learn to share."

Caedus grunted. The herd thinned as rivers of salt water and blood trickled off the ship's edges. Thunderous footsteps bent the floorboards just as he lowered his guard, however. A monstrous man, roughly the size of Captain Ammonladus, stood in the center of the deck, his bare torso and scarred grimace facing in his direction. Caedus placed one hand over the other on the hilt of his shortsword as the man loosened the slack on a massive chain in his hands. The Merrin sailor heaved the chain in the air, gained momentum, and whirled it over his head. Stepping forward with caution, Caedus waited for the right opportunity.

Once he moved within range, the giant sailor slammed the chain into the deck, nearly cracking the wooden boards in half. Caedus spun in a circle on one foot to dodge the brutish attack and then lept in the air at his enemy. His attack met one of the metal wrist braces with such force that it created fiery sparks falling to the deck. When he landed on his feet, Caedus ducked the chain slash aimed at his head and sliced at the man's inner left knee. Groaning in pain, the sailor dropped. Caedus slashed the other knee and rendered his opponent incapacitated.

After catching his breath, Caedus walked behind the Merrin, flicked his sword around to a reverse grip, and plunged it into his opponent's shoulder down through his heart. Heaving his blade from the torn flesh, Caedus shoved the corpse to the floor and glared at his kill.

He stepped back and watched his allies make short work of the rest of the Merrin crew. Caedus wiped the blood off his face with the back of his hand, chest heaving with adrenaline. The surviving Merrins surrendered moments later, offering him a victory at the hand of his perfected swordsmanship skills.

~ ~ ~

After the explosive bolt from the ballista punctured the hull of the Merrin galleon, Prince Lucien ran to the rail of the upper deck and watched the flames battle against the fog for dominance of the atmosphere. Captain Vederosa climbed onto the bowsprit, and several others followed her across. Lucien grabbed the hilt of his longsword and stepped forward to join them, but a firm hand grasped his forearm.

"No, Lucien," King Atlas said in a loud voice to overcome the commotion. "I need you here!"

"Why?"

The Leviathan rocked back and forth, and the shouting from the skirmish on the other ship drew the prince's attention over to it.

"The Merrins have advanced our plan to open the portal to Aeladaecia much farther than I had anticipated. We're running out of time! We need to open the gate before we are overrun by their boarding parties!"

Dazed, Lucien looked at Atlas with a lack of confidence.

"You have nothing to fear, Lucien," Atlas said. "Vederosa and her men are doing their job; it's time we do ours."

The prince nodded, still unsure of how to pull off this scheme.

Atlas descended the stairs down to the middle deck, and Lucien followed. Bursting into the Captain's chambers, he scanned over the ceremonial items laid about.

"Iluundi. (Illuminate,)" King Atlas said.

A bright green flame appeared in the palm of his hand, which he placed in the copper bowl as Lucien had seen before.

"Kneel," Atlas said with a hasty tone.

The prince lowered himself to both of his knees, teetering back and forth as The Leviathan swayed from the soldiers fighting above.

"Entering Elysia without a proper seal requires more ... sophisticated actions than merely showing it to you as I did two days ago."

Lucien waited patiently and watched Atlas close his eyes, take a deep breath, and recite several phrases in Aznogsi. Strange noises sounded off in all directions, but the prince couldn't pinpoint their origins. He glanced around in a mild panic. His vision of Vederosa's chambers shifted around like rippling water. Barely able to make sense of anything, Lucien felt the instinct to flee.

However, moments later, the rippling calmed to reveal the cosmic plane of the spiritual plane he had seen from Atlas's clairvoyant powers. Water seeped into his pants and soaked his knees.

The prince stood to his feet, shaking off the excess water and staring into the void of the sky. He expected the rocking of the ship to toss him off balance and adjusted accordingly, but he remained in perfect equilibrium. Sloshing footsteps approached him from behind. Lucien turned to see King Atlas standing before him in different clothing. A decorated spiritual robe covered him head to toe, and Atlas's glowing red eyes appeared from underneath a hood that stretched to the ends of his shoulders.

"How?" Lucien asked, scanning Atlas's apparel.

"To an Osirian," Atlas said. "Reality can be what we'd like it to be."

A whirl of energy wrapped around Atlas as he held out his hands. His normal clothing returned along with the Daecian crown on his head that caught Lucien's eyes with a sparkle.

"But, perhaps it's best to keep things simple for now," Atlas said.

Lucien stood motionless as Atlas turned his back to him.

"So," Lucien said. "Are you going to let me in on your plan or keep me in the dark until it's complete?"

"My plan is to open the gateway so we can resurrect Zededia and save our people," Atlas said with an edge in his voice. "That's all you need to know."

The shadiness of Atlas's answer twisted knots in Lucien's stomach. Whether Atlas hadn't told him because he couldn't comprehend the plan or because he would disagree with it didn't matter; it gnawed at his trust just the same.

"Bogrikrash, cost kar lett Eldarzenmilaosir. (Bogrikrash, bring me the Pool of Elders,)" Atlas said.

Lucien raised his eyebrow and waited, keeping his eyes open for any change in scenery. Suddenly, a vertical whirlpool of pure energy appeared in front of Atlas.

"Prince Lucien," the Daecian king said, "do you remember the sorceries I've been teaching you over the last two days?"

"Yes...."

"Recite the first one, please."

With a concerned look, he glared at his cousin.

"Aeles ... aelas ir arci. (Gods ... gods of old,)" he said, his tongue aching from speaking the ancient words. *"Zo meskag zant, cod orae, cod stnaka, ish cod dirizel. (I call unto you, for aid, for guidance, for wisdom.)"*

Moments after Lucien spoke, the energy pool swirled. A phantasmic hand with long, slender fingers breached the surface and turned to open its palm faceup. Mesmerized, Lucien stared as an orb hovered over the hand.

"Ozlent meskag zigni? (Who calls upon us?" several voices of differing pitches said in unison.

Lucien's rising fear forced the hairs on his arms to stiffen.

"Atlas Osiris, santir Olethrias Osiris. (Atlas Osiris, son of Olethrias Osiris," Atlas said. *"Zo meskag Zol'ngan lett Eldarzen sen lyasen os brunu disma zot comoseta. Zomed hastetageg ell the Neshkasokos oznag zo enve konkag ullagen zant shakla sen zot mesk. (I call unto Zol'ngan the Elder to perform a duty under my command. He is bound by the Seal of Neshka which I have placed before you to obey my call.)"*

Completely unaware of Atlas's words, Lucien felt helpless. His mind pulsed in intense pain from attempting to understand the situation. Despite watching Zededia undergo dozens of meditations, he never picked up on any of his brother's terminology. He simply idled by at the mercy of the gods Atlas spoke to.

"Lett gaarungal jhinnzo at nossek ag comosetegs, mytha. (The deathless spirits are not to be commanded, mortal,)" the voices from the orb said with a harsher tone. *"Zanto jolskalae ... agoza zant graova. (Your foolishness ... will be your demise.)"*

The portal shimmered. Lucien widened his eyes as the ground shook.

"Who were you speaking to?" he said. "What did you ask?"

Staggering from the vibrations, Lucien retreated from the portal. He glanced at the uncertain look in Atlas's eyes and started to panic. An ear-splitting shriek sang from the energy pool as a massive, shadowy hand broke through. It clawed at the ground, pulling the rest of its body through to reveal an arm wider around than the largest tree

Lucien had ever seen. The shoulders hosted an eyeless head as it wriggled its way through next. Hundreds of needle-like teeth lined a gaping mouth.

Lucien remained paralyzed in place, focusing on the monstrous being escaping through the portal. When it stumbled out and stood to its feet, it towered over him and forced him to tilt his head back as far as he could. Another shriek assaulted the immediate area from its nightmarish mouth, sending dozens of small waves through the water at Lucien's feet. His knees buckled once the titan turned its attention to him.

"What the hell is that?" he said, shouting at Atlas.

"Miliacas!" Atlas said. "Eater of Souls! She's a lesser god. The elders use her as their personal guard to watch over Elysia and devour those who are trespassing!"

"That's US, you bloody moron!" Lucien shouted.

"You have to trust me! This is the prime target I was looking for! I knew if I angered the gods, they would send her after me!"

The Daecian king ignored his jeer. A massive, shadowy foot stomped forward.

"Quickly, Lucien!" Atlas said. "Recite *Morvvos Menaeakae!*"

Choking on the dryness of his throat, Lucien fought to regain control of himself. His terrified eyes stared at the Eater of Souls. She reached her many-fingered claw toward him and growled.

"My-mythraedos ... terros ... avasalae.... (M-mind ... body ... soul ...,)" Lucien said in staggered breaths, watching imminent doom close in. *"Zanto ag zot sen comosetag. (Yours are mine to command.)"*

A trail of green essence flowed from Lucien's mouth. He watched it climb up the devilish spirit's torso and burrow into the side of her head. Miliacas struggled for a moment, clawing at the entry wound and whining in pain.

"What is it doing?" Lucien asked.

He looked at Atlas after his patience for an answer expired. The smile on the Daecian king's face disturbed him.

"Obeying."

The green essence covered the surface of the lesser god's head where its eyes would be. Lucien recognized the sight as the same phenomenon that occurred when he utilized his Osirian magic, though, this time, the aura was green rather than red when he controlled Thancred and Spymaster Rachtus.

"That's not ... possible," Lucien said in a low mutter.

The prince raised his right arm, and Miliacas mimicked him. A wicked sense of excitement flowed through him, and he toyed further by waving both of his arms in different directions. Each time, the spirit replicated his movements. Lucien started to laugh as he commanded the titanic being.

"I can't believe that worked," he said. "What do we do now?"

Atlas's sly grin gleamed at him.

"Raise hell."

Chapter 18

The Siege of Amuun Drall

Day 4 in the Month of Rain

The Hostellae marched across the open courtyard in front of the main gate of Amuun Drall like an imperial army. Thousands of shining silver boots stomped in unison, and every soldier narrowed their eyes on the city with murderous intent. Their king rode between the battalions of foot soldiers, chin high and proud under his helmet. The white feathers of his plume danced to one side with the blowing wind; a rainless thunderstorm cracked the sky between black clouds. Flaming boulders from Hostellian trebuchets pelted the main gate for hours over the early afternoon, forcing the Voluutian archers away from the crenellations. The city was ready to be taken.

Plumes of smoke developed into thick columns from the burning buildings just inside the wall and added to the darkening atmosphere. Bits of ash coated Matticus's helmet as soot floated down from above. He stared at the crumbling gatehouse, waiting for the final blow to bash it down and create an opening for his soldiers to enter. The architecture of the landscape reminded him of that of Vaedor Sellos's inner city. Commands from his officers ordered the first wave forward, and Matticus focused his gaze on the flying rocks above his head, watching for the one to crash into the gatehouse. A moment later, he found a winner. The trebuchet directly behind him launched its projectile square into the top of the gatehouse and collapsed it. Something strange caught Matticus's attention shortly after. A blob of red light glowed from deep within the city, and then it screeched through the air like a spear and smashed into the trebuchet, exploding on impact and consuming the nearby Hostellians in red fire.

Matticus squinted in anger. He knew where that bolt had come from.

Raed.

The Voluutian king revealed the presence of *Osirisigniros* and its terrible power. Matticus's obsession for it heightened and sent adrenaline pumping through his hulking body. Archers reappeared on Amuun Drall's wall where his siege weapons didn't target. They stabbed at the marching Hostellae with arrows of fire, taking out a handful soldiers here and there. Matticus cared not. A few dead men meant nothing to him compared to a conquered Voluutia.

"Forward," the king said, his tone deep and drawn out. "Forward."

The time for battle approached. Matticus felt his aggression flow through his limbs and leaned his head back to take in the aroma of war. Once the foot soldiers grew close enough, they broke formation and surged through the ruined gatehouse to clash with the Voluutian defenders. More openings appeared as the siege weapons continued to assault the wall. Hundreds of Hostellian soldiers rushed the fortress, clawing their way inside over whatever or whoever stood in their way. The first wave made quite the mess of things, drawing archer fire and the focus of the Voluutian cavalry charging from the city streets. An opportunity presented itself; the main causeway into Amuun Drall became clear and ready for a charge.

An elite platoon of knights restlessly awaited orders from their king. Matticus's fanatical mind thought back to his ancestor's holy wars across the valleys a thousand years ago. Manic, he obtained the delusion that he was Osiris reborn. The line between his personality and his forefather's blurred more with each passing day, the righteous quest to unite Osiria's kingdoms burning in his heart.

"'The gods look upon this day and rejoice, for their reckoner marches upon the sinful. Enter, ye righteous. Slay the impious.'"

The words of Ozamendelas fueled his fury and linked his spirit with Osiris. His ancestor smiled upon him yet again. Spurring his horse onward, Matticus led his cavalry in a steady trot, eyes glowing red, and heaved his longsword from his sheath. Hooves pounded the earth as they quickened to a gallop. Like angels, the Hostellian knights flew across the courtyard, carrying wings of white feathers on their backs. Matticus's reddened eyes shined through the eye slits in his helmet, and he closed in on the Voluutian soldiers battling to keep their city safe.

Matticus pulled his sword high in the air, held his head down, and glared at his enemy. He swung his arm backward and cleaved underhandedly, hacking the first soldier across the bridge of his nose clean through the helmet. The rampaging cavalry trampled the Voluutians with ease; they punctured a gaping hole in the front line of Amuun Drall's defenders and spread out into the next street. Matticus shifted focus from target to target, slicing at them as fast as he could. The sounds of tearing flesh from his holy steel echoed through the city, and the foot soldiers that initiated the attack followed behind the horsemen to finish off those they stampeded over. Arrows rained down from the wall, but Matticus paid them no attention. He only looked to the sky for another bolt of red lightning. He looked for Raed.

Thirty minutes of grisly warfare passed, and King Matticus pillaged the lower city of Amuun Drall with the aid of his daunting forces. Superior siege tactics and skilled soldiers won the first skirmish. The heart of the Hostellae would face the next. Two miles of densely packed buildings, winding roads, and frenzied Voluutians with their backs against the wall distanced him from his prize.

Ordering for the foot soldiers to surge ahead, Matticus stopped his horse in a large clearing at an intersection of two roads. He sheathed his sword and removed his helmet to better calculate his next move. The massive pack of his hundreds of knights split off into smaller teams to clear out the adjacent streets, leaving only the Vaedorian Guard around to protect their king from any harm. Matticus took a breath of cool air as the sun started its descent from its peak in the sky.

The metal shoes of a horse clicked against the stone road to his left, and he turned to see Commander Nysis approaching. He had sent his second-in-command to lead another division of the Hostellae into Amuun Drall from the north in a cohesive offensive with the Korzegi troops relinquished by King Raed. Nysis's presence here told Matticus that the other half of the advance went semi-smoothly at worst.

"Your Majesty," Nysis said. "I'm glad to see the siege has progressed on all fronts."

"Korzeg has stayed true to our accord?"

"Yes. Four thousand Korzegi warriors are assaulting the northern sector of the city. Their fire siphons are proving quite useful. Bloody brilliant engineering."

"What our forces?"

Nysis pulled out a map from the satchel on the saddle of his horse. Matticus rode closer to inspect it.

"Battalions three, four, five are moving through the city here," the commander said, tracing his finger along the layout of Amuun Drall. "Six and seven maintain a hold on the docks and are patrolling the harbor grounds. We moved eight, nine, ten, and eleven to the south—the Voluutians are focusing their efforts to keep the road to Merrinine open—leaving twelve to occupy the area here."

Matticus listened and followed Nysis's observations. The siege route to the keep had been as carefully chosen as the acolytes of Osiris. There was simply no room for error.

"Send twelve on," Matticus said. "There's no need for them here."

"As you command, sire. Our tunnelers have breached the enemy ranks closer to the inner city. The Voluutians weren't prepared to have their main line of defense exploited so easily."

"Leave the rest in the fields where they are. The Korzegi dogs will clean up everything else."

A thundering boom shook the ground from a great distance away. Matticus looked up and saw a massive dust cloud rapidly expanding over a row of buildings. He knew what had caused such an explosion; the aura of *Osirisigniros* hummed through the air and seeped deep into his soul.

"King Raed is holed up in his keep. Our boys won't be able to storm his castle so easily, it seems."

The veins in Matticus's face shined. Anger filled him through a hateful sneer.

"I will handle King Raed."

The first two battalions of the Hostellae pulled back to the fields after suffering heavy casualties, but ten thousand more soldiers pillaged their way through Amuun Drall at his command. Matticus pried his eyes away from Nysis's map and gazed out to the next obstacle he would have to smash through. He squinted at the border checkpoint that surrounded the inner city. These walls were thicker than the ones his engineers demolished earlier in the day. Worse still, moving his packed trebuchets through the rubble-filled streets took too long to maintain an efficient siege. Matticus stood his ground against such a challenge. He knew that once he penetrated the inner city, he grew one step closer to Raed.

"It will take the rest of the day to push the ram to the inner city gates," Nysis said. "What are your orders, sire?"

Matticus tilted his chin high, body tired of its rest and mind aching for bloodshed.

"We aren't waiting all day," he said, dismounting from his horse.

His feet hit the ground with a solid thud. Matticus loosened his shoulders and then placed a firm hand on the hilt of his longsword.

"Proceed with the assault, Commander Nysis. Move your men to the keep. There, you will find me bathing in glory ... and Osirian blood."

Nysis spurred his horse to ride out to the other side of the city. King Matticus crunched his boots against the stone road that led to Amuun Drall's keep, starting the long walk to victory.

The Hostellae battled their way through every alley, building, and street as they took more of the city. Matticus, with his platoon of heavily armored guards, marched over the ruins piled with corpses of Voluutian soldiers and citizens alike. A once vibrant fortress crawling with life turned into a razed hellscape of fire and ash. Dead faces looked up to him as he walked over them, but Matticus didn't so much as glance at their glassy eyes. He walked the path of righteous fury. No room to mourn a slaughtered enemy.

Eventually, Matticus gained ground on his men carving their way to the keep. Waves of shining steel caught his eye, and he heard battle cries and clanging metal echoing down the narrow street. The great walls of the inner city came into view; the Voluutians had dug their heels in to fight at the most defensible point they had left. Growing near, Matticus unsheathed his blade, and the Vaedorian Guard behind him followed suit. The common foot soldiers moved aside to let their king pass, reinspired by his presence in battle. Once he stepped out into the clearing just before the gradual climb up a stone ramp to the gatehouse that sealed off the inner city, Matticus carefully analyzed his surroundings. He needed to take the critical points leading up to the wall if his men had a chance of reaching it. On either side of the gatehouse, Voluutian archers rained arrows down on whoever came in range. Matticus then saw a small siege tower to his left that connected to the main wall via a smaller walkway halfway up. He found a way in.

"Protect your king," Matticus said, flicking his wrist toward the fray.

The Vaedorian Guard bolted free of their formation and stormed out into the open courtyard, twenty hulking soldiers in blue capes and thick armor thundering across the paved road. As the most skilled soldiers the Hostellae had to offer, they cut down the enemy troops like weeds, great shields in one hand and one-handed swords in the other. Matticus walked through the middle of battle unscathed, keeping perfect poise as he proceeded. None of the Voluutians even came close to touching him. Every time one tried to charge the king, one of his guards intercepted them and gutted them like pigs.

When Matticus reached the base of the tower as his men warred with the Voluutians, he took a deep breath and closed his eyes. He channeled his empowered magic into a balled fist, red auras whirling around it.

"Sunzer sen gol. (Stone to dust,)" he whispered to himself.

His hand started to glow. Matticus then planted his feet, cocked his arm back, and punched the dense tower with all his might. The stone exploded from his fiery impact. Once the dust settled, Matticus walked through the opening and marched his way up the tower, slaughtering all who stood in his way, until he reached the pathway that led to the main wall. The Voluutian archers turned their attention to him and fired, but most of their arrows missed by wide margins as they panicked at his presence. One met its mark and struck his right shoulder, penetrating his pauldron. Matticus winced as he felt a trickle of blood spill down his arm. That only angered him, though. His rage boiled through the shine in his veins, and he held up an open hand at the archers.

"Evverstas. (Sever.)"

A jagged crunch cracked an instant later, and each of the archers fell dead to the ground as Matticus summoned a spell that simultaneously snapped their necks like twigs.

Yanking the arrow in his arm free, he cast it aside and moved out to the middle of the partition wall. He cast the same sorcery he used to break a hole in the stone tower and slammed his palm into the walkway. The stone under his feet started to collapse, and after he stepped out of the way, the center portion of the partition crumbled down in a pile of rubble, creating a makeshift path for his soldiers to follow onto the main wall.

Point by point, the Hostellae pushed the Voluutians back and captured more territory. Matticus proceeded to the top of the gatehouse to secure it. A desperate enemy soldier rushed him, but he deflected the hasty strike of his sword and plunged his blade into the man's chest. Another sprinted forward, giving him no time to pry his weapon free, so Matticus let go of his sword, caught axe aimed at his neck by the handle, and ripped it away. He flipped the axe around and cleaved it into the side of the man's neck with such strength that he hacked right through the collarbone halfway across the other side of his ribcage.

"Quickly, the cauldron!" he heard a Voluutian say near a lever positioned next to the outward facing crenellation.

Matticus looked over as two men heaved on a crank to release a nasty surprise onto the gathered Vaedorians below. He stormed over, and as he did, one of the Voluutians fled in terror, leaving the other too weak to pull the lever. Hands surging to the engineer's throat and belt, Matticus lifted the man in the air, ignoring the pleas for mercy, and hurled him off the wall directly into a pot of boiling oil. Gagging, fluid screams chilled the air as the Voluutian flailed while his flesh melted from the bones.

Matticus glared at the writhing man, the sight of such cruelty pleasing his darkened heart. He then looked out at the horde of Vaedorian soldiers holding their blades high in the air to cheer on their king. Hostellian flags waved over thousands of silver specks. A few of his men that made it to the wall with him cranked on the gears to raise the gate. Metal churned and voices shouted. A Voluutian standard plagued his view to the right as he scanned the scenery. With a sneer, Matticus ripped the spear off the wall, tore the enemy flag off, and replaced it with his cape stitched with the gilded eagle of Hostellus. The king wriggled his fingers along the spear and drove it through the mortar between two stones to claim this territory for the Hostellae. A roar of excitement screamed from below, and the wind fluttered the newly planted flag a vigorous breeze.

"My king!" one of the soldiers near him said.

Directing his attention behind him, Matticus turned to see a finger pointed out toward the northern side of the city. He walked across to the other side of the gatehouse and surveyed the landscape. Flashes of red light soared through the sky and plummeted toward the northern side of the city. Watching them crash into fiery explosions, Matticus wondered why Raed had suddenly ceased targeting his armies with bolts of hellfire, and now he knew. The Voluutian king chose to fend off the attack from Korzeg, perhaps because they were the first ones to reach the inner city.

Good dogs, Matticus thought, praising the Korzegi armies for acting as his meat shield against Raed's power with *Osirisigniros* in hand.

"Isn't Commander Nysis advancing with the forces from Korzeg?" the soldier beside him asked. "Should we redirect our battalions to aid him?"

"No," King Matticus said, shifting his gaze to the Voluutian keep in the heart of the city.

Another beam of red energy screeched into the air from the center of Raed's fortified castle. Matticus narrowed his gaze to where he knew Raed waited for him.

"Our prize is there."

Chapter 19

Cradle of the Colossus

Day 4 in the Month of Rain

Prince Lucien shook awake from his voyage to Elysia. Heart racing, he darted his eyes around Captain Vederosa's chambers and saw Atlas waking just the same. Once he stood to his feet, Lucien held his hands out in front of them and examined them front to back to make sure he returned with everything in its proper place. The green aura that seeped from his body after casting Atlas's spell remained. Lucien frowned in confusion, wondering if he still maintained control over the horrifying goddess he encountered moments before.

The half dozen questions Lucien had prior to entering the spiritual realm expanded to thrice more. Time forced him to sideline them, however, and Atlas ushered him out toward the deck.

Once he stepped outside, the scenery had changed, but not by much. The thick fog still plagued the air, barring his vision of anything fifty meters away from the ship's edge. Towering rocks passed by from time to time and caught his wide eyes by surprise every time. He then looked behind The Leviathan as it sailed by.

The Merrin galleon sank in the murky water in the distance, its sailors nowhere to be seen. Captain Vederosa stood at the helm of the ship, face as stern as ever, and Lucien deduced that she along with Caedus and the others had fended off their pursuers. Or at least one of them. Though he spent mere minutes in his meditation state in Elysia. He walked over to the staircase, climbed to the upper deck, and searched for Caedus. His unmistakable blank expression stared off the port side of the ship. Thancred stood next to Caedus, alerted to Lucien's presence.

"Ah, my prince," Thancred said, "thank goodness. I was worried for a moment when Caedus told me you had entered Elysia in the middle of that scuffle."

Lucien opened his mouth to speak with a wide smile, but he couldn't begin to describe the experience Atlas drug him through.

"I take it that you found whatever you were looking for?"

"I suppose," Lucien said. "I wasn't really told."

Lucien's head throbbed as hastened footsteps pounded up the stairs.

"Lucien!" Atlas said, running up to him. "How are you—do you feel all right?"

He struggled to feel much of anything other than the cold chill in his bones and his headache.

"Define 'all right.'"

Atlas seized his wrists and examined them. An ecstatic grin broke out on the Daecian king's face.

"Brilliant, Lucien. Bloody brilliant."

"Okay, well what the hell am I supposed to do with this?" the prince asked, holding his hands up as the green mist slowly revolved around them.

"Think, concentrate," Atlas said. "Miliacas is at your command. She lingers in Elysia as she can't take physical form as we do. Not until I provide her a proper entrance."

"I'm going to pretend I know what that means."

"Just be ready to send her forth when I call for it. I'll take care of everything else."

While he didn't fully understand what Atlas was trying to do, Lucien had little room to try and argue.

Minutes passed, and the fog started to dissipate. Lucien regained view of the environment, and a daunting realization struck him. The Leviathan picked up speed at an alarming rate. He looked up to the masts, but they remained completely raised. A strong current propelled the ship forward, seemingly with a will of its own. Pillars of rock continued to stab at the sky, tightening in density. Lucien's anxiety grew as the danger did. The crew had calmed down from their adrenaline-fueled rage against the Merrin sailors, making the scene even more uncomfortable.

Shadows danced across the rocks cast by the lanterns of the ship, and an eerie feeling slithered down Lucien's back. He had no idea where Vederosa and Atlas meant to sail the ship. Lucien rested against the edge of the railing, trying to figure out what the sea held in store for him. Eyes glued to the rocks, he made sure the ship steered clear of them as if he could do anything to prevent it. Each of them looked as sinister as the last, but the prince became used to their presence after a while. Then, just as he lowered his guard, something jarred his attention. For a moment, he swore he saw something move between the massive pillars that looked identical to the plated carapace he saw crawling along the ocean floor several days ago. He searched intently, eyes nearly bulging out of his head, for whatever slithered under the water. The prince blinked rapidly, trying to separate an apparition from reality. Loose boulders tumbled down from one of the rocks in his peripheral vision, taking his paranoia to a new level.

"What the hell was that?" one of the sailors said.

Everyone jolted to life. A soft creak resonated from under the ship; the current changed course, pulling it slightly to the right, and the sounds of swirling rapids hummed through the air.

Suddenly, Lucien shuddered as a rock pillar toppled over and quaked the sea from a good way away. He along with the others near him rushed to the starboard railing, frantically scanning the mist for its source.

"We're getting close," he heard King Atlas say behind him. "Stay on course."

Lucien looked over his shoulder and met Captain Vederosa's squinted gaze. How she managed to navigate such impassable terrain eluded him. The ship glided over the churning water through the maze of rock and fog, gaining speed by the second. Lucien watched the bow dip farther below than the upper deck and noticed that The Leviathan started to descend. The water swirled faster, and then it hit him.

We'll summon the gate at the vortex of the Cradle, he remembered Atlas tell him.

He hadn't realized how literal the Daecian king meant to be.

Vortex of what? he thought.

Out of nowhere, the hull of the ship scraped against a submerged part of rock nearby. Lucien held tight to the railing to keep his balance. As the current's strength increased, control over The Leviathan grew harder to maintain. Captain Vederosa struggled to keep the wheel in its proper place as Lucien looked back at her.

Nearly falling over after letting go of the railing, the prince stumbled to the helm. His hand fell upon one of the pegs, and he used it to haul himself upright as the sea pulled the wheel the other way. A massive rock pierced the fog in the direct line of sight of the ship once Lucien gained his balance. Vederosa heaved on the wheel, unable to steer out of its path. Prince Lucien took hold of it with both hands, wrapping his left arm around the captain's back, and twisted it with all his might. The veins in his biceps and forearms glowed brightly. Lucien grunted, fighting the pain of exhaustion in his arms. Eventually, he and Vederosa combined enough strength to turn the ship to safety. They missed the rock by mere meters, and Lucien watched it fade in the distance, salt water and sweat dripping from his face and arms.

Vederosa gave him a softer look than she normally did, one that silently appreciated his efforts to save her ship. He nodded, the tension in the atmosphere sending everyone into shock.

Another pillar crashed into the sea out of view. Lucien heard violent splashing different than the rapids under the ship.

"Shouldn't we—"

"Never mind that!" Atlas said, cutting Lucien off. "Just look for—there!"

Lucien stared at a clearing between the rocks, and the fog cloud disappeared, revealing the vortex Atlas mentioned. The Leviathan titled down even further as it plunged into a massive whirlpool that the currents of the sea emptied into. When Lucien studied the vortex closer, he eyed a black void that swallowed all light that passed through it. He stared in horror.

"What ... *is* that?" Lucien asked, shouting over the raging sea.

"The Cradle of the Colossus!" King Atlas said. "Once a home for the waterborne gods, it's now a gateway site to the worlds beyond ours!"

The Leviathan struggled against the raging ocean but used the momentum of the whirlpool to keep along its edge. Lucien squinted through the spraying mist from below to study the blackened center where the water vanished. As he looked, a strange feeling overcame him as an intense pressure pushed out against his chest from inside. The prince coughed, choking on something clogging his esophagus, and grasped his neck. His mind panicked. The Leviathan rocked violently in the maelstrom, knocking him to his feet. Lucien gagged and scraped at his throat, and a trail of black mist seeped from his mouth, eyes, and nose.

"Lucien! No!" Atlas said. "Don't let her go!"

Siezing on the upper deck, he lost control of his body. His fingers twitched after his hands fell to the floor, eyes starting to roll into the back of his head.

"Save him, you bastard!" Caedus shouted.

"This was your bloody plan?" Vederosa said, looking over her shoulder.

Just when Lucien thought he would suffer one of the worst fates imaginable as he flopped on the deck, the pressure in his chest rose to the back of his mouth. He opened his jaw as far as he could, and a silent breath scraped out. Suddenly, his body stopped seizing, he inhaled as much as he could, and then screamed bloody murder as a mass of black energy spiraled out from every part of his face. The cloud blinded him, and the blood vessels in his neck and face bulged as they strained. After a moment, the mist flew through the air and pooled together on the other side of the maelstrom.

The prince, free of the hell that plagued him, leaned his head back against the deck with heart pounding and lungs starved for oxygen. Caedus helped him to his feet, and when Lucien stood upright, he focused his eyes on the ghastly sight in the distance.

"By the gods," he said. "What have we unleashed?"

Miliacas, the ancient horror he brought with him from Elysia, rampaged like a frenzied bear. It slammed its hands into the water, tilted its head up, and shattered the atmosphere with a deep, shrill scream.

"Lucien!" Atlas said. "You need to regain control of it!"

Still dazed in fright, Lucien glanced around and rapidly blinked. He focused on the angered spirit, holding his hands up and trying to remember the spell Atlas taught him. The Leviathan sailed around the whirlpool, getting into an effective range.

Before Lucien could speak, however, a blast from behind him knocked The Leviathan off course and deeper into the whirlpool. The prince caught himself against the railing and twisted around. A harpoon larger than he struck the side of the ship and demolished a portion of the upper deck. From its direction, a large, white mast with the insignia of a green gem broke the plane of the mist and sailed toward him. The rest of the Merrin fleet caught up to them. Another harpoon soared through the air from the ballista mounted on the enemy ship's bow and barely missed. The powerful currents of the sea battered the hull, Miliacas started to wade out away from the vortex into The Leviathan's path, and the Merrin pursuers closed in.

"Black powder in the water!" Captain Vederosa shouted. "Toss the barrels behind!"

The whirlpool gave The Leviathan a head start on the Merrin ship and allowed it to glide away. Lucien stood by as the sailors chucked small, reddish barrels with a large 'X' painted on them into the ocean. Seether and King Atlas rushed by him to the back of the upper deck.

"Iluundi. (Illuminate,)" Atlas said as Seether strung an arrow in his longbow.

The arrowhead lit ablaze with a green flame, and the immaculately skilled archer released it into the sky. As one of the barrels floated near the tailing longship, Lucien watched a faint green light strike it on its side. Instantly later, the barrel exploded right in front of the Merrin ship and forced it off course.

Seether continued to rain fire upon the longship as it sailed toward the center of the whirlpool, gaining speed and matching The Leviathan's angle. The other men around Lucien made haste across the deck, making repairs where they could and gathering arms to board if necessary.

Miliacas thrashed in the water, reaching its shadowy claws at The Leviathan and the Merrin longship each time they passed. Lucien felt helpless in the matter. He stood as firm as he could on the upper deck and faced the goddess while repeating the phrase Atlas had taught him. Unlike before, none of the green essence from his veins trickled out, and the spirit standing over the vortex remained unchanged.

"We need to get closer!" Lucien shouted. "I can't reach its mind!"

"If I sail further in, the currents will be too strong!" Captain Vederosa yelled back.

Lucien grunted in frustration. The Merrin longship took another pass on the outer side of The Leviathan, throwing spears and roped hooks on board. Most missed their mark, but one hook latched on the railing of the middle deck. The entire ship creaked, pulled by the enemy galley as it tried to sail away.

"Cut the line!" Vederosa ordered as she steered to loosen the tension from the rope.

The Leviathan's ballista fired at the Merrin ship, sending an explosive bolt flying into the enemy's hull.

"We're out, Captain!" the sailor mounting the great weapon said in a shout. "No powder aboard!"

As if matters couldn't worsen, Lucien saw two more Merrin ships sail into the whirlpool along with a number of rowboats.

"Lucien!" King Atlas yelled right next to him. "We need Miliacas! Now!"

Around in circles The Leviathan sailed, taking hit after hit from Merrin harpoons. The prince froze. Time slowed around him as he watched the sailors nearby tumble into the raging water from the harpoon impacts. Captain Vederosa fought with all her might to steer the ship in the safest path. Lucien lost his sense of hearing, the roars from Miliacas and the chaos among the crew fading out, and a blur started to cloud his vision.

A rough pair of hands grabbed onto his shoulders. Lucien glared at the man right in front of him, but he couldn't distinguish any features through the blurry haze.

"Lucien!" the man shouted at him.

The prince's ears rang, the voice jolting his hearing back to life.

"Lucien!"

As the man shook him violently, the blur disappeared, and Caedus's unshaven face stared back at him.

"Lucien, for shit's sake!" Caedus yelled.

The prince snapped back to life, clinging to Caedus's arms as his heart pounded in his chest.

"Caedus–I–I–"

Hooks grappled the side of The Leviathan along the entire outer side, cutting Lucien off from his thought. Moments later, a dozen Merrin soldiers boarded and drew their blades. Lucien reached down for his weapon, but Caedus stopped him.

"Do as Atlas says!" Caedus yelled, pointing at Miliacas as it smashed its fist directly onto an enemy dinghy. "I'll handle the Merrins!"

Lucien nodded and turned away, retaking his post at the railing of the upper deck and narrowing his sight upon the nightmarish spirit in the water.

~ ~ ~

Caedus gazed upon the boarding soldiers, weilding his shortsword in his right hand. He held his left at his side facing him, and a black mist seeped from the thick sleeves that reached his wrists.

"Cazak kar, Caedus. Ini kar lassamar aries tozi mozoco. (Free me, Caedus, let me loose against these heathens.)"

"Nossek dem. (Not yet.)"

The black mist slithered back up his arm. Five enemy sailors stood in front of him holding their weapons toward him. Caedus took a step backward near Prince Lucien and eyed each of his opponents. One flinched forward, trying to bait him into charging.

After taking a moment to concentrate Caedus sprang into action, slashing his sword and spinning closer to the Merrin sailors. Caedus carved his way through one of his enemies, severing hand from arm and thrusting his sword through the man's neck. The next Merrin swung at his head, but he ducked and tackled him to the ground. With a violent jab, Caedus forced his blade into his opponent's chest, practically ignoring the leather cuirass that covered it.

King Atlas raced to the upper deck from the fray below and made quick work of the Merrin soldier closest to him while Caedus shoved another overboard.

"We need-" Atlas shouted as he plunged his sword into an enemy. "To take out-"

Another Merrin threw himself at Caedus and nearly tackled him, but he hurled the man over his shoulder.

"That transport!"

Twisting his head around, Caedus eyed the deck of the enemy ship. He gained a daring idea.

Is that close enough? he said in his head, knowing Osinian could hear his thoughts.

"Sett, (Yes)."

He gave Atlas a slight grin.

"Leave that to me."

Stepping over to the railing, he studied the deck of the Merrin ship. Caedus concentrated, aligning his mind with Osinian's, and exhaled.

Go.

In that instant, Caedus vanished into thin air with a hint of Osinian's essence left behind. The first Osirian teleported him onto the Merrin ship right behind the captain at the wheel. Ten sailors dressed in green attire stopped in their tracks in disbelief and glared at him.

"Aesta? (Now?)" Osinian said.

After wriggling his shoulders, Caedus closed his eyes and channeled the soldier within him. He placed a firm hand on the hilt of his sword. As Caedus looked upon the Merrins once more, the whites of his eyes turned solid black. Osinian's spirit melded with his, and an evil grin stretched across his face.

"Aesta. (Now.)"

Caedus leapt into combat, prying his sword free from its sheath to slash at the closes Merrin. A shadowed silhouette sprang out of his back with two crimson eyes, took the shape of a man, and sliced a path through the enemy ranks. Caedus stabbed his shortsword into one man and then hacked at the legs of another while Osinian blinked from spot to spot, finishing them off with swift strikes. Cries of pain sang through the air as splatters of blood painted the deck. The puddles of sea water on the ship deck turned red around the corpses. Caedus put his masterful swordsmanship skills to work, dancing around the Merrin sailors and plunging his sword into any exposed flesh he could find.

Osinian cleaved a man in half right down the middle as Caedus severed the arm of another and kicked him down the stairs to the middle deck. More sprinted up from the other staircase and lunged at him. Caedus looked at Osinian and grabbed hold of his outstretched hand, instantly swapping places with him. The Merrins' blades sliced through the black mist to no effect. As he readied himself for another duel, Caedus heard a deep, raspy laughter nearby and watched the shade butcher the Merrins like cattle, splitting them in pieces long after they died.

"Menne, mothra canastis. (Worthless, filthy dogs,)" Osinian said.

With the upper deck clear for the moment, Caedus tried to control his beating heart. He looked around in search of what to do next. Several Merrin sailors climbed across the cables attached to The Leviathan.

"Cut the ropes," Caedus said. "That'll buy us some time."

Osinian faded into thin air and reappeared on the middle deck to spread terror while Caedus carefully descended the left staircase. With the shadow slicing and dicing his way through the Merrin sailors, severing the boarding ropes along the way, he took advantage of the commotion and snuck over to the opening that led to the lower deck.

Down inside the ship, Caedus peered over the edge of the wall attached to the stairs and saw rows of men pushing and pulling massive oars. He retreated back behind the wall and thought carefully of how to disable an entire crew.

Black powder, he thought. *There must be some here.*

Caedus crept down onto the oarsmens' level and used each crash of a wave to conceal his footsteps. The ceiling thudded every few seconds; trickles of blood spilled through the cracks in the planks. Muffled sounds of wisping air and flesh tearing open echoed down from above.

A pile of crates and boxes came into view as Caedus progressed to the back of the ship. He looked back and made sure no one had spotted him and then started riffling through the supplies. At the bottom of the pile, a small barrel with a black sphere painted on it stuck out like a sore thumb. Caedus grabbed it, popped the lid off, and sniffed. The strong scent from the volatile powder burned his nose. With the barrel in tow, Caedus coughed to clear his throat and headed back to the stairs to the open deck.

"Enemy!" one of the sailors yelled.

Caedus froze. Some of the oarsmen abandoned their post to take up arms, and he bolted out of his trance toward the stairs. The rusted edge of an ax missed his head by inches as he ducked and tumbled his way up the steps.

Back outside, he glanced around for his shadowy companion. Osinian continued to battle the Merrin sailors, but each one he cut down, Caedus saw two more emerge from the lower deck. Suddenly, a pleasant surprise appeared in his view as he scanned over the rest of the main deck. Dozens of barrels identical to the one in his hand jostled around in a cage near the bow of the ship. Caedus turned his head and squinted through the misty haze at The Leviathan in search of a particular ranged ally of his.

Caedus inserted his thumb and index finger between perched lips and sent a blaring whistle into the air. Seether recognized the call and directed his hooded eyes toward him. Waving his free hand, Caedus moved alongside the length of the transport ship and then lifted the barrel of black powder in his hand. Seether noticed him and waved in return. Caedus waited for his friend to gather Atlas's attention, and then he saw a faint flicker of a flaming-green arrow.

"Whatever you're doing," Caedus shouted at Osinian while facing The Leviathan. "You've got about ten seconds!"

After ensuring that Seether was prepared, Caedus hurled the barrel into the air at the others. A green flame soared through the sky toward the cage at the front of the ship.

"At zant inni ir zanto mythraedos? (Are you out of your mind?)" Osinian yelled.

"Shut up and get us out of here!" Caedus barked, keeping his eyes on the arrow screeching toward the powder kegs.

The barrel bounced off the cage, Caedus's nervous expression deepened, and the arrow neared its mark. Just as the flaming steel tip punctured the wood and ignited the black powder, Osinian emerged behind him and teleported them both away.

Right after landing on the upper deck of The Leviathan, a deafening explosion of fire and debris knocked him to his side. Ears ringing, Caedus pulled himself up to his feet and glanced at the enemy transport. He blinked the blurriness away and beheld the obliterated Merrin ship, its front half completely gone and its back quickly sinking to the depths below to be crushed by the maelstrom.

"By the stars, Caedus," King Atlas said with a wide smile. "When you said 'leave it to me,' I wasn't quite sure what you meant!"

Atlas grasped the inside of his forearm in a firm shake.

"But I suppose I should know not to doubt a soldier of the Legonae!"

Caedus nodded and looked at the prince who faced away from him toward the vortex of the whirlpool.

"Lucien!" King Atlas shouted. "We're going to sail closer to Miliacas. Cast *Morvvos Menaeakae* to take control of it! We can't stay in this maelstrom forever!"

As Caedus shuffled his way over to the staircase, Osinian retreated back into his body. The Leviathan sailed deeper into the rushing waters, Miliacas becoming wise on its presence.

Caedus helped one of the sailors toss debris overboard and made sure that any wounded found their way to the infirmary below deck. Miliacas's deep roar sang into the sky, paralyzing him for a moment while demanding his attention. Standing by and waiting for the goddess to crush the ship with its massive hand, Caedus darted his gaze to Prince Lucien, who remained in his post, trying his damnedest to recast the spell. The black void inside the vortex shimmered, and soon after, a horizontal stone barrier appeared.

"Now, Lucien!" Atlas shouted.

Just as Caedus saw a mist of green surrounding Lucien's raised hands, a deep, thundering roar, deeper than the cries Miliacas belted out, resonated across the entirety of the Cradle. The air stilled, chills raced down his spine, and The Leviathan shook under his feet. Tumbling rocks from one of the pillars that circled the whirlpool crashed into the water. Shadows danced in the foggy outskirts, playing tricks on his mind. Everyone froze, including Miliacas. A massive figure moved beyond the veil of the fog. Caedus's eyes then beheld a sight that haunted the darkest of his nightmares.

Wriggling antennas squirmed through the fog attached to a long, slender body covered in thick, armor-like plates. A gaping mouth opened at the head of the behemoth, revealing a circular jaw surrounded by needle-like pincers.

"By the gods ...," one of the sailors near him said in a hopeless tone.

"It's Nyaka Viaentas!" another shouted.

Raising its head to the sky, the beast released another bellowing howl that reached the deepest octaves Caedus's ears could pick up. The vibrations from the shockwave knocked him to his knees. Scrambling around, Caedus glared at King Atlas, Prince Lucien, and Captain Vederosa as they all glued their eyes to the titan in the distance.

Miliacas roared at the ancient sea serpent, seeing it as a rival, but Nyaka Viaentas responded with a concentrated beam of pure energy blasting forth from its mouth. Caedus watched as the transparent ray of light bore a hole in the spirit's chest, eventually melting it from the inside. A dying howl grated his ears, and the goddess disintegrated into the wind. Miliacas, the great avenger of the gods, evaporated to nothing in mere seconds.

Nyaka Viaentas turned its attention to the closest boat right under it. Caedus eyed several of the Merrin sailors abandoning ship to take their chances in the unforgiving seas shortly before another beam of light decimated the longship. That which remained burned and quickly sank into the whirlpool. The cries of drowning men fought against the currents' thrashing waves, adding to the chaos that had erupted.

Caedus panicked and searched for a solution. King Atlas and Captain Vederosa remained frozen in a trance.

"If we stay here, we'll be blown out of the water!" Caedus shouted. "Get us to cover!"

The sea serpent sprayed the Cradle with another attack, turning the rowboats caught in the light to dust. Trails of steam rocketed to the sky, and Caedus fell to the deck as Captain Vederosa swiftly turned the ship out of the line of fire.

The final Merrin longship sailed directly underneath the sea monster and launched harpoons at its underside, to which it skittered atop the rocky pillars and unleashed the fires of hell upon it with its mouth. The beam must have hit one of the black powder barrels; the Merrin ship exploded from within. Charred segments of the boat flew across the maelstrom. The dust provided cover for a few brief moments, blocking the serpent's view for just enough time to sail by one last time.

The Leviathan sailed alone in the Cradle at last. Vederosa gave no care to how she dodged the monster's attacks, tossing Caedus around the upper deck like a ragdoll. He slid back and forth across the wet planks until he collided with the railing.

"Can you bloody steer any more reckless!" Caedus shouted.

"Unless you want to fry like a hagfish in the blistering sun," Vederosa barked at him. "Shut your damn mouth!"

"Just take us out!" he yelled back.

With a swift yank of the wheel, the ship made way toward one of the exits into the fog. However, The Leviathan crashed into a submerged section of rock, beaching it and sending Caedus tumbling to the main deck. Grunting with pain, he felt a sharp pressure in his right side. When he looked down, the dagger he kept sheathed in his belt stuck clean through him on the edge of his oblique muscle. Blood splurted out from aside the blade, and he shakingly gripped the hilt with both hands. Preparing himself with a deep inhale, he jerked the dagger out of his side and yelled at the top of his lungs. He dropped the dagger, lungs sending out staggered breaths.

Caedus staggered back and leaned on the edge of the ship, holding his wound with one hand and the railing with the other. His clenched teeth ground against one another, and he glanced at the blood seeping through his fingers.

"Caedus!" Captain Redding shouted, rushing over to him.

"I'm fine."

"Come on, we need to find Atlas. He can heal you"

Just as Caedus shoved himself away from the railing, a low-pitched chittering noise clicked right above him. Slowly, he titled his head to the sky. Staring right at him was the great leviathan, its pincers twitching back and forth.

Nyaka Viaentas's body pulsed from its midsection to its opening mouth, and Caedus's mouth dropped agape at the sight of a massing pool of energy between its circular jaw. With a sudden twitch from the beast, Caedus covered his head with his arms out of instinct. All his earliest memories came to life behind clenched eyes; all the regrets he ever had flooded back. Nyaka Viaentas chittered again, forcing the hair on his neck to stiffen and his stomach to knot.

Certain death loomed overhead. He prepared himself for the worst.

"Mythraedos, terros, avasalae! Zanto ag zot sen comosetag! (Mind, body, soul! Yours are mine to command!)"

Caedus opened his eyes in shock. He glanced around, frowning with disbelief, and saw Lucien standing right beside him holding his arms to the sky. He then saw wisps of green essence flowing from the prince's hands. An aura of the same energy circulated around the creature's head; Caedus stared at the sight with an astonished face. He looked back at Lucien, who lowered his arms to shoulder height out beside him. Under the prince's control, Nyaka Viaentas turned its head away from The Leviathan stuck on the rocks, looked to the black void in the center of the Cradle, and paused. Caedus heard booming growls echoing from deep within its lungs. Lucien then forced his hands forward, and Caedus watched the giant beast unleash a devasting attack directed at the vortex.

Caedus limped over to the other side of the ship, able to feel the intense heat emitting off the beam of energy. The power from Nyaka Viaentas broke the seal protecting the gate. The way was open.

A grin appeared on Caedus's face, but it shifted to a wince shortly after as the bloodied wound at his side reminded him of its presence. Lucien walked over to him with his focus still wrapped around controlling the titan.

"Hold on," Lucien said.

Bracing himself against the railing, Caedus stood by as the giant creature lifted The Leviathan off the rocks with several of its appendages. The ship rocked in the water and slowly gained speed at the edge of the whirlpool. Nyaka Viaentas shook away the prince's control as Caedus remained astounded by the entire situation. With several short, pained clicks of its pincers, the beast wriggled its way off the rocky pillars and receded back into the fog, one final roar of frustration resonating across the ocean.

The green aura around Lucien's eyes faded as Caedus approached him.

"Marvelous, Lucien!" King Atlas shouted with glee as he jogged beside Caedus. "You're as brilliant as you are mighty. Your brother would be proud."

Caedus saw the fake smile on the prince's face and smirked.

"Captain!" Atlas said. "Sail for the gate! Get us out of here!"

The remaining crew of The Leviathan returned to their posts as if nothing had happened

"You're injured," Lucien said.

He grinned and looked down at his bloodied hand.

"I've weathered far worse."

Lucien nodded in respect. After a sigh of relief, Caedus turned to see the open gate to Aeladaecia.

"How did you know that would work?" he asked Lucien.

The prince raised an eyebrow at him.

"I didn't."

Caedus glared at the prince, strangely proud of his heroism despite the insanity that came with it.

"I'm bloody glad you're on our side."

Lucien chuckled.

"Me too."

The Leviathan sailed for calmer waters. After surviving the Cradle, the storm of chaos disappeared for the time being, but Caedus wondered when it would return. Aeladaecia brought endless unknowns. For now, though, he focused on not bleeding out, appreciating the temporary peace before the next leg in the journey.

Chapter 20

The Duel of Tyrants

Day 4 in the Month of Rain

Forced to retreat, the Voluutians gathered all remaining men they had to fend off the unstoppable onslaught of the combined forces of Hostellus and Korzeg. Matticus choked his enemy back to one point: the keep. He marched through the final city block, his army at his side shouting battle cries. The glimmer of the moat shined along the wall of Raed's castle, Hostellian flags waved high above silver helmets, and the winds of war invited a bloody conclusion to this siege.

However, as Matticus and the Hostellae ran out into the street surrounding the keep, something seemed off. Silence filled Amuun Drall as his men stopped their charge and looked around in confusion. The Voluutians were nowhere to be found. Matticus expected a heavily defended keep, but not so much as a single arrow flew from the battlements. An eerie atmosphere fell over the street. Looking around, he noticed that his enemy had raised the drawbridge but left no soldiers to defend it. The metal armor of the Hostellae grinded together as they stood by with no enemy in sight.

Where are you, coward? Matticus thought.

Raed had shown no restraint in using the power of the Sword of Kings prior to now. He suspected a ploy.

"Perhaps the Voluutians have surrendered, my liege," one of his men said.

Matticus shifted his eyes. A chill in the air alerted his senses.

"No," he said. "They're here."

A strange sound pulled his attention upward. Matticus frowned and looked up to the black clouds covering the city in a veil of darkness. His eyes widened at the sight of bursts of electricity shooting across the sky, forming a massive pool of energy. In a single flash of white, a thousand individual bolts of lightning streaked down from above like hellfire and vaporized every single Hostellian that stood in the street. When

Matticus rose upright after flinching to defend himself, he surveyed his surroundings in disbelief. Hollow pieces of armor rolled along the stone road, and piles of black dust scattered by with the wind. An entire battalion of Hostellian soldiers gone in an instant. Raed had acquired his attention, but Matticus sneered at the castle rather than flee. He had come too far to simply tuck his tail and run. While standing alone amongst the graveyard of ash and metal, he heard a soft click followed by churning gears. Matticus looked to his left and watched the drawbridge to the keep slowly lower. Skeptical, he studied it for a moment, fearing another trap. However, he quickly realized that the Voluutians had sent him an invitation.

Matticus paced around the edge of the moat until he neared the drawbridge that hit the other side of the street with a thud. Sword in hand, he stared through the shadowed haze of the gatehouse with glowing eyes. There, in the center of the courtyard beyond the castle wall, he saw enemy standing like a statue with a golden blade in his grasp. Raed waited for him, for a duel to end this war right here and now.

Pausing inches away from the drawbridge, Matticus took a moment to glare at King Raed, who returned his gaze with red eyes of his own. Two of the most powerful men in Osiria locked eyes with each other in a harrowing showdown.

The drawbridge creaked as Matticus stepped onto it, never breaking sight of Raed the entire way. He wriggled his fingers on the hilt of his longsword, and loose stones crunched under his heavy boots under the cover of the gatehouse.

When he walked out into the open courtyard, mind seething with rage to fuel his aggression, dozens of Voluutian soldiers rushed from the outer wall and drew their weapons, cutting him off on all sides. Matticus froze, lowered in his stance to prepare for an ambush, and waited. He glanced from side to side and studied the men around him.

"Surrender, Hostellian!" the lead soldier said. "You're surrounded by the Voluutian Guard."

Matticus lowered his chin and chuckled, the deep vibrations echoing off the insides of his helm. He found Raed's intimidation tactic rather amusing as if he hadn't laid waste to the entire Voluutian army over the last few days. Channeling his strength, he took a deep breath and held it in. Matticus then closed his eyes.

"All I am surrounded by ... is fear," Matticus said while raising his head.

A brighter red glow shined through the eye slits of his helmet.

"And dead men."

Whispering an ancient sorcery, Matticus raised an open palm with his fingers curling inward toward it. Each of the Voluutian soldiers except for the captain suddenly levitated off the ground. A faint aura of red seeped from Matticus's face, and, after a moment, he dropped his hand. In the blink of an eye, the Voluutian soldiers plummeted to the earth and splattered like rotten apples against a stone wall.

The Voluutian captain stared at him in terror. Matticus stepped forward, placed his hand on the man's shoulder, and shoved him aside; he wanted Raed.

His cousin sneered at him and held the Sword of Kings pointed forward. Matticus's breath shot out through flared nostrils. Seeing his ancestor's mighty blade after searching for it for so long sent him into a brewing frenzy.

"That sword you're carrying," Matticus said, voice darkening as the power of Osiris corrupted his physical body, "that's mine.

"In a thousand years, when future kings look back on this day," Raed said in an increasingly rageful tone, "there will be no record of your existence. I will eliminate you from history! When scribes analyze your bloodline, all they will see is 'King Nameless, son of Matias!'

Raed's eyes glowed darker.

"I will cast you into the darkest pits of *Ozek Monns* the gods can conjure; you will be erased from this world and the next!"

"'The gods smile upon me. Their favor runs through my veins,'" Matticus said, reciting a quote from Osiris spoken during his war with the Aznogs. "'History will remember those who shackled the world ... and the redeemer who freed it.'"

"You are no Osiris!" King Raed shouted.

"No, I am not."

Matticus planted his feet in his *Igni* stance and held his longsword up by his chin pointed at Raed.

"I am stronger."

The fury of hell in his eyes, he stormed forward, ready to end his feud with Raed for good. While he marched with torso twisted and arms cocked, Matticus watched King Raed start to move toward him as well. The courtyard seemed to lengthen with each step he took. Raed's dormant power revealed itself soon enough through the same red glow that coursed through his veins. Matticus, the mighty and powerful king of Hostellus, closed in on his foe.

Once in range, he heaved his longsword from the right after whirling it around his head, slashing at Raed's neck. The cold edge of his longsword crashed into the Sword of Kings, bolts of red lightning stabbing through the air from the golden blade. Matticus battled the vibrations shooting down into the hilt of his sword and swung again, missing just barely as his opponent stepped out of reach.

The savage nature of his attacks tossed him off balance. When he regained his footing and looked at Raed, a wave of energy burst from his enemy's hand, throwing him to the ground with force. Matticus grunted with each impact and coughed to clear his throat. He rose to his feet and held his sword with a firm grasp. A lesson quickly learned, patience overtook aggression.

"Hasty and arrogant," King Raed said. "Just like your father!"

Raed invoked another sorcery as he shouted and channeled the energy into *Osirisigniros*. A wall of fire raced across the paved ground toward him. Matticus quickly cast a spell of his own, resting an open palm against his other clenching his blade. As he spoke, the Vaedorian king sank in his stance and swiped his arms to his sides, sending a gust of wind rushing forth in front of him. The approaching wall of fire split in two and crashed into the buildings behind and engulfed them in flames. Wood splintering and stone cracking, the heat of the blazing ruins pressed against his back through his armor.

Matticus peered back through the slits of his helmet, gazing at the destruction. The round tower built into the inner wall toppled over in a fiery crash. Shaking the dust off, he turned to face his enemy once more.

King Raed speared the Sword of Kings into the ground in a burst of rage, tremors rippling in the earth. Matticus stammered for a moment and fell to his knee. When he rose, his eyes widened in shock as his opponent leapt into the air toward him. Dodging

Raed's aerial strike just in time, he lunged to the side. Raed exploded toward him, the power of *Osirisigniros* gifting him with incredible athletic abilities, but Matticus hadn't fully collected himself. The searing energy from the Sword of Kings pierced the dense armor on the side of his arm. Luckily for him, the sword's corkscrewed edge hindered its slicing capabilities.

Matticus winced and retreated, holding his bleeding wound with one hand and his longsword in the other. After a moment, he returned his bloodied hand to his sword and regained his focus. Raed advanced again, and Matticus sidestepped the attack, planted his heel firmly against the Voluutian king's shoulder, and shoved him to the ground with all his might. On the offensive, Matticus channeled his wrath into a downward swing that Raed struggled to deflect. He continued to assault his foe with relentless strikes. Each consecutive hit wore down Raed's strength, and Matticus readied himself for a lethal blow. As he raised his arms above his head, however, a blast of red energy from Raed's hand struck him in the chest. The impact knocked him in the air, and he crashed to the ground a good distance away. Feeling the burnt indent on his breastplate, Matticus heaved himself upright.

Angered furthermore, he stomped back toward the Voluutian king. Matticus parried Raed's next attack, shoulder charged him square in the chest, leapt toward him, and thrusted his sword forward. Raed staggered before answering his onslaught with a blind swipe. A clink echoed through Matticus's cuirass, and he looked down and observed the slight nick across his abdomen. He paused for a moment, noticing Raed's shift in fighting style the more threatened he became. Matticus took careful note of his opponent's status and reengaged with fresh fury.

The two Osirian kings battled with one another across the courtyard of Amuun Drall for several minutes, trading nicks and cuts here and there. Matticus held the advantage for most of the fray, forcing Raed into every corner he could. Eventually, he herded him back to the steps leading up to the keep. The broadened barrier behind gave Matticus the perfect opportunity to overpower him, but he wasn't ready to end things now; the cruelty infecting his mind wanted more. Matticus obsessed over this day for years. It deserved a proper fatality.

Matticus clashed his sword against the Sword of Kings for a brief second, whirled both blades around in a circle, broke away from the lock, and heaved his sword in an upward arch from his feet. He sliced a massive gash in Raed's right hand, cutting clean through the bone of his little finger just above his wrist.

Matticus stared at the warm, thick blood spilling down both arms as Raed yelled in agony. It enticed him like a deep ocean predator. He stepped forward in the image of wrath itself. However, just as he raised his sword to strike again, Matticus paused and witnessed the other side of the powers *Osirisigniros* blessed its wielder. The golden blade glowed light red, and the hemorrhaging wound on Raed's shaky hand started to heal until the damage had been fully repaired after the trickles of blood retracted and seeped back through the gash. Rumors of the Sword of King's healing capabilities had reached Matticus's ears in his youth, but he never valued them when compared to its destructive nature.

"You may tear at my flesh ... and crack my bones," King Raed said with a dark voice as Matticus watched his veins glow red. "But the power of Osiris shields me. You cannot strike at me in a way that matters."

Matticus squinted in anger.

"We'll see."

Though he hated to admit it, the taunt baited him. Matticus became more careless with his attacks and risked his positioning for an increase in damage. His superior strength knocked Raed back with each strike. Eventually, he abandoned the core of his swordsmanship skills and cleaved at his target, using every muscle in his torso and arms to twist and swing over his shoulder. Like the first time he crossed blades with Raed, sparks of red lightning shot from the Sword of Kings, and Matticus sent his opponent hurling across the open arena.

Immediately after, Matticus winced at a sharp spark of thunder in his ears. When he opened his eyes, his attention shifted to the blackened sky and light gray cobblestone below his feet. He blinked several times as the courtyard of Vaedor Sellos appeared all around. The white walls of his city surrounded him with the keep behind him where he expected the Voluutian stronghold to be. Matticus's lungs pounded, and his heart raced. Confusion blurred his focus while the aura of the illusion around him felt like a bad dream. Shifting his eyes around, he couldn't discern what was real and what was a figment of the guilt his subconscious rocketed forth.

"Matticus?" a voice said.

He turned to his right, and he froze at the sight. A young version of Zededia, no more than ten years old, stood a dozen feet away from him; one that ignited the first memories of his childhood when he and his younger brother were close. Zededia's worried expression pained him in a way he couldn't explain, the emotional turmoil he felt for Lucien days ago slamming into his thoughts.

"W-why are you pointing your sword at me?" the apparition said.

Matticus looked down and realized he had held out his father's sword toward his brother in a hostile fashion. Snared in his own hallucination, he struggled to speak, think, or even move. Matticus's anger vanished replaced by the guilt he had kept dormant for so many years. Expelling his brother, slaying his father, neglecting his family—each memory stabbed at him. His heart split in two, torn between the monster he had become and the child he used to be. He didn't recognize himself in that moment and nearly let go of his sword. The vision of Zededia stared at him with large eyes, the eyes of a younger brother who feared what they saw.

"Are you going to fight me?" it said.

Slowly shaking his head, the angered sneer he showed to Raed melted to sadness. The ghost then vanished into thin air.

"Are you going to fight me?" the apparition said again after it reappeared in a different spot.

Matticus turned and took a step backward as an eerie feeling crept across the back of his neck. As his brother moved closer, the knot in his stomach sank lower and lower. Again, Zededia disappeared as quickly as he appeared, leaving Matticus in a pool of confusion.

"Are you going to fight me?" the ghost said as it popped up before blinking away.

He heard another voice along with his dead brother's, like another spirit was present inside.

"Fight me."

Insanity crept in.

"Fight me."

Each time the voices spoke, a new one joined in, becoming more demonic by the second. Zededia's expression grew angrier with each appearance, and Matticus retreated every time it spawned. Soft thunder echoed across the landscape as the spirits of his brother closed in.

"Fight me. Fight me. Fight me."

Losing track of them, Matticus spun around in circles. The hair on his neck stiffened. The spirits kept appearing from all sides, and Zededia grew in age into adulthood.

"Fight me. Fight me."

A hellish version of Zededia appeared with solid black eyes.

"Fight me!"

Matticus tripped over the loose rubble as he flinched from the swing of a sword his brother carried. The same crack of thunder from before followed right after.

Reality returned. He panicked, darting his eyes back and forth at the burning landscape of Amuun Drall. Looking at his free open hand, he clenched it repeatedly to test his motor control. The rage driving his fury flooded back to him, dispersing all notions of the guilt his vision showed him. Raed staggered in his direction across the arena. Matticus, reengaged with the duel, took his *Igni* stance once again.

"Even with the Sword of Kings, you cannot hope to best me," he said.

A sneer intensified through the Voluutian king's thick beard.

"You've seen nothing yet."

Raed's suggestive remark left him confused. Suddenly, a gust of wind swept over the courtyard, wisps of faint green mist fluttering along with it. Matticus watched as they flew toward the Sword of Kings in Raed's hand and his opponent's eyes began to glow.

"Oustranag sen kar, slalyasae, abast sen rogtang arie. (Return to me, felled ones, rise to fight again,)" the Raed said as he raised the golden blade.

A wave of green energy pulsed away from the sword. Matticus stood firm to brace for the impact, but as it passed, he remained unaffected. He looked around, the eerie silence of the battlefield creeping in.

Next to Raed where he had entered through the gatehouse, a sharp crack alerted him. Matticus glanced over at one of the dead Voluutian soldiers he had smashed into the ground. The corpse began to move, realigning its shattered limbs and mangled flesh back into their proper places. Matticus took a step backward in shock. As the dead soldier sluggishly rose to its feet, he heard the others around him follow suit until they all stood.

A swarm of glowing green eyes glared in his direction after they all snapped their heads toward him in unison.

"You see, boy," King Raed said, the reanimated soldiers stumbling forward. "I don't have to best you. The might of Osiris will do that for me."

The army of dead Voluutians surrounded him as they did before when he first walked into the courtyard. King Matticus held his longsword tightly and sprang into action. Able to dispatch the shambling corpses with ease, he realized they had lost their agility and strength in their undead state. Slow, inaccurate swings of their weapons fell by the wayside, and each time he met blades with one, he pushed them back onto the ground.

Matticus fought the horde of undead men for a good while, each of them returning to the fight after he cut, skewered, and tossed them around. No matter how he severed or incapacitated them, they came back as if nothing had happened. However, those he butchered to pieces took longer to put themselves back together. Taking note of his observation, he adjusted his strategy and cleaved at the staggering Voluutians, granting much more lethal results. As less than half remained, Matticus looked beyond to his primary target and realized that Raed had summoned his men back to life to buy time. His anger grew while he watched Raed use the Sword of Kings to heal all his wounds and channel his power into the undead.

Tearing his way through the Voluutians, Matticus pursued Raed in his vulnerable state. He charged forward, forcing Raed to shift concentration. The Voluutian soldiers dropped to the ground once the spell had ended shortly after.

Raed broke from his healing state and thrusted the Sword of King's forward. Matticus quickly parried the attack, pushing Raed closer to the burning buildings behind. He advanced, trading strikes with his foe until the support column that held up the outer covering cracked and collapsed. Matticus then sidestepped as Raed lunged at him, grabbed the thick section of the wolf pelt on his opponent's back, and heaved him back toward the center of the courtyard with all his strength.

The sun started to lower, and the clouds of smoke rising from the ruins blotted out any light that remained. A faint red glow shined brightest from the gaps in Matticus's armor and the eye slits of his helmet. The caged demon inside started to break loose. He hastened in pace as he marched toward Raed; he hadn't finished toying with his prey.

Matticus swung his longsword at Raed overhead repeatedly, bashing down the Sword of Kings Raed held up to defend himself. The brute strength of the Hostellian king started to overpower his opponent. Sheer rage fueled his attacks, and he sensed that Raed's energy began to deplete. Matticus's ferocity peaked, and he slammed the heel of his boot in Raed's chest and kicked him onto the staircase of Amuun Drall's keep.

Matticus heard Raed spit a mouthful of blood onto the stone steps as he approached. His enemy lay broken and beaten; victory neared.

"I told you," King Matticus said as he gripped Raed's long, gray hair. "You cannot hope to best—"

A shrill gasp burst from his mouth as Raed twisted and plunged the Sword of Kings into his lower abdomen. Matticus staggered back, groaned as Raed yanked the corkscrew blade from his body, and fell to one knee. Blood dripped out from the holes in his helmet in front of his mouth. Vision blurring, he concentrated on staying conscious. He held his right hand firm on his gaping wound and struggled to hold his longsword with his left.

Footsteps sounded off in his ears as he felt his heartbeat pulse through his entire body. Raed stood directly in front of him. Matticus couldn't move.

"You are no conqueror," Raed said after lowering himself to Matticus's ear level. "And you are no king."

Matticus tried to pull himself upright, but an empowered blow from Raed's fist struck him under the chin and sent him tumbling across the courtyard.

On his back, he tried to summon the strength to rise. He coughed several times, grabbed his weapon from beside him, and used it as a crutch to stagger to his feet. When he looked up, a blanket of red energy wrapped around the Sword of Kings, and he glared at King Raed with a defiant frown.

"And now ...," Raed said. "You are ... ash."

The sword glowed brightly, and a beam of burning light exploded from it in his direction. Matticus widened his eyes, dropped his longsword, and lunged to the right to save his own life.

Raed's sorcery leveled a section of the inner wall as it bore its way through the stone and wood. Clouds of smoke and dust filled the courtyard, crawling their way into every crevice in the arena. The wind settled soon after, and King Matticus found himself peering up from his back into a hazy sky yet again.

An intense pain burned across the side of his face, but when he tried to raise his left hand to feel it, he frowned. He received no response from his arm, looked over, and realized that it *wasn't there.* The edges of his shoulder armor were black with char. His eyes darted back and forth in disbelief. He then tried the other and brought his right hand to examine the pain on his face. Cold metal touched blackened skin around his eye. Raed's beam of light had vaporized the left section of his helmet from the bridge of his nose to behind his ear. The thick metal of his armor had spared his eye, but it torched the skin around it like paper.

Matticus groaned and rolled over to his side. Without his left arm to help him balance, rising to his feet proved more difficult than ever. He stood upright after staggering for a moment and scanned the dusty arena. The cloud settling in around him barred any noise outside of it from seeping in, creating a dead silence save his muffled footsteps.

Body nearing complete exhaustion, Matticus trudged across the courtyard with ragged breaths. He searched for his opponent, but the debris cloud limited his sight to a few feet in front of him. Stones crumbled in the distance to his left. Another blast of red light erupted from the Sword of Kings, giving Raed's position away immediately. Matticus sank in his stance and saw his enemy's outline in the brightened haze. The dust provided a perfect cover for him to sneak by, so crept across the loose rubble under his feet as quietly as he could. Eventually, a silver shine caught his attention. As Matticus looked down, he glanced at the hilt of his longsword that scattered away from him in the blast. It felt much lighter in his hand as carefully picked it up from the ground. He brought it closer to his face, glared up and down the length of the blade, and came across the crude edge about a foot away from the crossguard. Matticus eyed the sharp point the edge came to like a dagger and tested the weight of his new weapon with his right hand. Another bolt from *Osirisigniros* rang off closer to him on his left. Again, Matticus stared at Raed with a deep concentration in the game of cat and mouse.

"The smoke can't conceal you forever, Matticus," Raed said in a loud voice throughout the arena.

Matticus steeled his focus and kept his keen eyes on Raed's direction, slowly approaching the clearing. Raed fired again, missing him to his right close enough for him to feel the heat from the ray of light. Tensing his shoulders, Matticus crept closer and closer. His opponent's lumbering footsteps guided him. Raed's outline became clearer through the dust, giving him a clear target. As Raed paused at the base of the staircase, so did he. Staring down his rival, he flipped his broken sword to reverse grip, planted his feet, and waited for the right moment to strike.

King Raed pivoted away from him, and Matticus exploded from his stagnant position, taking massive strides to close the distance in just over a second. Yelling with a hoarse voice as he leapt into the air, he simultaneously stabbed the shortened blade of his sword into Raed's shoulder and pressed his knee into his back. The dagger barely managed to penetrate the thick fur armor, but it sank in enough to give him a grip and force Raed to the ground. On the way down, Raed blindly fired another ray of light, missing Matticus's head by inches. He wrestled with the Voluutian king, releasing his grip on his shattered sword wedged in the pelt armor and resorting to his sheer strength to restrain Raed's hand with the Sword of Kings to the ground. Matticus struggled to contain his prey with his one arm. Eventually, he knocked the golden sword away and reached for his weapon in Raed's shoulder. Just as he pried it free, his opponent kicked him off and sent him rolling across the dusty stone path leading to the keep.

He climbed back to his feet, feeling the pain of his wound in his side claw at him even more. Raed regained control of the Sword of Kings and fired a beam of energy at him. Sidestepping the attack, he then somersaulted forward and rose up within striking distance.

Focused and steady, King Matticus assaulted his opponent with a flurry of differing attacks. He sliced his dagger across the midsection, skewered it in Raed's upper thigh, and struck his knee into the thick leather chestplate. Matticus then yanked his dagger out, slashed through the inside of the opposite knee, and punched Raed square in the mouth with a haymaker enforced by the metal grip of his sword behind his closed fist. Raed haphazardly swung downward, but Matticus stepped aside, wrapped his arm under his enemy's, spun on his heel, and hurled him into the wooden support column lining the staircase.

Raed yelled in pain as he crashed into the column; Matticus approached. He heelkicked the Voluutian king back into the terrain, punched him again, ducked under a backhanded slice, and carved his dagger across the torso from hip to opposite shoulder. With a brutish force, he bashed his elbow into Raed's chin and drove his dagger through Raed's arm that held *Osirisigniros* in one powerful blow, piercing clean through the forearm guard and pinning it to the cracked wooden column behind.

The Sword of Kings fell to the ground with a metallic rattle and rolled away. Matticus's veins in his right arm and exposed portion of his face shone red as he collected himself and stared at his opponent squirming in agony, and the fires on the outer edge of the keep's walls raged on.

Matticus took a step forward as Raed writhed like a trapped animal. He heaved his broken blade from the column with a firm hand, blood spilling across the ground and staircase like a sack of spilled dye. Flicking his sword to forward grip, Matticus struck Raed in the side of the head with the pommel, threw it down, and tossed his enemy to the ground.

Raed hit the cobblestone like a corpse. Matticus walked over and flipped him upright before standing over him with one leg on each side. Taking a moment to savor the act of murder, he glared at Raed's bruised face and concussed eyes. He slowly knelt with fiery eyes, plumes of smoke and dust spiraling toward the sky from every part of the castle grounds. Matticus wriggled the fingers on his remaining hand as Raed lay broken against the staircase.

"I will regret killing you, Raed," Matticus said with a demonic voice that echoed off the inside of his helmet as he grabbed hold of his enemy's bloodied beard. "Not because I will mourn or feel sympathy for you."

He pulled the mangled Voluutian king toward him, his blaring red eye shining through the cracked opening in his helmet.

"But because I can only kill you once."

Matticus shoved Raed's head back to the ground and proceeded to beat him to death with a clenched fist. Each strike cracked his opponent's skull more and more, spurting blood onto his arm and torso, until Raed's face caved in completely and he pounded his brain into a slurry of blood and bone.

Chest heaving with shortened breaths, Matticus loomed over the dead king with pride and fury. A deep roar bellowed from the depths of his lungs like a bloodthirsty animal completing a glorious kill. Raed had been slain; Voluutia had a king no longer.

As Matticus rose to his feet, he shook the blood and gray matter from his knuckles, a glimmer of gold gleamed in his peripheral vision. The fabled Sword of Kings rested peacefully against the earth, longing for a Son of Osiris to hold it once more. The blade called to him. Years of his fanatical quest for it had reached a climax. Matticus staggered towards his ancestor's weapon, the injuries pushing him closer to the brink of death. He had sacrificed everything for this moment—his time, his army, even his arm. Holding *Osirisigniros* was all he craved. Nothing else mattered.

Matticus reached down, wincing from the gash in his side, and wrapped his shaky fingers around the decorative hilt smothered with Raed's blood. As soon as he strengthened his grip around the Sword of Kings, all Osiris's power erupted from the blade in whirling auras of energy. A strange sensation coursed through his veins and over his skin, like he had simultaneously caught ablaze and plunged into an icy river. He grunted in agony as the essence of his ancestor fused with every fiber of his being.

A dark fluid leaked from the jewel in the guard of the sword and crawled up his hand. Matticus flinched as it constricted him after penetrating the armor on his forearm and wrapping itself around his wrist. Like a thousand tiny needles, the fluid seeped into his skin. Osiris's holy spirit intertwined with his soul and nearly caused him to faint. Matticus fell to one knee as he couldn't withstand the transfusion, holding himself up with a clenched fist around the hilt of the golden sword. As the fluid moved across his body, an excruciating pain overtook him as if someone had pressed a heated branding iron against his side. Matticus sent a staggered shout echoing across the courtyard. However, when the pain receded, he regained his strength, stood to his feet, and glanced at the split in his armor on his lower torso. To his amazement, his hemorrhaging wound had healed, washed away like sand on a rock by ocean waves.

Matticus stared in awe. Shortly after, the fluid spread toward his shoulders and reached the strands of burnt flesh just below his left deltoid. Tracing the outline of what his left arm used to be, a mass of red energy crawled out from under his charred skin and rebuilt his appendage in the form of a solid beam of light. A wicked smile broke out on his face. He had finally found the power he so desperately chased. The corruption infesting his mind doubled, sending him further down the path of madness. His ambition for a conquered Osiria soared to new levels, and a new vision of blood and bodies consumed his thoughts. Taking over Voluutia wasn't enough anymore—he wanted the world.

He held his new hand up in front of his face and watched the crimson aura remake his fingers. Matticus tested his strength and senses, opening and closing his fist and wriggling his ghostly fingers. Nothing stood in his way to domination. Paired with the might of *Osirisigniros*, his fury knew no bounds.

King Matticus drew in a full breath, charging the power coursing through his body, and held it with closed eyes. After a moment, he released in a gasp as a massive wave of energy shook his body and scattered away from him in all directions.

The Voluutian landscape burned with the flames of Matticus's hatred, and the Hostellian Empire grew one step closer to completion.

Chapter 21

Black Beaches

Day 4 in the Month of Rain

The Leviathan erupted from the portal in the Cradle and bobbed up and down until it found equilibrium atop the sea. Huge waves of salty mist coated the entire ship from the sides, and Lucien his squinted eyes to clear them of water.

Silent and calm, the ocean reflected a faint white light from all directions. Lucien looked up above, but he found no trace of the sun or any celestial body. Though the skies mimicked the blue hue painted above his kingdom, he knew he trekked in a different world. Something about his surroundings unsettled him, like it didn't quite match in a way he couldn't explain. As the ship sailed across the glassy waters, Lucien stepped over to the portside and scanned for any type of landmark. He heard and saw nothing, not even a breeze.

"This is a strange place," he said.

Appearing like ghosts, a massive cloud of white fog crept over the horizon. Lucien studied it intently and made his way down the stairs to the lower deck where the sailors worked back and forth under Captain Vederosa's orders. The white cloud neared; Lucien's gaze started to pierce through.

"Shore!" said a sailor up on the top mast cried out.

The prince leapt up onto the railing and held himself by the rope of the pilot ladder. A great shadow emerged through the cloud, casting a haze over a giant landmass in the distance. All the sailors rushed to the bow of the ship beside him.

Lucien stood firm; his eyes took in a marvelous sight of a vast island shattering the flat surface of the deep ocean. A towering peak centered the island and speared over the scaling landscape. Below, Lucien's eyes traced down the cliff sides to the treeline where fields of green that resembled moss on rock covered the rocky base down to the beaches. Crashing waves met dark shores in soft embraces, flocks of birds soared above the mountaintops, and the swaying canopies of the vast forest gave life to the island.

Scanning the perfectly clear water of the sea, Lucien caught a glimpse of the colorful reefs and sandy ocean floor. He had never seen such a sight before. He fancied it and watched the schools of fish swim about as the wooden hull of The Leviathan delved through the shallow tides.

"Bring in the sails!" Captain Vederosa shouted behind him.

The great ship slowed to a crawl and turned with its port side facing the island. It sailed parallel to the coastline as Lucien remained in a trance with eyes locked onto the paradise in front of him. Pure, clean, and perfect, the island upheld its reputation as a home of the gods. The dual anchors plunged into the shallows, and Lucien dropped down from his position and walked toward the middle of the deck.

"We're here," Caedus said. "I hope."

"This is the right place," Lucien said. "Though, for some reason, that doesn't make me feel much better."

Several of the pirates gathered near the edge of the ship as the prince peered over his shoulder. The unease in their expressions unsettled him.

"Gather your belongings, boys," King Atlas said as he walked by. "We've gods to meet."

Lucien secured his pack on his shoulder, feeling for his brother's letter in his tunic pocket and his sword fastened to his belt. Atlas's soldiers loaded into a longboat after their king, and the captains of Anzagaar Nostir climbed into another. The prince paused and looked around. He met eyes with the sailors nearby as they seemed to be in no hurry to vacate the ship. Captain Vederosa descended from her perch and walked toward him.

"You're staying?" Lucien asked.

Vederosa wiped a strand of red hair out of her face.

"My sailors are," she said, placing a hand on her hip. "I am not."

Lucien watched Caedus step into the second longboat after Commander Ursa and then shifted his attention to the island behind.

"I made an oath with my king to see this journey to its completion," Vederosa said.

"So, you're coming solely to fulfill an oath sworn to your king?" Lucien said. "There's no part of you, a revered captain of the high seas, that's curious about the adventure or danger that lies beyond the beach?"

"Perhaps ... but someone needs to make sure no one fucks this up."

Lucien raised an eyebrow.

"You've no faith in me?"

She turned and gave him a sullen look.

"I've no faith in anyone."

Daunted, the prince stood there on the deck for a moment. He proceeded to the boat with caution, wondering what the captain had experienced in her past to force that level of distrust in the world.

"My prince," a voice said behind him.

Lucien turned to see his old friend standing nearby.

"Thancred, are you joining us? The longboat is about to depart."

"I'm afraid not. This island is no place for my old bones. I will remain here with the crew and the ship."

A smile cracked in Lucien's expression. For a moment, the thought that Thancred had reached the age where he couldn't travel with him on his adventures saddened him. He knew the old man had earned his rest, though, and grinned, nonetheless.

"I'll be back soon," Lucien said. "With Zededia."

"I know you will. May the gods favor your journey, Lucien Osiris. Bring peace back to this world."

Giving his friend a sincere look, Lucien climbed over the railing onto the longboat, took his place next to Caedus, and glanced at Vederosa's fierce yet beautiful eyes. The boat dropped into the ocean; Aeladaecia awaited.

One longboat full of Atlas and his guards sliced through the shallows next to Lucien's with the soldiers of the Legonae and Captain Vederosa. He looked over Caedus's shoulder at the mystical island in the distance. A deep hum vibrated in his bones as he neared one of the many realms of the gods. His anxiety increased, feeling his destiny inching over the horizon.

When both parties landed on the shores, Prince Lucien hopped out onto the loose soil with watchful eyes. He looked down and observed the black beach that swallowed his boots as he sank into the earth. Trudging over the damp ground, he noticed Caedus kneeling to his right as he sifted the sand through his fingers and slowly floated back down like feathers.

"Strange," Caedus said.

Lucien frowned. Further down the shore, he noticed that a section of the beach shifted against the rest like a river flowing downhill.

"I think it's safe to say we're a long way from home," he said.

The prince progressed toward the treeline as members of his cohort readied themselves on the edge of the beach. Ursa, Ammon, Seether, Redding, and Caedus all followed him in a line, and Captain Vederosa walked beside him and matched his stride. Lucien glanced at her from the corner of his eye and traced her jawline down to her strong chin.

"So, Osirian," Vederosa said. "What's your plan after we resurrect your brother?"

Lucien thought hard on her question and allowed his eyes to trail off. He hadn't really given much attention to that up to this point.

"Bring him home," he said. "Let him fight."

"What makes you think he'll fight Matticus a second time?"

"Hmph," Lucien said with a smirk. "More like the thousandth time."

Crunching sand under his boots replaced the pauses in his thoughts.

"And, uh ..., where there is one, the other will follow. Or so my father put it."

"What did he mean by that?" Vederosa asked.

Lucien released a deep exhale.

"My brothers have been locked in a feud for years, for most of their militaristic careers. Both rose to prestigious ranks in Hostellus's armies, Matticus as the *Soll Minoros*, or Second King, who acted as the chief of all generals when my father was away, and Zededia as the Commander of the Black Legion, the most elite fighting force Osiria has ever seen. Often, Zededia disobeyed or altered the commands given to him by Matticus, but his results on the battlefield saved him from treason on almost every occasion."

"Almost?"

Lucien's expression became joyless as he remembered what Thancred had told him about the northern raiders. He blotted out his brother annihilating the region of Konkour, the darkness of that winter bringing back the memories of when his family fully fell apart.

"There was, uh, there was one time when Zededia ... went too far."

He paused, feeling Vederosa's eyes boring a hole in the side of his face.

"And? Are you going to tell me what happened?"

The prince's joyless expression brightened to a grin as he shoved those memories back in the bottle they lived in.

"Maybe one day."

The crashing waves behind faded in his ears as the wooded terrain cast a gloomy shadow over the party. Lucien stood at the edge of the treeline and studied it. No clear path presented itself. Only a dense jungle lay ahead.

"Where to, Your Majesty?" Captain Vederosa asked.

"There should be ... a road here ... somewhere," King Atlas said, walking up to the prince with his ancient tome in hand.

Lucien relied on Atlas's translations to lead them in the right direction. So far, he had no reason to distrust him.

He scanned the thickness of the jungle in search of the right way to go. Something about the strange looking forest caused his skin to crawl. Flora he had never seen before wrapped around each other in twisted knots, vines slowly slithered like snakes, and the old wood of trees groaned as they swayed. Lucien took a step forward, the sense of caution in the back of his mind pulling him back. Just as the prince's foot touched the shadowed ground, the plant life near him curled back to reveal a paved road. Lucien squinted as a ray of light shined through the opening in the canopy. While the rest of his party gathered behind him, he traced the path to a pile of fallen stones that reminded him of the precisely cut marble architecture of his home. The stones came to life soon enough, rising from the ground with no aid or explanation. Amazed,

Lucien allowed his mouth to fall agape. The marble segments slid together and fit perfectly against one another to form an archway high enough for the tallest man alive to walk under. Runes from an era long before his time in the sides of the stones lit with a light blue hue.

"If that's not an invitation," King Atlas said. "I don't know what would be."

The Daecian king stepped in front of him and marched forth. The others followed, leaving him there to ponder who had sent the aforesaid invitation. Stories of the spiritual lands beyond his world had entertained him greatly as a child, but he never imagined he'd observe their mystic nature in person. The wonders of Aeladaecia entranced him completely, and he had barely stepped foot off the beach. He barely noticed that Vederosa had pressed herself against his arm as the archway constructed itself in the distance, but he quickly missed her presence once she pulled away.

"We had best make haste, Lucien," Caedus said, urging him onward. "I'd prefer not to wander an unknown land in the dark."

Prince Lucien proceeded over the stone road while keeping a keen eye on the dense forest closing in on both sides. As he walked, twigs snapped, and he looked behind to see that the vines had retaken the open space and cut him off from the shore, the ship, and an any means of an escape.

Flowing streams of water soothed his ears as the suffocating forest shifted to the paradise he had seen in his vision. Rows of towering trees coated with thick, smooth layers of bark stretched their branches out far and wide. Plump, enriched pieces of fruit dangled from their blooms and tempted him for a taste to wet his dried lips. The light above reflected off them and caused them to twinkle. Lucien walked under the marble arch and eyed the runes on the sides before heading deeper into the jungle.

After the party traversed the natural utopia of Aeladaecia for half an hour, booming, heavy footfalls shook the ground shortly after. The prince darted his attention in their direction, and the rest of the party drew their arms in preparation. Out from the darkness of the forest, a pair of jagged antlers speared through the trees atop a massive head that hosted two glowing green eyes. It resembled a man from its midsection upward and a horse from the waist down as it balanced itself on four thundering hooves. Lucien, eyes wide with panic, noticed that the beast's entire body was made of wood and vines, as if it were a walking tree. The creature stepped forward after pushing the branches out of its face, cracking them with ease. Though it easily stood taller than three of him, it stared at Lucien without presenting any hostility. The prince eased the tension in his shoulders as he watched Atlas lower his weapon.

"By the gods," Atlas said. "A Haellusette."

The beast raised its left arm, wriggled its fingers around the shaft of a wooden scythe, and rested the heel against the ground.

"A what?" Lucien asked, eyes glued to the massive beast.

"Sentinels of the forest ...," Atlas said as he motioned for everyone to sheathe their swords. "Ancient spawns of Haellus, god of nature and harvest."

Another Haellusette pushed its way through the vines on the opposite side of the path; Lucien turned his head to study it.

"Come," Atlas said.

Lucien followed the rest of his party while King Atlas remained to escort them by the elder spirits in their presence.

"They've allowed us safe passage," Atlas said as Lucien walked by.

"And that's a status that will remain?"

"Yes. Just don't bloody touch anything."

Lucien met eyes with one of the Haellusettes, and it gave him a stern gaze from a mouthless face. Careful of his footsteps, Lucien progressed along the stone road until the great beasts faded from view behind him. The forest thickened, but a clear path remained. Songs of whistling birds echoed through the swaying branches and dancing leaves. Occasionally, small creatures skittered across the gap and looked as unfamiliar as the foreign giants he had just encountered.

"Why the hell does everything look so ... different?" Lucien asked.

He met Atlas's turned gaze a few feet ahead of him.

"Aeladaecia is home to all things made by the gods," King Atlas said. "I've read countless stories about this place ... it's even stranger than the texts led me to believe. Everything that hasn't spread to our world ... remains here."

"Hmm."

After scaling a small hill, Prince Lucien and the rest of his company stepped into a clearing in the forest. Toppled columns lined the outskirts of the stone floor that resembled the base of a ceremonial structure at one point in time. Atlas's men dispersed while Lucien wandered over to a large pond to the left where he heard a running spring. When the prince stood along the bank, though, he frowned. The ripples collapsed toward the spring instead of the edge of the pond, and when Lucien followed their direction, he noticed that the waterfall flowed against gravity in reverse. Droplets broke free from the rising stream and floated upward until they bounced off the undersides of the leaves on the overlooking trees.

"Remarkable ...," Lucien said.

The light shining overhead dimmed, though it didn't fade near the horizon like a usual sunset. The prince looked around and saw that everyone had started to settle down for a moment to refresh. Atlas approached him.

"This may a good a spot as any to rest," the Daecian king said. "What do you think?"

A deep exhale left his nostrils. Lucien scanned the dense jungle around and the trees that provided an acceptable barrier around the clearing.

"I suppose. Do you have any sense of how close we are to where we need to be?" he asked.

Atlas shook his head at him.

"I'm afraid not," he said. "The legend of Osiris's ascension didn't exactly come with a guidebook. Even the tome I have that describes it is vaguer than anything I've ever read."

"Have you deciphered anything about where we are now?"

"Not really. 'The acolytes walked the path of silver stones through the vastness of Aeladaecia,'" Atlas said, reading from the marked section of the tome. "'They entered the cave of Nazkala and Abbendae to perform the ascension for the Holy Uniter.' And that's as far as I've gotten."

"Well, I don't see a cave of any sort nearby. Maybe once we get closer to the mountain."

"Agreed."

Lucien sank his teeth into his lower lip. Glancing up at the mountain peak that jutted above the trees, he knew that was where he needed to go. He felt Neshka's presence in his heart trying to steer him in the right direction.

Everyone around him started to unpack their belongings, and he saw Caedus and the other officers of the Legonae attempting to start a fire.

The prince walked over, grabbed a hefty stone from the ruins of the columns, and placed it near the hearth. Darkness overtook the land far quicker than he had expected or was accustomed to. The strikes from the flint in Caedus's hand echoed in his ears, and Lucien took a seat and looked around the camp. He saw Atlas and his soldiers who pitched a tent for their king on the other side of the clearing. Alone and distant from the others, Vederosa lured his attention. For the first time on the journey, he realized that his party had outnumbered hers in a great amount. The fierce sea captain kept her gaze hidden by her cascading hair, but he caught a glimpse of her face through the silky red strands. She paused as he locked eyes with her while sitting on the bank of a small pond next to the clearing. Lucien noticed her cold expression and guessed she felt more like an outlier than a member of the company. With a half-grin, the prince nodded at the low fire, beckoning her to come and join in. However, she rejected his invitation by turning her focus back to her pack. The prince's grin faded in disappointment.

Atlas and the captains of the Legonae started to converse with one another, trading stories and their thoughts of the journey so far. Lucien overheard Caedus ask about the next step in the plan. He, too, wondered where the path ahead lay. His focus pulled his eyes back to Vederosa shortly after. She chose to conceal herself from everyone else. The bare skin of her pale shoulders appeared soft and smooth in the gaps of her cloth shirt after she gathered her hair on one side of her head. Lucien looked back at the men near him to ensure they were occupied. He then quietly stood to his feet.

The prince's footfalls echoed across the stone clearing in the dead of night. Bright, luminescent lights of the forest of Aeladaecia twinkled all around. As he approached, the corner of Vederosa's eye gleamed at him. The rough, rigid exterior he had first seen on the docks of Skulpos crumbled away. Lucien sensed a deep pain in her, one that hit rather close to home.

"You don't have to isolate yourself," he said, stopping a foot behind Vederosa's hunched position.

Silence followed.

"You're welcome to join—"

"I'm fine where I am, thank you," Vederosa sharply said.

Lucien braved her harsh words, holding his ground.

"You belong over there. With your people."

A deep breath escaped him. Lucien took a few steps forward and gazed into the pond in front of Vederosa. The glassy water mirrored the expression she allowed to rise in the moment of peace, giving him a glimpse of the saddened eyes that replaced the fierce aura she usually presented. Slowly, the prince sat down on the bank next to her. She kept her face hidden, tilting her head slightly down to drape her red hair across her cheek like a curtain.

"And where do you belong?" Lucien asked.

He lost sight of her reflection once he was on the ground, but he looked at her at eye level.

"Nowhere."

"What makes you think that?"

Vederosa lifted her chin, revealing the tip of her short, button nose.

"The seas have been my watchers for twenty years. I haven't had a stable place to call home in all that time. Just my ship. Every time I set foot on land I ... it doesn't seem right. I've just been running, regardless of how much I don't want to admit it."

"Running from what?"

"I don't know," Vederosa said. "My father sold our home in Skulpos when I was four. We became fishermen then. Made the most sense as there's no shortage of work in that industry."

Lucien tried to connect the dots in her family tree, thinking back to what she had told him in the tavern in Talluna.

"How did your brother make it to Ehthilia?"

She sighed.

"He volunteered to aid them in handling the bandit lords that revolted. That was years ago now, I barely remember his face. And ... I doubt I'll see it again."

Lucien's thoughts wandered to his memories of Zededia. Hearing Vederosa talk of the distance from her family forced him to realize how separated he was from his own. The wound of his brother's death reopened, the optimistic smile on the prince's face fading.

"It's funny," Lucien said. "The only thing I see when I close my eyes ... is Zededia's face."

The forest murmured. Old, ancient species of trees creaked and swayed.

"I never thought my days without him would come so soon," he said with a slight scoff. "I was grossly unprepared."

"You're going through an awful lot to bring him back."

The prince grinned.

"There isn't a thing in this world I wouldn't do for him."

"Your love for your brother runs that deep?"

Lucien paused. He studied the pond, noticing its clarity as his sight adjusted. His eyelids faintly trembled.

"He was my hero," he said as his throat tightened. "I looked up to him more than anyone else. My father and Matticus were idols as well, but they didn't ... see me ... like Zededia did. He always watched over me. Always steered me right. Always had my back."

A soft chuckle rose unexpectedly as a particular memory came to mind.

"One time, when we were young, I found myself in quite a bit of trouble with the older boys training to be soldiers. They cornered me and showed a great deal of hostility. I think they were just jealous I was royalty. Anyway, Zededia stepped in at the last moment and defended me."

The prince slipped into a trance as he tried to keep a grasp on the scene from his youth, picturing himself feet away from his brother and the Vaedorian trainees.

"They beat the shit out of him," Lucien said, turning the chuckle into a healthy laugh. "He was a great fighter, but he weighed probably half of one of those boys. I went running to my father after that, thinking he would send out a wrath worthy of the gods. When I told him what happened, though, he scoffed with a grin. He was proud of Zededia, but he told me I need to learn to fight my own battles."

Lucien returned his gaze to Vederosa, who remained slouched with arms over her knees. Struggling to determine if his anecdote had helped ease her pain, the prince kept his mouth shut. He received his answer shortly after, however, as Vederosa shifted and inched closer to him until her shoulder touched his. A warm rush rose in his chest. She still closed herself off in every other way, but he had a foot in the door.

"You belong right where you are," Lucien said. "Right here with me."

"And where are we, Osirian?"

The prince took a deep breath.

"At the edge of the world. Fighting for what good is left in it."

"You still think there's good to find here? After everything your family has been through?"

He thought back to motivation his old friend had given him after finding him in the run-down village in Merrinine. Thancred's advice had never failed to pull him from the depths of depression. Lucien looked up to the sky and admired the luminescent canopies that twinkled in his green eyes.

"Always."

Out of the corner of his vision, he noticed Vederosa turn her head and gleam her wide eyes at him. He met her gaze with a sincere expression. The calm atmosphere of the mystical forest lulled Lucien into a romantic mood, and Captain Vederosa leaned her head down on the top of his shoulder. The prince felt a joyful flutter in his stomach. Looking out to the faint lights of Aeladaecia, Lucien savored the connection he made with the woman who captured his heart from day one.

~ ~ ~

Around the campfire the Legonae soldiers had lit in the clearing, Caedus glanced over his shoulder at Lucien and Vederosa sharing a tender moment. The captain nodded with a faint smirk, proud of the prince's efforts to crack the enigma of her callous nature. He then looked back to the fire near his feet. Dancing sparks erupted from the flames and died on the cold stone ground. Caedus couldn't help but think over his journey to the Temple of Osiris with the fair woman he traveled with. Raeza's soft skin and playful embrace teased him in his memories. He wondered if she had made it out of Osiria, if she had started a new life for herself. The agony of releasing her from his presence stung him. As he thought, his eyes wandered and fell out of focus.

"Caedus," Commander Ursa said, breaking his train of thought.

Caedus raised his head.

"Hmm?"

He studied Ursa's awkward expression and waited through the hesitant pause.

"You ... you never told us what happened. After you vanished."

The other captains of the Legonae turned their eyes to him. Caedus took a moment to collect himself.

"There's not much to say. Commander Zededia gave me an order."

"To protect the Sword of Kings?" Captain Redding asked.

Caedus nodded.

"Why not tell anyone of his order?" Captain Seether asked.

Fearing this conversation would arrive at some point, Caedus knew he had to play his hand carefully.

"The fewer who knew of my location, the better chance I had at hiding. Keeping *Osirisigniros* out of Matticus's grasp was more important than anything else. Not that that turned out so well as I was forced to relinquish it to the Merrins."

"How were you able to slip through Hostellus so easily? The Hostellae patrol nearly every inch of land outside Anzagaar Nostir's reach."

Caedus glanced down to the trail of black mist seeping out from sleeve. He thought back to the numerous occasions where Osinian had used his godly abilities to teleport, shift, and blink him past any guards he came across.

"I ... met a few friends."

"Well, whoever they are, they did the trick," Ursa said. "The entire Order went looking for you. Atlas himself nearly joined the search had the Meeting of Sons not been summoned."

"I was where I needed to be," Caedus said. "That's all that matters."

The conversation died off as the Legonae soldiers made themselves comfortable for sleep. Caedus shifted against the hard ground, used to having to find a bed in the most uncomfortable of places. Captain Seether then stood from the circle and walked over near him, and Caedus glanced over. The fearsome longbowman remained quiet as he took a seat on the ground. Caedus had grown accustomed to Seether's peculiar personality ... or lack thereof. Though sealed off from most, including the other captains, Seether had become a great friend of his.

Caedus raised an eyebrow. Seether's dark yellow eyes studied his arm, and he held out an open hand after understanding the silent request. Caedus watched as his friend traced the lines of his palm with his fingers, following the faint wisp of black mist.

"You are ... tethered to this being," Seether said from behind the wrap covering his face. "A shade. How is this possible?"

Reluctant, Caedus closed his fist and pulled it back.

"When Commander Osiris died," he said, "his bond with Osinian passed to me. And if he returns—"

"*When* he returns," Seether said, correcting him.

"Yes," Caedus said slowly. "*When* he returns ... well, I'm unsure what will happen. Zededia brought it back with him from Elysia—a king of old just after Osiris's passing. Almost as menacing as you."

"Can you understand him?" Seether asked.

"Vaguely. I'm understanding more every day."

"What possessed you to try and learn that crude language?"

Caedus lightly scoffed.

"Two months on the road alone with a being that hardly speaks any Eldish provides ample motivation."

The cloaked captain slowly nodded, and Caedus grew tired from the journey.

"You should get some sleep," he said. "Who knows what tomorrow has in store for us."

Seether rose to his feet and walked over near the edge of the woods. Caedus watched the longbowman take a post next to a ruined stone wall. With Seether's keen sight on lookout, he gained the strongest sense of safety he had felt since his departure from Hostellus.

Leaning back on the rock that propped him up, Caedus slowly closed his eyes. He took a deep breath, quieted his thoughts, and fell asleep.

Two hours passed, but the darkness of night remained as thick as ever as Caedus stirred awake. He glanced around with hazy eyes and noticed that Seether hadn't left his position against the section of stone. Caedus pushed himself upright and looked across the clearing. Everyone laid still in their slumber.

Caedus shook off his lingering exhaustion by wiping his face, stood up, and carefully stepped through the gaps of the sleeping men. The foreign calls of Aeladaecia's creatures hiding deep in the denseness of the trees haunted him.

"I'll take watch," he said to Seether as he approached.

"This forest makes strange noises."

Stopping once adjacent to him, Caedus crossed his arms.

"So I've noticed," he said. "I'll be glad to get out of here if I'm being honest."

As Seether started to turn in his sideview, a ghastly hum boomed through the trees, causing their branches to shake. The noise mimicked that of a massive whale singing through vast, empty oceans. Caedus focused intently, scanning for any movement. A higher pitched screech chirped in short bursts in response.

"What the hell is that?" Seether asked.

Caedus darted his eyes back and forth.

"I don't know."

He scoured the treeline just yards away. The shadows and faint lights between the tree branches confused him. However, when he stumbled upon a particularly dark gap directly in front of him, two of the specks of light floated toward each other, turned bright white, and squinted. Something's eyes fell upon him. Fear chilled his spine.

Out of the blackness, a creature burst forth. Howling, it leapt through the air and crashed right in front of Caedus. The captain tumbled backward, and Seether helped him back to his feet. Glaring in shock, he saw a four-legged beast snarling at him with a featureless face except a gaping mouth revealing several rows of teeth. A thick shell covered its entire body like an exoskeleton. Powerful forearms and a hulking torso crept forward. In shock, Caedus retreated. The other members of the party jumped from their sleep during the commotion.

"Protect the king!" a Daecian soldier yelled.

Caedus back peddled and drew his sword. Lucien and Vederosa joined the group to his right. The beast halted just outside the clearing, sinking its sharp talons in the earth. Another being emerged from the woods, the same being that first glared at Caedus with sinister white eyes. It walked like man but looked akin to the first creature with shiny, gray skin. The humanoid smiled at him with an evil grin. Others rushed out from the shadows, each holding crude, misshapen weapons, and formed a perimeter around the clearing. They inched closer, forcing Caedus and his allies to group up and surrender precious ground. He had never seen such an enemy before, but that didn't intimidate the weathered captain of the Legonae.

"Stay together," Atlas said. "We're outnumbered."

A light chuckle hummed from Caedus's closed mouth.

"We've been fighting the Vaedorians for years," he said. "We're always outnumbered."

The tension shattered in that moment as the assumed leader of the humanoid crab men pointed at Caedus and roared, signaling the rest of his kin to charge. Readying himself for a fight, Caedus widened his base and strengthened his hold of his sword. The eyeless behemoth pounded its way across the stone clearing, crashing through the low stone wall with its shoulder. Everyone around clashed in combat, and Caedus sidestepped the beast's advance and slashed at the soft spots in its armor. The twinkling light from the stars above illuminated the shell, but the joints remained dark and nonreflective, giving him a clear target to strike. Caedus aimed his next attack at the crease in its elbow, spilling dark purple blood on the ground. The beast howled in pain and limped around.

Before Caedus could attack again, it turned in a fit rage and pounced on one of Atlas's men. The beast ripped through the metal armor of the Daecian in savage, frenzied bites. Blood splattered the clearing, and Caedus watched it thrash its prey from side to side like a dog would a rabbit. Bones cracked and body torn open, the Daecian slipped out of its mouth and slopped onto the ground. Caedus traced its sight to King Atlas battling with one of the crab men and bolted to save him. Caedus jumped onto the beast's back, slipping on its smooth exterior, and eventually hoisted himself up to straddle it. Bucking with ferocity, the creature tried to throw him off. Caedus took a firm hold of the edge of the shell that covered its back and flipped his sword in reverse grip. With a swift strike, he plunged his sharp steel into the exposed flesh of its nape until the tip tore out through the bottom side of its throat.

The beast trembled, choking on its own blood, and crashed to the ground. Caedus then plucked his sword free and assessed the situation. Many of island's inhabitants lay dead across the clearing, but, one by one, Atlas's guards met their end, weakening the defensive barrier around the king. Caedus ran over to him to form a plan of action.

"Can't you do anything to stop this?" he shouted. "You're a bloody god to these people!"

"I've tried!" Atlas yelled in return. "My sorceries are of no use here! I can't conjure anything!"

"Shit," Caedus said under his breath.

He glanced around for a solution to come about, but more shelled enemies appeared behind their master at the treeline. Prince Lucien and Vederosa fought off their attackers together separated from the others. Caedus quickly understood they didn't need any help and elected to focus on the other captains. Ammon forfeited his weapon and resorted to strength, tearing the limbs of his opponents like sticks off a tree. Everyone else held their ground as well thanks to a few well-placed arrows from the snap of Seether's longbow. The humanoids outnumbered them still, showing no sign of an end to their ranks. Caedus dispatched one and tossed it over his shoulder, but another took its place and reengaged.

We need to break through their perimeter, he thought. *We can lose them in the trees.*

Suddenly, the earth shook with a chilling roar much deeper than the one he heard before. The crab men stopped in their tracks and turned their attention to the source of the rumble. Atlas approached behind while still on alert.

"That doesn't sound good," the Daecian king said. "That sounds like a much bigger problem."

"That sounds like a much bigger problem," the Daecian king said.

"If these bastards fear it," Caedus said between rapid breaths, "I think we should be, too."

Trees snapped in the distance. Booming footsteps shook the island. The humanoids forgot all about Caedus and the others around him, fleeing for their lives.

"What in the world is that?" Lucien asked as he jogged up to him.

Another thundering footfall sounded off.

"I don't exactly want to be here to find out," Caedus said, starting to run away.

Caedus ushered the Legonae captains to the woods. Atlas and his remaining men tailed shortly behind. As Caedus jogged to the tree line, Lucien and Vederosa passed him. He paused, though, hearing a faint chittering from the clearing. Resting his hand against a tree, he peered back to see one of the humanoids staggering to its feet. An eerie silence arrived as the creature limped toward him.

A flash of teeth sprang into view from above, a massive jaw clamping around the crab man and cracking its shell in an instant. Caedus jolted in his skin. Larger than any living thing he had ever seen, the monster in the clearing sparked a primal sense of fear he didn't know he had. Caedus sprinted through the mountainous forest of Aeladaecia, his party members a good distance ahead of him. Some of the crab men ran about as well. He gave little care to them, though, knowing a much graver enemy pursued him close behind. The footsteps quickened in pace; the monster caught onto his trail.

Short, sporadic breaths pounded out of Caedus's lungs as he ran. He lost sight of Lucien and Atlas, hopefully because they remained far enough away to be safe. Another staggering roar erupted. Caedus found himself sprinting next to one of the humanoids, and he flinched in surprise as it swung its shoddy spear at him. The captain caught the sharp end of it on his outer thigh and yelled. Crippled enough to become the slowest prey of the pursuing beast, Caedus had only one option.

He removed a dagger from the small sheath in his boot, held it by the blade, and hurled it through the air as he limped for dear life. A soft crack followed by a flurry of chitters sang out from the crab man running in front of him, and it stammered, clawed at its back, and twirled around in circles. Caedus rammed his shoulder into the creature, knocking it to the forest floor. The sharp pain in his leg hindered his retreat and forced him to stop behind a tree. Leaning against the wide trunk, he held his hands around his leg and felt a trickle of warm blood soak his fingers.

Another soddin' injury, he thought. *And Atlas can't fix this one.*

Caedus pressed to try and stop the bleeding to no avail. He gritted his teeth and let the back of his head hit the tree. The titanic monster closed in with a guttural growl. Hesitantly glancing around the tree, he saw the crab man crawling away on the ground.

For a moment, he regretted wounding it. The sentiment vanished in a heartbeat, though, as a talon-like appendage broke through the canopy of the forest and skewered it in the torso. Caedus swallowed his mouthful of spit in absolute terror. More talons stabbed the earth all around him, and Caedus realized whatever monster rose above the trees walked on six legs, each capped with a spike that resembled teeth of a giant. The leviathan hissed like a reptile, its outline barely visible through the shaking branches under the starlight. It searched for him. The fresh blood seeping through his pants gave off a potent scent.

As the giant predator lowered its head to find him, he heard it sniff around. Caedus quieted his panicked breathing, praying to whoever could hear him for a savior.

Suddenly, someone answered his prayers. A burst of white light exploded in the air above the forest. Nearly blinding Caedus in the process, the distraction burned bright enough to damage the beast's eyes. A new wave of confusion flooded Caedus's thoughts. More explosions lit up the sky a few seconds later, and the monster roared in defiance before withdrawing from the scene. A figure scurried between the trees toward him. Caedus held his sword up to defend himself, but he felt more confusion than anything as he observed the strange being. Dressed in loose rags, it knelt in front of him and held out a two-fingered hand.

"Come! Quickly!" it said. "Before she comes back!"

Chapter 22

Locals

Day 4 in the Month of Rain

With a slew of questions running through him but no time to answer them, Caedus reached out and took the hand of his alleged rescuer. His palm gripped cold, damp flesh almost like clay. The two-fingered figure heaved him up to his feet and ushered him on. A hood covered the being's head attached to an assortment of rags it used as clothes to wrap itself in. Caedus limped as fast as he could, the deep gash on his outer thigh searing with pain.

"Your friends are ahead," the figure said on the move. "You'll be safe in Hoslentos."

Wondering what the hell was going on, Caedus traversed over the flattened part of the forest. The trees, massive and towering, spread far out from each other, wide enough for a standard road to fit between them. Their roots dug deep into the earth and hid under the hard topsoil. As Caedus frantically ran to wherever his cloaked guide led him, he occasionally looked up to see their branches twisting and moving much like arms as if they were sentient. Aeladaecia provided ample mysteries that challenged the laws of nature Caedus had become used to.

A minute later, the figure slowed to a stop, and Caedus bent over on his knees to catch his breath. He leaned up, panted, observed a worn-down trench lining the ground from left to right.

"All right, the Naaklings won't follow us beyond this point," the being said. "Neither will she."

"Who is *she*?" Caedus asked between breaths.

His guide turned to reveal two glowing blue eyes misaligned with each other on either side of a wide, flat nose.

"Phae'Raxya."

Caedus studied the stranger, noticing the odd complexion of its skin. He quickly deduced that it was made of earth, not of the same flesh as him.

"We call her 'The Devourer.' Very nasty creature. Eats anything she can catch. When the Architects made her, all races went into hiding, the Naaklings included."

"The Architects? What the sod are you talking about?"

"Come," the guide said with grin. "You've much to learn."

Caedus's guide continued to lead him across the island where he hoped the familiar faces waited for him. He walked through the trees, on alert as ever as his paranoia told him that creature meant to lead him into an ambush like some sick game. Several minutes later, faint blue lights caught his attention through the dense foliage. As he walked closer, he saw Prince Lucien's unmistakable green eyes.

"Caedus!" Lucien said with great excitement.

The prince stepped forth and embraced him.

"We feared you had fallen," Lucien said as he leaned away.

"The gods aren't through with me yet, apparently."

Caedus saw King Atlas over Lucien's shoulder along with the rest of his allies. Around them, several beings akin to the one that had saved them stood by.

"It seems we found the locals," Atlas said.

Turning around to his savior, Caedus took a better look. His eyes hadn't deceived him before; a face made of clay grinned back at him.

"The prime specimen has returned at last," the clay man said.

Caedus raised an eyebrow.

The what?

"What? Just who are you, exactly?" he asked.

"My name is Tog," he said. "I am one of the *Varas Zogad*. These are my family."

As Caedus met the unique, molded faces of the clay people, he noticed a worried frown on Atlas's face after Tog spoke. The Daecian king knew something he didn't. Now wasn't the time to chase his curiosity, though, sensing that whatever information caused an Osirian to have doubts would best be talked over in private.

"Now, let us leave this desolate place," Tog said. "Hoslentos isn't far."

Caedus traced Atlas's skeptical stare to the leader of the clay people as the company started to move with their escort.

"Tozi at os znakas domoane, Caedus. (These are a strange people, Caedus,)" Osinian said in his mind. *"Ag maskos. (Be wary.)"*

The warning flags rose higher than all others, but Caedus felt no need to doubt them just yest, especially after Tog had rescued him from the horror he previously encountered. He followed the path through the open door the island had given him.

An hour passed, and Caedus started to think he had been led around in circles. Each tree appeared the same, the windless, dark aura of the forest making it hard to keep track of his surroundings. Up ahead, a trickle of water broke the silence. Tog and a few of the *Varas* stood at the edge of a cliff basking in the pale light of the moon above. Caedus stepped out from the shade of the branches, walked forward, and nearly gasped at the sight below.

A bright, vibrant river flowed through the valley sourced by a waterfall that poured out of the mountain at his level. Splitting the flowing water into two streams, a small city rested on a rocky isle. Caedus glanced over the decorative stone buildings. Clouds of mist hovered out from the bottom of the waterfall and surrounded the city in a haze, and flocks of winged creatures native to Aeladaecia skittered about. The dim light of the night reflected off the rooftops and gave depth to the streets.

"It's ... marvelous," Lucien said to his left.

"It's more than marvelous," Tog said. "It's our home."

Caedus allowed an astonished half-grin to appear on his face.

"Welcome to Hoslentos."

Tog beckoned for the party to follow; Caedus lingered. A wave of caution kept him in place. In his sideview, Lucien approached.

"Everything all right?"

"Hmm?" Caedus said, turning his head to the prince. "Yeah, I'm fine. Just ... admiring the scenery."

"Something's wrong, isn't it?" Lucien asked. "What is it?"

"I don't know," Caedus said. "But Atlas does."

Feeling Lucien's concerned gaze on him, Caedus glanced off to the clay people taking everyone else to the city below.

"Do you think he'll inform us of what that is?" Lucien asked.

"I'm sure we'll find out one way or another. For now, just stick to the plan ... whatever it is. Let's go."

Caedus caught up to the rest with Lucien beside him. Tailing the pack, he descended the stone ramp built into the side of the cliff toward the waterfall. Sprays of mist caked his skin as he walked by. When the party reached level ground of the isle, the *Varas* were greeted by their loved ones. Smaller figures Caedus assumed to be children ran out to their mothers and fathers. The wholesome encounter touched him.

Limping still, Caedus made his way into the open town center in the middle of the city's buildings. The Legonae captains kept close together next to him. He held his hand over his wound as best he could, the pain becoming visible through the expression on his face. He stopped to take in the full beauty of Hoslentos and everything it entailed.

Homes, storehouses, and marketplaces filled the circular platform on the risen earth between the bisected rivers. Almost like Vaedor Sellos, the light gray stone the *Varas* used to build their town emitted a friendly yet sturdy invitation to foreigners. From what had seen so far, Caedus realized how connected the clay people were with each other. A true sense of community bonded them together. At the heart of the town center, a beam of yellow light pulsed from the ground into the sky before branching out in all directions like leaves of a lily. An aura of protection guarded Hoslentos, and Caedus thought for a moment about what the *Varas* needed protection from. He counted himself lucky to have found possibly the only non-hostile race living on the mystic island of Aeladaecia.

"You are injured," Tog said, approaching him from behind. "Your leg it ... it is leaking?"

Caedus frowned in confusion.

"You mean bleeding?" he said.

"Ah, yes. I forget that humans are filled with soft, squishy flesh, not stone or clay like the *Varas*."

He glared at the clay man.

"We must tend to you," the clay man said. "Our healers are not familiar with your anatomy, but they should be able to stop your ... bleeding."

"My healer is of no use here it seems. But you talk as if you have seen humans before?

"Oh, of course!" Tog said as he signaled for him to head toward a stand alone building on the other side of the courtyard. "We've been waiting for your people to arrive for a thousand years! After all, we were made to serve you."

"Ter nossek ozno dorzga ozi sil cod. (That's not what they were made for,)" Osinian said in the place of his conscious.

Intrigued by the open nature of the *Varas Zogad* people, Caedus set his course for the medical building ahead.

He stepped inside, and several feminine figures greeted him. They took a liking to him, inspecting every inch of his exposed pale skin. Caedus flinched as one of them grazed his wound with her earth fingers.

"Be careful with him," one of them said in an authoritative voice.

She stepped out from the rest and embraced Tog; Caedus still struggled to fully understand his surroundings.

"This is my mate, Holna," Tog said. "She will care for you so you are ready to travel for your journey tomorrow."

"My journey?" Caedus asked.

"Your journey to *Elysimylos*, the Eye of Elysia! That's why you are here, are you not? You seek the cave of Nazkala and Abbendae?"

Caedus played along and nodded after a moment. Two of the *Varas* women helped him into an adjacent chamber to lie down on a cold stone table. The moonlight above shimmered down through a circular opening in the ceiling.

"Forgive us," Holna said. "Our home doesn't contain much comfort for your kind."

"I've been in worse places."

The *Varas* healers waited on him hand and foot, offering sweet wine and massaging his tender muscles. After a few minutes, Caedus lowered his guard and slipped into relaxation.

"Here," Holna said, handing him an alien-like leaf. "Eat this."

The clay woman practically forced it into his mouth. Munching on the succulent plant, Caedus felt a rush of numbness slither down his body and over the nasty cut on his leg. He groaned as the intense agony melted away in seconds. Holna brought forth a blue-ish paste in a bowl and smeared a healthy coat on the laceration.

"This," Holna said as she spread it around further, "is one of our most sacred possessions."

"What is it?" Caedus asked.

"Mother's Clay. The island blesses us with a unique type of earth near the top of the waterfall. It's healing properties are wonderous on its own, but when we mix it with Naakling blood, it can mend the deepest of injuries."

"Naakling blood?" Caedus said. "That-that ... *thing?* That's what bloody cut me in the first place. That's supposed to heal me?"

Holna nodded.

"Brilliant," Caedus said with a sarcastic tone.

Surrendering to the hospitality the clay people had shown him, Caedus closed his eyes and loosened the tenseness in his shoulders. The calm moment allowed him to clear his mind of his racing thoughts. Whatever creatures he had battled in the stone clearing of the forest and the horror that hunted him seared its image into his brain. He tried his best to scrape that memory away, praying he wouldn't ever see something like that again. As he lay on the stone table, he lost a grip on his consciousness. The *Varas* women eased him into a deep sleep with tender caresses, an experience he had well deserved.

~ ~ ~

On the other side of the town, Prince Lucien followed the clay people whom he had met in the forest into a grand manor. Immaculate statues, fountains pouring water toward the ceiling instead of the floor, and tapestries decorated the interior.

"Please, make yourselves as comfortable as you can," one of the *Varas* said. "This is your home as much as it is ours."

Lucien studied the masterfully crafted artwork. The figures in the paintings stuck out to him as ones he recognized. Osiris in all his glowing might stood in the foreground of each of them. A mask with many holes covered his face like he had fifteen eyes spread about from chin to forehead. Wrapped in tight cloth under a flowing tunic, Osiris's body glowed a faint yellow wherever the skin showed. In his grasp, he held *Osirisigniros* as clear as King Raed had back in Voluutia several days ago.

He was here, Lucien thought, finding delight in the fact that he strayed at least somewhat close to the path his ancestor followed.

Whoever these people were, they obviously knew of him and his lineage. Hopefully, they could shed some light on how to perform the ceremony he had set off to complete.

He scanned the room further, and one painting in particular caught the prince's attention. Osiris demonstrated a daunting display of his magic, torching unknown enemies with holy fire from his hand. The singed bodies on the ground unsettled Lucien. He hadn't seen such a powerful image of his ancestor in all his life, simultaneously fueling him with pride and fear. Looking down to his open palm, he weighed the sorcery waiting to be summoned at his fingertips. The prince struggled to resolve the inner conflict storming in his heart. Spymaster Rachtus's slashed neck at the hands of his magic forced him to question his morals or if he could even control them.

Am I capable of such fury? he thought.

"This way, Your Grace," one of the *Varas* said, breaking his line of thought. "The one you call Atlas has asked that we place you as close to him as we can."

Wondering the intentions behind the Daecian king's request, Lucien joined his escort in a luxurious room that easily rivaled the finest chambers of Vaedor Sellos. The clay man vanished in a hurry, leaving Lucien alone behind closed wooden doors. He explored the room, noticing the missing fourth wall opposite the entrance that gave a clear path to the vibrant river. The bank lay a few yards away from the stone platform Hoslentos stood upon. As he neared the edge, he looked down to the soft grass swaying back and forth. Tiny bugs crawled between the blades, luminescent like much of the environment. The blue and green glows bounced off Lucien's pupils. Like a slow, melodic symphony, the flowing water of the river tempted him to take a dip. Dirt and grime covered his body.

Lucien leaned out and looked to his right and left. All was quiet save the calm rush of the stream. Everyone turned in for the night, the lamplights of the city dimmed to darkness, and the murmurs of jovial conversations met their ends. The prince released a deep exhale, taking the opportunity to fully appreciate the comfort of solitude. He missed roaming the streets of Vaedor Sellos like a rogue. A half-grin rose to reveal his white teeth while he revisited those memories, but it fell as soon as he thought of Matticus. Being this far away from the real world in such a strange place nearly made him forget why he was here to begin with. His eldest brother's angered sneer glared at him in his mind. Zededia's lifeless eyes came next. Lucien found no escape from his guilt, even in the middle of the most beautiful part of the most beautiful place he had ever seen. The blissful water of the river called for him evermore to wash away his worries.

Taking a seat next to the steps that emptied into the small grass field, Prince Lucien jostled his boots free from his feet. He lowered his legs until the delicate flora tickled his soles. The earth remained firm under his full weight as he stood. His racing mind calmed, distracted by the serene nature of the river. Soil shifted to sand after a few careful strides. Lucien unfastened the straps on the sides of the thin leather armor he wore to protect his torso, slid it off, and tossed it aside. Next, he pulled his shirt off over his head. The light breeze soothed Lucien's dense, chiseled muscles. Loosening the stiffness in his shoulders and upper back, he neared the water. The bright blue river glowed in a manner he couldn't understand, and its incredible clarity allowed him to see all the way to the bottom. Lucien wriggled his toes in the sand, the damp grains clinging to the hairs on his feet.

After pausing to watch the ripples of the current flow by, Prince Lucien untied the string of his pants. He stepped over near a looming, willow-like tree shading the bank and unclothed himself completely. He then dipped his feet into the river, the cool sensation shooting up his leg. A flash of horror struck him like lightning; the harrowing encounter with the depths of the Orlestian after he tumbled overboard held him hostage.

Lucien persisted, though, easing his fears by convincing himself that no real danger lurked by. Only the refreshing river enchanted by the gods lied in front of him.

Lucien waded against the currents, submerging himself at mid-thigh. He flinched once the water reached his groin. Goosebumps rose across his nape and shoulders, and he dove into the river to acclimate completely.

When he rose, Lucien wiped his hair back, kept his eyes closed, and let the water trickle down his face, over his powerful chest, and between his prominent abdominals. The prince balanced himself in the loose sand, his flawless skin pure and clean of the filth from his journey. Lucien lowered to his knees to let his shoulders sink below the surface. Time ticked by, but he lost track as he focused entirely on allowing his mind and body to ease away from the harshness they had been exposed to over the week prior.

Fifteen minutes of isolation in the stream drowned his worries and gave him clarity. Taking one last look at the scenery, Lucien panned over to the towering waterfall that poured into the river and then to the bank on the other side lined with beautiful flowers.

Exhaustion set in after his depleted muscles finally had the chance to recover. Though used to the chill of the river, Lucien longed for the warmth of the bed waiting for him in his chambers. Nothing sounded finer than surrendering to the comfort of soft fabrics and a feather pillow.

Lucien rose from the water and made his way back to the bank, droplets raining off his lean, naked body as tiny waves cascaded away from his ankles. He neglected to collect his gear piled in the grasses and wearily proceeded to his room. As he walked, something in the corner of his eye startled him wide awake.

Motion stirred from a shadowed corner of his chamber. Lucien squinted, and his heart started to race. A familiar figure stepped into the moonlight, silky, red hair bouncing with each step. Captain Vederosa stared longingly at him with a shy yet curious expression. Embarrassment flushed Lucien's face. He froze. Trying to make himself decent, he pivoted to gather his clothes lying out next to the river.

"Don't," Vederosa said.

Lucien slowly turned back, making sure his most prominent feature could be seen at her request. Vederosa's unmoving gaze watched him as he stepped closer and ascended the short steps to his room. Standing a few feet away from her, the prince locked his sight onto her eyes, eyes that held a firm lust behind them. It wasn't just a carnal lust, though. It was a lust for his soul, for his heart along with his perfect body. Vederosa gracefully slipped the straps of her outer shirt off her shoulder, allowing it to fall to the floor after she untied the string that held it in place over her torso. Lucien's mouth cracked open in awe. The gorgeous woman in front of him gracefully neared him, pulled her inner shirt off, and lightly shook her head to give life to her hair.

The prince's gaze fell to her bare chest. Free of any blemish, Vederosa's perky breasts lightly jiggled as she moved in. Lucien then studied the rest of her physique that matched his in athleticism and perfection. He reached out and brushed her toned, powerful arms up to her pointed shoulders. Sinking into the embrace, she placed her hands on his stone-like chest while his moved across her wide latissimi. The urge to wrap her up with all his strength increased, and he did just that as her soft lips gently suctioned his collarbone. Vederosa's fingernails dug into his upper back as he squeezed.

Searching for her mouth with his, Lucien passionately kissed her. He slid his hands down her hourglass figure until he reached the sides of her hips. The prince wiggled his fingers under her pants, growing more aggressive as she did. Once naked, Vederosa pressed herself against him. Lucien squeezed her firm, rounded ass, feeling the small divot in her glute muscles before hoisting one of her legs up around his thigh. Vederosa pulled on the back of his neck, urging him to dive deeper into the affair. He pushed her against the wall, pinned her to it, and balanced her on his leg. With one hand stretched out on the cold stone, he used the other to press on her lower back. Soft moans sang in his ear. Ecstasy fueled his sexual desires. Lucien then picked her other leg up so she could straddle him, irises shifting to a bright red hue along with the veins in his neck and arms.

Lucien leaned his head back, pulling away from her lips nibbling at his ear, and looked deeply into Vederosa's eyes once more as he pressed his full erection into her inch by inch. Soft gasps trickled out and shifted to moans the deeper he went. His hip bones reached hers, and Vederosa squealed. The prince started off slow to ease her into his pace. Sweat gathered and glazed his skin.

After he saw the shock in her expression fade away, Lucien picked her up, his thumbs firmly delved into the creases between her thighs and hips. Vederosa rocked in tandem with him, growing faster and faster. Lucien, focusing on spreading her open with each thrust, staggered his way to the bed, and toppled over on top of her. She pushed him away, sinking her nails into his chest, flipped over, and taunted him by leisurely wobbling her ass at him. An excited sneer flashed on his face. Lucien then squeezed the back of her thigh with one hand, sliding it up to her lower back and across her spine. He balanced himself on the bed on his knees locked outside her legs. Vederosa's begging gaze beamed back at him over her shoulder.

His careful touch snapping to aggression, Lucien planted his hand around the back of her neck and sifted his fingers through her hair, took a handful, and pulled to force her head up with a taught hold. The prince then spread her cheeks apart with his other hand and plunged into her once more. He gave her little chance to prepare for him this time, though, vigorously sliding in and out as fast as his flexibility would allow him. Vederosa's moans elevated to subtle cries. Lucien titled her head to the side and took great pleasure in the pain shown in her clenched eyes and trembling jaw. She squealed louder at one of his deeper advances.

"Shhh," Lucien darkly said, lowering himself parallel to her while decreasing his pace. "We must be courteous to those around us."

She shakingly nodded.

"Don't worry," the prince said, fluidly swaying his hips back and forth, trading strength and speed for a bit of finesse in his strokes.

He drove himself further inside her at an almost teasing rate.

"I'll go nice ...," he whispered against her shudders, sliding in as deep as he could, "and slow."

The prince filled her with sexual euphoria until she started to breathe harder and harder.

"Lu ... Lucien...," she said between pants. "I ... ah ... ahhh...."

Lowering her head to the bed, Lucien smiled. Vederosa bit down on the cotton pillow, sent staggered exhales out her nose with each wince, and grasped at the silk fabrics around her. Lucien gained speed with the same intensity. A quiver shook through her body from head to toe. Heavy moans escaped every time her abdomen contracted, forcing her shoulders to cave in toward the bed each time. Lucien felt her clench around his erection as she reached climax. He couldn't hold the urge back any longer; Lucien relaxed himself and climaxed as well, fighting back the roar climbing in his throat. The prince pumped her full of his semen, all his energy immediately left his body, and he pulled himself out. He dripped onto the sheets as his chest heaved with exhaustion. Satisfied, empty, and tired, Lucien rolled over beside Vederosa, and grinned.

The gorgeous woman next to him lifted her head up, hair frizzy and in her face. Lucien noticed her wide grin through the strands and caressed her upper back with his knuckles. Vederosa pulled herself up to him a moment later. Shifting himself so she could comfortably lay on his chest, the prince lifted his arm around her.

Lucien exhaled as delicate yet sturdy fingers rubbed over the valley between his strapping pectorals carpeted by sparse black hair. In the silence of his chambers, the sounds of the flowing river nearby echoed in once more. The twinkle of the night sky caught his attention from beyond the stone awning.

"The stars above us are beautiful. Truly fit for paradise." Lucien said in a low voice. "But ... they're quite disappointing if I'm being honest."

"Oh?" Vederosa said, turning over to rest her chin on her arm laid across his abdomen. "Why's that?"

Lucien scanned over the specks of white in view.

"There's something here that outshines them."

"What would that be?"

Twisting his head, inches away from her, he studied Vederosa's slender face and button nose.

"You. Your smile."

Vederosa's blushed as she looked at him.

"You should show it more often," Lucien said.

"That's not exactly an option. I didn't get where I am by smiling."

"Is that why you're all grit and attitude?" he said with a grin.

"I suppose. As a girl, I had two options: be another pretty young face at the mercy of the fate set before me or ... create my own."

Lucien softly raked his fingers through Vederosa's hair.

"And how did you do that?"

"By taking what I want. And beating the shit out of anyone in my way. Seemed to work until I attracted Neptabyss's attention."

"What happened then?"

A subtle pause delayed Vederosa's reply.

"Well, after I muscled my way into a fleet of marauders picking off fishing vessels along the coast, earned the respect of the crew, and overthrew the captain, I became Skulpos's number one enemy. My luck ran out, though, when Neptabyss himself showed up to put an end to the show. He spared me, to my surprise. Said my talents could be used elsewhere. Apparently, the Skulpin navy had been lacking a fleet commander for decades, and he offered the spot to me."

"So, you changed sides just like that?"

"It was a promotion ... if you want to call it that," she said. "I didn't care what side I was on. The fewer men I answered to, the better. And now, I only answer to him. Better than being against him. He's an Osirian, after all."

"So am I," Lucien said.

Vederosa hoisted herself up with her forearms on the bed next to him.

"Yes, but there's a much different reason you've gotten as far as you have."

A light chuckle mumbled behind his closed lips.

"And what reason is that?"

The look in her eyes acted as a window to her bleeding heart as she gawked at him.

"I ... I don't feel alone ... with you."

Lucien sunk his eyebrows, the bitter surroundings of her statement touching his heart.

"I've always had to keep my guard up, to fight against the pressure put on me. I've always had to maintain the stigma that I'm more masculine than any man around me and that I can exactly what they can," she said.

A warm hand rose to the side of his face.

"But with you ... I don't have to. You see beyond what I show the world. You see *me*. And you're the only person who ever has."

"I see you because ... I do the same thing. In a way. My life has been given to me and planned out at nearly every turn. Vastly different that your upbringing, yes, but I hated not having the choice to be who I wanted. I've had to present myself as a royal, as my father's son, to carry his legacy. And, because of that, I ... I haven't had the chance to find myself. The lost look on your face behind closed doors is the exact same face I wear every day. I know that kind of loneliness."

Lucien sighed, holding the woman in his arms tighter to him.

"It's rather damning, isn't it?" he said.

Vederosa sniffed; Lucien noticed the thin veil of a tear cresting her eyelid.

"Yes," she said, lowering her head to his torso. "Yes, it is. Captain Vederosa has been my name, my reputation, and my legacy for eighteen years. No one who's alive knows me any different or even knows my first name."

"What is it?" Lucien asked.

Vederosa hesitated. The prince knew she held onto the secrecy of her real self more than anything else. Getting it out of her required an advanced level of trust. Her index finger slowly moved up and down his jawline as he studied her beautiful face.

"Lilian."

Warm feelings rushed through him as he realized the weight of her revealed name.

"You're safe with me, Lilian," he said, rubbing the back of her head.

Vederosa closed her eyes and held him tighter, allowing him the chance to take in her full beauty. He had heard stories of love in all the heroic tales of his youth. Maybe this is what it felt like. The prince dismissed the intense emotion warming him. Vederosa had only been a part of his life for nine days, not enough time to fall in love with someone by a fair amount. He couldn't help his attraction to her, though, the same she held toward him. No one had ever dissolved his loneliness like her before.

His eyes started to close as well, fatigue setting in without the distraction of sex or a meaningful conversation. Relaxation came quickly in the comfort of his bed. Lucien circled his fingers on Vederosa's back until he fell asleep, and he slipped into a dream state in the safety of Hoslentos.

~ ~ ~

The prince laid flat on his back in his illusion. A faint breeze washed over him and chilled his skin. Running water alerted his ears, and for a moment, he thought of the river outside the city in Aeladaecia. When he fully came to, though, a much different environment surrounded him. A sun shined overhead in the middle of a bright blue, cloudless sky, and marble columns lined a circular arena barely wider than the streets of Vaedor Sellos. Tropical trees leaned over through the gaps between the pillars, shading parts of the clearing. Beyond them, Lucien studied the thousand-foot drop to the landscape below of ancient ruins scattered across grassy hills and shallow streams.

"You're a peculiar individual, Lucien Osiris," a heavenly voice called behind him.

Slightly startled, the prince faced the source of the voice. Cascading platforms jutting out from a natural rock wall came into view. On the centermost one, Lucien fixed his gaze upon a feminine figure laying on her hip and elbow on a mound of pillows. The top half of her face remained hidden behind a decorative, eyeless helm with three white feathers sticking out of each side. Flawless skin, an inviting smile, and hands covered in assorted jewelry caught his attention. Upon closer inspection, the prince noticed her tall stature even in her laxed position. The exaggerated curves of her hips and her thighs as thick as his entire torso gave evidence of her size.

"Neshka," Lucien said in amazement. "Where ... what is this place?"

"This is my home," the goddess said in a graceful yet booming voice that carried others behind it with a brief echo. "Or what's left of it."

"What's left of it?"

"Yes," Neshka said. "This is where the first civilization I created used to roam. But, as you can see, they're no longer here."

Lucien took a step forward, shifting his eyes to the empty beds around the great goddess.

"Are you alone here, then?"

"My siblings return from time to time," Neshka said, holding her hand up to marvel at the glimmering gold wrapped around her wrists and fingers. "But, for now, yes. You're all mine to play with."

A bolt of nervousness shot down his spine.

"Play with?" he asked with a frown.

"Indeed."

Neshka propped herself from her elbow to her hand, bending her legs to the side.

"Like I said, you're ... a peculiar individual."

"How so?"

"You're different than all my other children. You are stronger."

"It doesn't really seem that way."

"Who else would I have trusted to receive my message?" Neshka said. "Only one of your kind has made this journey before."

Lucien scoffed.

"I'm no Osiris," he said.

"No," the goddess said, whirling her free hand in the air.

Suddenly, lifeless clones of Lucien's forefathers appeared all around him in tiers. The holed mask of Osiris himself glared at him on the closest statue.

"You are better."

Glancing over Osiris's covered face, Lucien raised an eyebrow.

"No other Osirian would make the journey you have to bring back one of his own," Neshka said. "No other is so ... selfless."

"Zededia is the only one who can stop Matticus," Lucien said. "This is the only option."

"Hmm, perhaps," Neshka said. "But there is more behind your desire to bring him back than that."

The prince wove his way between the motionless mimics of his family.

"Yes."

"The love you have for your brother has compelled you to change the world. A quality rarely seen in my children. Osirians are typically driven by power or greed. But not ... not you."

"Power and greed have destroyed my family," the prince said. "The bond of brotherhood has been long forgotten, and men are dying for the wrong reasons. There is corruption where there should be honor. Betrayal where there should be loyalty. We as a race have failed the world. We are supposed to be the leaders of men, not their enslavers."

A thin smile widened on Neshka's face.

"That, my dear child," the goddess said in a soothing voice, "is why you are different. You have the heart of a true Osirian. The heart of Osiris himself. Your people have created the idea that your ancestor is due to return to the earth one day. Perhaps he has chosen to do so through you."

Refusing to give himself credit, Lucien dismissed that idea. He condemned any thought that compared him to Osiris, the Holy Uniter who freed the world. Halting his pacing between the Hostellian kings, he shifted his view from the former Hostellian kings to the goddess perched on the platform.

"You're nearing the end of your path," Neshka said. "Once a lost little boy running away from his grief ... is now the man responsible for saving the world."

"Zededia will save the world," he said, arguing against her claim.

"And you will save Zededia. You are his tether to your world. He needs you over all others."

The task to resurrect his brother from Elysia still remained, and Lucien had less than no idea of how to proceed. He frowned with concern.

"Where do I go from here? How do I bring him back?"

"The *Varas* will know what to do," Neshka said. "Let them guide you."

Behind him, a swirling portal opened like a phantasmic doorway back to the physical realm.

"The Naaklings will try to stop you," the goddess said as he started to turn toward it. "They seek the Architects just as you do—only for a much different reason."

The Architects?

The memory of the black shadows in the vision Neshka blessed him with in Voluutia crawled back into his mind. Lucien paused to process Neshka's warning. He then put one foot in front of the other to make his way to the portal.

"I'll be watching you, dear Lucien," the goddess said, her voice starting to fade as he broke the plane of the blue shimmer. "Do not disappoint me."

~ ~ ~

Lucien woke from his dream and glanced around. Vederosa's arms still clung to him while she stirred in a deep sleep. A dim, orange sunrise crept in through the openings of his chambers and outshined the bioluminescent flora outside Hoslentos. The day he had worked so hard for over the course of the journey lit up the sky. Beyond the closed doors, he heard footsteps and mingling voices. Lucien had several questions for Atlas, and he assumed the Daecian king would want to hear of his latest encounter with Neshka.

Chapter 23

The Architects

Day 5 in the Month of Rain

After conquering the capital city of Voluutia, the Hostellae marched through the ashen ruins as proud as their king, waving Vaedorian banners high in the air for all to see. Broken, beaten, and leaderless, the Voluutians had no choice but to submit to the power of *Osirisigniros* and its carrier.

Matticus entered the great hall of Amuun Drall the morning after slaying King Raed. Larger than its Hostellian counterpart, the inner keep's sanctum boasted an array of artwork portraying Voluutia's history. As Matticus stood at the center of the glossy floor made from dark green tile, he stared at the mural painted on the inside of the domed ceiling. All the previous kings of this land stuck out with their unique features. Matticus cast his eye over Raed, and, to his surprise, the anger he felt for the Voluutian king didn't cook his veins like any other time he thought of his rival. Instead, the same emptiness that plagued him after Zededia's death dampened his brutality. Taking a deep breath, Matticus reflected upon the strange state of peace that came with the lack of an enemy to defeat. The other kingdoms remained for the taking, but he preferred having a challenger in front of him to the political nature of plotting another invasion.

The charred skin tissue on the side of his face choked his eye. *Osirigniros* had healed his vaporized arm, but it left the patch of blackened skin near his nose as a reminder of its true power. Through the gap in his helmet, Matticus shifted his squinted eye to the scenes of glory above.

Footfalls echoed off behind him, but Matticus kept his gaze focused on the painted depictions of the Voluutian kings.

"Your Eminence," he heard Commander Nysis call from near the entrance of the great hall.

Matticus turned to face his warlord. Beside Nysis, several other officers of the Hostellae walked toward him. Once they stood in front of him, he took a deep breath.

"The day is won, sire," Commander Nysis said. "The Voluutians have offered their official surrender."

Matticus lowered his gaze to the floor, taking a moment to savor his victory.

"Amuun Drall is yours," Nysis said.

He looked over to his left hand made of red energy from the sword. The sharpened edges that replaced his fingertips intrigued him. As he studied his new hand, Matticus thought deeply of his campaign to conquer Osiria.

"Do you know why we came to Voluutia, Commander Nysis?" he asked in a dark voice. "Do you know why we are really here?"

"The Voluutians are our greatest rivals, sire. They pose the largest threat to our plan of unification."

Matticus paused, keeping his eyes on his ethereal fingers.

"We came ... because this is the last unconquered city in the entirety of mankind's existence. For three thousand years, these walls have withstood the northern raiders, the Raoans, the Archelects. Not even the mighty Aznogs could maul their way to where we are. This is where the remnants of the Old World made their final stand against the men from the mountains. This is the rock that could not be broken."

Turning around, Matticus walked across the tile floor, hands behind his back, toward the decorative throne King Raed governed from. He stopped at the base of the staircase leading up to the raised platform and scanned the grand statue behind the throne.

"And now, I stand here in the ruins of this ... timeless nation ... as its champion. What else proves that I am Osiris reincarnated?"

The marble statue depicting King Raed stared down at him with a lifeless gaze. It mocked him. For a moment, the blank expression in the carved stone shifted to Matias's unapproving scowl. Anger filled Matticus's heart; he glared at his father with disdain.

"What more must I do to win your favor?"

Just as Matticus started to sink into the depths of his fury, the doors to inner hall opened once more. A familiar sound caught his attention—the marching of soldiers. As

Matticus turned, he eyed a platoon of warriors from Korzeg carrying their kingdom's standard atop pikes. From the middle of the pack, King Holthiem appeared. Matticus made his way passed his men to confront his unexpected visitor.

"Why have you come here?" he asked, a slight hostility in his tone. "You dare bring your army into my presence without my summons?"

"I don't recall needing your summons to go where I please," Holthiem said.

Matticus stared at the old king and his thick, white beard. Holthiem had sat upon the throne of Korzeg for over a century ruling as far back as his great-great grandfather. He gave little care, though; he had lost respect for all Korzegi people for not being able to defend themselves against the northern raiders.

"There is nothing for you here," Matticus said. "Our accord is complete. Go back to your home."

"Ah, our accord," Holthiem said. "Yes, I've been reflecting over the terms we agreed to."

"Be wise with your next words," Matticus said, tightening his grip on the Sword of Kings. "I was generous to spare your pathetic kingdom. Pray to Neshka I do not change my mind."

"My men bled for this day, Matticus, as I know yours did as well. But you have no need for Voluutia. It belongs to Korzeg."

Matticus clenched his jaw and took a step forward, his veins starting to glow red.

"You don't seem to understand," Matticus said darkly. "All kingdoms belong to *me*. Ehthilia, Voluutia, Korzeg, they have ceased to exist. Only Hostellus remains. All else is mine to command. We are not equals. *You* serve *me*, your men serve *me*."

The Korzegi guards around King Holthiem sensed his aggression and took defensive stances.

"You are a fool to think I will serve you so quickly," Holthiem said as he stood his ground. "Just because you wield *Osirisigniros* does not mean you are a greater king than—"

Matticus raised a half-closed fist to his chest level, and a wave of energy pulsed from his red hand. Holthiem and each of his warriors floated helplessly in the air, eyes widening with panic. Taking heavy steps as the power from the sword coursed through him, Matticus sneered under his helmet until he stood a yard away from the Korzegi king.

"I am no king," Matticus said through his teeth, eyes glowing red. "I am ... the Holy Uniter."

Closing his fist, he enacted the second half of his spell and siphoned the life from each man in front of him. Trails of ghostly mist seeped from their mouths, Holthiem's included, and pooled into a ball above. Soon, Matticus reduced the Korzegi soldiers into piles of skin and bone, and they slumped to the floor. King Holthiem's life force resisted with more success, but Matticus increased the intensity of his magic. The wrinkled skin of the old king's face shriveled and turned as white as his beard, and the eyes dried up and retracted back into his skull. Matticus released his hold of his prey and focused on the mass of energy hovering in the air. Holding his hand up to the swirling cloud, he sucked it into his palm, adding to his already overwhelming power.

Calmly, Matticus glanced over the corpses on the floor, turned back to his men, and walked toward the throne. As he climbed the stairs, the wails of the souls trapped inside the Sword of Kings softly hummed through the hall. Eerie and crooked, the dark atmosphere clouding Amuun Drall gave life to a new form of wrath in Matticus's changing nature. He took a seat on Raed's throne. After raising his head to survey his conquered territory, his vision turned red. The tattered banners of Voluutia and Korzeg fell to Hostellus's might.

"Hail, Emperor Matticus," Commander Nysis said as a flag bearing the gilded eagle dropped down along the wall behind the throne. "Hail the Great Osiris."

Four nations were under his control, and the entirety of the Hostellian Empire awaited his command. With each conquered foe, Matticus's lust for power grew bolder. Daece's borders lay a day's ride away, a new target for his ramping aggression; Skulpos's a short distance after that. All signs pointed east, and those who remained to challenge him had nowhere to run.

~ ~ ~

Prince Lucien emerged from his chambers after dressing himself. He glanced over his shoulder as Captain Vederosa made herself decent. Slipping into the street, the prince made his way toward the gathering of men near the town center. King Atlas and the captains of the Legonae formed a circle to discuss their plans. Lucien found a spot next to Caedus, who gave him a welcoming nod.

"What's the plan?" he asked.

"Atlas and Tog are devising it right now," Caedus said.

Lucien peered between Seether's cloaked head and Ammon's towering shoulder. The clay man who had led him to Hoslentos held a cheery smile, but Atlas's expression of confusion concerned him.

"There seems to be a little problem, though," Caedus said.

"What's that?"

"I'm not quite sure Tog understands why we are here. He keeps mentioning 'the holy creation' as if it was prophesied or something. No one here could have known of our intentions up until now, though."

"Hmm," Lucien said. "That seems in line with their expectation of our arrival. Maybe there's something more at play here."

"I hope you're wrong," Caedus said with a gripe. "That's the last thing we need."

Pushing his way to the front of the crowd, Lucien cleared his throat amid the conversation.

"We are not here for some holy ritual," Atlas said in an impatient tone. "We are here for an ascension ceremony."

"Oh yes! Yes!" Tog said. "We are so delighted you've come after all this time! Neshka will be pleased!"

Atlas's raised eyebrow gave Lucien the cue.

"Neshka has spoken to me," the prince said. "She has shown me our path."

"Wonderful!" Tog said scurrying up to him. "Then you have seen the ceremony! You've seen the Architects!"

Lucien hesitated, trying to recall the exact details of the vision given to him in Voluutia. The ghastly figures of his vision he could barely comprehend haunted him with their featureless faces.

"Actually ... I have," Lucien said.

"What?" Atlas said, stepping forward. "You know what he's talking about?"

"I believe so," Lucien said.

"That's something you neglected to mention."

"Well, it didn't exactly occur to me at the time. I saw many strange things."

"What a glorious day for the *Varas Zogad*!" Tog said. "We are most happy to take you to them!"

Without a competing option available, Lucien shrugged. Tog and a large group of other clay people met together near the road leading out of the city, and the prince turned to face King Atlas.

"I thought you were supposed to be the expert on Aeladaecia?" Lucien said. "You're the religious one here."

"In all the texts I have ever scoured about this place and the originations of our ancestral line, there's not a single mention of these people or the creatures they call the Architects. This is not where I thought our journey would lead us."

"Best we just keep moving," Lucien said.

"Agreed."

Lucien started to follow Atlas then noticed a bundle of bouncing red hair out of the corner of his eye. Vederosa still held a slightly cold expression to him in public, a necessary evil in their current situation. Matching her stride, the prince walked with her to bring up the end of the envoy.

"Do you trust these strange people?" she asked.

Pausing to reflect, Lucien reanalyzed everything that had occurred over the last day.

"I do," he said. "Atlas seems to be on edge, though. He suspects something."

"Well, if there's one thing I know, Osirian, it's that no one shows this kind of hospitality without an ulterior motive."

Lucien smirked.

"That's rather misanthropic."

"Perhaps, but I'd rather be skeptical and alive rather than naïve and dead."

"I suppose."

Up ahead, Tog stopped everyone at the main bridge to cross the river near the waterfall flowing from the cliffside.

"Be ready, Osirians," the clay man said. "The journey from this point on is one you will not return here from. This is the last you will see of Hoslentos; if there are any final matters to attend to, you should do so now before we depart."

Everyone kept quiet as Lucien scanned the crowd.

"Excellent! Then there's no reason for further delay!" Tog said.

The party moved on over the bridge, Lucien walking with Vederosa at his side once more. Tog escorted them back up the stone ramp from whence they came. Lucien still wondered why the *Varas* were so eager to lead them to the ascension ceremony. Something about their mood and the cynicism from his group members allowed him to see through the side smiles and excited tones.

Nearly running into Captain Ammon directly in front of him, the prince abruptly pulled himself to a halt as Tog stopped about halfway up the ramp. Lucien stepped to the side to investigate. Two of the clay men around Tog faced the densest part of the waterfall.

"What are they doing?" Vederosa said in a mutter.

"I don't know," Lucien said, noticing their outward stretched arms.

Suddenly, a platform jutted out from the cliff, and the waterfall parted down the middle. A whirling, multicolored aura surrounded the shifting stone as the *Varas* seemed to pull it toward them as they retracted their hands.

"They're using ... magic? No, that can't be," Lucien said. "Osirians are the only mystical beings on this earth."

"But your sorcery doesn't work here, right?" Vederosa said.

"Right ... that's what Atlas said. For some reason, we are unable to use our powers here. That would make sense, though. Ever since we arrived here, the laws of nature that govern this island are not aligned with the ones back home. Things are different."

Lucien eyed Tog as he motioned for the party to proceed across the platform.

"*They* are different," he said.

The prince followed as instructed. As he ventured through the waterfall, he glanced up to the ceiling of the massive cave carved into the side of the mountain. A hidden passage revealed itself and stretched on for as far as Lucien could see. The *Varas* guides summoned orbs of light in their palms to illuminate the path. Tog lingered until everyone had passed, and Lucien gave him a fake grin as he caught up to him.

"This is a wonderful day, isn't it?" the clay man said. "The gods will be pleased we have finally fulfilled our purpose."

"What exactly is your purpose, Tog?" Lucien asked.

"Why, to serve those who are chosen, of course, those who are of the blood of Osiris, the Lightbringer! He was made from the gods, and you were made from him."

"What were you made from?"

Tog's hesitation puzzled Lucien.

"Just as you were created from water, we were created from stone."

Lucien struggled to understand anything that came from Tog's mouth.

"That doesn't exactly answer my question," he said. "Care to elaborate?"

"When the Architects made the first *Varas* people, they did so under the command of Neshka herself following Osiris's ascension ceremony. Your father abandoned his physical form to seek divinity, and we were molded by what was left behind."

"I see...."

"You are born of Osiris's blood; we are born of his flesh."

Lucien added another piece of lore to his growing collection.

"Hmm. Thank you, Tog."

Through the gaps between his company members, Lucien eyed Atlas with his nose buried in the text he had been studying since the prince told him of his dream of Aeladaecia. Lucien had questions for the Daecian king, ones that needed answers.

The journey through the mountain tunnel led Lucien and his team back into the forest they had ventured into from the black shores. Several hours passed as the party traveled over a winding stone road with only the sounds of creaking trees muffled footsteps to distract him. The wide trunks of the trees created an endless maze that swallowed anyone who strayed from the path. A heavy morning fog rolled in, the decaying road became more twisted, and swaying branches blocked the small amount of light piercing through the dense clouds above.

A sudden sense of paranoia shocked the prince's spine as he sensed a strange presence. Something was watching him. A twig snapped in the distance; the party stopped.

"What was that?" Captain Redding said.

Lucien scoured the fog, unable to see much of anything. He stepped to the edge of the road, leaned over, and squinted. A shadowy silhouette advanced toward him with great speed, and then, a screeching figure leapt through the mist onto the road. The prince staggered back, planted his feet, and drew his sword just in time to block the shoddily made axe from hacking his thigh. After casting the attack aside, Lucien peered up into the cruel, beady eyes of a crab-like humanoid. The Naaklings had found them.

More Naaklings followed the initial charge and engaged the company. Though it caught him by surprise, Lucien's enemy proved to be an unworthy opponent as the prince drove his blade through the hardshell torso with great force after dodging its next swing. The Naaklings were no match for his hardened experience formed by years of training in the Vaedorian military academies. Another sprinted at him on the road from Hoslentos's direction; he sneered and faced the combatant with ferocity in his strides. Lucien sliced upward from his side and cleaved the crab man's leg off. As it crawled in agony, the prince skewered it through the soft spot on the back of its neck.

Clanging steel echoed through the forest as all members of the party fended off the ambush, and Lucien turned back to see Captain Vederosa challenging three Naaklings at once. The fare woman he saw as a mate sneered just as he did—the aggression in her eyes fanned the flame in his. Lucien advanced, stabbed one of the Naaklings in the back while Vederosa finished the other two, and pried his weapon free before searching for the next target. A group of crab man cut them off from the rest of the company and circled them. Lucien pressed his back to Vederosa's, arms readied in the *Promaast* fighting stance.

"We're outnumbered," the prince said, calculating the odds.

"If they wanted a fair fight," Vederosa said as she cleaned her saber of the Naakling's dark burgundy blood, "they should have brought more."

Prince Lucien and Captain Vederosa danced together in battle, sending the crab men to the dirt in quick succession. When one turned, the other moved to cover their back. A Naakling swung at Lucien's head, but he ducked the attack as Vederosa thrusted her saber over his shoulder into the crab man's chest. The prince then pivoted to parry an attack aimed at Vederosa's back, heel kicked the enemy away, and hacked at another to his right. Soon, Lucien filled the gaps of Vederosa's attacks and supplemented her with his own. As if they shared a mind, the two moved perfectly in sync with one another, whirling across the stone road like a tornado of steel.

The Naaklings retreated after a moment to focus their efforts on the other company members. Lucien watched them flee with courage in his heart and anger in his eyes, and Vederosa stood proudly beside him. Their bond strengthened over a pile of corpses at their feet, power and domination leaking from them both. The others needed his help; Lucien bolted toward Caedus and the Legonae captains swarming them. However, as he sprinted back into the fray, a towering Naakling, larger than all the rest, leapt onto the stone road, cutting him off. Vederosa lagged behind unable to provide immediate assistance.

Lucien sneered and swung his longsword across his body, but the behemoth in front of him snatched it with its claw and slowly pulled it away. The prince widened his eyes as Naakling snapped the forged steel clean in two, destroying the sword his father had gifted him. A low chuckle rattled from the creature's throat. Lucien ducked the beast's claw aimed at his neck, slid between its legs, and popped up on the other side. Using its size against it, the prince danced around in search of a weak point. He kicked the exposed joints of its knees, forcing it to kneel. As Lucien came around front, he sent a haymaker at its gut. The hardened shell of the Naakling nearly cracked his knuckles, but Lucien's enhanced strength from the power boiling in his blood sent the beast crashing on its back.

Captain Vederosa took control right after, slicing at the Naakling like a savage. As it fought its way back to its feet, the prince joined his fair maiden in battle once more, punching and prying to knock the Naakling off balance as Vederosa slashed at the soft flesh between the gaps in its shell. It stood no chance against the might of Lucien and Vederesa's ferocity. Weakened and injured, the Naakling staggered around, and the prince found himself several feet behind it. The beast wobbled, unable to defend itself any longer.

"Osirian!" Vederosa yelled.

Lucien looked under its arm and met her stunning, powerful gaze as she heaved her sword in the air. He followed the gleam off her saber as it soared over the Naakling. Understanding her set up with a smile, the prince took a step back, jumped as high as he could like a leaping predator, and firmly grabbed the hilt of Vederosa's blade. Lucien twirled it upside down as he fell back toward the earth and drove it through the center of the Naakling's head with all his strength. The behemoth groaned a dying breath, leaned forward, and collapsed on the road, shaking the path as plumes of dust erupted from the cracks in the stone.

Captain Vederosa gave him a sly grin as a portion of her red hair covered half her face. Lucien pried her saber from the Naakling corpse and handed it to her hilt first. He shared a moment of sincerity with her amidst the eye of the storm, his forefinger grazing against hers as she took her sword from him.

"There are three things I love above all else," Vederosa said as she stepped closer. "The sea ... gold...."

She placed one foot between his, her hips an inch away from his and her chin tilted up at him.

"And powerful men...."

Lucien grinned back, watching Vederosa's swaying hips as she walked toward the rest of the company. Caedus and the others had dealt with the Naaklings surrounding them. The prince approached the group, took note of the lone casualty of one of Atlas's soldiers, and stood next to Caedus.

"We are lucky," Tog said. "The Naaklings travel in large groups, but never this large."

Lucien watched Atlas lean down and pray for his fallen guard.

"There are surely more to follow," Tog said. "They've picked up our scent–they know we seek the Architects."

"We need to keep moving," Lucien said.

Caedus nodded at him.

"Right, let's be on our way. The fog is clearing, and it's not much farther."

Up the road, Lucien walked side by side with Vederosa, keeping his eyes keen on the dissipating mist as his paranoia ate at him. He had seen enough of the island's creatures for three lifetimes; he longed for the long voyage home across the Orlestian Sea despite maintaining a moderate dislike for the constant rocking and sleepless nights aboard The Leviathan.

Half the day lay behind Lucien, and his feet ached from the tiresome climb to the cave of the Architects. However, just as he wanted to complain, the trees of the forest grew thinner in number, and a towering peak cast a dark shadow over the stone road. Lucien squinted and observed a gaping entrance into the mountain under an archway scribed with runic signs he didn't recognize. Osiria contained many mystical arches to many a spiritual place, but none were this size or carved with the same symbols. Torches bearing blue flames flickered on each side. As he stepped closer, Lucien felt an enchanting presence calling to the divinity in his blood. He looked down, watched his fingers tremble against his will, and took a deep breath.

At the entrance to the cave, Tog stopped everyone; Lucien made his way to the front of the pack.

"At last, we have arrived!" Tog said excitedly. "The rest of the Naaklings will not be far behind, and we cannot offer our services to protect you as we are needed to perform the ritual."

"We'll stay here," Caedus said.

Lucien turned his head.

"Are you sure?" he asked.

The rest of the Legonae captains gathered around Caedus, and the prince met their prideful gazes.

"You've brought us this far, Prince Lucien," Commander Ursa said. "Let us uphold our duty on this journey."

Caedus took a step toward him. Lucien stared deep into the captain's bloodshot eyes and all the silent pain they held behind them. He felt a sturdy hand on his shoulder.

"I wasn't there for your brother when he needed me," Caedus said to him, a hint of agony in his broken words, a rare display of emotion from the stoic captain. "I wasn't able to save him from his fate."

Lucien frowned in confusion as a tear pooled in his eye.

"But you can. You can be there for him now. You can bring him home."

The torment from Zededia's suicide Lucien kept buried screeched through the cracks of his heart. He hadn't ever realized Caedus blamed himself to such degree. Thinking back on their conversation in Amuun Drall, Lucien deemed his outburst at the captain rather foolish and misplaced. There were more than just he who were affected by Zededia's death. Lucien remembered that now, here, at the final stages of his odyssey.

"Go," Caedus said. "This is a place for gods, not men. We will be of more use to you here to guard the entrance."

Lucien nodded after a moment. He then looked to Captain Vederosa.

"I will follow your lead, Osirian," she said.

Her tone contradicted her words as the prince knew she didn't take orders so easily, but something about the sincerity in her eyes told him she meant it.

"Stay with me."

The smallest of smiles cracked across the side of Vederosa's face; Lucien sensed it immediately.

"Here," Commander Ursa said, pulling his attention back to the Legonae soldiers. "This may help you ... find him."

Lucien held out his hand and took a firm hold of Zededia's longsword protected in its sheath. As he scanned the hilt, flashes of his youth raced back to him, mainly his brother's graduation from the military academy when he received this sword. The prince hesitated for a moment as he remembered how much blood this sword had spilt. The world needed it, though, now more than ever.

"Alert us if you are in need of aid," Lucien said as he looked back to the soldiers in black armor.

Caedus boasted a proud grin and chuckled.

"The Legonae are never in need of aid."

Nodding once more, Lucien turned to delve into the secrets of cave of the Architects. Tog and half a dozen of his people beckoned him along the path, and King Atlas and the rest of his guards followed. The dark tunnel brought memories of Vaedorian prison where he searched for Zededia after his capture. The *Varas* waved their hands above their heads, using their arcane sorcery to light the torches lining the cave walls with blue flames just like those outside. A deep hum echoed down the corridor, one that rattled Lucien's ribcage. He felt Vederosa's fingers grab for his, and he locked hands with her in the cover of the dimly lit tunnel. Lucien lightly squeezed her to ease both her fear and his own.

A faint light ahead pierced through the veil of shadows engulfing the cave; the ritual chamber came into view. Lucien noticed Atlas with his attention buried in the tome he carried once more and wondered what held the Daecian king's focus in such a tight hold.

"Have you reached the passage that speaks of the ascension ceremony itself?" the prince asked.

"Well," Atlas said, "I ... think so. But, this part of the text isn't written in Aznogsi. It's written in a language I hardly recognize."

"You can't decipher it?" Lucien asked.

"I didn't say that. Though I can't read much of it, there's one phrase in particular that repeats itself over and over."

"What would that be?"

"Free ... the mind," Atlas said as he decoded the unknown language from his knowledge of Aznogsi and Eldish, "find ... the soul ... build the body."

"What the hell does that mean?" the prince asked.

Atlas hesitated to answer him, forcing his concern to spike.

"I don't know, exactly."

"Well, that's promising," Vederosa said.

Lucien frowned at her sarcasm.

"Free the mind. Find the soul. Build the body," Lucien heard Atlas mumble. "Free the mind. Find the soul. Build the body."

While he let Atlas prod for clues hidden in the ancient tome, Lucien focused on the chamber ahead. The tunnel opened to a massive corridor with a ramp descending to a stage-like stone platform in the distance. On either side of the ramp, depressions in the ground sloped downward and created clearings that appeared were made to hold gatherings of some sort. Something crunched under Lucien's foot, and when he looked down, he saw a dusty pile of dried clay in his wake, a rather strange sight this deep in a cave made of solid stone. Before the prince could investigate, however, Tog stopped the group just before the ramp reached the stone stage.

"Arise, my brothers and sisters!" the clay man shouted as he turned to face the party. "At long last, the Day of Ritual is here!"

Stone crumbled all around Lucien; he glanced to either side of him to study the commotion. From the ground, several sets of arms and legs shakingly reached up at the ceiling, a sight that disturbed him greatly. Dormant members of the *Varas* people slowly came to life as they freed themselves from their rocky prisons. Dozens of them rose from the earth, each of them staring at Lucien where he stood.

Smiles on their faces, the awakened *Varas* men and women raised their open hand toward him. A gleeful giggle poured through Tog's clenched jaw; Lucien looked back at him, his tiny, glowing blue eyes expressing an eerie sense of eagerness. Lucien sensed the fanatical attitude grow within his earthy guide.

"Come! Come! We must wake the Architects! They will be so happy to see you!"

Flashes of Lucien's vision from Neshka flew by, bringing an intense migraine with their passing. The prince bent over in pain as the veins on the side of his head glowed bright red.

"Lucien!" Atlas said, holding him by his arm to keep him from falling.

With the other arm, Lucien brought his hand to his head, squeezed his eyes shut, and gritted his teeth. A presence overcame him almost as if someone had climbed into his thoughts to plant their own. Lucien's mind raced with visions of Aeladaecia. From his first footsteps on the black sands through the forest and into the cave of the Architects, the divine message slowed and focused upon the flat platform in the distance. Runic symbols panned down his eyes like raindrops falling from the sky; Lucien gasped for breath as he struggled to perceive what he saw.

Eventually, he saw a glimpse of the two faceless beings from his first dream. They sat cross-legged as giant, phantasmic shadows much like Osinian under Caedus's command. Their large heads in proportion to the rest of their body slowly turned and looked at him. Each of them pointed a misty finger at a section of the floor with the same runic symbols carved into it, and a glossy, cosmic portal appeared above it. The deep hum he heard upon first entering the cave grew louder, deafening his ears. Lucien screamed in agony as the passing symbols in his eyes flew by faster and faster until they blurred together and shined like white torches in his skull. He felt the Architects' presence pull at his soul the longer they stared at him. The prince violently shook his head in his hands. Just as he thought that he could no longer bear the pain, though, the vision stopped.

Lucien returned upright, heart pounding and head throbbing. He shakingly looked around, met Vederosa's concerned gaze, and then shifted his attention to Tog.

"What did you see?" Atlas asked frantically.

The prince frowned in confusion as he tried to piece everything together.

"I saw them," he said. "They were guiding me to ... a portal of some kind, a gate. Much like the one we traveled through to get to Aeladaecia."

A lengthy gasp seeped from Tog's dry throat.

"They ... they have shown you ... *Barad Dorr*," the clay man said as the excitement nearly erupted out of him.

"The gate to *Ozek Monns?"* Atlas said in translation. "You know what that is?"

"Yes! Yes!" Tog said. "Oh, what a special occasion to be blessed with such a sight!"

"What does it mean?" Lucien asked after waiting for Tog to calm down.

"It means this is no ordinary ascension ritual," the clay man said. "They wish to ascend one of the ascended!"

"What?" Lucien said, just as confused as before.

"The ascended," Atlas said. "That's a nickname for us. Same thing as Osirian, just far less common. Since we are of the blood of he who ascended, we are kin to him in the eyes of the gods."

"They know who you wish to bring back! Of course they do, his soul beckons for revival! Oh, a special occasion indeed to witness such power!" Tog said. "But we must wake the Architects before they can begin! Come, my brothers and sisters, come!"

All the *Varas* men and women grouped together and walked up onto the platform below the ramp. Lucien followed Tog with Vederosa right beside him, and Atlas paced one stride ahead. Several of the clay people stepped out from the rest and formed a line. Curious, Lucien watched them fluidly and slowly wave their arms in the air. Tog removed something from a pouch attached to his belt, something too small for the prince to make out. A round pedestal centered the stone clearing, and soon after the leader of the clay people neared it, a large white pillar of fire erupted from it. The flame danced in Lucien's eyes and spiraled up to the ceiling of the cave as if it burned inside an invisible pipe.

"Maahett oovos meaenta!" Tog shouted in a language unknown to Lucien. *"Saavi nesttresta mayya Varas Zogad! Koas naiia brassahi!"*

"What the hell is he saying?" Lucien whispered to Atlas.

"Something about ... 'we are here'? Or 'we have come'?"

"Johovvat vahan borraam."

As Tog spoke, his voice became increasingly unhinged, almost like a village chieftain chanting an ancient spell. Soon after the invocation ended, though, the ceiling started to rumble. Lucien turned his attention to the gaping holes in the cave above, noticing the vast darkness seeping from within. Loose rubble trickled down next to his boots. As he studied the shadowy depths of the tunnels in the ceiling, he noticed a subtle movement.

Trails of black mist seeped down like the tentacles of a great sea beast. They wriggled toward the ground, pooled into a larger mass, and took the form of the two massive humanoid beings Lucien saw in his vision. The prince stood motionless, slightly paralyzed at the sight of the Architects as he stood just yards away from actual gods. Their heads turned to him, and they sat along the cave floor with legs crossed as they were depicted in his dream.

Lucien's mouth cracked open in shock as his shifted his gaze between their blank faces aimed directly at him as if they meant to single him out from the rest. A deep, slow murmur softly echoed through the cave, almost undetectable by his human ears.

"Hahaha!" Tog shouted. "They have answered our call!"

The clay man jogged back over to Lucien.

"Aren't they marvelous!" Tog said.

"These are ... the Architects," the prince said, eyes still focused on the towering gods before him.

"Yes! It is an honor to introduce you to Nazkala and Abbendae, our true creators!"

True creators? Lucien thought.

"I thought Neshka created man?" he said.

"We were made in Neshka's image," Atlas said, intervening. "It's never been determined who *actually* made us. Well, until now, I suppose."

"That's right, wise king!" Tog said. "Neshka turned to her brothers thousands of years ago to create the race of men so they may inherit the physical plane. Neshka created the world, and Nazkala and Abbendae made all living things that crawl or sprout upon it!"

Lucien wanted to retreat inside himself as he felt the terrifying gaze of the Architects glare at him. Their towering, shadowy bodies nearly reached the ceiling, and though he saw no eyes, he knew they singled him out from the pack. They weighed his worth, one moving its shadowy head closer for a better look.

"So," Lucien said, searching himself for all the confidence he could find, "let's begin."

Tog started clapping rapidly and turned to face the gods sitting on either side of the white pillar of flame. As the leader of the clay men and women reached his arms up and chanted another foreign phrase, the rest of the *Varas* people assembled into lines just before the platform all the way to the back of the cave. Lucien twisted his head over his shoulder and watched them take a seat on the floor. The prince stepped back, ushered by Atlas to make room for the ritual to begin.

A ghostly aura fell over the crowd of *Varas Zogad*, and they began to hum a low tune as they slowly swayed their torsos side to side.

"Hassllastos maa annsa morr!" Tog shouted to the gods. *"Iihaeya kaos nholas!* Bring forth ... the gate!"

The prince held Vederosa's hand as tight as he could, locking his eyes on the Architects as they each hovered a hand over the seal inscribed in the center of the platform. They then leaned their heads back. Lucien nearly lost his balance as the cave started to tremble. Larger chunks of rocks fell from the ceiling. Out from the abyss of their mouthless faces, the Architects released a blaring cry kin to the ringing of a massive, low-pitched church bell at the top of its tower. Lucien planted a firm foot behind him as the vibrations from their roar pounded his chest. The white pillar of flame flared on all sides in response. Another loud rumble echoed through the cave shortly after; gusts of wind gravitated toward the seal like forming tornadoes. Lucien squinted as loose debris soared through the air in circles above the runes.

"What the hell is happening?" Lucien shouted over the commotion.

The hums of the *Varas* shifted to symphonies of a choir. Their melodic chords rose and fell in pitch in separate groups, making their voices sound like there were ten times as many of them.

"Look!" Vederosa yelled as she held a finger at a black speck floating in the air.

The prince narrowed his gaze to the speck, watching it grow in circumference as sparks of static shot out in different directions.

"The portal!" Atlas said.

"Yes! The portal of *Barad Dorr* is here!" Tog shouted as he ran back to the group. "There, you will find whom you seek!"

The circular void widened to form a cosmic doorway. Lucien stared into the blackness, focusing on the white specks of light that resembled stars and the dark colored celestial bodies floating between them. The gate allured him. The divine power in his blood called for the spiritual planes.

"But I must warn you, my friends," Tog said.

Lucien snapped out of his trance.

"Only spirits are able to wander through this gate. Your physical bodies cannot make the journey."

Atlas looked at him.

"Free the mind ...," Lucien said under the whirling commotion surrounding the portal. "That's what it means."

He turned to Atlas

"We must project ourselves into the spiritual world!"

"But our magic doesn't work here, Lucien!" Atlas said. "How are we to astrally walk without it?"

Stuck in thought, Lucien sifted through possible solutions.

"Tog!" he said as an idea came to mind. "Do you think you can separate our bodies from our spirits? Can you induce us into such a meditation?"

The light in Tog's eyes lit up brighter than ever.

"Oh, yes! Yes!" he said. "Our sorcery is plenty capable of doing something like that! It would be such an honor to aid you with this task!"

"Then ... that's our only option," the prince said, sharing nervous eye contact with Atlas.

"Very well," the Daecian king said.

With the portal to *Ozek Monns* at its full might and the *Varas* people in the middle of their ceremonial incantations, Lucien followed King Atlas to a flat portion of the cave floor. He felt Vederosa's grip on his hand tighten, and he turned to her. Her words remained dormant behind parted lips, but the look of worry in her deep, beautiful eyes spoke for her. As Lucien opened his mouth to speak, she changed her wide eyes to the same stern expression as always. No time for fear now, no time for weakness.

"Be safe, Osirian," Vederosa said as if Lucien barely knew her.

The prince gave her a half-grin.

"For your brother," he said. "And mine."

Vederosa nodded in approval of his dedication.

"I will protect you should the need arise," she said.

Before Lucien lowered himself to the cave floor, he raised Vederosa's hand to his lips and kissed the tops of her knuckles. The prince took a seat with Atlas next to him, crossed his legs, and placed his palms on the sides of his knees. The phantasmic doorway ahead waited for his spirit to enter; Zededia waited beyond the veil.

"Deep breaths, Lucien," Atlas said.

Following his advice, the prince took in as much air as his lungs allowed. He focused on himself, driving out all sounds and external stimuli. Tog started to cast a spell over the two men, and Lucien closed his eyes, calmed his heart, and faded into the void.

When he cracked his eyelids open, he flinched. An identical image of himself sat across from him, and Lucien realized he now faced away from the portal. The air still whirled with the energy pulsing from the Architects and the gateway they summoned, but the cave fell silent as if he were experiencing everything from a separate place. Lucien held up his hand and noticed its slight transparency.

"Interesting ...," he whispered.

"Welcome to the other side," Atlas said.

Lucien looked to his right and watched the Daecian king rise to his feet. He stood as well, still perplexed by the concept of spiritual projection. Studying his body lingering in the physical world, the prince moved his attention to Captain Vederosa with her eyes glued to his meditative self.

"Let's go," Atlas said. "Who knows how long Tog can keep us here."

"Right," Lucien said. "Any idea as to what we do once we go through that door?"

"Well, we freed the mind," Atlas said casting his gaze to the portal to *Ozek Monns*. "Now we must find the soul."

Chapter 24

Ozek Monns

Day 5 in the Month of Rain

Caedus leaned against the side of the cave entrance as Ursa, Seether, and Ammonladus wandered around next to him. Keen eyes on the road leading away from the mountain, he wriggled his fingers with anxiety slowly creeping in. He knew the Naaklings were out there somewhere in the forest. He knew they would come to challenge him once again. For now, though, the air stilled, leaving only the creaking of the trees to fill his ears.

The other men kept quiet, fiddling with their weaponry in anticipation of a skirmish. Suddenly, a deep resonation bounced through the cave tunnel and emptied into the open space outside the mountain. Caedus leaned away as the intense ringing rattled him.

"I suppose they've started," he said, pushing himself off the side of the entrance.

Eerie chittering followed the ringing from hidden spots behind the tall trees. More chittering responded to the first, and soon, the dead leaves on the ground rustled with staggered footsteps.

"Ish dorzga enve lett violae. (And they've alerted the horde,)" Osinian said in Caedus's head.

Caedus, standing in the middle of the path now, drew his blade and squeezed the hilt. Each of the other captains readied their arms as well. Squinting to scan the landscape, Caedus watched for movement between the trees. He heard the Naaklings surge from hiding, but he still couldn't see them. Only glimpses of greenish-gray shells blurred by in the distance.

"We cannot allow them to reach Lucien," Caedus said.

"Hold your ground, boys," Ursa said.

Soon, the Naakling's beady eyes popped out from behind the cover of the trees a hundred yards away. Caedus lowered his hips and took his *Serrast* fighting stance, the preferred style of combat for one-handed swordsmen. The Naakling's snarled and chittered as they sprinted without coordination.

"Steel yourselves, brothers," Caedus said, focus locked on the charging enemy. "Fight for our commander."

The hardened feet of the crab men clicked against the stone road as they approached, swords flailing and earth shaking.

"Fight for Zededia."

One of the Naaklings broke free from the pack, barreling toward Caedus at lethal speed. Captain Ammon stepped in front of him and bashed his rectangular great shield into the creature's head, shattering the shell and spurting blood and gray matter in all directions. Caedus then stepped around Ammon as Seether launched an arrow at the next closest target. He cocked his arm, leapt off the stone road with his sword pointed at a Naakling, and drove the piercing metal right between its eyes. After pulling his blade free, he looked to the next. Commander Ursa and Captain Ammon battled with a group of them to the left while Seether remained tucked inside the cave firing arrow after arrow.

Caedus engaged another, ducking the crude first strike, and stuck the Naakling in the side where its shell was thinnest and up through the opposite shoulder. One by one, the crab men challenged the finest swordsman in all Osiria, and they each were cast to the ground dead and in pieces. As the minutes passed, Caedus grew more gruesome with his executions, sacrificing his careful precision for brutality the more his rage fueled him.

They tried to catch him off guard by attacking his sides, but Caedus's expert training and agility saved him from death and allowed him to defend himself.

"Fel! (Behind!)" Osinian said, watching the captain's back.

Caedus ducked instinctively, feeling wind off the slice of a sword just above his head. He then jolted around, hacked at the ambushing enemy with fluid, circular strikes, and shoved it to the ground.

The next Naakling that approached him tried to impale him with a spear, but the quick captain sidestepped the thrust, grabbed the wooden shaft just below the serrated metal edge, and severed the spearhead with a clean hack of his sword. Caedus, with a new weapon in reverse grip in his free hand, pivoted on one foot, spun completely around to the Naakling's right side, and plunged the tip of the spear into the back of his enemy's head. A gurgle choked out from the crab man's mouth as he collapsed.

"Come on!" Caedus screamed, face covered in the blood of his vanquished enemies.

The Naakling's hesitated, though, seeing the enraged soldier of the Black Legion slaughter their friends with ease. An order barked from what appeared to be the leader of the Naakling's assault. Caedus met the pair of angered eyes and smiled at the sword his enemy held toward him. The menial drones did as commanded and chose to charge at Caedus, a must unwise decision in their case. Captain Ammon rushed to his aid, and the two men picked the Naaklings apart like gods slaying the nonbelievers.

The initial wave of the Naakling assault thinned in numbers. Caedus backed up to the cave entrance to regroup with the others amid a calm moment. Seether stood behind him, bow aimed and ready, and Ursa stood to his right with Ammon to his left. Caedus wiped the gritty Naakling blood off his hand with his pants and waited for this enemy to advance. They stalled, though, forming a front line at the edge of the treeline.

"What are they waiting for?" Captain Ammon asked.

"A new plan," Seether said.

A hundred Naaklings gathered as their reinforcements arrived. Caedus knew they craved the power of the gods within the mountain; he knew they would willingly throw themselves at death to find it.

"Whatever they try," Caedus said, "we will hold them here."

Caedus froze in place as a booming roar thundered through the forest from behind the Naaklings. He scanned the trees and then the line of crab men on the road, noticing their turned heads to the source of the cry. They were just as ignorant of it as well. It wasn't from one of them. A heavy footstep shook the forest, and the memory of the horrifying beast he saw yesterday haunted his thoughts.

Oh no.

Anxiety filling him, Caedus took a step backward as the Naaklings abandoned their formations and sprinted for the cave tunnel.

"New plan," he said frantically. "Run!"

In a desperate attempt to escape the one the *Varas* called 'the Devourer,' Caedus sheathed his sword and bolted for the safety of the cave's deep interior. The other captains followed him in his wake, the Naaklings poured into the mouth of the cave as titanic appendages slammed into the ground. Caedus heard a shrill cry followed by the sound of teeth puncturing the hard shells of an unfortunate crab man.

"Holy Neshka," he said, a chill running down his spine from the agonizing shriek of the Naakling.

Without a torch to guide the way, Caedus struggled to keep a straight line down the tunnel. He bumped shoulders with Captain Seether, knocking both off balance.

"Shit!" Caedus yelled. "Go, go, go!"

For a moment, he peered over his shoulder. A dozen Naaklings crawled over each other trying to find shelter. The mountain quaked, chunks of stone falling from above. Caedus nearly tripped over his own feet and stopped for a moment. As he scanned the tiny hole of light beyond the fleeing Naaklings, he saw one of Phae'Raxya's legs near the tunnel entrance. The ground shook again, and a loud, frustrated roar blistered his ears.

"It's clawing at the mountain," Caedus said with a panicked tone. "It'll dig right through it."

Part of the tunnel collapsed, hindering the Naaklings' retreat and forcing them in a bottle neck. While Caedus knew they fled to stay alive, he also knew they'd hunt him down if they got close enough. The deeper he ventured into the mountain, the more the titan outside roared with ferocious hunger.

Several minutes passed, and Caedus's lungs begged for mercy. Thankfully, the distant light of the chamber he assumed to be the one Lucien had found caught his eye. Captain Ammon slowed in exhaustion beside him. Caedus tried to usher the large captain onward with a few words of encouragement. Seether and Ursa stopped at the doorway to the ceremony chamber, and once Caedus reached it as well, he stared down the long, stone ramp and eyed Lucien and Atlas seated on the floor. The next sight took the breath from him as he shifted his gaze to the towering black beings on either side of a flaming pillar of raw energy.

"Ell lett aelas ... lett Hyastreynya, dorzgad venni. (By the gods ... the Architects, they're real,)" Osinian said in just as much awe as he.

Caedus couldn't believe his eyes, especially when he noticed the void-like portal hovering between Lucien and the column of white fire. He then looked down at the sides of the chamber where hundreds of *Varas* people swayed side to side in the middle of their ritualistic mantra. Their hums soothed his ears, but the strange cries from the Architects stunned him with a primal sense of fear he didn't know he had.

The hasty footsteps of the Naaklings spurred him back to the immediate problem.

"Close the doors!" he shouted at the other captains while pointing at the massive stone barriers that looked like they hadn't been moved in centuries.

Caedus and Ursa pried on one while Ammon and Seether heaved the other from its spot. The heavy stone doors scraped against the cave of the floor, and as Caedus pushed, he gritted his teeth while watching a horde of crab men barrel down the tunnel. After a mighty effort, Caedus sealed the chamber off from the tunnel and leaned against the door until Ammon slid the large, iron bolts into their locked position. As Caedus rested his head on the damp stone, a sudden jolt lightly vibrated it followed by an angered snarl.

"This should hold them off," Caedus said to Ursa leaning as well, "but I don't know for how long. If that ... *thing* ... brings down the mountain, we are doomed to an eternity in this cave."

Captain Vederosa sprinted up the ramp toward him.

"What the hell is going on?" she asked frantically.

Caedus boasted a sarcastic smile.

"We have company," he said.

A sudden bang jolted the door. Caedus lost his footing for a moment and scrambled back into position.

"The Naaklings? What happened to keeping them away from here?" Vederosa asked.

Phae'Raxya released another bone-chilling roar, and the mountain shook once again. Caedus watched Vederosa's annoyed expression melt to fear.

"*That* happened," he said.

The cosmic portal over the platform shimmered, sending ripples out from the center to the borderless edges.

"They've started the ritual?" Caedus asked.

"Yes," Vederosa said. "Lucien and Atlas severed their spirits from their bodies. It's the only way they can find Zededia in Elysia."

"Well," he said with a grunt, flinching from another try at the door from the crab men, "let's hope they find what they're looking for. Wherever they are, they need to hurry."

~ ~ ~

Lucien stepped into the glassy void of the portal before him, nervous to explore the depths of an unknown plane. He had trusted the *Varas* people up to this point, but an eerie feeling in the pit of his stomach kept him on edge. On the other side, his eyes beheld a dark sky of bleeding stars and shattered planets. The craggy landscape stretched on for miles in nothing but red mountains, cavernous canyons, and lakes of liquid silver. This wasn't the Elysia he and his brothers had traveled to before; it was an entirely separate world.

"By Neshka," Lucien said. "Where are we?"

"This is *Ozek Monns*," King Atlas said. "Where tarnished souls wander in limbo."

The prince scanned his surroundings atop a small plateau that overlooked a rocky valley. He compared it to a destroyed version of the place Neshka pulled him to in his most recent dream. The layout seemed familiar, only all that was lush and green was nowhere to be seen.

"Tarnished?" Lucien asked. "Why would the Architects send us here? Did they summon the incorrect portal by mistake?"

"Gods don't make mistakes, Lucien, we're here for a reason."

"But ... that only means—"

"That your brother's soul is blacker than you think."

Lucien didn't argue. In fact, he started to doubt the perfect image of Zededia in his mind. If the gods truly felt he deserved to linger in such a place in the afterlife, perhaps there were things about his brother he didn't know.

"Look," Atlas said. "Over there."

Following Atlas's point, the prince glanced to his left and saw a massive white orb menacingly floating above the landscape.

"What is that?" he asked.

"They're referred to as the *Vaostas*, or the Sentinels," Atlas said. "They're loosely mentioned in the texts I've read about *Ozek Monns*, but from what I've gathered, they act like shepherds tending to their herd of souls. They are acolytes of Morgost, god of the dead and guardian of this realm."

"I'll bet you they'd know how to find Zededia's soul," Lucien said.

"Yeah, I don't know about that," Atlas said, peering down at the closet orb below the plateau. "Something tells me they won't be so willing to give up their flock so easily."

Lucien stepped over to the edge and watched the white sentinel hover over what appeared to be small, wandering shades. Blackened souls just like Atlas explained, these once living shadows meandered their way under the protection of the orb.

"Okay, think, Atlas," Lucien said. "How are we supposed to find one soul in a pool of ... well, countless others?"

The Daecian king stood in deep thought. Lucien waited patiently, hoping his spiritually wise cousin could offer some insight.

"We start looking."

Lucien disliked Atlas's cryptically simple answer, finding it hard to believe he actually thought they would find Zededia's soul in an endless landscape of drifting shades by sheer luck.

The prince followed Atlas off the plateau and down into the valley. He kept a firm eye on the closest white orb floating high above, watching it wander like a cloud in the sky. As he walked out into the red valley, a group of shades meandered by, seemingly by force, on their eternal march through *Ozek Monns*. Instinctively, Lucien ducked and searched for cover. He and Atlas crouched and snuck their way over to the closest one. The white guardian in the sky irked Lucien, but he pressed on.

"Hello?" King Atlas whispered to the shade. "Can you understand me?"

The shade turned and stared at Lucien with red eyes in a black, shadowy face. It lacked a mouth and nose, but the prince saw the sadness in the fading pools of crimson that beckoned for release of this prison. Lucien froze, an eerie memory flooding back to him. He thought of Zededia's day of execution in Vaedor Sellos, and while he couldn't remember much from how his crafty brother managed to escape, the sight of Osinian standing on the stage stuck to his subconscious like thick honey. The wicked laughter the resurrected shade sang through the city haunted him to this day. Lucien gathered his courage, though, convincing himself that the shade in front of him was a completely different being.

The black shadow took a step toward Atlas and spoke in a language neither of them recognized. It stretched a hand out toward Atlas, and Lucien retreated. A soft wail crept out from where its mouth would be as it begged for help.

"It looks in pain," Lucien said. "Is there nothing we can do?"

"Who are we to interfere with the punishment of sinners, Lucien?" Atlas asked. "No, we cannot act in the gods' stead for the sake of one person. We will leave that to Morgost."

"But ...," Lucien said, frowning, "aren't we doing that already? With Zededia?"

Atlas gave him a conflicted look.

"Yes, well ... this is different."

While Lucien agreed, ignoring the damned soul's cry for aid knotted his stomach.

"Come on," Atlas said.

The prince and King Atlas spent what felt like hours scouring the jagged plains of *Ozek Monns*. Each time they encountered a group of shades, they quietly interrogated one of them, but each either spoke a different language or didn't speak at all. Taking too long to question one of them increased the risk of unwanted attention.

Lucien rounded the bend of a pillar of rock with Atlas behind him. He glanced back at the portal upon the plateau, sighing at its tiny size the farther he ventured away from it.

"There must be a better way to navigate this plane," Atlas said in annoyance. "How can my feet hurt if my body isn't even here?"

The prince softly chuckled. A sound of water shifting alerted him just ahead. When Lucien glanced up, he saw a shade kneeling down next to a lake of boiling silver. Squinting to observe, he waited.

"Atlas," Lucien said. "What's it doing?"

The Daecian king walked over.

"I ... I don't know?" Atlas said. "Have we seen one that hasn't been marching?"

"No," Lucien said. "No, we haven't"

Enticed by his curiosity to discover why this shade hadn't been forced to roam the rocky plains, Lucien stealthily tip-toed toward it. As soon as he neared it, though, the shade stood from the lake, turned around, and stared at him.

"Eldish?" Lucien asked. "Do you speak Eldish?"

The shadow remained silent, but Lucien watched it scan him up and down.

"What about Aznogsi?"

As soon as Lucien mentioned the language of his ancestors, the shade's eyes widened with fear and scrambled to flee.

"Wait!" Lucien yelled, running after it. "Wait a moment!"

The spirit's ghostly nature allowed it to traverse the terrain with ease. Lucien struggled to keep up with it and nearly tripped over himself.

"Wait just a damn moment!" he shouted.

The prince gave up his chase and frowned. He turned back to the boiling lake of silver and fell into a mild trance of thought. After a few seconds, the shade reappeared in his peripheral vision, stepping toward him with caution. Lucien twisted his head to greet it.

"You, you are not of this world, are you?" the spirit asked.

"No. I come from Osiria," Lucien said.

"Osiria?" the shade asked. "What kind of strange land is that?"

Without the time to explain, Lucien sighed.

"Why did you run when I said 'Aznogsi?'" he asked, disregarding the first question.

He detected a bit of hesitation from the shadow.

"The Aznogs are responsible for the death of my people. Many of them wander here, but they can't hurt me. I still fear them, though. I thought you were one of them coming to hunt me even in the afterlife."

Several questions whirled in Lucien's head, reminding himself to neglect the fact that he *was* Aznogsi by blood.

"The death of your people? The Aznogsi tribe has been disbanded for a thousand years."

"What?" the shade said. "Then they were defeated?"

"More or less," Lucien said. "But we aren't here to hunt you."

"Then ... why are you here?" the shade asked.

Lucien noticed how young the voice sounded. Estimating that this man had died somewhere between the ages of fifteen and twenty, he received a firsthand account of how ruthless his ancestors were before the days of Osiris.

"We seek a soul," King Atlas said, stepping forward. "Zededia Osiris, Prince of Hostellus."

"I do not know that name," the shadow said. "And you're not likely to find someone you know so easily. There are millions of souls imprisoned in *Ozek Monns*."

"That's what I was afraid of," Lucien said. "Well, if you can't help us, can you tell us why you are not shackled to the guardians above?"

"My time here nears its end," the shade said. "Those who complete their sentence given by Neshka are given more freedom. But, while I walk without the chains of the sentinels around my neck, I am still not free. I cannot join my brothers in the Meadows for another hundred years. I am bound by—"

Before the shade could continue, a light tremble in the ground interrupted him.

"Oh no," the shadow said. "He is wise to your presence."

Lucien darted his eyes around in search for the 'he.'

"Wait, who is?"

"Flee while you can, my friends!" the spirit said, gliding away. "Trespassers are not smiled upon!"

One of rock columns behind the prince toppled over, and Lucien swiftly turned around. A chunk of rock levitated across the landscape high above his head and descended toward his position. Stealth remained out of the question; something had found him. Lucien studied the approaching platform, trying his best to hold a courageous front. Whatever stood upon the red rock ahead sent a thick dose of terror through the shade at the shore. Lucien only guessed what an immortal being could fear so heavily.

"My, my, my," a deep, strange voice said with a soft echo trailing behind. "What would possess a spirit of the living to invade the land of the dead?"

A chill shot down the prince's spine. As the platform lowered, his eyes struggled to take in exactly what he saw. A humanoid being composed entirely of small shards of obsidian centered the flat stone hovering a foot above the ground. The flat, reflective stones that acted like tiny scales shifted with each movement like the waves of an ocean. Lucien stared into the shining black orbs of its eyes.

"Lucien," Atlas quietly said with a hint of panic in his voice. "Kneel. Now."

"Lucien?" the glimmering being said. "Lucien Osiris?"

The echo behind its voice bounced off the crystalized interior of its throat. Despite the harrowing sound, it spoke with complete clarity.

"Ah, you must be one of Neshka's," it said.

Lucien blinked rapidly and locked eyes with the obsidian man as the rock it stood upon revolved slowly around his position.

"I've heard about you. You're the one my sister decided to bless with her precious vision."

Sister? Lucien thought while frowning.

"She spends so much time with you humans, and for what? To watch them die in twenty or thirty years?" the being said, its tone increasingly smooth and menacing. "You all return to me in the end. Your lives hardly matter."

"You must be Morgost," Lucien boldly said. "God of the dead."

A low, devilish laugh pulsed from the god's hollow chest out its wicked smile.

"Most of your kind flee when they hear my name let alone look at me."

"I am not like most of my kind," Lucien said.

"Clearly not."

The obsidian god continued to circle Lucien on his rock; the prince remained firmly in place, keeping his eyes pointed forward until Morgost appeared on his other side.

"And so, the question stands," Morgost said. "Why ... are you here? Surely Neshka's glorious dream didn't lead you to my home by nature."

"I ... we ... are here," Lucien said, referring to Atlas, "to seek one of the dead. We mean to resurrect him to walk among the living once more."

"Hmm, a fallen friend? In war, perhaps?" Morgost said, slightly mocking the prince. "Or a father who succumbed to disease in his later years?"

Lucien kept quiet.

"No ...," Morgost said slowly. "Neither of those."

Suddenly, the morbid god zoomed to right in front of Lucien, nearly causing him to flinch. The prince glared at Morgost, the widening smile on his face revealing teeth just like his, except they were shiny black stones instead of white bone.

"You seek ... a brother."

The prince paused.

"Yes, you're here for Zededia."

The stone platform slowly receded away.

"Plenty of people go looking for the dead, but few of them ever make it this far," Morgost said. "And even fewer are able to find Aeladaecia so easily. With that being said, I'm afraid your road leads to a dead end, chosen of Neshka."

"Zededia isn't here?" Lucien asked.

"Oh, he's here. But you're a fool to think I would relinquish such a worthy soul from my legions."

"Why is my brother here in the first place?" Lucien asked, placing one foot in front of his other in slight defiance of the reality of Zededia's fate. "The damned roam this plane—Zededia was no such thing."

Morgost stilled his tongue, his sly grin taking shape.

"Maybe you don't know your brother as well as you think," the god said, his voice quiet and cryptic.

Lucien's lips parted slightly. The disbelief of his brother's place in *Ozek Monns* started to dissolve. Perhaps Zededia held a darker secret than he suspected. Every single one of his brother's wrongdoings in the nearly twenty-six years he had known him raced through in his thoughts, and every single time, Lucien failed to understand how Zededia deserved to suffer in this desolate wasteland.

"No," the prince boldly said, his tone growing more confrontational. "You're wrong. Zededia has paid for his transgressions as a living man, he does not belong here with the dead. Why is he here?"

Speaking such a way to the gods typically earned swift retribution, a fact Lucien kept in the back of his mind. Morgost's calm demeanor lingered to his surprise.

"Clever boy," the god said, seemingly proud of Lucien's astute perception. "'You have the heart of a true Osirian.' Isn't that what Neshka tells her pets now?"

Lucien loosened the tension in his shoulders after calling Morgost's bluff.

"You're right," Morgost said. "Your brother did not come to me naturally."

"How did he get here?"

"Zededia owes me a debt. Not one like the others here have to repay. This one is personal."

"How so?"

Morgost held an open hand near chest level and summoned a seeing stone in his palm. The orb appeared larger than Lucien's head, and he glanced through the transparent center at the vision the god wanted to show him.

"You see, Zededia was here not long ago," Morgost said, revealing an image of a man standing before a large door. "Somehow, he managed to craft the Seal of Elohiir, the seal which all spirits are bound to."

Lucien watched as the door opened, a black mist pouring out from within. Red eyes appeared in front of the man and took the form of a shadow just like all the others the prince had passed during his time in *Ozek Monns*.

"Your brother stole something from me, simply put," Morgost said. "A soul of far greater value than any other."

The shade from the doorway whirled around Zededia in the vision for a moment, and then both vanished completely.

"The shadow that followed him around, Osinian, he belongs to me. Since he is gone, Zededia is his replacement."

That's why you won't give him up?" Lucien asked.

The orb in Morgost's hand disintegrated to ash and blew away. No words came from the god of the dead. Lucien only received the same pompous look he had been given over the entire conversation. Seeing the dead end Morgost mentioned earlier, the prince desperately tried to think of a solution. Overcoming the trials of Aeladaecia was one thing, outsmarting the gods was another. Suddenly, an idea sprouted amidst the dozens of thoughts passing through his mind.

"You talk of souls as if they have worth," Lucien said, bolstering his confidence. "That means they have a price."

He watched Morgost slowly raise his eyebrows. The god then crossed his arms.

"Perhaps."

Lucien took a step forward.

"Then bargain with me," he said, glaring at Morgost with a fierce expression. "For Zededia's soul ... I will give you something of greater value."

"What could you possibly offer me that's worth more than the soul of a mass-murdering Osirian? And don't waste your time offering your own. Nobility is not the currency of the dead, boy."

"What is?"

Morgost appeared slightly surprised by his question.

"Pain," the god said after a moment.

Lucien took a deep breath, trying to formulate the second half of his plan that failed to come to him.

"What on earth can we give him, Lucien?" Atlas said, stepping closer. "Morgost deals in human life. Unless you are prepared to sacrifice others to bring Zededia back, we don't have anything."

The conversation he had with Atlas aboard The Leviathan when the two discussed their plan for breaking into Aeladaecia rose to the center of his thoughts.

You will be king, he thought. *Moments like this will define your legacy.*

Lucien weighed his options. Sacrifice others to bring Zededia back, that was the deal on the table. The prince exhaled, looked at Atlas, and gathered his moxie.

"Then that's what we must do."

As soon as the words left Lucien's mouth, a sour taste coated his tongue. Trading one life for others contradicted every ounce of his being. It sounded so selfless to even suggest. Lucien stood on trembling legs, his physical body rejecting the decision his mind had made.

"Morgost," he called to the deity hovering above.

The god moved in, and though his arms were crossed, Lucien knew his ears were open. Dry and sandy, the prince's mouth struggled to produce the words.

"Release Zededia's soul to me, and I will trade you ... ten thousand others."

"What the hell are you doing?" Atlas shouted under his breath in protest.

Morgost let a sudden laugh burst out.

"Oh? What a surprising offer, Lucien Osiris," the god said. "But I am ever so curious. Indulge me, then, how you propose to deliver *ten thousand* souls to me in place of Zededia."

Lucien swallowed an arid breath, locking his gaze on the black marbles in Morgost's face. He pondered over the bargain he imagined, using a perk of Matticus's campaign as a bargaining chip.

"If you allow me to resurrect Zededia, war will come to Osiria," he said. "The eldest of my family, Matticus, has declared himself the sovereign ruler of all eight kingdoms, and, until now, no one has been able to stop him. As he progresses, conquerable lands dwindle in number, and so do the souls passing on to you."

Lucien paused, watching Morgost's grin widen in amazement at his cruel suggestion.

"If Zededia returns, though, the war will continue. More will die."

The harsh truth Lucien spoke pained him to confront. For a moment, he questioned his motives. He questioned if carrying out this task would lead to less catastrophe than if he simply let Matticus unite all kingdoms under one flag. Over everything else, he questioned if he could ever turn back from this mentality.

"So ... you want to revive Zededia ... to *start* a war ... instead of end one?" Morgost said to clarify. "You're willing to let ten thousand more die just to prevent this-this ... unification?"

"If it means the people of my world are truly free of the darkness brought by tyranny," Lucien said, pulling from a quote that Zededia had said to him a few years ago shortly after his banishment, "yes."

Morgost remained speechless as Lucien waited for a reply. Instead, the god of the dead slowly shook his head and stared at him in amazement.

"You truly are intriguing," Morgost said, leaning toward Lucien to take a more observant look. "Maybe your soul isn't so perfect afterall."

Lucien lifted his chin to hold his ground.

"Fine," the god said, pulling away. "I'll give you Zededia for your little ritual."

At last, the end was in sight. Lucien couldn't keep the euphoria off his face. The obsidian god stretched out his hand like before, but he held his palm facing the ground instead of the sky. Morgost's eyes briefly glowed a bright white, and gusts of wind whooshed to a forming cloud of mist under his hand. Soon after, a small orb similar to the shape and composure of the Sentinels floating around appeared. Lucien stared inside, and he saw what looked like a miniature hurricane of white mist. The prince reached his hand out to touch it, eyes mesmerized by the swirling essence inside.

"But," Morgost said, retracting the orb away from Lucien.

The obsidian god bent over, inching his face closer until the prince could see the back of Morgost's eye sockets.

"You will give me a war worthy of the Osirian name," Morgost said in a low, sinister voice. "Should you disappoint, know what awaits you once your pathetic life finds its end."

Lucien nodded as smoothly as he could after hearing such a threat. He knew he could uphold his end of the deal, though. While he aimed to trick Morgost for his brother's soul, there was truth in his reasoning. With Zededia returning, the piles of corpses left in Matticus's wake would turn into mountains as the divide between the eight kingdoms would create two evenly matched sides led by the most destructively powerful beings in all Osiria.

"Deal," Lucien said, sealing the pact.

Morgost allowed a sly, hoarse chuckle to slither through his black teeth. Lucien stretched out his hands as the orb containing his brother's soul floated down to him. The whirling mist entranced him as he held it. For a moment, the prince took time to treasure what Morgost had given him. All Zededia's thoughts, memories, experiences, feelings, everything. It all rested between his palms. The life he shared with his brother, the one he had lost and what had broken him, it was obtainable yet again. A tear formed in Lucien's eye as he cherished the orb.

"The portal is far, Lucien," King Atlas said. "We need to go."

Snapping away from the nostalgia usurping control, Lucien nodded. He looked up at the plateau where the gateway to the cave in Aeladaecia faintly glowed. Lucien kept both hands around Zededia's soul as he started the journey back to the physical world. Morgost moved aside on his hovering rock.

"Don't lose your head ... watching the dead ...," Morgost eerily sang as if reciting a ballroom tune while the prince walked away. *"The shadows follow wherever you tread."*

Lucien's skin crawled as the sinister god hummed the same tune. Though Morgost's voice grew fainter the farther he walked, it seeped deep inside and infected his mind. The prince twisted his head over his shoulder and watched the god's glowing eyes fade away in a black mist that swept over the landscape.

"What tears you will shed ... what terror you'll wed," Morgost sang, his black teeth shining. *"As the darkness bites ... and misery spreads."*

Morgost disappeared in the cloud of fog. Lucien tried to pry the creepy smile out of his thoughts, but it lingered like a plague. He shook his head to refocus, held Zededia's soul close to his chest, and marched over the crooked rocks of *Ozek Monns.*

Atlas walked beside him the entire way back to the mystical portal waiting atop the plateau. Once he stood in front of it, Lucien paused to reflect over his time in the most hellish part of Elysia.

"Lucien?" Atlas said.

The prince looked at the Daecian king.

"Do you believe in what you said to Morgost? Sacrificing a few to save the many?"

"I don't really know," Prince Lucien said.

He shifted his focus to the swirling orb in his hands.

"But Zededia did."

After all these years, he realized that a piece of his older brother had rubbed off on him. A faint grin appeared on his face.

"The others are waiting," Lucien said, eyeing the portal to Aeladaecia. "We have a god to create."

Chapter 25

Build the Body

Day 5 in the Month of Rain

Lucien crossed the threshold of the portal brought forth by Nazkala and Abbendae. The air remained silent like before, and he glanced at his body sitting on the cave floor. King Atlas hurriedly walked over; the prince followed. Unsure of how to exactly return to the physical plane, Lucien took a seat and matched the exact position of his body, closed his eyes, and concentrated.

The quiet atmosphere slowly transitioned back to the commotion of the ascension ceremony. Deep, melodic hums of the *Varas* people gathered in rows throughout the cave softly rang in his ears, and the energy pulsing from the Architects and the white pillar of flame rattled his chest. Lucien opened his eyes like a newborn taking his first view of the world. The cosmic gateway collapsed on itself and disappeared, and the black giants channeling their divine powers startled him despite knowing they were there.

"Haha! You're back!" Tog shouted. "And you've found the soul!"

Lucien looked down at his lap. Just like his time in *Ozek Monns*, the orb in his hands swirled like a storm of mist. It wasn't a dream; he had brought Zededia's soul back from the dead.

"Quickly! Quickly!" Tog said. "Bring the soul!"

A violent thud behind alerted him. Lucien twisted his head around, his faint smile shifting to a panicked expression as he eyed Caedus bracing the stone door to the chamber along with the other Legonae soldiers. Right after, Lucien froze in terror as a monstrous roar horrified him.

"We've less time than we thought," Atlas said as Lucien turned back to face the Architects.

"Then we've no time to lose."

Lucien carefully walked closer to the flaming pillar carrying the orb of his brother's soul. As he neared, both gods on either side eerily cast their gaze upon him. Nazkala, on the left, held out his shadowy hand, seven spindly fingers unraveling around a black palm. The prince stared up at the faceless god with widening eyes. Slipping out of his grasp, the orb between his hands floated up until it rested just above Nazkala's open hand. The god wrapped each of its fingers around the orb, savoring it like a thief would a priceless gem, and let loose another ringing cry like before. The earth trembled under Lucien's feet, the Naakling's savagely threw themselves at the stone door, and the Architects leaned their heads back to further channel their divine energy.

Ghostly wails screamed out from the flaming pillar as the blackened gods summoned the essence of creation. Lucien's heart pounded furiously in his chest. As the white fire flared more vigorously, an opening appeared in the middle of the column high above the prince's head. He glared at the vortex hidden within, and then, spirits of the dead screeched, flew out of the opening, and sporadically raced throughout the cave like a pledge of wasps swarming around their hive. Lucien ducked and covered his head to protect himself from their crazed frenzy.

"Ahahahaha!" Tog shouted as he held out his arms. "And so! The Eye of Elysia awakens!"

Lucien noticed a harrowing change in Tog's demeanor. The leader of the clay people became more fanatical than ever, yelling like a mad priest addressing his crowd of faithful with sermon.

"Our time of deliverance is here, brothers!"

Taking a step back to distance himself from Tog, Lucien watched Nazkala place the orb containing Zededia's soul in the heart of the opening. Shortly after, the white flames engulfed what Tog called 'the Eye of Elysia' once more. The Architects' fingers shook with sheer energy as they held open hands pointed toward the ceiling.

"Alas, chosen of Neshka! Witness the might ... of ascension!"

The Seal of Elohiir in front of Lucien jaggedly split down the middle, waves of light rippled from the fiery column, and the blood in Lucien's hands started to glow. The prince studied the red shine in the veins of his arms, puzzled about the reaction causing the divinity inside him to suddenly arise.

"Step back, Lucien," King Atlas said, pulling on his arm.

"What? What's wrong?" he asked.

"Something's spooked me ever since we arrived here," Atlas said, cautiously observing the ancient gods at work while keeping an eye on Tog. "Something that tells me that performing a ritual such as this requires ... a price."

Caedus's statement earlier about Atlas being wise to an ulterior motive here made sense.

Lucien retreated to the base of the stone ramp with Atlas. Stumbling over himself, he watched Caedus continue to stave off the Naakling's prying at the chamber entrance. The stone doors cracked open, allowing the crude iron heads of their spears to stab through.

"What's going to happen, Atlas?"

"I don't know!" the Daecian king said. "Stay close to me! The *Varas* might try to—"

"Maaless ... dorrmess...."

Lucien's eardrums nearly imploded at the depth of the combined voices of the Architects. He could barely understand the cryptic words they chanted at all, much less what they meant.

"Carrnak ... Myaa Duuuuuuu...."

After reciting the incantation, Abbendae, the giant on the right, looked out across the chamber. The hairs on the back of Lucien's neck stood straight up, and a pointed finger stretched out.

"Ahahahahaha!" Tog laughed, insanity sprouting out through the leaks in his composure. "Come, Osirians! Bow to the might of Abbendae!"

"Back, Lucien," Atlas said. "Back!"

However, to the prince's surprise, Abbendae reached his shadowy finger to the crowd of *Varas*. Lucien's eyes followed the god's hand as it hovered over a clay woman in the front row. She raised her hands over her head, begging for the god to touch her as if she desperately welcomed what was to follow. As soon as the tip of Abbendae's finger brushed against the *Varas* woman, she screamed in blood-curdling agony. The others around her roared in ritualistic ecstasy; Lucien faintly gasped and watched in horror as the clay woman began to disintegrate. Her eyes spread to complete circles as she shrieked. Abbendae turned her to dust in seconds and drained her essence. Lucien fought to comprehend what just happened, scanning over the group of *Varas* who all stretched their arms over their heads like the first woman.

"What the hell ...," he said in complete shock.

Seven ghastly fingers spread out and found their own target. The *Varas* accepted their fate with a creepy sense of glee. Like the clay woman before, each of them touched Abbendae's finger, howled like slaughtered cattle, and allowed Abbendae to siphon their energy.

"Yes, brothers and sisters!" Tog said, jumping around on the platform. "Return to your makers!"

One by one, the *Varas* people crumbled into tiny pieces and faded away into the abyss of Abbendae's hand.

"Now I understand ...," Atlas said in a stunned tone.

Lucien pried his gaze away from the dying *Varas Zogad* and glared at the king standing at his side. The terror in Atlas's eyes chilled his core.

"All this time, I suspected a sinister plot devised by these people that ended in our demise," Atlas said. "Their name ... *Varas Zogad...*"

"What? What does it mean?" Lucien asked urgently.

"When we first met them, I thought their name translated to 'feeder of the gods.'"

The prince frowned in confusion.

"I thought they were going to feed us to the Architects in some twisted scheme of their own."

More than half of the clay people seated in the cave had been absorbed by Abbendae, leaving few to remain. The god searched for other targets to fuel the ritual while the other wrapped his hands around the flaming pillar; the prince watched with the same astonished look he held since Zededia's soul rose to Nazkala's palm.

"But ... I realized something just now," Atlas said.

Lucien turned his attention back to the king.

"Their name, it doesn't mean feeder," Atlas said, his thousand-yard stare glued to Abbendae. "It means food."

"Don't you see, my friends!" Tog shouted, facing Lucien and Atlas as the last of his people released their dying wails. "This! This is our purpose! This is why we were made!"

Taking a step forward, realizing what was about to happen, the prince locked eyes with the leader of the clay people.

"To serve the gods as the ultimate sacrifice! Where life is given, life must be taken!"

Tog kept his hands spread out wide. A part of Lucien hunted for a way to save the clay man, but he understood the sacrifice that must be made.

"Free the mind! Find the soul! Build the Body!"

Abbendae's finger moved over Tog's position as Tog shouted.

"Build the body! Build the Body! Build the Body!"

Lucien noticed a swirling mass forming in the center of the flaming pillar.

"The unsurpassable evolution! The perfect being!" Tog yelled as loud as he could, eyes nearly bulging out of his head. "Ring the bells! Your ascended is here!"

The top of Tog's head decayed into fragments, Abbendae's finger grazing the dry clay as his wicked smile remained.

"Behold!" Tog screamed. "Zededia! The SHADOW GOD!"

Chapter 26

The Shadow God

Day 5 in the Month of Rain

The sound of Tog's crooked laughter scraped Lucien's eardrums as his face cracked apart and broke off to be sucked into the pillar of flames. As soon as the final *Varas Zogad* vanished from the chamber, silence filled the cave. Lucien struggled to adjust to the sudden change, but the Naakling's ramming at the stone door kicked his hearing back into gear. The Architects returned to their dormant, level-headed state, and the subtle glow from the mass inside the white column shaped into the form of a human.

Lucien took a step forward, seeing the outline of his brother's body for the first time in months. Out from the thin veil, he saw a glowing white foot. The rest of the figure followed, emerging like phantom from the middle of a placid lake. Wanting to run to his brother, the prince stopped himself, unable to recognize his face. The glowing white being levitated across the cave floor with grace, hands open at its side and toes pointed toward the earth.

Locked in a trance, Lucien stood with his feet cemented in place. His eyes reflected the bright light of his brother's spirit. The hand nearest to him reached out, but Zededia's head remained level and aimed at the stone door at the end of the ramp. Lucien glanced around, trying to figure out what the hand wanted. After a moment, the sword on his back that Caedus had given him softly vibrated and pulled free from the sheath. Lucien couldn't believe his eyes as his brother called the sword to him. The true divinity of the ascended Black Prince of Anzagaar Nostir came to fruition. The Shadow God was here.

~ ~ ~

Caedus could hold the door no longer. His failing strength gave way to the Naakling's ravenous assault. The door broke free, and the captain stumbled to his back. A dozen Naaklings poured through from the tunnel, each armed and ready to maim.

Unable to draw his sword to defend himself, Caedus shut his eyes and prepared himself for the beyond. The charging Naakling stopped, though, as a faint white glow caught Caedus's attention on the ramp. He looked over, observed the vibrant entity floating toward his location, and stared in awe.

The Naakling nearest to him snarled and started to charge, but a bolt of lightning flashed from Zededia's raised hand and vaporized the crab man just feet away from Caedus. The captain lied there completely stunned and watched the rest of the Naaklings immediately drop their weapons and flee. They feared the Shadow God more than Phae'Raxya tearing down the mountain outside. A thick mist seeped from the earth and the inside of the tunnel as the crab men sprinted away. When Caedus stood, he eyed Zededia's resurrected form and watched him summon an army of black shades. Like demons from the darkest pits of hell, the shadows barreled down the tunnel and eviscerated the Naaklings into piles of shells and guts.

A euphoric smile grew on Caedus's face as Zededia floated by him. At last, he laid eyes upon the friend he thought he had lost forever.

~ ~ ~

Prince Lucien ran up the stone ramp as fast as he could to catch up with Zededia. He heard the shrill cries of the dying Naaklings but lost sight of his brother's white glow.

"Lucien!" Vederosa said as she jogged up to him.

Stopping to greet her, the prince gave Vederosa a half-grin and softly laughed.

"We ... we did it," she said, matching his smile.

Lucien placed his hands on the sides of her shoulders.

"We did it."

Sounds of slaughter echoed down the tunnel. Lucien chased after his brother again, following the glowing light in the distance as best he could. His leather boots stomped over shattered shells and steaming viscera, but he didn't care. The prince's desire to embrace Zededia and mend the tear in his heart urged him on.

Once Lucien reached the entrance to the mountain, he slid to a stop. His brother commanded the army of shadows to hunt down the remaining Naaklings and struck down all in close proximity with bolts of holy fire. Lucien stood by in awe of Zededia's sheer power, unleashing the full might of the gods upon the crab men.

Phae'Raxya leapt off the side of the mountain and crashed its six pointed legs into the earth facing Lucien with Zededia in between. The great beast retracted its lips to show its thousand needly teeth. It sent forth a guttural hiss and lowered its head. Lucien waited for it to strike, but, before it could, the Shadow God flew high in the air, forcing the prince to search for him against the blue sky, and unleashed a focused beam of light at the beast's head. Phae'Raxya bellowed a fluid, deflated cry as Lucien noticed the gaping hole burrowed clean through the top of the hard armor of his forehead down through the lower jaw. Phae'Raxya, the feared devourer of Aeladaecia, collapsed to the ground vanquished with ease.

Zededia lowered back down to the ground facing away from Lucien. The white glow of his brother's body faded to reveal the light color of human skin. A tear rolled down the prince's cheek, a tear he had finally shed out of joy.

Lucien took a step forward out of the tunnel, and his brother turned his head, revealing his radiant hazel eyes, and smiled.

- Epilogue -

Shortly after the death of Zededia Osiris

Like a soothing song, gusts of a cool breeze blew over a field of endless green grasses. A pair of sullen, worried eyes on Zededia's face gazed out over the viridescent sea, slowly blinking in a daze. Looking down after a moment, he broke his confused search to observe his coarse, bloody hands held out at his side. Instinctively, Zededia felt his abdomen for the fatal wound Matticus had delivered, the memory of their duel fresh on his mind. The realization suddenly stuck him.

The Meadows, he thought. *I ... I did it.*

Zededia took a deep breath to inhale as much clean air as he could despite a lack of need to. His soul required no air with his physical body burning to ash in the physical realm. The Black Prince held a disturbed expression on his face, the hell he endured in life breaking through the mask he wore around others. A strange sense of grief overcame him as he moved through the phases of realizing the world he had left behind. The Legonae, Caedus, Livia ... Lucien ... they were gone. Death hadn't spared him from that grief. The pain he felt in life vanished for the most part, lifting a heavy burden off his shoulders. No worries to face, no reminders of his failures, no guilt of the slain. Still, that wasn't enough to free him what truly ailed him.

The void in his heart where his mother once resided ached with a burning intensity. He longed to see her more than he willed to live; the very mentality that drove him to his suicide. Zededia studied the flat horizon for any sign of life, the desperation to find his mother that he felt since her death urging him on like an addiction.

Amidst his search that led him to wander around the field in circles, a woman's voice serenaded the Meadows behind him. Zededia turned, expression as broken as shattered glass, and saw a rise in the ground. He remembered that hill. It was the same one he climbed when he traveled through Elysia to visit his favorite memory before he found Osinian.

Zededia followed the voice toward the hill as it sang a pleasant song. The grass under his footfalls rose after he walked by. Legs becoming numb, he started the gradual incline. The soothing melody floated on the wind and allured him like a siren.

Cresting the hill, tears filled his eyes as they beheld an immaculate garden of purple flowers. His lips trembled. It had been twenty-one years since he last saw the violet tulips of the Vaedorian Gardens. Their unmistakable scent seeped into his nostrils, unlocking the door to the memories of the days when he would wander through the gardens and let his worries disappear in the rows of flowers.

As he stood in a trance, shuffled footsteps sounded off behind him. A younger version of his older brother sprinted over the hill and down to the gardens.

"Matticus, wait!" another voice said.

Zededia then stared at the younger version of himself. A strange sense of Déjà vu riddled him, and he remembered the same interaction from his trip to the spiritual plane. This time, though, he and his younger self had switched positions.

"Wait ...," the Black Prince said, almost forced to.

He couldn't pry his eyes off the small boy on the hill with him. After a moment the child's body started to fade. Zededia frowned and wanted to step forward out to save him, but his feet remained planted in place. The younger version of himself disappeared completely seconds later.

"Zededia!"

Slowly turning his head to the woman's call, Zededia scanned the field of tulips.

"Come on! What are you doing up there?"

Ushered forth, he started his descent. Everything from this point was new territory, and he tried desperately to replay the memory from his childhood. His feet pushed aside the loose gravel of the garden grounds that crunched under his boots. Zededia searched through the rows of flowers for his mother, but he saw no one in his immediate view. As he walked, he subconsciously held out his hand to graze the sides of the flowing tulips. One then appeared in his other hand. His fingers wrapped around as if muscle memory had forced him to. When he looked down, it crumpled in his palm from its pristine condition all on its own.

His mother's song echoed through the decorative flower beds and gave him a clearer path to follow. Zededia turned the corner around a stone pillar and studied the clearing in the center of the gardens. There, standing with her back turned, a woman full of life and joy swayed gently side to side. Her soft, delicate hair shined under the sunlight in its tight bun, and her silk garments draped her in the essence of beauty.

Zededia's mouth cracked open. He struggled to decipher if he actually saw the spirit of his mother he so desolately yearned for. The closer he walked, the more elegant her song became. Just yards away, Zededia focused on the back of her head.

Twenty-one years since he had felt his mother's embrace. Twenty-one years since the light of his life was taken.

The tear in his eye streamed down like a river. Zededia, tulip in a shaking hand, reached for Queen Niike.

"Mother...."

Emperor Matticus, the Conqueror

- Acknowledgements -

This book is dedicated to my father, Tony. Never have I known a man more invested and loyal to his children and their dreams—mine is no exception. My father has supported my dream to become a writer since I made my first story way back in grade school. I couldn't begin to tell you how many books he has read in his entire life, that number would be in the thousands. So, when he gave me advice on how to improve my work, especially as a fantasy writer, I listened. He has aided me in the more logistical aspects of being a writer, such as guidance in grammar, diction, and world-building as a former English teacher and editor of other authors, but, more so, he has aided me in the emotional side of this journey.

Since I was born, my father has sacrificed all but himself to give me a happy, successful life, even going to such lengths to reach out to friend of his who is a New York Times bestseller to ask for personal guidance to which I have tried to implement religiously. Every chapter I have ever written, every event I've ever gone to, every achievement I've ever obtained—my father has been there for me to share those moments with.

He isn't just a dad to me. He's Superman. Never quits, completely unyielding to everything life has thrown at him, and stronger in heart than anyone I've ever met. My father has always told me ever since I could understand what he meant in saying that his children are his legacy. He's not a man of material possessions that most people seek. Instead, he chooses to dedicate himself to his family and his community. I have to live knowing that I am a part of the legacy that he wants to leave behind, and I couldn't imagine a more honorable way to spend my life.

My father is my hero, plain and simple.

I love you, Dad.

The Sons of Osiris series continues with

Book 3: War of the Osirians

Look for the third installment of Michael Westmoreland's Epic Fantasy series coming late 2025/early 2026

Sign up for the reading list for the most up-to-date details!

www.michaelwestmoreland.com

A Tennessee native, Michael Westmoreland grew up in the foothills of the Appalachian Mountains where roving hills and vast forests sat in view from his backyard. This upcoming inspired the setting for the Sons of Osiris universe.

Before pursuing a career in publishing, Michael began his writing journey from the early age of nine when he wrote a short fiction story for his English class. His love for literature and the more artistic aspects of life blossomed in the support of his parents, who both studied language intensively and implemented it in his youth.

Michael takes great pride in his ability to shape a world with his experiences, but none of his achievements would be possible without the overwhelming amount of support he received from his friends, family, and colleagues in the publishing field. As a self-published author, he's building his brand from the ground up, learning how to better master his skills as a writer and entrepreneur on the way.

Join him on his publishing journey at www.michaelwestmoreland.com. Sign up for the reading list, check out his other works coming soon, or simply leave him a message with your thoughts. He takes great delight in talking about any topic related to writing and language (and Tennessee sports). Be sure to keep an eye out for *Sons of Osiris: War of the Osirians* to come out sometime in late 2025/early 2026!

Made in the USA
Columbia, SC
06 August 2025

fc3741c3-5c12-401e-b7b2-e12fbf6bcc69R01